The Patagonia Files

An International Legal Thriller

Mary Helen Mourra

PUBLISHER'S NOTE

This book is a work of fiction. Names, characters, places and incidents are the product of the author's imagination or are used fictitiously. Any resemblance to actual events, locales, or actual persons, living or dead, is purely coincidental.

Copyright © 2016 by Mary Mourra

ISBN: 978-0-9982975-0-7 (mobi)
ISBN: 978-0-9982975-1-4 (epub)
ISBN: 978-0-692-78920-9 (print)

ACKNOWLEDGEMENTS

I would like to thank all of my close friends who read and commented on the early drafts of this novel—especially Carolyn Clark, Kathryn Johnson, and Alexandre Bouton. I also want to thank Graeme Hague, my editor, and Marina Anderson and Jessica Holland of Polgarus Studios for their incredibly professional services. A special thank you to Arturo Bernardo Grandon for sharing his insight and knowledge of the Fuerzas Armadas de Chile, Policía de Investigaciones and Carabineros de Chile. I express my deepest gratitude to my mother and my daughters for their support, patience, and inspiration for this story—especially Emmanuelle Valentina Grandon Mourra (Emmy), the brilliant and creative author waiting in the wings.

Book cover design by Laura Moyer
Formatting by Polgarus Studio

Printed in the United States of America
Cavatina Publishers 2016
www.cavatinapublishers.com

To my loving mother and daughters

This book is dedicated to my loving mother—whose sense of respect and responsibility to others and to the earth has been an inspiration to me throughout my life—and to my incredibly wonderful daughters, Haneine Ramadan, Manelle Ramadan, and Emmanuelle Valentina Grandon Mourra who are my reason for being.

This book is also dedicated to the Kawésqar Indians of Chile. Their civilization, like so many other civilizations of the past, is being extinguished in silence as modern society unrelentingly adopts more destructive, farther-reaching methods of environmental degradation, threatening the very existence of the human species.

We do not inherit the earth from our ancestors.
We borrow it from our children.
Native American Proverb

Prologue

Land of Fire was the name Fernando de Magallanes gave to the archipelago off the southernmost tip of South America when he fortuitously discovered the secret passage through the straits connecting the Atlantic Ocean to the Pacific Ocean. It permitted a passageway between the two oceans, without which he would have been forced to go around Cape Horn—battling massive waves and being chased by peals of thunder, violent gusts of wind, rain squalls and hail—probably never to have returned.

The inhabitants of the Tierra del Fuego—who had subsisted in the freezing, wet climate since the last ice age—managed to maintain fire to warm themselves in their sand-lined canoes as they wafted through the icy channels. Magallanes and other explorers were mesmerized by the floating firelights illuminating the misted world of fjords and glaciers nestled between the two oceans. The Fuegians reportedly covered their bodies with whale and sea lion blubber and dove into icy waters to gather giant mollusks upon which they depended for survival.

Eventually explorers returned to Europe with several of the Fuegians, who were kept in cages for public exhibition in Brussels, Hamburg, London, Paris and Zurich. They claimed the monstrously tall, broad-shouldered, brown-complected tribesmen were 'animals that resembled humans.' By the end of the Eighteenth Century, most of them had been killed off by diseases such as syphilis or smallpox that were brought by European explorers and colonialists. In the 1930's, the Chilean government 'assisted' the settlement of the Kawésqars—the last surviving

1

members of this tribe—in Puerto Edén, a tiny village on the remote Wellington Island in the Región de Magallanes. The mysteries of their existence have, for the most part, been abandoned to the shadows of history. Today, they tend to disappearance...

Chapter 1

THE SKY OVER the tiny fishing hamlet on Wellington Island was black and starless. A dense layer of clouds poured down from the mountains above Puerto Edén, blanketing it in moisture-filled obscurity. Two men dressed in hooded neoprene dry-suits cruised toward the shore in an inflatable Zodiac watercraft. Cutting off the engine several hundred feet away, they paddled their way quietly to the two-hundred-foot scientific expedition vessel resting off the port. They wore fins, masks, and oxygen tanks with double-hose regulators to keep the tanks functioning in the icy waters.

One of the men eased himself into the dark sea without making a ripple. The other handed him a twenty-pound explosive and slipped into the water holding a rope and a clamp. The divers swam under the ship and attached the limpet mine to the hull, next to the engine room. They then placed a twelve-pound bomb into the propeller shaft of the ship. Then, one of the men climbed aboard the ship and placed a smaller explosive near the helm, directly under the radio communication system. It would be the first to explode, severing communication with the *Capitanía de Puerto*. A fraction of a second later, the propeller explosive would blow, crippling the ship. Seconds later, the limpet mine would shatter the hull, sinking the ship rapidly.

3

The bombs were timed to detonate several hours after the ship left Puerto Edén—just as it was navigating the Southern Patagonian Ice Field. The vessel would go down so quickly no one would suspect it had been rigged with explosives. Reaching Bernardo O'Higgins National Park by land was impossible. Flying over the two-hundred-mile expanse of glacial ice was also unfeasible under the prevailing circumstances. Rescue efforts would be frustrated by the storms, gale force winds and stinging snow, characteristic of the austral winter. There would be no survivors; the countdown to death for someone thrown overboard was a matter of minutes. It was a perfect plan for ending the Antarctic Expedition Team.

Chapter 2

EMMANUELLE SOLIS FOUGHT panic as she kicked against the current of the icy water. Stephan Henri Brent was below her, sinking into the shadows of the ocean. She groped for his hands but his fingers slipped away. He was convulsing frantically, trying to say something to her. Bubbles gurgled from his mouth. His eyes blazed with terror. Suddenly, the current dragged him deeper into the darkness. In seconds, he was gone. A stream of bubbles rose to the surface from where he'd been. She tried to scream, but she choked and gagged instead. Her legs were numb from the cold. The pressure on her lungs was unbearable. She would die if she didn't return to the surface immediately.

Emmanuelle started from her nightmare gasping for air, her tangled bedcovers drenched in cold sweat. She stared at the ceiling as reality, in fitful gusts of memory, set in. A chill crept across her body, prickling her damp skin. She knew things would never be the same. Her life was about to take a violent turn. She lay there clutching the sides of the bed for several minutes, as though the floor underneath were about to give way. As though in doing so, she might thwart the vicissitudes that laid in store.

Breathe, she told herself. She glanced around the room without moving her head, trying to assess where she was. A cold, damp hotel room in Puerto Montt, Chile. She shut her

5

eyes tightly, willing her heart rate to slow. *He's not going to show up*, she told herself. She sensed impending ill fate. He was in grave danger. Freezing wind and rain had pried open the glass panes, and an icy breeze sifted into the room. Shivering, she rose to close the window, staring at the hazy skyline above the bay. Being there seemed surreal. Everything Stephan had told her when he called three days earlier to tell her he'd escaped his abductors now thundered through her mind.

In the bathroom, she turned on the shower, letting it steam before getting in. She wiped vapor off the mirror, staring into the eyes of someone she barely recognized. Her usual creamy, olive complexion was pale now, and her brown, almond-shaped eyes were turgid with fear. Her long, brown hair looked bedraggled now. She leaned against the tiled walls of the shower for a long while, eyes shut, steamy water running from her head to her toes until she finally conceded she couldn't wash away the cold terror that seized her. Questions clamored in her head. Should she have told the authorities about the call? Had she made a mistake by leaving Washington, D.C. to meet Stephan without telling anyone?

Emmanuelle had been in Puerto Montt for two days now and there was no sign of Stephan. Not knowing what happened to him was torturing her. She stepped out of the shower and wrapped a towel around herself. Had they caught up with him? *You could be next,* he'd warned her. What was she doing here? Her instincts were telling her to get on the next plane and go back to Washington, D.C.

Something on the television caught her eye. *Televisión Nacional* was broadcasting a breaking news segment. A blond-haired reporter, struggling with the wind, was covering the story from the *Región de Magallanes*. Emmanuelle dropped the towel and pulled an Alpaca blanket around her shivering body. She'd seen the same images the night before on the television

6

but hadn't caught the story. She sat on the bed and turned up the volume.

Only hours after its departure from the tiny fishing hamlet of Puerto Edén, a scientific expedition vessel has sunk. It was carrying forty-five scientists and a dozen volunteers working with the Olofsson Antarctic Institute. The Chilean Navy suspects the ship struck an iceberg, but it's still investigating the incident. Rescue helicopters have been searching the area since early this morning, but the weather has made it nearly impossible. Authorities are concerned that if there are any survivors, they won't last long in the brutally cold water. The team was studying the geological consequences of climate change in the area. It had planned to present a report on the Patagonia at the upcoming United Nations Climate Change Conference and the State of the Antarctic Conference in Reykjavík, Iceland. All passengers and crew aboard the ship are feared dead.

Her eyes went to a stack of files on the desk, then back to the screen. Scenes of the glaciers, misty fjords, and the bow of the sinking ship protruding from the ice fields sent a chill of premonition through Emmanuelle as she recalled her nightmare.

When the news report was over, she walked over to the window, wiping condensation off the pane. The clouds in her head seemed as opaque as the fog outside. The hazy city below was just beginning to stir. Fishermen, sailors, priests, and others connected to the sea were gathered on the dock below to celebrate the *Fiesta de San Pedro*. Many were decorating their boats, lighting candles and floating the vessels along the coast in honor of the saint. Two men carrying a statue of Saint Peter led a procession through streets, which were filling with tourists. The men loaded the statue into a boat beside the dock and pushed off into the bay. Dozens of other small vessels, festively adorned, floated behind it.

Passengers aboard the boats threw crowns of flowers onto

the water and prayed for the intercession of the saint: *San Pedro Divino, Pescador de hombres... May the sea and the elements show benevolence ... May the sea harvest be abundant ... May we have fortune and good health in the upcoming year.* Candles and lamps flickered like fireflies in the mist. From afar, foghorns blasted, saluting Saint Peter as he passed.

Chapter 3

SEVEN YEARS EARLIER, Stephan Henri Brent sat staring at the dossier on his desk. He was waiting for ten o'clock before letting Emmanuelle Solis in for her callback interview. She'd applied for an associate position in the Washington, D.C. office of Oliver & Stone.

Stephan, the Canadian-born partner of Oliver & Stone who headed the firm's Arbitration Group, flipped through her file again. He'd been through it tens of times before. She was intelligent and had experience in arbitration. Her references were outstanding. She was fluent in French, Spanish, German and Portuguese. *Magna cum laude* from New York University Law School in 2008. She wasn't married, so presumably she would be available to work late and travel frequently. His department was accustomed to receiving applications from young lawyers with excellent credentials. *But something about this one*, he thought, skimming the documents one last time, *stands apart from the rest.*

He wanted someone to assist him with his arbitrations. The Arbitration Group was divided by ambition and greed. Stephan needed somebody capable of loyalty. Someone he could trust with information of the highest level of privilege and confidentiality. Lately, he'd begun to question the trustworthiness of some of his staff.

He would take Solis on as his *protégée*, he decided. She

wanted to work with him. *Why wouldn't she?* He smiled to himself. Anyone with any knowledge of international arbitration knew about Stephan Henri Brent. He had represented major corporations. Only a few select arbitrators decided the vast majority of high-profile investment cases across the world and he was one of them. He was recognized as the world's top arbitrator by *North American Lawyer* magazine. He gazed now at the article framed on the wall. He was eloquent and effective, fearing nothing and no one. He negotiated with the most powerful men in the world. He arbitrated billion-dollar disputes involving reconstruction projects for war-torn countries, the building of transcontinental oil pipelines, oil, gas, and mineral exploration and exploitation in South America and the Middle East.

He checked his watch, picked up the phone and told his secretary to bring Emmanuelle to his office. Stephan stood up, smoothed out his black pin-stripped suit and ran a hand through his stylishly trimmed hair.

His secretary tapped on the door before opening it.

"Ms. Solis." He extended his hand, staring at Emmanuelle for an awkward moment. He'd forgotten how attractive she was. "So nice to see you again," he said, breaking into a smile. Her perfume floated in the air. He liked the way she looked. Her long, silky, brown hair was loose now, cascading off her shoulders. She had an upper-class elegance although Stephan knew Emmanuelle was struggling. He'd checked her out through a friend in Homeland Security. Both her parents were deceased; her half-brother, an employee of the Inter-American Development Bank, had supported her throughout law school. She was on a student visa and had graduated with over $250,000 in student loan debt.

"So tell me, why do you want to work for Oliver & Stone? What do you think you can contribute to our firm?" He studied her as she assessed the question. She laced her fingers through her hair nervously and straightened out her posture.

When she finished answering, Stephan knew she was knowledgeable about his cases and the cutting-edge issues. She seemed genuinely interested in the awards he'd rendered and had definitely done her research on the firm. He liked that.

"So, you lived in Europe, Togo, Haiti, and Costa Rica…" He pretended to make a note. "You did the Vis Moot Competition in Austria?"

"Yes. I was the principal drafter of my team's memorials." Excitement flickered in her eyes. She took pride in her work.

Albert Thorman, a heavy-set man with white curls and a pasty complexion came into the office. He was one of the firm's senior partners. He'd been with the firm since graduating from law school over thirty-five years earlier. He took an interest in the recruitment of associates, feeling entitled because of his seniority and his role as entrepreneur for the firm—although recently some partners questioned his pathological optimism and complained he was gambling the firm's assets.

"Albert, this is the young lady I was telling you about." Thorman was the kind of lawyer who believed politeness and agreeability were tactics of last resort to be employed only when all else failed, but Stephan hoped he would like Emmanuelle Solis and behave.

They made introductions. Stephan reluctantly handed Thorman her dossier.

"I hear you worked in the Securities Investment Arbitration Clinic at New York University," Thorman said, stepping between them and reading through her application.

"Yes. Under the supervision of professors, I represented investors in small claims against brokerage firms."

"Did Stephan tell you I served as Commissioner to the

11

United States Securities and Exchange Commission?

"I knew you would fill her in on your life accomplishments," Stephan said, suppressing his anger with a moment of feigned distraction on his cell phone. The truth was he wanted to strangle the pompous, high-handed, fat man in his ill-fitting suit for compulsively trying to dominate everyone in the office. But he would confront Thorman another time. Privately.

Emmanuelle had withstood forty-five minutes of aggressive and probing questions—mostly from Thorman—with impeccable calm and responses that reflected her self-confidence. She peered at Stephan through a delicate pair of rectangular spectacles. She was serious. Something told him she was a workaholic.

All good, Stephan thought.

He shook her hand. "Welcome to the Oliver & Stone Arbitration Group."

***

"THAT'S ONE IMPRESSIVE young lady," Stephan said after Emmanuelle left the office.

Thorman was reviewing the dossier again. "She'll be a big income producer. My instincts are never wrong about these things." He handed it back to Stephan. "She's nice looking, too."

"Yes, she is," Stephan said quietly, walking over to the window thinking about how her distinctly feminine mannerism complimented her intelligence. He gazed out at the white granite United States Treasury Building across the street. The image of the building with its thirty-six-foot Corinthian columns never ceased to fascinate him. 'It's the world symbol of financial stability,' he told clients.

Thorman followed him. "Yes. As I said, she is *one* nice-looking girl. I know when you have your eyes set on a woman," he laughed.

Stephan turned and shot him a cold glance. "This one is different. I have no intention of getting involved with her. She may end up being my protégée. She might just be the lawyer I've been waiting for. She's a perfect fit for the Arbitration Group," he added, his voice drifting with his thoughts. The special plans he had for bringing Solis into the group churned in his mind. She would work exclusively with him and apart from the others. There was too much rivalry among the attorneys.

Soon, Emmanuelle would travel with him across the world. He would introduce her to the most influential lawyers, businessmen and government officials. He liked the thought of having her at his side. There was something different about her. Her dark eyes radiated when she talked about the law. But she was beautiful and sexy, and that was another reason he would have to keep her distant from the rest of the team.

Just to be sure.

***

Emmanuelle struggled to maintain her composure as she left the office. She was bursting with excitement. She'd landed a job with one of the best international arbitration firms. The threat of having to leave the United States after law school had terrified her. She was still on a student visa, and several of the firms that interviewed her frowned on the prospect of having to go through the immigration process to hire her.

Now she would work directly with *Stephan Henri Brent*. It was more than phenomenal.

She looked around the room, imagining what it would be like to work for Oliver & Stone, half-disbelieving it was all coming true. It was an exceptionally elegant place with high ceilings, bay windows, Seventeenth Century Dutch and Flemish paintings and Belgian silk tapestries displayed on the walls. It was located in the central nervous system of Washington, D.C., next door to the world's most powerful financial institutions. The thought of working there was exhilarating.

She stepped out onto the street, pulling out her cell phone to call her half-brother Camilo. They would celebrate the beginning of this new chapter of her life.

Chapter 4

EMMANUELLE SOLIS WAS born in Washington, D.C. Her father, Diego Solis, well integrated into the D.C. socialite circle, had been posted there for many years. Her Swiss-born mother, Gabrielle Karrer, had been an environmental lawyer whose tenderness in the face of human suffering often clashed with her husband's black-and-white vision of life, politics, war and, in general, the world.

They met after the Great Earthquake of Valdivia in 1960 when Gabrielle was an intern at the UN Relief and Rehabilitation Administration. Her team provided support to the government and assisted those displaced by the earthquake. She was quickly attracted to Diego, a cigar-smoking, Economics major at Catholic University in Santiago. He recited poetry and sang ballads, boleros and tangos to her. Like hundreds of other students riveted by news of the disaster, he volunteered with the relief effort.

Diego had always been a man of extremes. In him, the world's opposites collided. He didn't *like* anything; he either loved it or hated it. He could be gentle and loving or cruel and aloof. Abstemious or extravagant. A conservative or a bohemian. His politics was sometimes left-wing, sometimes right-wing. He cursed social injustice, the inequitable distribution of wealth and the lack of opportunity for the poor. In the same breath, he banged his fist on the table in support of the military. It was a symbol of law and order, not corruption like the military and police of other Latin American countries. He was often moody and brooded for days. Or he could be the life of the party, singing loudly, drinking heavily, dancing heartily. He was revered by his friends, despised by his enemies.

Emmanuelle's mother, being from a reserved Swiss family and nine years younger than Diego, had been enraptured by his eccentric character. Their lives, however, led them separate ways. Diego finished his doctorate in Santiago in 1963 and began working for the OAS. Gabrielle graduated from the University of Lausanne and worked for the UN Development Program joining their missions in African and Central American countries.

Years, distance, other lovers and oceans separated them until finally, in 1975, Gabrielle returned to Diego and they were married in Valdivia—where they had met fifteen years earlier. Their marriage was as passionately charged as Diego's moods and Emmanuelle suffered through the tumults of the relationship. She grew up struggling against Diego's unrelenting exigencies. Through her, he seemed to compete with the rest of the world. Her childhood afternoons were occupied with ballet, piano and fine arts lessons. She had tutors for every subject even though she did well in school without them. Nothing she did was ever good enough for Diego.

After her mother succumbed to cancer, Diego wanted to return to Chile. Emmanuelle, then sixteen, rebelled. They'd lived in the United States, the Caribbean, Central America, and Africa. Finally during Gabrielle's treatment they'd settled in Geneva for two years. Emmanuelle had a boyfriend and had finally found her niche among a few school friends who had spent their childhood in exotic faraway places with jungles and roaring waterfalls.

Her mother's death shattered Emmanuelle's life. She

grieved inconsolably and didn't want to move again. She fought against her father fiercely. Then, less than a year after her mother passed away, Diego died unexpectedly of a heart attack. In one swift blow, any connection she'd once felt to the many worlds they'd lived in dissolved. She became convinced she truly belonged nowhere at all. After her father's funeral in Chile, it was decided she would live with her aunt in Santiago.

Thankfully, her half-brother, Camilo—Diego's son from an earlier marriage— rescued her and brought her back to the United States on a student visa.

Now with the opportunity this job presented, she could embark on a career path far greater than anything she'd dreamed of.

For the next seven years, every waking hour of Emmanuelle's life would be given to an all-consuming career in international arbitration.

Chapter 5

STEPHAN'S HOUSEKEEPER LED Emmanuelle through the living room of his four-level estate on River Road in Potomac and into the spacious kitchen. She hesitated at the door. "I'm sorry... I didn't mean to interrupt your breakfast."

Stephan was shirtless, in pajama pants, and sitting at the granite-topped kitchen island. "Good morning," he said, walking over to her. "You look radiant as usual." He kissed her on both cheeks.

"Thank you." The aroma of breakfast foods filled the air. "Am I too early?"

"Not at all. I was hoping you'd join me."

The housekeeper was already arranging two place settings at a table next to the bay window overlooking the rose gardens. A small bird chirped on a branch outside.

"Thank you. I'd love that."

"So, you finished the memo, eh?" Stephan asked.

"Yes. I have it with me." She put her briefcase down on the kitchen island. "Would you like to see it now?"

"Let's have breakfast first." He ushered her to the table, snatching a piece of toast from a tray the housekeeper was stacking with pastries, coffee cake, bread, breakfast meats, jam and cheese.

"Are you planning to entertain the entire office?"

He held his toast out to her. She took a bite. He finished off the rest as he pulled out a chair for her.

"Just the two of us, my dear. Just the two of us." He sat facing her, smiling. She liked the way the corners of his eyes crinkled when he smiled.

"I'm not sure you are going to be able to decide this case the way you want to," she said carefully.

Stephan gave her a cold glance that made her breath falter. For a moment, the room fell silent except for the sound of percolating coffee. The little bird seemed to have flown away.

She thought for a second before saying another word. Stephan was arbitrator in the case. The mining company, their client, claimed the government's environmental laws adversely affected its investment. Emmanuelle had read all of the relevant cases—most of which had been decided in favor of corporations—but public criticism was flaring because of the environmental devastation they caused.

"The government will claim the public health and safety exception. The evidence is strongly in their favor," she said.

Stephan bit into a chocolate pastry. "If a government passes a law that makes foreign investments valueless, it's effectively an expropriation." He took a large bite now. "Isn't it?"

She'd seen this before. Whenever he was angry, he chewed faster. She reached for a croissant.

"Mining won't be economically feasible under the new law. It doesn't matter what they argue," Stephan replied. He was definitely pissed off. The housekeeper set his cup of coffee down in front of him. Black. No sugar. He picked it up.

"I know," Emmanuelle said, biting into the croissant. "But arguably, the regulation was for a valid and compelling public purpose. Several environmental organizations are trying to intervene in the case. They have evidence hundreds of people living close to the lakes are sick from chemical poisoning. Several died. The cyanide level in the lake is way above internationally accepted standards."

He shook his head. "This arbitration is about the investment treaty and the concession agreement. This isn't an environmental case. They can take that elsewhere. You know that. Non-profits are filled with people driven by a leftist agenda. They just want to humiliate corporations." Stephan looked irritated, but his voice was calm. "They make up shit or grossly exaggerate the facts. Do you seriously think they care about the welfare of the poor? They're not just in it for their own fame and glory?" The muscle in his jaw twitched. "Amicus submissions are *not* evidence. They're absolutely irrelevant."

Her throat knotted. She poured herself some orange juice and drank it quickly.

"Some tribunals in recent cases acknowledge the importance of amicus interventions. I summarized them. Do you want to go through my brief now?"

"I'll read it later. I appreciate your hard work. I'll worry about the rest from here out." He winked at her engagingly but she sensed it took effort. The conversation was over.

He got up and walked to the living room, interested in something on the television. She followed, bringing her cup of coffee. *Gold climbed for a third day, gaining alongside equities and other commodities before German and French leaders meet today to discuss the euro and as China said it will focus on aiding growth. Platinum and palladium gained. Spot gold rose as much as zero point three percent to $1,598.25 an ounce, the highest price since May tenth, and was at $1,596.25 at 11:00 A.M. in Singapore. Bullion last week rebounded after a twenty-one percent drop from an intraday record in September. The metal ended the week up zero point nine percent, the first weekly advance in three.*

"Yes!" Stephan said, throwing a punch in the air. He flipped channels between Bloomberg financial reports before tossing the remote control onto the couch. "I'm going to shower. We should take a drive through Rock Creek Park. Maybe get lunch somewhere. It's a magnificently beautiful day, and I'd like to spend it with you, my sweet Emmanuelle." He walked up to her, his eyes sparkling in the sunlight.

Her stomach fluttered. She was relieved his mood had brightened. Was he finally showing an interest in her? "Sounds wonderful," she said softly.

"Good. I'll be back down in ten minutes," he said, heading up the spiral staircase.

A while later, the fax machine rang. "Stephan," she called up the stairs. She could hear the shower running. She checked the machine as it clicked and buzzed. A light breeze stirred through the room. A page came through and then another. One fluttered to the floor near her feet.

Emmanuelle picked it up, intending to put it right back when she noticed it was an article in Portuguese from *Brasil em Folhas*, a Brazilian newspaper. The headline read: Geologist From The National Institute For Space Research Gunned Down In Broad Daylight. She glanced up the stairs and then quickly read it. There was no fax number to indicate where it had been sent from. *Why would someone send this to Stephan?* The machine clicked again. More pages were coming through.

Stephan appeared in the doorway, a towel wrapped around his waist. "What are you reading?" His lean, muscular physique glistened with beads of water.

"A newspaper article was just faxed to you. It's in Portuguese."

He took the page from her hand. His face looked strained. "You know I don't read Portuguese. What's it about?"

"A scientist from Brazil's National Institute for Space Research." She moved closer to him. "He was murdered in Rio."

He flipped through the pages. "It has no address, no telephone number. No indication of who sent it. That's odd." He picked up the other pages that had just come through. "Weird."

"Why would someone send this to you?"

"I don't know. Wrong number?" He shrugged disinterestedly. "It has to be a mistake. Hey, why don't we get lunch at Angler's Inn and talk about the future?"

The future? "That sounds wonderful."

"I'm thinking it's time to make some changes in my life." His voice was low. He was facing the window.

Throughout her years at the firm, most of the time they spent away had been strictly business. Any free time on a trip had been occupied with lunches, dinners or receptions with other attorneys. The conversation had always been about work. But two weeks earlier, things shifted. They had gone to Paris together for arbitration hearings at the International Commercial Court and every evening after the hearings they'd spent all of their time together. Stephan was unusually melancholy but kind, thoughtful and endearing the entire trip. He barely mentioned the hearings. He revealed to her that his mother had passed away a few weeks earlier. For the first time in their relationship, he talked about his childhood. Stephan exposed a deeply personal, affectionate side to his high-octane nature, being attentive to Emmanuelle in a different way than before. He took her to Galleries Lafayette and they shopped together. Later that evening he invited her to the Paris Opera. They had a quiet dinner in a high-ceilinged, open-space restaurant overlooking the city where he gave her a gold bracelet. They were truly alone for the first time in seven years. They talked through the evening, taking a long walk along the *Jardin des Tuileries* and the Seine. For the first time, Emmanuelle felt they held much in common.

Much to Emmanuelle's disappointment, when they returned to Washington, D.C. their relationship was quickly defined by the grind of work again, as though Paris had been imagined. Stephan was agitated and preoccupied with upcoming hearings.

According to rumors they were lovers, but in truth they had an intense work relationship with no romantic or physical involvement.

Emmanuelle's brother Camilo reproached her for the long hours with Stephan. "If you fall for this guy, it could ruin your career," he said. Once a week he walked from New York Avenue to her office to take her to lunch. "He's at least fifteen years older than you are! You talk about him as though he were God. He's just a lawyer. *Un simple abogado. Nada más.* Just another pinstriped suit walking down K Street in Washington, D.C. Seriously, Emmy, I think you are still traumatized by Papá's death."

"That's ridiculous, Camilo. And you've never liked anyone I dated."

"You never dated anyone I liked," Camilo laughed, ruffling her hair as though she were a child. "My guess is you're transferring emotions from the past that you never resolved."

She denied it, but Emmanuelle knew he was probably right. She was still wrestling with the death of their father.

Chapter 6

STEPHAN HENRI BRENT SAT at the head of the antique mahogany conference table in Oliver & Stone's meeting room. "Are you sure you want to do this?" he asked the executives of Hébère International Energy Company, tapping his pen on a legal pad. "Latin America has had so many water fiascos."

The afternoon sunlight gleamed on the table between them.

Mark Hollister, the CEO of Hébère International—Albert Thorman's biggest client—sat to his right. To his left, Leandro Piñeres, a young lawyer in the Arbitration Group who he'd brought in to take notes.

"When you mention privatization in Argentina, all hell breaks loose," Stephan told them. He wore an expensive navy blue suit, a white, tailored, silk shirt with gold cuff links, and a silk tie held in place by a gold clip. He glanced over at Thorman, who appeared to be holding his breath. The bastard wanted the deal so badly he couldn't have cared less how much hell broke loose in Argentina. He just wanted more billables.

Stephan reached for the crystal carafe of water. A hush fell over the room. The only sound was that of water pouring into his glass.

Thorman had a problem, which was why he dragged Stephan into this meeting. Thorman couldn't negotiate deals in

Argentina. He believed it was a country plagued with ideological disorder and a diseased economy. That affected his thinking. Thorman needed Stephan to close this deal with Hébère. The firm couldn't afford to lose any big clients now and Thorman was acting like the greatest kiss-ass the world had ever known. He'd even fixed Hollister's coffee himself.

Thorman's eyes were searing him now, practically pinning him against the wall. But Stephan decided to let him stew a bit. Thorman had been ducking financial matters that needed to be panned out. Stephan sipped his drink.

Hollister took the carafe and filled his own glass, locking eyes with Stephan. "We know the risks in South America. We just want you to feel out the situation. See if it's doable."

Hébère had an edge on Middle Eastern and African water markets. They wanted in on the Latin American region. "Argentina *needs* foreign investment."

Thorman broke in, "Fresh water is a scarce commodity." In other words, it had a big fat dollar sign on it.

"South America has an abundance of renewable freshwater resources. As long as countries privatize, we'll take the risk."

Stephan put his glass down and stared into it as though it were a crystal ball. He would accept, but he had to make Thorman suffer a little more. "Its just… I have an aversion to the demonstrations and chaos there. You know how it is in Argentina." His tone was mild, but he made sure it was sincere. He looked at his cell phone. It was lit with a new text. He scrolled through his messages, aware all eyes were on him. "Especially San Miguel de Tucumán," he continued without looking up. "Doing business in Argentina's a stressor. Remember what happened twenty years ago?" He put his phone down and looked at Hollister. "Massive protests. The French company flew out of there like a bat out of hell. The arbitration was one of the longest, most expensive ever." He thought for a few seconds. Was this his opportunity to turn things around? He picked up his phone again and thumbed out a text message: *On schedule as planned.* "Since 2000, Argentina's become more acclaimed for its picketers, riots and expropriations than for its tango. Ask Vivendi about the last tango in Tucumán."

Everyone laughed. All except for Thorman, whose eyes were fixed on Stephan. His expression said, *If you screw up this deal, I'll make the rest of your life very miserable*

"Risks are what political risk insurance is for, right?" Hollister said. "How can we lose with the world's savviest lawyer on our side?" He patted Stephan on the back.

Thorman was still holding his breath.

Stephan wondered for another moment. Maybe the opportunity he'd been waiting for *was* falling right into his lap? "Why not?" he said.

Thorman sighed in relief, breaking into a smile that exposed his incisors.

Stephan turned to Leandro Piñeres and whispered, "Make arrangements for me to get from Buenos Aires to Tucumán." Leandro's family chartered flights between South American cities.

"Sure," Leandro said. "No problem."

"Chile's a safer bet, but I'll go," Stephan said to Thorman.

Thorman nodded. "We should press forward in Chile as well. That country should be the economic model for all Latin American countries. Water can be bought, sold and traded there just like any other commodity. The majority of Latin American countries depend on hydro-electricity. With all the roaring rivers there, it's a huge potential money maker."

"True, true. We are making progress in the Patagonia," Hollister said. "Thanks to Thorman, we should move to the next phase of the dam project soon."

Leandro said, "But… you know there were massive protests over the dam proposals in Chile recently, right? There's intense public opposition to foreigners owning water resources."

Stephan kicked Leandro under the table. *Was he nuts?* He just broke an unspoken office law. That was associate suicide. Albert would go ballistic.

Leandro kept talking. "Ninety percent of the world's fresh water is trapped in ice sheets and glaciers. That leaves a small percentage of the earth's water for human consumption. More than one billion people in the world have no access to clean water. Water can't be treated as a commodity. Governments have to regulate water resources for public health and safety reasons."

Leandro's sorry ass would soon be airborne.

Thorman dropped his hand loudly on the table.

Leandro sat upright, startled.

"Corrupt third world governments can't manage water systems. Privatization is the only way to improve public health and safety." Thorman's complexion was splotched with rage.

Thorman was known to bellow expletive-laced tirades whenever someone challenged his notions of democracy, the free world, fair market and free trade. In other words, the world according to Thorman. The situation was spiraling dangerously out of control. Stephan had to break in.

"So, who am I meeting with in Argentina?" he asked Hollister.

"The head of the Tucumán municipality, Guillermo Santos," Hollister said, patting Stephan on the back again. "If anyone can cut us a clean and fast deal, it's you."

That was, after all, Stephan's style.

Thorman relaxed back in his chair.

Chapter 7

THREE DAYS LATER, Stephan asked Emmanuelle to drive him to the airport after work. "Keep my car till I come back," he said, handing her the keys.

"I'd rather drive it back to your place," she said. The Mercedes sports car was only one of several expensive cars he owned.

"Alright, but keep the keys and fetch me from the airport next week. You drive. I need to make a few calls on the way."

"If you insist." She watched him select files and pack them into his briefcase, noticing the perspiration stains near his armpits.

"I insist." He glanced back and smiled at her, but his tired, perhaps even worried eyes betrayed his enthusiasm. He hadn't opened up since their Paris trip. She assumed his mother's death had dredged up long-suppressed emotions. In Paris, she learned that his childhood had been difficult, marked by the death of his father when he was nine. His mother eventually remarried to a man who managed a mining project in Calgary that had failed a year later. His stepfather used his mother's money to pay off debts. The family was soon forced to move to a poorer neighborhood in the northeast region of the province. Stephan confided he had few fond memories from childhood to adolescence after his father died. He'd struggled through law school with a night school arrangement that permitted him to have day jobs. When he finally began earning money, he took pleasure in the fact that the 'mediocre fools'— as he called them—from the better neighborhoods of Calgary finally respected him.

He was now revered by the legal community. He gave generously to charities. Recently, he'd mentioned wanting to retire from law, perhaps leave the D.C. area. Financially, he could afford to.

Fifteen minutes later, they were on the George Washington Memorial Parkway headed to the airport. They rode with the top down through smooth-flowing traffic. After several calls, Stephan put his phone away.

"Emmanuelle…" He turned away from her, taking in the view of the Potomac River.

She judged from his tone he had something important to tell her but was now deciding against it. "You seem distracted lately," she said softly. "Is everything okay?"

"No, things are *not* okay." His tone startled her.

"What is it?" she asked, veering onto the exit.

No answer. They drove in silence for a few minutes.

Emmanuelle pulled up to the curb in front of the Reagan International Airport departure terminal. "Are you worried about this trip?"

He glanced at his ticket and then tucked it into his coat pocket.

She lowered her voice to a whisper. "*What* is not okay?"

He was staring ahead.

"Are you sick? Is it your health?"

"Nothing like that." He reached for his briefcase. "Look, I have to get to my plane." He was shutting off to her again.

She reached for his arm. "Don't leave like this. Are you alright? What's going on?"

He sat back, releasing his grip on his briefcase. "I've been

29

thinking, I wanted to tell you …" He turned to her and touched her cheek lightly. "You know there have been many women in my life, but I don't think I've ever felt…." He took her hand and caressed her fingers as he spoke. "You've been good to me. You've been *very* loyal to me. I don't think anyone I've ever worked with has ever been there so selflessly for me. I wanted to thank you for that."

"That's sweet, but … what's up? Why did you say things aren't okay?"

"Well, you know, I was pressured into taking the trip for Thorman. You know how that is. But … well, it's more than that."

"What is it? You're worrying me."

"I just want you to know, should anything ever happen to me, I would roll over in my grave if I hadn't told you what you mean to me and how grateful I am for all you've done for me." He stroked her face pensively. "Never doubt that."

Now she *was* worried. "What could happen to you?"

"Nothing." His signature smile returned. "I'll be back on Tuesday. Put a Dom Perignon on ice before you pick me up." He leaned over and kissed her gently on the lips. He'd never done that before. In seconds he was out the door.

She watched as he quickened his pace and disappeared through the terminal doors.

An hour later, she was parking his car at his house in Potomac. Searching her purse for her cell phone to call a cab, Emmanuelle noticed a USB drive on the floor in front of the passenger seat. "Oh no!" He would probably need it.

She dialed Stephan's number. It immediately switched to voicemail. She looked at her watch. *He must be on the plane by now.* She put the USB stick in her purse and called a taxi.

Chapter 8

AT 8:30 A.M., Stephan Henri Brent adjusted his tie in the mirror and smoothed his hair. He was dressed in an Italian-tailored cashmere jacket and matching pants. He picked up a cigar, lit it and blew a ring of smoke to himself in the mirror before stepping out of his hotel room.

Outside, a black Mercedes sedan pulled up and he got in. The meetings were being held in the offices of the Municipal Directorate of Water Services of Tucumán.

The car rolled through the center of town. Flyers were pasted to the walls of buildings in colorful mosaics, announcing music festivals, cultural activities, and political demonstrations. The city was a hub for Argentine culture. It was the birthplace of a host of folk singers, literary scholars, authors, musicians, botanists, and painters renowned throughout South America. Streams of little blue and white flags, now looking rather tattered and dirty some weeks after independence day celebrations, were tangled around street polls.

Stephan heard shouting, chanting in the near distance. The car slowed as it cut the corner. Picketers were clustered outside the municipal building. The noise spiked as the car crawled through the crowd.

"What's going on?" he asked the driver.

"*Piqueteros.*"

"*Obviously.* What the hell are they protesting?" he groaned, biting off the end of another cigar and clamping it between his teeth.

The driver shrugged.

Stephan cracked the window and struck the flint of his lighter, puffing until the cigar was lit. "Bullshit anarchy is what it is. Who has time for this shit? *Compadre,* your country's got great restaurants and nightlife but this shit pisses your country away."

"*Che viste. Las puta madres que los parió.*" The taxi driver raised a hand in disgust as he cursed the whoring mothers of the demonstrators and police. "It's the thieving government's fault. *¡Boludos corruptos!*"

A picketer slapped his palm against the car door.

His driver blasted the horn in response. "*¡Criminale!*"

Stephan craned his neck to read the signs. "Oh, Jesus Murphy. Fucking *lovely.* They're protesting water privatizations, eh? Bloody coincidence, is it? Stinking anarchists."

"Yes. Stinking anarchists," the driver echoed, looking at Stephan in the rear view mirror. The car crept through the traffic jam. "All they do is figure out ways to block traffic and keep everyone else from working."

They pulled up to the entrance of the building. "*¡Que suerte!* It's your lucky day. The police aren't protesting for higher wages today. Maybe those *boludos* in military boots can help you get into the municipal building."

A cluster of officers of the *Policía Federal Argentina* dressed in riot gear pushed through the crowd to get to the car. The shouting grew louder as they opened the door. As Stephan got out, the police protectively surrounded him.

Two men got out of a car behind them. They were dressed in bureaucratic suits and shiny shoes, carrying leather briefcases deformed by the enormous volume of papers they held. "Señor Brent?" one of them said.

"Yes," he said, eyeing them skeptically.

The police shoved him forward. Protestors were breaking through the perimeter. A security officer at the entrance of the municipal building opened the door and pointed in the direction of a large conference room. "Mr. Santos will be with you shortly."

Stephan paused in the doorway, inspecting the spacious, high-ceilinged, rib-vaulted room before heading over to the French windows and peering out at the *Casa Histórica de la Independencia*—the historic building where the first *Congreso Argentino* met in the 1800s to proclaim Argentine independence from Spain. The city was then a cradle of independence movements against the colonialists in South America who'd come to exploit the region's abundance of sugarcane, rice, tobacco and fruit. It was later reconstructed as a national monument to symbolize the expulsion of the Spaniards.

A subtle reminder of how swiftly they throw foreigners out, Stephan thought.

The two bureaucrats took seats at the conference table and stared at Stephan who was pacing, shoes clipping sharply on the marble floor.

A thin, balding man in a grey suit came into the room, his arm extended in greeting. "*Buenos días*, Señor Brent. I am Juan Carlos Santini, *asesor legal* for the municipality." Stephan eyed the man and judged from his attire that the man ranked low in the hierarchy of the municipality. His shoes were worn and dusty, coat too long, pants baggy and wrinkled. A long strand of greying hair was combed from one ear to the other and held in place with a shiny emollient of some sort.

"Some of the negotiators haven't arrived yet."

"It's not likely they will now, is it?" Stephan retorted. "This is a bloody waste of my time."

The man shrugged, looking at his watch. "*Mirá vos*, for me, too. It was dark when I got out of bed this morning. I drive two hours in traffic to get here. With this parade outside, we won't start before noon." Getting to work was more upsetting than the crowd raging outside.

"How did they find out about the meeting?" Stephan demanded, narrowing his eyes.

Santini shrugged again, running a hand along the top of his head slowly, as though verifying things were in place up there.

The noise suddenly grew louder. Picketers were crying, *¡Abajo la Privatización! Water isn't a commodity. It's a fundamental right. Governments shouldn't allow privatization of something so critical to human life. ¿Qué sigue ahora? ¿Privatización del aire que respiramos?*

Santini grimaced. His eyes darted to Stephan and then back to the scene outside the window. Then he gasped, as though he'd just realized the demonstration wasn't merely the everyday rally that cluttered city traffic. This was serious.

"No one was supposed to know about the meeting. Who leaked information to the press?" Stephan asked angrily. He loosened his collar and patted the breast pocket of his jacket in search of cigars.

He found his phone and thumbed out a text message. *Where the bloody devil are you?*

Chapter 9

TINY RAYS OF light gamboled in the chiseled crystal of the liquor glasses on Guillermo Santos' desk. A shot of whiskey at the end of the day had become habitual for the chief representative of the Tucumán municipality. But the day had only just begun and he was ready for it now. His political enemies had just consigned his career to oblivion. He was certain of that. This *smelled* like the work of his enemies. They'd orchestrated the demonstrations to turn the mobs against him. *¡Hijos de la gran puta!*

"*¿Qué es eso?*" he cried, slapping the newspaper down onto his desk, sending a passel of papers fluttering to the ground. He got up and paced back and forth, hands behind his back like a prisoner awaiting execution. The mob outside was making him panic. Visions of his political demise filled his head. He patted the breast pocket of his black and white pinstriped suit, pulled out a pack of unfiltered Gitanes and lit up.

The *Gaceta*—Tucumán's principal daily paper—bore the headlines, The Water Rats and Blood-Suckers Return. It depicted a caricature of a fat, bloated rat extending a fistful of United States dollars. In the background, thirsty and desiccated Tucumán citizens were covered with slugs.

"Look at the papers," he said to his secretary, picking them up and tossing them across the table.

The papers conjectured that a certain water company—driven out of the country by Argentine protesters years before—was back to take over the facilities and water would soon become inaccessible to the poor again.

Guillermo sucked in a dramatic breath and blew out a stream of smoke as he watched the picketing mob now chanting anti-World Bank and anti-IMF slogans. They blamed globalization and the world's financial institutions for sinking the country into poverty.

Everyone knew Guillermo had been positioning himself to become the minister of justice. This scandal would certainly disqualify him. He spotted several members of his staff leaving the building to join the dissenters.

"Bloodsucking Assassins! ¡Sanguijuelas ¡Asesinos! ¡Sanguijuelas Asesinos." They shouted in the direction of Guillermo's window. Appalled, he slipped back, away from their view.

"How did they find out?" Guillermo roared, smoke blowing from his nostrils like a basilisk. He glared at his assistant, an elegant, fair-skinned woman who wore a cream-colored business suit with a Latin-styled flair.

"How would I know?" she said, indignant.

She marched over to him, stopping so close he felt her minty breath on his face. She slid a hand across his chest—the way a police officer frisks a suspect—until she found the Gitanes in his pocket. She yanked them out.

Guillermo took the box back from her and offered her a cigarette from it. "We didn't agree to anything. Just a meeting." His voice dropped to a conspiratorial whisper. "They'll say we're hypocrites."

"I warned you," she said, snatching the cigarette and his lighter. She struck the flint and waited for a moment as the flame sparked before lighting it, staring into his eyes through a cloud of smoke with a lingering sort of look. A look that said she would never sleep with him again. Her tortoise-shelled spectacles reminded him she was probably smarter than he was. "*¿Ché, viste?* What did you expect?" She blew smoke in his face. "You never listen to me."

"Someone set this up. I'm certain." Santos dropped the butt on the ground and lit another cigarette for himself.

He looked out at the mountains above the city. South America was experiencing a fierce winter, breaking records of the last half-century. The blizzard blew thick, white clouds of snow, obscuring the sky over the Aconquija Mountains.

"*S'acabó.* My career is over." He picked up a fat file crammed with yellowing, wrinkled documents and headed to the conference room, cursing the whoring mothers of his political opponents.

The clamor outside was deafening. Several men were trying to force their way into the building, banging pipes loudly against the wrought-iron gates. Suddenly, the gates burst under the weight of the protestors. People surged forward, shoving police officers to the ground.

In the conference room Guillermo radioed security. "We need to get out of the building," he told Stephan who was now looking at his cell phone.

"My security people are here," Stephan replied.

A large, smoking object crashed through the window.

Stephan and the negotiators scattered for safety. A disheveled-looking man with a battered briefcase pushed past Guillermo, nearly toppling him as he fled.

Two heavily armed men dressed in black arrived. Stephan hurried to them.

The wailing of police sirens reverberated through the business district as more trucks teemed with police rolled into the area.

Chapter 10

ALBERT THORMAN WAITED in the sitting room behind his office. It was nearly 9:00 A.M. FBI Special Agent Samuel Jackson would soon arrive. He debated whether or not to let Jackson into this part of the office. It was a private area he shared with Stephan.

Few people had the privilege of being allowed in. It was filled with antiques and relics from Europe they'd collected over the course of their practice. He stared at the still-life porcelain painting by the early Nineteenth Century Austrian artist, Josef Nigg. It was one of his favorites. His eyes shifted to an oil painting by Franz von Stuck. A recent addition to the office's collection, a portrait of Sisyphus, the mythological King of Corinth, naked and struggling to push a boulder up a hill. Stephan would have laughed if he were here. Was it the truth? Did all of man's efforts to climb to the bitter peak inescapably come plowing down to destroy him? Would all he'd worked for come plummeting down on him? Was that the rule of life? He would fight until the bitter end. Stephan was going to learn a lesson. And it was coming soon. *He'll soon find out who the real king is...*

His gaze traveled the room, perusing every one of his possessions in it. Thorman decided he couldn't let the FBI in here. They wouldn't understand. He deserved these luxuries. He had worked hard all of his life. He was a trail-blazing pioneer in natural resource exploitation contracts. It was his mission to ensure that the world's resources were in the right hands. A mission that nothing and no one could stop. A new economic world order was emerging. With Islamic fundamentalism on the rise and leftist nationalism resurgent in Latin American, the industrious had to maintain control. Everyone was created equal, but some were more equal than others.

Chapter 11

EMMANUELLE OPENED THE double-stained-glass entry doors of Oliver & Stone. Before she could greet the secretary, the large flat-screen television in the reception area caught her attention.

A CNN news report displayed a picture of Stephan Henri Brent, with "Breaking News" scrolling underneath. A foreign correspondent was reporting from outside an Argentine government building in Tucumán de San Miguel. *Stephan Henri Brent, a Canadian-born international arbitrator is apparently missing after demonstrations against the privatization of a water facility here turned violent yesterday. Brent came to negotiate on behalf of water conglomerate, Hébère International. Angry protestors stormed the gates and closed in on the negotiators here inside of the municipal building.* The scene switched to clips of the protesters.

"Oh my God," Emmanuelle gasped. Her briefcase slipped from her hands. She checked her cell phone for messages. Stephan hadn't responded to texts she'd sent him the night before.

The news traveled through the office like wildfire. Within minutes, there was buzzing everywhere. A handful of fashionably dressed lawyers appeared in the reception area, their assistants and office staff less than a step behind them, all wearing expressions of shock. One of the lawyers picked up the phone at the reception desk and dialed someone. "Turn on the news. It's about Brent."

Before the broadcast was over, a small crowd had gathered in front of the screen. Someone switched the channel to BBC News.

Emmanuelle stood frozen, briefcase and files scattered at her feet, watching. A British correspondent reported from Buenos Aires. *American officials and representatives of the Argentine government are in disagreement over what happened to one of the world's most prominent lawyers. US Embassy officials here today are suggesting someone in the Argentine government leaked information to the public about controversial plans to privatize the city's water facilities, sparking protests that may have resulted in the abduction of Stephan Henri Brent.*

The news shifted to an interview with the United States ambassador to Argentina, a graying man wearing a blue suit with a U.S. flag pin and a red tie. *We believe Mr. Brent was abducted, and we will do everything in our power to find the perpetrators and bring them to justice.* The Argentine minister of foreign affairs writhed in response to the US ambassador's invective. *There's simply no evidence Mr. Brent was abducted. We know for a fact he was personally escorted from the building by his own private security.* He spoke in clear but accented English. The anger in his eyes flashed through his modern, half-rimmed eyeglasses. *He left the city on a private jet that hasn't been sighted since it took off. With the blizzards of the past few days, it's very possible the plane went down in the Aconquija Mountains on the outskirts of Tucumán.*

When the broadcast was over, everyone began speaking at the same time.

"Has anyone been in touch with the US embassy in Argentina?" a young associate asked.

No one answered.

A French attorney who'd joined the Arbitration Group as a partner a few years earlier asked, "Are search efforts under way?" He looked at Emmanuelle for an answer.

"I don't know." Her first collected thought was of the

strange conversation she'd had with Stephan before he left. Had he sensed something was going to go terribly wrong? "This is the first I've heard of this." She tried to suppress the panic in her voice. "Shall I try to call the embassy?"

"I'll talk to Thorman and see what's going on," he said calmly, looking pointedly at her briefcase and papers scattered near her feet.

She bent down and picked them up.

"Thank you," he said.

***

Emmanuelle stood outside of Thorman's office. A half hour had passed since he'd asked her to wait there, but he continued to ignore her. Through the open door she could see he was on the phone furiously punching in numbers, making one call after another.

Her knees trembled.

He finally slammed the phone down angrily. "Are the Hebérè International files in Stephan's office? I can't find them anywhere."

Was he directing that at her?

"Did he take them with him? I need them *now*," he shouted.

There was no one else near. "No idea," she responded. Why would he raise his voice at her?

"I want a list of all his contacts in Argentina. Who the hell arranged his flight?"

"Which flight?" she asked, walking into his office.

"San Miguel to Buenos Aires." He spoke slowly, as though he were addressing an idiot. "I assumed you would know."

His tone and attitude were insulting. Her pulse accelerated. "He didn't mention anything to me." She forced herself to stay calm. "I can ask Martha." Martha was the staff person who generally took care of travel arrangements for the office.

"Maybe Michael Ross knows," Thorman said.

She'd heard the name before. *Ross...Ross.* Managing director for the Argentine water project. She swiped the touch screen of her phone twice. "I've got his number in my phone."

He wrote it down. "Don't just stand there. Get me the files."

She lingered for a moment. He busied himself with the computer screen. The hostility in his voice was clear. Where was it coming from? He'd never been so aggressive before.

The intercom buzzed. "Mr. Thorman, the American Embassy is on line two. The Ambassador will speak to you now."

"Ambassador Goodall, it's so good to hear your voice," Thorman said, abruptly smooth and polite. With an impatient gesture he motioned for Emmanuelle to leave his office. He didn't want her to hear the conversation. What was the secrecy about?

Emmanuelle walked to Stephan's office as quickly as possible without calling attention to herself. She searched for the files.

Thorman was still on the phone when she returned. She waited by the door again, cradling the files, straining to listen to the conversation. In the corner of her eye, she saw he was signaling for her to go away. Emmanuelle pretended to be reading something in the files, shifting weight from one foot to another.

He ended the call and she went in. "Is there any news?"

"Nope. No news." No eye contact.

Her ears started to buzz. She sensed he'd learned something.

Thorman stared at his computer, scrunching his porcine features into an ugly squint—his alternative to wearing reading glasses. "Thanks. I'll let you know if I need you," he said.

"Okay." *Asshole.*

***

A while later, Thorman's secretary tapped lightly on Emmanuelle's office door. She was an older woman with a slight drawl who had worked there for more than thirty years. Associates quickly learned she was the kind of employee who was accustomed to being the scapegoat for Thorman's mistakes.

"Ms. Solis, Mr. Thorman wants a list of the cases you're working on. He asked me to copy your files."

That would be madness. "All of my files?" Emmanuelle asked. Her stomach cramped with anxiety as she stood. What was going on? Without Stephan, she felt vulnerable. He'd been her sole contact point for everything she worked on since he hired her.

The secretary took her glasses off and folded them, regarding Emmanuelle caringly. "Are you okay, hun?"

"I'm fine," Emmanuelle said, softening her tone. "He wants *all* of the files?"

"I guess." The secretary looked perplexed for a moment. "He wants the FINRA files immediately."

"What FINRA files? What's he talking about?"

"I don't know. I don't even know what FINRA is."

"It's the regulatory body for securities. Was there a FINRA arbitration going on? How would I not know of that?"

She shrugged. "He just said to copy the FINRA files. I assumed you would know. So I…" her tone was apologetic. "I didn't ask questions."

"I'll bet you didn't. You were probably afraid to, right?" Emmanuelle whispered as she opened the cabinet beside her desk and sifted through files, even though she knew it was pointless. "Tell Thorman I don't have any FINRA files. I'm not aware of anything pending in FINRA."

"He mentioned contacting FINRA to postpone the hearing."

Emmanuelle shut the file cabinet. "What is Thorman talking about? Was Stephan representing a company under investigation? Was he seated as arbitrator in a FINRA hearing?" That would be hard to believe. She would know if that were the case.

She shrugged again. "He's on the phone with FINRA now letting them know that Stephan won't be back in time for the hearing."

Emmanuelle's insides went icy. Stephan wasn't dead. No one knew what had happened. He could surface at any moment. Why was Thorman acting as though Stephan were never coming back?

"Martha, are you sure it's one of Stephan's cases?"

"Hun, I only know what Thorman tells me. Oh, and Thorman wants you to keep working on the Ecuador memorial. Does that make sense?" The secretary canted her head to the side.

Emmanuelle nodded.

"He'll be gone all next week for an arbitration hearing in Bonn. He's still trying to prepare despite all of this news. Can you imagine? I am sure he'll talk to you when he gets back."

Emmanuelle sat on the edge of her desk and listened as the secretary chatted away. "I know you must be devastated. My heart stopped when I saw the news. Stephan is such a dear. Always so kind and generous. Especially with my family." She was whispering. "You know, I almost lost my house when my husband died."

"Did Stephan help you?"

"Yes. He's a rare breed in this office." She was barely audible now. "I think he's the only truly good man among the partners." She glanced behind her to make sure no one overheard. "Look, just take your time and when Thorman leaves, I'll come help you figure out what he needs. Here," she said, picking up a pen from Emmanuelle's desk and writing something on a legal pad. "My home phone number. If you need anything, don't hesitate to call me. When Stephan gets back, everything will return to normal." She smiled affectionately before leaving the office.

Emmanuelle closed the door. All she could think of was her last minutes with Stephan. She spent the rest of the day scanning the Internet for news about the protests in Argentina, calling colleagues in South America and responding to inquiries about Stephan.

***

The jolt of the elevator brought Emmanuelle's attention back to reality. As the doors opened, she saw frenzied journalists and media people in a shoving match with security guards at the entrance of the building. She jabbed at the elevator button and rode down to the parking lot, leaving through a side door. She stopped at a newsstand on K and 19th Street. Pictures of Stephan caught her eye. His disappearance had made front-page news across the world. She grabbed a copy of every paper with his face on it and handed the newsstand boy a fifty-dollar bill. Not waiting for the change, she flagged a cab home.

Inside her apartment, Emmanuelle was conscious of how empty and quiet it was. She kicked off her heels, dropped her briefcase and headed to her bedroom with the newspapers. She sat there until the sun rose, churning over her last conversation with Stephan, reading the news reports, flipping between all-night news channels. The CNN, Bloomberg, MSNBC, and BBC talking heads all conjectured about Stephan's disappearance.

Dear God, what could have happened to Stephan? She prayed for his safety.

Chapter 12

CHIEF SCIENTIST NILS Giaever stood on the observation deck of the *Antarctic Mist*. It was 8:00 A.M. and the ship was positioned west of the Southern Patagonian Ice Field. The Norwegian glaciologist raised his binoculars, assessing the desolate fishing hamlet ahead.

The fog-enveloped Nothofagus forest lining the island's mountaintops gave the place a mystical aura from a distance. But if the name 'Puerto Edén' had been given to it as a biblical allusion, it fell miserably short of the reference. There was nothing heavenly about the place other than the fact that it was situated in a remote location that was very difficult to access.

Most of the island's inhabitants lived in rustic wooden houses with no running water or electricity. The houses lining the wharf were mounted on rickety-looking stilts to prevent them from sinking into the perpetually rising waters. *Palafitos*, they were called.

The island was perched on the cliff of a mountain that, over the course of thousands of years, had become almost entirely submerged in rising seawaters. A few hundred people lived there now, mostly fisherman. Among them, the last surviving members of the ancient Kawésqar tribe that had inhabited the Patagonia since the last Ice Age. There were now less than ten of them in the world and little was recorded about their history—which now seemed mythological. The unfortunate creatures of circumstance once kindled fires in their sand-lined canoes in defiance of the fiercely cold climate and swam in glacial waters, hunting for food among seals and whales.

Nils continued to scan with his binoculars. Morning was inching up the horizon. Islanders in red and yellow wooden boats were making their way to the ship to bring team members ashore. He focused on faces, searching for Juan Carlos Messier. He was one of the last Kawésqars. Unlike anyone else in his tribe, Juan had taken advantage of a government grant for indigenous Indians, moved to Santiago, and gotten a degree in glaciology. For years, he had solicited Nils' help to put together an expedition. Three years ago they began putting that dream into action.

The *Antarctic Mist* was several hours off course. The eighty-knot winds of the night before hadn't rattled Nils as much as the stillness around him now did. Not a breeze stirred and the world seemed to be holding its breath. The sea ahead of Nils mirrored the snow-peaked mountain range like polished glass. The silence was so absolute Nils could hear the sound of the slightest movement. The rustle of clothes, the flutter of distant birds, his own breath—as time ticked away the last days of the expedition. This would be his last expedition. He had organized many over the past twenty years, each one involving lengthy periods away from home.

Before each journey, his time was consumed soliciting grant money. Competition for funding was fierce. When he returned, there were reports to finish, conferences to attend, papers to publish. There was never enough time. Leading an expedition used to be exhilarating. Somewhere along the course of his career, the allure had been lost. With heightening governmental debate about climate change, his work, along with that of thousands of other scientists had been thrown into a massive political shit storm.

The media distorted the debate, demanding evidence beyond any margin of error. *As though science were a crystal ball,* Nils thought grimly. Lost in the confusion was the basic consensus of the majority of scientists—climate change was a reality that demanded an urgent response. It was causing catastrophic changes in the environment. Yet politicians expected one hundred percent proof before enacting any reforms. What were they thinking? Scientific conclusions on climate change were based on years of observation and analysis of the past. *It presents a clear and present danger to civilization.*

The ice cores Nils and his colleagues had painstakingly retrieved from retreating glaciers confirmed their existence for hundreds and, in some cases, thousands of years. And clearly, the conditions that sustained glaciers for those periods were rapidly changing. The current warming was unusual and adversely impacted by human activities. And yet, countries were not taking action.

A shrill, grating noise pierced Nils' thoughts. The rusted metal stairs behind him were clanking under someone's weight. He lowered his binoculars and glanced back.

A young man, olive-complexion, tall and strong, with a crew cut, black beret and thick wind pants was coming up onto the deck.

"Sir, the commanding officer's been looking for you."

"Tell'im to bugger off," Nils mumbled. "He's a pain in the ass, your captain. He's got a Napoleon complex, you know? The short bastard. The entire trip's been a blasted test of wills. Arguing 'round every bend in the fjords."

"Sorry?" the young man said, looking startled.

"*Bueno, ya.* Okay. Thank you." Nils dismissed him with a slight wave. "Tell him I'll be down in a few."

"Been out here all night?"

"Since the storm passed."

"Everything alright?"

The question disarmed Nils. No one ever expressed concern for him. "Fine. You are? Remind me please."

"My name is Belisario Araya."

"With the Chilean Navy, are you? *La Armada?*"

"No, sir. Just a volunteer."

"Ah, yes. That's right. The conservation mission?" Nils asked, referring to a private nature reserve dedicated to conserving rare plant and wildlife species of the Patagonia. It supported the expedition team with research and volunteers.

"Yes, I'm hoping to learn about isotropic analysis on this trip. I'd like to go with you when you collect the ice core samples from the Pio XI Glacier," Belisario said. "I'm thinking about maybe studying to be a glaciologist." He smiled. "Like you. I just applied to the University of Concepción. My brother, Martín, graduated from there this year."

Nils often puttered through the ice-choked waters in his skiff alone. But this time, he and several others were planning to collect, label and analyze snow and ice samples from the Pio XI Glacier. They would then package and send the samples to the International Ice Core Laboratory in Norway for analysis.

Belisario was muscular and energetic-looking. They needed help lugging the equipment. The drill they used to penetrate the ice weighed a ton. "Sure. Could use some help transporting and managing the drill."

"*Excelente.*" Belisario smiled heartily.

Nils shielded his eyes from the rising sun. "Pio XI might be the only glacier still standing when you finish your studies."

"Is that so?"

"Unfortunately, yes. Pío XI's an anomaly in a melting icescape." He waved his arm. "Of the forty-eight glaciers in the

Southern Patagonian Ice field, forty-six are losing mass quickly. Only one is stable. Pío XI. It's advancing like a demon and shoving several centuries of forest out of its way. Uprooting the Magallenic Subpolar Forest lining the mountains."

"Why *is* it advancing when the others are melting?"

"Who knows? That's why we're out here. Could be related to Lautaro," he said. This was an active volcano from which the Southern Ice Field radiated. "Or the tectonic plates pressing together. The South American, Nazca, and Antarctic tectonic plates are colliding and lifting those massive mountains," he said pointing to the Andes Mountain range running behind the island. "That's why they're all crinkled up like that. Stress causes the volcanoes scattered throughout them. The ice here is almost always at melting point. This area gets thirty feet of snow or more a year."

Belisario listened intently. Nils examined him for a few seconds. There was a quality in his eyes he couldn't quite place. Innocence perhaps, or youthful ardor. Nils guessed he was about the age of his son, Aimar. A sudden wave of guilt crashed over him. Aimar had been born deaf. Having a deaf son had been foreign to everything Nils had known and expected about child-rearing. No one in his family had been born with any disabilities. And he'd never had the time to understand Aimar's world. That was his wife's job. And his expeditions had only further put a rift between them.

Nils pulled off his wool cap and ran a hand through his fine blond hair. "It's a lonely business, this one. Especially for a young man like you. You could end up spending most of your life alone in this vast field of emptiness. Then, you get back to reality and find out politicians are makin' cock'n bull stories of your research for their own political gain. It's a bite in the ass, this business."

The solitude and distance of these journeys used to have an

anesthetic effect on Nils. Fading memories, distancing emotions. Nils was fifty-five now. He was tired of spending so much time alone. In spite of his journey to rescue the world, he'd hardly ever been there for his son. He couldn't think about Aimar now. He had to focus on the final expedition. It was important, he told himself. This was mission to end all of his missions. He knew this expedition would bring closure to his scientific searches as well as personal ones. He'd calculated it precisely. He would finalize his research, fill in the gaps of missing data, submit the report, and from then on out it would be home. There wasn't any more he could do that would impact the state of the world. Then he would spend more time with Aimar. Make up for his past absence. "This all seems like a massive expanse of emptiness now. No limits, no boundaries."

"Emptiness, sir? To you, this is emptiness?" Belisario said. The rising sun cast diamonds of light on the water behind him.

"Yes. I do see it that way. I used to like it. It's been my escape from the dissonant sounds of the world. I liked the quiet. The vast open spaces." They were both leaning against the ship's rail, staring out at the island in the distance. "It's grown too quiet. It's become a deadly sort of silence. Too empty." He turned and faced Belisario. "What draws you to this? You running from something, *compadre?*"

"I am not running from anything," he answered with a wholehearted laugh. "To me, sir, all of this is the nexus between the tangible and the intangible. The connection between man and the stars. The connection between man and the angels. There's an energy about it. That's what I feel out here."

"What you feel are massive, rumbling volcanoes and shifting tectonic plates. No angels. Just volcanoes and a shifting planet." He turned to study Belisario.

Belisario smiled. "I expected that kind of a... well, clinical explanation from you, sir." He shrugged innocently. "I see it differently though."

The ship's commanding officer appeared on the deck. A few steps behind him, Philip Sands, a New Zealand volcanologist who worked for the Smithsonian Institute. He spent most of the year examining the earth's crevices, craters, fissures and cracks in vastly uninhabited places of the world. Expedition team members were streaming up the stairs behind them.

"Nils, we're at the base of the cliff," the captain said. "The ship can't weave through the rock bench any farther. It will rip this vessel in two." His posture was rigid, his expression void of emotion.

"I'm aware of that, Martín."

"The anglers are coming to take us ashore."

"I see them. Thank you." Nils raised his binoculars again, spotting fisherman on the wharf. Impoverished, weather-worn men staring back at them. *Hoping we're interested in their gigantic smoked or pickled mussels, king crabs, and sea urchins.*

"We may be here longer than you planned."

Nils lowered the binoculars and faced him. "What do you mean?" Nils was paying for every day of ship-time and for the investigations. The grant money was barely enough to cover the expedition. If they were delayed, the expenses would run over the budget.

"There's a storm to the south of us." The thrust of the commanding officer's chin said *he*, not the chief scientist or any other scientist on board, would have the last say on whether or not they would sail.

Nils let out a hollow laugh. "This vessel was built for navigating ice-encumbered waters in all kinds of weather. It's been through much worse in Norway."

Philip pulled him aside. "The trip through the Strait of

Magellan is extremely difficult to navigate under normal conditions," he whispered. "The currents are unpredictable. Thirty-foot waves. Gale force winds. Don't push it."

"That's easy for you to say, Philip. You're not stuck with the tab when the expedition is over. I'm paying for ship time."

Andres Saavedra, a Chilean seismologist who studied the thousands of tremors rocking the Aysén Province, came up the stairs. "We lost three of the ocean-bottom seismometers last night. They were recording underwater earth motion before the storm broke."

Two female volunteers kept close to his side. One was pale and had dark circles under her eyes. Seasick, Nils guessed.

"They just wouldn't release from the sea floor in time," one of the girls said.

"The Argos satellite tracking system has just located two of them," someone behind her called out. "They came back up to the surface through the back-time release. We are checking our options to see if the Navy will help us recover them."

"We'll risk more equipment," Philip said.

"That's right," the captain added. "The Navy may close the port. If it does, we aren't going anywhere."

Nils winced at the thought of losing more equipment. He did some quick mental math. Losing equipment could be more costly than extended ship time. No matter how hard he struggled with it, he knew it was the captain's call.

"This place isn't called the Province of Last Hope for no reason," Andres said, unzipping his wool-insulated jacket and stroking his moustache. "It's called that because this is your last chance to turn around. You keep on going and you'll get a lesson in atmospheric sorcery." He gave the sick-looking volunteer a beguiling smile.

"It's amazing the sun is out," Andres said. A school of dolphins whooshed alongside the ship. "This place gets inundated with six meters of rain a year. It rains 363 days a year and today is no exception. It looks like last night's storm followed us here."

Dark clouds rapidly filled the sky again.

The entire team crowded around Nils and the captain on the deck.

"It might do us some good to rest. I've slept about six hours in the past seventy two." Nils conceded.

"You can expect seventy knot winds farther south," Philip said, looking at the girls still clinging to Andres. "Ten meter waves as we pass through the strait. It's enough to turn your stomach inside out."

Both girls groaned.

***

It was exactly 6:00 P.M. and the sky over Puerto Edén was black. On shore, team members and volunteers were filing into the Armada building. All eyes were fixed on Nils. They wondered whether he'd gotten permission from the *Armada de Chile* to continue the journey. Naval officers were still reviewing the team's paperwork. Nils and the captain had been with them all day as they inspected the ship and its equipment for seaworthiness.

One of the officials finally approached the captain and handed him the paperwork. "*Listo.*"

Nils and Philip exchanged glances and went over. Nils asked the captain, "So … does that mean we're cleared?"

"Yes, they're done."

"And the weather?"

"The port reopened. We're cleared to proceed."

Nils felt a rush of relief. "Good news, everyone," he called, raising his voice over the chatter. "We're cleared to go on."

Loud cheers went up.

"So, let's relax and have a drink," Philip said, wrapping his scarf tightly around his neck and rubbing his hands. "It's freezing in here." He pointed to the woodstove, but Nils didn't budge.

"Where is Karl Gustav?" Nils asked, looking around. Karl Gustav Madeiro was a scientist who worked for Brazil's National Institute for Space Research. He had just completed a study on climate-altering pollution caused by large dams.

"Wasn't he with you when the *Armada* was inspecting the ship?"

"He left to get insurance papers from his bungalow. He said he'd be right back. We're lucky the *Armada* didn't insist on seeing them. With their one-size-fits-all rules, they could have held us here all week." He looked at his watch. "That was five hours ago. Where the hell is he?"

"My guess, he's put on his night-vision goggles and gone ahead of us to monitor some late-night glacial calving." He grinned, glancing around the room.

"Very funny."

"It's possible. He's just as anal as you are. The two of you are insomniacs. Work like demons day and night. Relax, for Christ's sake." He motioned for Belisario to join them. "Can you bring this bloke one of those little shots of whatever it is they're passing around?"

"Pisco. Distilled liquor. Pretty strong stuff."

"Strong, you say? Make that two shots."

"Certainly." Belisario disappeared into the crowd.

Team members had gathered around the woodstove. Some circled around *Armada* officers asking questions, sipping drinks. Nils and Philip joined them.

A senior research scientist from an earth observatory institute was sitting on the floor next to Andres Saavedra. They were discussing the hundreds of recent tremors and earthquakes in the area. Her work involved monitoring the activity of submarine volcanoes. The two were flipping through satellite images on her iPad.

"Has anyone seen Karl Gustav?" Nils asked.

Shrugs and blank faces. Johan Bahr, a German scientist who often accompanied Nils on expeditions offered to go look for him. He headed to the door.

Belisario handed Nils a shot of Pisco.

He took a sip and grimaced. "You haven't seen him either?"

"Not since the inspection."

The door opened and several locals came through carrying trays of food. They walked to the back of the room where others were arranging tables. A lanky figure bracing a pile of firewood stacked to his chin marched in behind them and headed to the stove. He set the wood down and began poking at the fire. It crackled and hissed. Sparks flew out. A small burning ember rolled close to one of Nils' colleagues.

She jumped quickly to her feet. "You almost wouldn't mind if your ass caught on fire here. It's so damn cold," she said, rubbing her hands close to the fire.

Others laughed.

Nils summoned everyone to gather around him.

Some of the chatter subsided.

"As many of you know, we chose to meet here in Puerto Edén as a tribute to the Kawésqar tribe. I'd like to introduce my long-time friend, Juan Carlos Messier. Some of you already know him. His perseverance made this expedition possible. He's been coordinating with Chilean government agencies on our behalf to get the authorizations we needed." He motioned to a towering man with square shoulders, a flat, abundant nose, protruding lips, a prominent brow, tan leathery skin moving across the room to join him. The crowd applauded heartily.

"My ancestors spent most of their lives in canoes, fearful of nature's malevolent spirits—the violent wind, the furious sea, the incendiary lightening, the deafening thunder, the fire-spitting mountains, the trembling earth. Their days were a continuous struggle against these forces. Today, our entire civilization is threatened. The exploitation of the earth for human use is irreversibly altering life, decreasing species' diversity, and rendering uninhabitable or unproductive vast regions of the planet. Keeping further heavy industry out of the Patagonia is critical. Instead of using his ingenuity and his inventive technology for his benefit, man is using it to his own destruction. Industrialization and resource mismanagement threaten to destroy the Patagonia. The people of the Patagonia are grateful for your efforts to help us."

Nils wrapped his arm around Juan Carlos's shoulders. "Our Chilean colleagues can count on our efforts to help them save the Patagonia. The most difficult part of the journey is still ahead of us." He pointed to a map on the wall behind them and used a marker to carefully delineate the travel route they would follow in the morning. "The weather's been bad," he added, gazing at the team members over his bifocals. "Our ship leaves port at 3:00 A.M. so we can take advantage of the limited sunlight. We'll continue monitoring undersea seismic and volcanic activities. When we collect the ice cores from the Pío XI glacier, the expedition is complete. The onus is on *each of you* then. September 15, 2016 is the deadline for the United Nations Climate Change Conference and the State of the Antarctic Conference in Reykjavík. Ours will be the most comprehensive study of climate change in the Patagonia to date. So let's give this all we have." Determination was etched on his face. "The next few weeks are critical. Make yourselves available by phone, email or Skype so we can get our report on the table."

More cheers went up.

Team members began instructions on how to operate safety

equipment and inflatable life rafts, how to avoid hyperthermia, how to detect an approaching blizzard. Younger volunteers listened closely, asking questions.

Suddenly, the door swung open and Johan Bahr entered the building. He quickly found Nils and Juan Carlos.

"Did you find Karl Gustav?" Nils asked.

Bahr was visibly shaken. "He's not well. I'm afraid if we don't get him to a hospital immediately he'll die." He took his fur cap off.

"What? How could that be? He was fine a few hours ago." Nils cried, clutching his empty glass.

"There were two men with him when I got to his bungalow." He lowered his voice and shrugged. "One of them said he was Karl's friend from Brazil. He said they'd been drinking and eating shellfish and Karl suddenly got sick. They think its *marea roja* poisoning. You know, paralytic shellfish poisoning. Karl is already showing signs of cardiac distress. There's no antidote. I'm going to the ship for cimetidine. Maybe we can stabilize him until we can get him to a hospital."

They all knew there were no hospitals nearby. The only way to reach Puerto Edén was either a three-day ferry or by helicopter.

"I'll ask the naval officers if they can radio a rescue helicopter to take him back to Puerto Montt."

"He won't make it if we don't get him out of here soon," Johan Bahr said.

"Where is he now?" Juan Carlos asked.

"Still in the palafito. Belisario's brother Martín is with him." Juan Carlos hurried out.

Chapter 13

Emmanuelle Solis' phone rang shortly after midnight. She groped for it, still half asleep.

"Hello?"

"Emmanuelle?"

She held her breath. "Stephan?"

"Yes, it's me."

She bolted upright. Was she dreaming? She reached for the lamp on the night table. "Stephan, where are you?"

"In Argentina. Close to the Chilean border." His words came out in strained whispers.

Emmanuelle's fingers searched for the lamp's push-button switch. "My God! Are you okay? Where are you? People have been saying you were killed."

"I just escaped, but they're after me. They'll kill me if they find me … but they want … Uhh, Christ … I … I don't have time to explain now." He sounded out of breath, as though he were moving quickly as he spoke.

"Who did this? Who are they?" Her heart pounded.

"Look, I need your help."

"Where are you?"

"You have to listen carefully. I need files from the office. I tried to tell you before I left. I discovered something about …

a partner." He hesitated. "I found out about some huge wire transfers … someone in our office. I felt like my hands were tied. I came across evidence in the course of the proceedings."

"Which proceedings? Which case?"

"I can't explain now. But … the wire transfers … I suspect some partners are involved in money laundering. The last arbitration I adjudicated … the dispute seemed bogus."

"What? I don't understand."

"It seemed like the parties were engaged in simulated disputes to legitimize a cross-border payment. You know, money laundering."

Emmanuelle's brain accelerated. She knew how complicated it could be if evidence of an apparent crime surfaced in the context of an arbitration proceeding. They were confidential proceedings. Arbitrators were bound by that confidentiality. She had read of instances in which one party submitted a claim and the other didn't contest it, and a judgment was entered. The 'winner' would receive a cross-border payment that, on the face of it, looked clean and legitimate. In many countries the judgment was exempt from taxes or judicial scrutiny. Parties could stage fake disputes to transfer money in what appeared to be a legitimate transfer.

"I'm talking about some high-level fraud," Stephan said. "As soon as I started poking around, things started spinning,"

"Which partner do you suspect is involved?" She swallowed hard, clutching the phone.

"The day before I left, I received a subpoena to appear as a witness in one of the biggest securities arbitrations of the century."

"Oh my God, the FINRA arbitration?"

"You know about it?"

"I just know one is pending. Thorman wanted the files. He contacted FINRA and he told them you wouldn't make it to the hearing."

"Yeah … they want to make sure I don't testify for that one," Stephan said grimly.

"Were you supposed to testify against someone in our office? Who is under investigation? Tell me!"

"I … I can't explain it all right now…. It's complicated. Messed up." There was a pause.

"Stephan? Are you there?"

"I need your help. I was collecting records to build a case against them. The evidence was on my computer. I had copies of wire transfers, different transactions. Hundreds of files. You know … getting closer to closing in on them. I suspected … Jesus Murphy, I spent my whole life working hard. You think you know the people you associate with. Then you find out how truly evil they are." His voice was haunted. "Most of them, they have the law in their hands."

Emmanuelle shut her eyes tight. She couldn't believe what she was hearing.

"They know everything about us. Every move. You have to be careful. You could be next. I'm sure they suspect I shared information with you. Don't talk to anyone in the office. These guys are thugs. One of the bastards who held me hostage …" He was whispering. "He kept his gun pointed at my head for hours at a time, laughing. I was bound to a chair—just a click away from death. They're brutal. They wouldn't hesitate to kill you."

The thought sent a shudder of fear up her spine. "How is this related to the Argentine government? And the protests …"

"Listen to me. I need your help. I have to get out of here before they catch up with me."

"Tell me where you are."

"*Listen* to me." His voice was imperative. "I need you to bring me files. We'll go straight to the authorities. But you need to be careful. I have the proof. It's the only reason why they haven't killed me yet. They know it's out there. They want to destroy the evidence I have on them."

"Stephan, just tell me where you are." She reached for a pen and paper from her night table, almost knocking the lamp over. "I can get help to you immediately. I'll call the American Embassy in Argentina. Thorman's in touch with someone there. They have search teams out looking for you."

"Don't go to Thorman! Don't go to anyone until we talk. You can't trust him. It's extremely complicated. I discovered most of the information during the arbitration. Unless I can prove it's criminal, I could be sanctioned for violating the privileges of the proceedings. Do you understand? They have me in a straitjacket. We have to do this intelligently. If they suspect we're in contact, you could be next." His voiced hitched. "Wait until I explain what's going on."

"Okay. Okay. I understand. I think I understand."

"We're talking about multibillion-dollar deals. Governments rise and fall over these deals. Do you understand? Countries go to war over these issues. Government officials get bought out quickly. We have to go to the authorities, but the *right* authorities and I need the evidence. I need the proof. It could backfire on us if we don't do this right. I'm going to cross the border soon. Meet me in Puerto Montt, Chile. Bring the files and leave tonight."

"Tonight?"

"Yes. I have to go to the authorities immediately. This mess can implicate you and me. If I don't get killed first."

"Why Puerto Montt?"

"My contacts there promised to help me. There's law and order there. I'll meet you at the airport. If you leave tonight you'll be in Puerto Montt by tomorrow. I'll wait for you at the airport."

Stephan then instructed her to retrieve documents from a

file cabinet in the Special Documents Room, explaining where he hid a key. "They took everything away from me. My laptop, camera, my phone. Everything."

"Stef … I found a USB memory stick in the car. I have it with me."

"My USB? *You* have it? It was in my briefcase."

"It must have fallen out in the car. I tried to call you, but I guess you were already on the plane."

"Bring it. We have to take it to the authorities. I know who … we have to play this smart." His voice was low, breathy. "If not, they'll turn this around and implicate me. Maybe even you. And don't let anyone know you spoke to me."

"Is Thorman involved? Do you think he's behind this?"

"If anything should happen to me, just know … I love you." The phone went dead.

"*Stephan!*"

She yanked the sheets off her legs and checked the caller ID on her phone. That wasn't his number. Her thoughts spun wildly. Where did he call from? She put the number on her cell phone contact list. She wondered if the number would work after he crossed the border into Chile? She struggled to process what she'd just been told.

It had been a week since his disappearance. The story still received significant press coverage. FBI agents had interviewed many people in the office, including Emmanuelle. But they revealed nothing to her about the investigation. Her colleagues didn't seem to know much either. If they did, they didn't talk about it. Now she knew he *was* alive. She breathed deeply. She'd nearly lost hope.

She booked a flight to Chile and then opened her closet and anxiously selected some clothes for the trip. *Slow down and process this*, she told herself as she folded her clothes and placed them in her travel bag. Why didn't Stephan want Thorman to know he'd escaped and called her? She wondered which FINRA hearing he was supposed to testify in. There were hundreds of investment fraud proceedings in FINRA. Why did Thorman want the FINRA files? Who'd arranged for Stephan's security?

In the bathroom, she selected toiletries and dropped them into a large cosmetic travel bag. She thought about how Thorman had been acting since Stephan's disappearance. Secretive and purposefully alienating her. He took her off cases she'd been working on with Stephan and offered no explanation. Worse yet, he seemed to be monitoring her every move. She hadn't understood why until now. She never liked Thorman. He was a myopic ideologue.

She had always trusted Stephan's instincts. Doing what needed to be done was intuitive for him. Everything he'd just revealed was spinning in her brain like a spool of thread, weaving more thoughts into her imagination. She tried to imagine where he was, what he was going through, what it would be like when she saw him again.

She thought about her colleagues. Despite her seven years at the firm, she hadn't made close friends there other than Stephan. How could people she worked with be involved in criminal activity? Especially involving abduction and maybe even murder. Stephan feared for his life *and hers*. Everyone was a potential suspect. Investment fraud was like that. What kind of office did she work in? Even Stephan seemed to trust only her.

Thank God he's alive, she thought, kissing the gold medallion of the Madonna she wore around her neck.

By 5:30 A.M. her bags were packed. She was ready. She had it all planned. She would get to the office early, before anyone got there, retrieve the files, and leave. Then she'd call in and say she had to leave the country for a family emergency. Her plane would leave D.C. at 7:30 P.M.

She adjusted her dark dress suit in the mirror, placed her leather suitcase and matching carry-on by the door of her apartment, and turned off the coffee machine.

She walked quickly down the corridor toward the elevator. Images of Stephan filled her head. The thought of seeing him the next morning overwhelmed her.

Chapter 14

EMMANUELLE SOLIS LISTENED for voices before swiping the security card and opening the door to Oliver & Stone. Stephan's call the night before was still fresh in her mind. She prayed no one was in the office. It was shortly after 6:00 A.M. She would retrieve the files from the Special Records Room and go. She made her way down the corridors. The only sound was the low thrum of computers and office equipment.

Stephan had showed her into the Special Records Room many times before. Oliver & Stone's most important documents were kept there. It was tucked behind the partner offices. Only certain partners had keys to it. She gripped Stephan's keychain tightly in her fist.

A voice startled her. "What are you doing here so early?" Donaldo Moreno, a Brazilian lawyer, was approaching from the opposite end of the corridor.

Her pulse erupted in her veins. She feared he would shoot a barrage of questions at her. She tried to convince herself to be calm.

Donaldo's father was partner at a Brazilian law firm that Oliver & Stone teamed up with for São Paulo arbitrations. After Donaldo graduated from the Georgetown Law Center LLM program, Thorman agreed to let him work at the firm temporarily as a gesture of friendship to his father. When he first started working there, he made advances on Emmanuelle and felt jilted when she resisted. Donaldo grew resentful and their relationship soured. He became more aggressive after Stephan disappeared. He was now approaching with long strides. "Emmanuelle? Why are you here so early?"

"I came in early to finish a memorial." A cold sweat broke out between her shoulder blades.

"Oh …" His eyes rolled down her body, making her uncomfortable. "So, what's going on in the Brent case? Any new developments?" He was following her down the corridor.

"All I know is what's in the press. You work with Thorman. What did he tell you?" She turned around and headed to her office, conscious of his eyes on her back. She felt his footsteps at her heels.

"The Argentines *say* they're cooperating with the investigation, but the US Embassy suspects they know what happened to Brent and aren't saying." His voice was low, as though they were in collusion.

She turned to face him. "What do you mean? Who told you that?" She remembered the desperation in Stephan's voice when he told her he was trying to get out of Argentina. She wondered if he had gotten out safely. It had been seven hours since his call.

"I have my sources. Have you finished the memo on expropriation for the Egyptian highway case?"

She hesitated and then opened her office door. "Why?" She flicked the light switch. It wasn't a case Donaldo had worked on. She cleared papers from her desk and sat on it, facing him. Donaldo's eyes slid down to her legs.

She self-consciously tugged on the hem of her dress, uncomfortable with his presence. "What do you want Donaldo?"

Donaldo crumpled his face and pushed his glasses up the bridge of his nose. "We need the memo for the upcoming jurisdictional hearing."

Heat rose from her chest to her neck, flushing her face. "We? Are you going to be working on the case with us?"

"No. Thorman and I are handling it now."

"What?" Thorman had taken her off the case, but they were planning to use *her* memorial.

"Albert asked me to get it from you."

What was that bastard up to? She debated whether to argue or just move forward with what she needed to do. She had to get out of the office with the files. Emmanuelle was powerless to protest anyway. She was only an associate and ultimately, unless Stephan were here to say otherwise, Thorman could take it over if he so chose.

"Fine. I'll email it to you as soon as you leave my office." She was going out of the country anyway. It would be one less thing she had to worry about while she was gone. That arbitration was certain to be contentious and protracted. "Anything else?" she asked dryly.

"Not for now," he said with a smirk.

She locked the door after he left and stood still, willing her heartbeat to slow down to normal.

A few minutes later, she peered out in the halls again. Something told her it wasn't going to be easy getting Stephan's files with Donaldo in the office.

***

Glancing behind, Emmanuelle turned the key in the lock, opened the door to the Special Records Room and slipped inside. It was a sumptuous place with elegant furniture and oil paintings on the walls. Stephan had explained that the files were kept in an Eighteenth Century file cabinet with inlaid polished bone and intricately carved claw feet. She spotted it immediately and tugged lightly on the drawer, checking it was locked. In the middle of the cabinet, there was a small door flanked by classical pillars.

She unlocked it, pulled open the top drawer, and thumbed through the labeled tabs. The ones he wanted weren't there. Maybe he was mistaken? Maybe they were in the second drawer. She opened the bottom one, searching anxiously through its files. *Wait!* What was she doing? Wasn't this like stealing? Wasn't she taking property she shouldn't be taking? Her heart thudded. People might start coming into the office soon. More heat rose from her chest and neck. An accordion file filled with manila folders labeled *The Patagonia Files* was at the back of the drawer. *That's it. Breathe.* She pulled it out, slid the drawer back in place quietly, locked the cabinet and headed out.

Donaldo reappeared as she was closing the door behind her.

An electric jolt surged through her body.

"What were you doing in there?"

She struggled to collect herself but her legs felt weak. "ICSID scheduled memorials for the Nicaraguan mining case. That's what I'm working on." Her mouth was dry. She licked her lips, clutching the files tightly against her side with one hand.

"Stephan could be dead for all we know. Albert's in charge of that case now. I'll be working with him on that as well."

She felt hairs on the back of her neck rise. *Think,* she urged herself. "Well ... before he left, he asked me to prepare the memorial and he told me to check the original documents in the file. He gave me the key to this room." *Think harder.* She knew Donaldo wasn't capable of drafting the memorial and Thorman was in London. He depended on her to finish it. "If it's not finished this week, you'll have to request an extension. It will probably be denied at this point. That could cost the firm dearly. But if you don't need me to write the memorial, no problem. I'll stop working on it. You'll write it yourself, right?"

He looked stressed. "That's what you are working on?"

"Exactly. That's why I came in early. But since *you're* now in charge, I'll delete my files from the system and let you do the work."

"No, finish it by all means. Email it to me as soon as possible."

It worked.

"Will do." She walked past him, turned straight into her office and closed the door behind her, locking it. She flipped through the files nervously before putting them in her briefcase. *Was that idiot going to call Albert and tell him I was in the Special Records Room?* The preliminary hearings in the European Community Pharmaceutical Imports case were about to begin in the London Court of Arbitration. He would be gone for at least five days. He would probably be too tied up to answer a call from Donaldo.

***

Later that afternoon, the phone rang in Emmanuelle's office as she was about to leave for the airport.

"What the hell were you doing in the Special Records Room?" Albert shouted. "Only senior partners are allowed in there. Who gave you the key?"

"Stephan did before he left. I'm working on the request for discovery in the Nicaraguan mining case." She forced confidence into her voice. "The preliminary hearings are set for July fourteenth and discovery hasn't been requested yet. Albert, you know there are two European arbitrators on the panel— neither of whom is fond of American-style discovery. The Nicaraguans are arguing that there was an agreement signed that prohibits certain types of discovery. I was checking to see if there might be a copy of it in the original files. We may have to ask for an extension or put the case in jeopardy. This is a multimillion-dollar client. They might block your discovery." Her voice was steady. *Stand your ground. Your career could be on the line,* she told herself. The more he pressed her, the more she knew she could pull it off. She had to. It had come down to saving Stephan and herself at this point. And everything she'd worked for over the past seven years.

"I'll see you in my office on Monday."

"Fine."

It was getting late. She had to get to the airport.

Chapter 15

NILS GIAEVER STOOD on the deck of the *Antarctic Mist*, pointing to the magnificent mountain of blue ice towering in the distance. "Pius XI," he shouted, inhaling the icy air. The wind bit through his balaclava, stinging his face. The ship was laboring through the Straits of Magellan. Katabatic gusts of wind were blowing clouds of ice and rain about.

Philip Sands—several yards away clutching the rail of the deck with both hands—was trying to say something to him, but all Nils could hear was the whipping and gusting of the wind. Nils edged closer to him. The ship pitched dangerously sideward, spraying the deck.

"We need to go inside. We've been out too long. I'm numb. I don't want to lose important body parts."

"I still can't understand what happened to Karl," Nils said, reaching his side.

"Shellfish poisoning. It's rampant in these parts now. He'll be fine. Stop worrying. Juan Carlos has probably gotten him to a hospital by now. The locals know how to treat endemic poisonings better than we do."

The mass of ice ahead of them stretched for miles in length and over one hundred feet in height. He had certainly timed it right. Morning was about to break. A hundred shades of blue and white light refracted through the chiseled surface of the glacier as a thin ray of sunlight broke through dark clouds.

"He was fine earlier. When in hell did he eat shellfish?"

"Oh, please. When did we *not* eat shellfish? I've eaten so many of those smoked foot-sized mussels that I'm sweating hickory under my parka. Last night I dreamt I was moving into an empty mollusk shell." He blinked his frosty eyelashes repeatedly before rubbing his eyes with his thick gloves.

"Very funny."

"Seriously. Toxins proliferate in shellfish here because of the changing temperature. For Christ's sake, you know that. Diarrheic shellfish toxins are endemic in Chilean mollusks."

"He had symptoms of paralysis and cardiac arrest."

The thunderous sound of glacial calving clapped in the air. They watched as chunks of ice split from the glacier and fell splashing into the sea ahead.

"Those are symptoms of *marea roja*," Philip insisted. His running nose matched his red parka.

Nils wasn't convinced.

Masses of ice hung on the mountains around them.

"My eyes are burning." Philip blinked again. "Hey, if I die out here in the next few minutes, would you tape my eyes shut before rigor mortis sets in? Once it sets in, no way I'm getting these lids shut. Can barely shut'em now." Nils could see Philip's silly grin under his balaclava. "We need to go *inside!*" Sands shouted over the wind.

"Not yet." Nils studied the sky, gauging the storm. "Something isn't right."

"We're in for a big storm. *That's* what's not right. We can survive *if* we go inside." In spite of the parkas, fur gloves, and boots made for polar climates, the cold ate through to their skin. "My body's numb."

74

"Something's wrong I'm telling you." Nils knew it wasn't just the storm. The captain and his crew were native to the Patagonia, skilled at navigating fjords and ice-encumbered waters.

"You're right—these waves can send this ship hurling into an iceberg or put enough pressure on the hull of the ship to crush it," Philip shouted.

"Do you think Karl will make it?"

"He'll be fine. I'm not going to freeze out here while the rest of the crew is sipping coffee and keeping warm below." Philip headed down the stairs.

Chapter 16

THE JOLT FROM the first blast confirmed in Nils' mind his presentiment of an impending tragedy. It came from the lower deck of the ship. He clasped the ship's railing for support and struggled to the stairs. A gigantic wave thrust the ship sideward. He heard equipment and machinery smashing below.

In a flurry of frenzied activity, one of the Chilean Naval officers appeared at the foot of the stairs. "It's the communication systems. *S'explotó!*" His horror-stricken expression said it was fatal. "Some kind of explosion." A stream of smoke rose from the communications room.

"What the hell is going on?" shouted the captain. Nils reached for his cell phone. His numb fingers struggled to dial the *Armada* in Puerto Edén. Could he pick up satellite activity from this position?

The next blast came.

Simultaneously, a terrifying jolt propelled the ship's stern violently downward, knocking him overboard. He plunged into the water, his head striking a chunk of ice. He had the sensation of air being sucked from his body. He couldn't breathe. The cold burned. He knew that anyone who went overboard in these waters had next to no chance of survival. A body submersed in freezing water lost heat twenty-five times faster than one in air.

He felt his life and his connection to the rest of the world slipping away. In fleeting images, he saw his wife and son, and all of their days together. He saw himself in panoramic vision, limbs freezing in the ice-laden water. He couldn't move. He felt the weight of all of his years compressing into his bones, like snow packed into a glacier.

Within seconds again, the third blast ripped through the hull. The stern of the *Antarctic Mist* was rapidly being pulled under. The ship was now at a fifty-degree angle. Screams of horror filled the dense cold air.

Survivors still aboard, knowing they had to abandon ship immediately, scrambled for inflatable life rafts.

This was one of the most desolate regions of the world. But nothing could compare to the sense of separation Nils now felt from the rest of the world. The ship's whistle blasted a piercing shriek through the wailing wind. An electric bell began to toll, but was quickly silenced as the freezing sea dragged the ship under.

Nils' vision blurred, the images dimmed. He wasn't sure if he was floating in the sky or sinking into the blue water. He was losing consciousness.

Chapter 17

THE CAPTAIN OF a whale-watching ship grappled to maintain his balance on the slippery, foam-covered deck. He focused his binoculars on the Pope Pius VI Glacier. He and his crew had heard a blast in that direction. The binocular-camera caught an image of a small section of ice breaking from the glacier and collapsing into the water.

"It was glacial calving," he said calmly.

His ship often cruised the treacherous Straits of Magellan as part of an environmentalist crusade reporting on commercial whalers who furtively invaded the area for illegal whaling. It was a historical breeding ground for endangered species of whales, dolphins, porpoises, and elephant seals.

A second blast sounded in the distance.

He scanned the area again, this time catching sight of a sinking ship. "*Por Dios!* There's a ship on fire out there. It's going down. Call the *Gobernación Marítima! Al tiro!* They're going down fast." He zoomed in on the submerging ship, its bow now skyward.

One of his mates radioed authorities. "They're dispatching rescue teams. They say the Antarctic Expedition Team was headed here earlier this morning. It could be them."

"How did it go down so fast?"

The men looked at each other in silence. They had all heard the blasts.

"How long can they survive? Some of them must have immersion suits on."

"You can't survive for more than a few hours in these waters, even in a dry suit."

Chapter 18

EMMANUELLE SAT FOR hours on a cold metal bench in the unheated, immaculately-clean terminal of the El Tepual airport in Puerto Montt waiting for Stephan to appear. She was afraid that if she moved from where she was—directly outside the glass doors of the bag claim area—the only way for arriving passengers to exit the terminal—she might miss him.

She'd landed in Santiago, Chile at 6:00 A.M., but her connecting flight to Puerto Montt had been delayed due to fog shrouding the port city. She scanned the airport waiting area again, certain Stephan had been there hours earlier waiting for her plane to arrive. Her mind was still trying to process what he'd said to her yesterday. It seemed unreal that a network engaging in high-level investment fraud in North and South America could be connected to their office.

Compulsively, she opened her briefcase to check. *They're there.* She'd brought the Patagonia Files to Chile, just as he'd asked. For most of the nine-hour flight to Santiago, she read through their contents. They contained reports on an eleven million dollar project proposal involving the construction of dams along Patagonian rivers. Most of the correspondence in the files was addressed to or from Albert Thorman. Nothing appeared markedly unusual. She wondered how the files related to the crime Stephan spoke of. She had to trust his judgment. It would all make sense soon. *He'll be here any minute.*

She checked herself in her compact mirror, carefully lined her lips with lipstick, adjusted her collar, and buttoned and unbuttoned her trim-fitting coat. Another group of passengers collected their luggage and left the airport through the crowded waiting area. She searched their faces. Had she missed him? *Please, let him appear.*

She hoped they would go to the authorities with the files quickly and get this nightmare over with. *Everything will be fine,* she told herself. Stephan was a stickler for doing things in accord with the law. After scouring her brain for days, it was now clear why Stephan had been taken hostage—to prevent him from testifying at the FINRA hearing. But he'd escaped. And she had the files with her. *This will resolve. It has to,* she thought.

As the minutes had ticked away into hours, she was climbing the walls and a debate began to thunder in her mind. Had she just made the worst mistake of her life? Should she have gone to the police even though he said not to? Was she the only person who knew he was still alive? What if his captors had caught up with him? Killed him? Left him dead on the side of the road in some deserted place in the middle of nowhere. What then? She slid her phone out of her coat pocket again and dialed the number he called her from yesterday. *Answer. Please. Please.* An automated message in Spanish came on again after ten rings. *The person you are trying to reach is not available at this time. Please try your call again later.*

Damn. Shifting in her chair, her mind sifted through thoughts of her colleagues at the office and conversations she'd had with them. She wondered which of them were involved. She'd put in seven grueling years of sixty to eighty-hour weeks at Oliver & Stone, and Stephan had reassured her she would make partner this year. Now everything was on the line. Her thoughts shifted to Thorman. Her instinct told her he was the mastermind behind a sinister plot to get even richer at the expense of others. The files confirmed his involvement. He was a monster.

She watched as the waiting room emptied out again and passengers of another flight moved briskly across the marble floors and filed out the doors into the rainy morning. With mounting frustration, she found herself desperately wishing one was Stephan.

She unfolded the Chilean newspapers she'd read on the plane from Santiago. They had articles about Stephan's abduction the week before. She ran her finger along a picture of him that was next to one of the articles. The handsome blue-eyed, forty-five-year-old lawyer with a distinctive cleft chin was impeccably dressed and smiling in the picture. *Please let him be safe somewhere. Please.*

The Chilean newspapers *Tercera* and *Mercurio* reported the same story as the *New York Times* and *Washington Post*; they claimed Stephan disappeared after riots erupted in San Miguel de Tucumán and that US officials believed that Stephan was being held hostage by a radical self-proclaimed Bolivarian, anti-imperialist organization that wanted to drive foreign corporations out of the region. *Movimiento Patriótico Revolucionario Arribeño.* Argentine officials denied the supposition, insisting that Stephan left the city in a private jet that crashed in the Aconquija Mountains on the outskirts of Tucumán.

It was odd reading the news now. She knew neither account was true. *He's alive and will be showing up any minute.* She tried to recall every word he'd said to her in their last conversation, desperate for clues as to what she should do if he didn't appear. She hadn't a clue.

Where is he? she wondered, checking her watch for the hundredth time.

***

Hours later, clutching her briefcase, Emmanuelle sank into the back seat of a taxi. "Hotel Interamericano, *por favor*," she told the cab driver. She wondered what kind of hotel it was. An airport tourism agent had suggested it.

"Are you on vacation?" the driver asked as the taxi pulled away from the curb. She saw him looking at her in the rear view mirror. Averting his eyes, she didn't answer. Soon enough he would figure she wanted to be left to her thoughts.

They continued in silence along the coastal road toward the *Santuario y Cruz Monumental de Isla Tenglo*. She'd never been to the south of the country before. She stared out the window, taking it all in. The landscape seemed oddly familiar. She felt she'd seen it before, perhaps, in the faded snapshots of her family album. Like a fog rolling in off the coast, distant memories came back to her.

The sun was breaking through the clouds. A colossal cross became visible through a scrim of mist. It was mounted on a sanctuary on the hilltop of an island across from the port. The snow-capped Osorno and Calbuco volcanoes appeared in the distance as the fog lifted, unveiling the port speckled with colorful boats.

She clung tightly to the door handle as her taxi cut between cars, skidded down hilly roads, and whizzed past a mish-mash of modern buildings and middle-European gabled homes with high and low-pitched roofs, unpainted shingles, ornate balconies—abandoned to the cold.

The taxi, swerving to avoid crossing pedestrians, glided past the Amphitheatre, the buildings of the Courts of First and Second Instance, the offices of the *Diario El Llanquihue* newspaper, and finally pulled up to the entrance of the seven-story, modern-style hotel overlooking the bay.

***

The lobby was decent, but nothing luxurious. Emmanuelle guessed it was a hotel for businessmen, not rich tourists. A picture window near the reception overlooked the port and the afternoon sun shimmered on the port.

"Good afternoon. Ms. Hernandez from the Esquerre Agency made a reservation for me." She put her purse down on the reception counter, keeping a tight grip on her briefcase.

"You are Señorita Solis?" the fair-skinned, well-groomed receptionist asked.

She nodded.

"May I see your passport?" He addressed her politely, examining her thoroughly.

She handed him her passport, glancing around the room. Where would she go from here? She didn't have a Plan B. She'd counted on Stephan meeting her at the airport. She hadn't planned for this.

"Are you on vacation or business?" he asked in a tone of light-hearted chat. He flipped through the pages of her passport, appearing more interested in the countries she'd visited than confirming her identity.

Good question. "Business. Have you got a room or not?"

"Yes, I have the perfect room for you. Seventh floor. View of the port. *Espectacular.*" He handed back her passport and began typing away on his keyboard, looking up at her every few seconds, a smile on his lips. "How long will you be staying?" he asked, handing her forms to fill out.

"A few days, maybe more," Emmanuelle replied, staring out at the port. Something told her she was going to be there for a much longer time than she'd planned.

***

An hour later, Emmanuelle sat on the hotel room bed trying not to yield to the rising tide of panic spurring her. Her instincts told her this was dangerous. *Get back on the plane. Head back to D.C. Talk to the FBI.* Her imagination was wild with thoughts of what might have happened to Stephan since the call. She needed air. She got up and pushed open the window, for a split-second feeling ready to throw herself out. Just being here had the curious effect of bringing the past into the present, blurring the lines.

She knew she was out of her element in Chile. She hadn't been back since her father's funeral fifteen years earlier, and a barrage of emotions discharged from someplace she'd long held under lock and key. Chile was a world she never felt she belonged to as a teenager. She now wondered whether that had just been part of her rebellion against her father. She'd avoided accepting work trips here.

Her adolescent panic attacks seemed to be waiting in the trenches, preparing to fire. She'd gotten them under control as an adult. After law school, she'd become cool, calm and collected. *I just need to remind myself of that,* she thought as she stared at her reflection in the mirror across the room.

She dialed Stephan's number again. *No answer.* How would he find her? She dialed again and left a message with the hotel address. She had already sent him more than twenty text messages with no reply.

She had to get out of her hotel room. The blast of horns and traffic noise from the streets below were cluttering her thoughts.

It was still light outside. She decided to shower, dress and walk around the town. She peered into her suitcase wishing she had packed warmer clothes. It was colder and wetter than she'd imagined.

It was now obvious she would be here for more than a few days.

Chapter 19

WITH QUIVERING FINGERS, Emmanuelle fastened the buttons of her double-breasted cashmere overcoat and walked out of the hotel onto Calle Illapel. It was drizzling again. Her consciousness adrift in her thoughts, she turned up her collar and put her freezing hands in her pockets. She waited on the street corner as a cluster of cars passed. Crossing the street, she ran through an inventory of alternatives. She would go to the authorities alone, if Stephan didn't contact her soon. But which ones? The FBI? The US Embassy? Chilean Carabineros? She wasn't sure. Stephan mentioned Chilean authorities he trusted. *Just wait a little longer,* she told herself. *He'll show up. He knows what he's doing.*

She paused to look around for a refuge from the cold. A rough-looking man with a scowl on his face, maybe in his forties, was standing near the gate of the courthouse defiantly smoking in the rain. He seemed vaguely familiar. Had she seen him somewhere before? At the airport, perhaps? Was he following her? His eyes locked with hers before he tossed his cigarette to the ground. Leaves whirled at his feet. She lengthened her stride down the hill, glancing back to see if he was following. He had disappeared.

As she continued down the road, she remembered that her brother Camilo's maternal family owned an *estancia* in Puerto Aysén where they bred horses for the rodeo. But she barely knew them. She quickly decided against calling on them. The farther she walked along the crowded streets, the more mixed-up her thoughts and feelings became. The landscape that had formerly stirred disquiet in her now overwhelmed her with a sense of belonging. She leapt across puddles and stepped into the *Casa del Arte Diego Rivera*, the Mexican-Chilean cultural center, to escape the cold. Her overcoat was rain-soaked. Shivering, she stared emptily at the work of local and foreign artists displayed on the walls.

The center hosted theatrical shows, dances and films. A crowd clustered at the entrance was slowly filing into the room. Women in cocktail dresses passed through the door, shedding their coats. They wore stilettos and their cheeks were thickly powdered, their lips painted red. Emmanuelle looked down at her drenched boots, her pant legs soaked to the knees. She suddenly felt embarrassed and left.

For a moment, she stood under the awning of a theatre as rain fell in sheets. Memories of the past were shifting in her mind like color and light in a kaleidoscope. She didn't know whether to go back to the hotel or keep walking. She wasn't going to find Stephan on the streets. But he was a survivor. He was Stephan Henri Brent. Emmanuelle knew he was alive. Somehow she would find him.

Chapter 20

ISAURO SALAZAR STOOD behind the reception desk of the Hotel InterAmericano, pondering what he would say to the new guest. She had just ordered her dinner. It was unlikely any guests would be checking in tonight. He would lock the doors, leave the lobby for a few minutes, and take the dinner to her himself. He couldn't resist the opportunity to find out more about her. That was one of the duties his position entailed, he told himself reassuringly. *Policía de Investigaciones* had cautioned him to study hotel customers. "You don't want to be harboring criminals. Be aware of the habits of the people who stay in the hotel," he'd been told in security trainings.

He summoned the room service girl to bring him her tray. Not that he believed the new guest was a criminal or the likes of one. It was that, since she'd checked in, Solis kept calling the front desk and asking if anyone had phoned for her. She was obviously expecting someone who'd not yet come to call. She seemed troubled. He would try to talk to her. Few tourists came to this part of the country during the winter. He'd find out why she was here.

He rode the elevator to the seventh floor. When the doors opened, he checked himself in the hallway mirror, smoothed back his hair. He was here six days a week. He had to make a boring job interesting. It was about making the right eye contact with the customers, saying positive things to them, keying in on their emotions. Maybe she would take a liking to him. *She is one fine-looking lady.*

He knocked.

"Oh," Ms. Solis said, opening the door. She was plainly startled to see Isauro.

For a split second, Isauro felt self-conscious. How conspicuous was he? There was an awkward silence.

"*Permiso.* Your dinner."

"Thank you, come in." She pulled the door wider and stepped aside.

He pushed the cart over to the desk. Her laptop and files were spread about, as though she'd been working. He wondered what she did for a living. "I thought I would take the opportunity to bring you your dinner and make sure everything is okay."

"*Si, si. Por supuesto.* Everything is fine," she said, fumbling through her handbag and pulling out her wallet.

"No, no tip for me. *Por favor,*" he said, proudly. Did she assume he was from the same social class as the other staff? "Save that for the room service girl."

Ms. Solis stuffed the money back in her purse and sat down on her bed. Her attention was on the screen of her cell phone, scrolling through messages. She seemed to have forgotten he was still in the room.

He was careful to take time arranging the plate, napkins and utensils on her desk.

Solis finally slipped her cell phone into her sweater pocket and glanced at him, her almond-shaped eyes flickering with suspicion. She was wondering why he hadn't left.

"Thank you." Her tone was far from gracious. She wanted him to get out.

"Can I get you anything else?"

"No," she said, removing more files from her briefcase.

His eyes browsed her belongings. *Leather briefcase. Nice. Italian, perhaps.* She seemed like the kind who would work while having dinner. *Expensive, stylish clothes, shoes, coat. Prada handbag.* He noted the color combinations of the shoes and suits in her open suitcase. *Leather suitcase, too. Nice jewelry. This one has money. What did she do for a living?* He watched as she fiddled with the clasp of her gold watch and laid it on the desk. *Piaget.* The soft light of the lamp reflected on her glossy hair. *Bonita la galla,* he thought, his eyes skimming her slender figure.

She turned around quickly, as though she felt him staring at her. "Thank you. That will be all." Her tone was curt.

He returned to the tray with her dinner. "Your *cortado*," he said, picking up a steaming Chilean version of *café au lait* and setting it down on the desk. He uncovered the dish with her steak, tomato, string bean and hot pepper sandwich, still inspecting her from the corner of his eye. "Your *chacarero*."

She didn't look at him or the tray. She swiped the screen of her phone again, irritated and muttering to herself.

He finally mustered the nerve. "May I ask what brings you to Puerto Montt?"

"Are you sure there were no calls for me?" Now the tone suggested he might be incompetent.

"*Si. Segurisimo.* The Hotel Interamericano phone didn't ring once today," he said quietly, offering a polite, apologetic smile. "I wish it would ring." He sighed lightly and stood there in the awkward silence. If she didn't want to talk to him, he would have to leave immediately. "Is there anything else I can do for you?"

"No," she said sharply. She opened an expandable file and removed manila folders from it. He walked to the desk and lit the red lacquer lamp. It stood out against the dull-colored room with tan walls, a brown carpet and brown bedspread.

"Be careful," he told her. "There will be protests in the Plaza de Armas tomorrow."

"Protests against what?"

"A supreme court ruling in favor of building dams in the Patagonia. You should avoid the plaza. The protests get rough."

"Dams on Patagonian rivers?"

"Yes. The country is divided over the issue."

"In the plaza?"

"Yes. The papers reported today that the judge who decided they could proceed with the dams had a big investment in the water company." His eyes lingered on her files, which were open on the desk. They were in English. *Pucha*, no chance he would understand them.

"I scanned every newspaper online today except the Chilean papers." Her voice trailed off into thought.

"*¡Lástima!* What a pity. I hope the protests don't last all day. Tomorrow is *Fiesta San Pedro*. You know, a celebration in honor of Saint Peter—the patron saint of the fisherman. There will be celebrations all along the coast. It might be the biggest celebration in years. The fisherman are praying for the intercession of the Saint because *marea roja* devastated the coast earlier this year." Emmanuelle had read that a virulent algal bloom had killed off more than two million fish along the southern coast.

"Unfortunately, in the plaza you can expect trouble tomorrow," Isauro said. "If it gets bad, Carabineros will come in with the water cannons. Maybe even tear gas. Whenever there are protests, troublemakers show up. Masked protestors throw stones and Molotov cocktails. You should stay away from the area."

"Where is the Plaza de Armas?"

"In front of the cathedral."

"Thank you." She gave him a look that made it clear he needed to leave.

"Call if you need me," he said, retreating through the door.

Chapter 21

EMMANUELLE WALKED IN the direction of the Plaza de Armas, her breath puffing out in little clouds of vapor. Her dream of Stephan drowning haunted her. Hope of finding him rapidly faded.

Police sirens blared from all directions. She wondered to what extent she was putting herself in danger. But she had to search for anything that could bring her closer to finding Stephan. Why had he asked her to bring those files? What connection did they have to his abduction? Could they contain evidence implicating individuals in the office? She had no answers to any of these questions.

The demonstration was set to take place at 10:00 A.M., but people had begun pouring into the Plaza de Armas an hour earlier, crossing the congested streets, halting cars, carrying banners that said *Patagonia Sin Represas*: Patagonia Without Dams. She guessed there were thousands of demonstrators now gathered in front of the cathedral.

She retreated under the awning of the courthouse, deciding not to get any closer. On the other side of the plaza, a Carabinero van skidded to a halt on the wet pavement, nearly striking a group of young men who refused to get out of its way. The streets and sidewalks were littered with flyers and notices. She picked up as many as she could, stuffing them into the pockets of her coat. Maybe they had names or contact information she could use to find out more about this unraveling mess.

A tall man with a craggy, but youthful face spoke through a loudspeaker, waving a fist in the air. "The Patagonian dams will flood our rare temperate forests and rich ranchland. They want to generate more energy than several mid-sized nuclear energy plants from the rivers of the Patagonia. They will run two thousand kilometers of high-voltage wire through our national parks and the wilderness of the south, threatening rain forests and rare plant species. And the *sin verguenza* judges who gave them the authority to do it are big stockholders in water companies," he shouted with the self-righteous air of authority that only politicians or aspiring-politicians assumed.

Cars weaved around demonstrators, some nearly running them down. Environmentalists distributed literature explaining how more than fifty percent of Chile's plant species found nowhere else in the world was threatened by the project. How the operation of the dam would result in 40,000 tons of carbon monoxide, which was contributing to the climate change that was already posing serious threats to the environment. Picketers carried signs in favor of wind, solar and geothermal energy alternatives. Others held up signs with pictures of millions of dead fish washed ashore months earlier. The government's commission had approved the project and judicial appeals against the decision were rejected. The demonstrators accused the commission and judges of corruption and favoritism toward the corporate interests at the stake of the country. Emmanuelle wondered where Thorman fit into the scheme.

A cluster of protesters broke into the cathedral. Riot control vehicles rolled into the plaza to disperse the crowd with tear gas and water cannons. Panicked demonstrators ran for safety. A young man in soiled jeans hurled a Molotov cocktail. It hit the ground and smashed. Flames spread across the street and under a police van. Two Carabineros ran after him and tackled him. Two others joined them, dragging the man by his arms and his legs. More protestors smashed windows and destroyed property. A masked group emerged in the crowd, brandishing signs denouncing the arrest of indigenous leaders. They shoved their way through the police barricades at the entrance of the cathedral.

Emmanuelle retreated from the plaza, glancing back at the drama unfolding on the streets and recalling Stephan's words several nights earlier. *There is law and order in Chile.* But the chaos raging on the rain-slick streets of Puerto Montt said differently.

Chapter 22

THE NOISE OF the demonstrations buzzed in her head long after Emmanuelle returned to the maddening quiet of her hotel room. It was midmorning and she had been in Chile for a little over twenty-four hours. The whole situation was setting off more alarms in her mind. It was apparent she was not going to find Stephan and only now was the magnitude of her predicament becoming evident. For a long while, she stared at the stack of files on the desk afraid to touch it. As though it were a snake ready to uncoil and strike her.

So, this is the deal, her legal mind kicked in. *A little too late,* she conceded. She'd taken files that belonged to a senior partner, and they pertained to one of the most controversial investment transactions in South America, and it involved Oliver & Stone's wealthiest client, Hébère International. If Stephan didn't show, she wouldn't look very good. She ran her fingers along the edge of the stack and then opened the file on top again, flipping through the pages, but the words seemed to be jumping around and running off the sides of the page.

If the files indicated criminal activity and if Stephan never appeared, authorities might assume she was trying to obstruct evidence. That alone could implicate her. Not to mention imply possible disbarment for unauthorized removal of confidential files. Her mind scampered with fear. She needed to turn this over to authorities urgently, but she didn't have a clue whom she should speak to or what she would say. She pushed the files away. She wasn't even sure *what* the crime was.

She logged onto the Oliver & Stone server and downloaded information about the companies named in the files. She picked out a letter Thorman sent to an engineering company contracting its services to conduct an environmental impact study for the dams. She tapped on her laptop's keyboard and the screen lit up. She searched for it on the Internet, jotting notes on a pad of paper.

Then she noticed, for the first time, a manila envelope tucked in the inner pocket of the file folder.

Her heart thudded. It was sealed. *Invernex, Calle el Otoño 11, Vitacura, Santiago, Chile* was printed on the corner of the envelope. She did another search. It was a Santiago Brokerage Firm. She ran her fingers along the sealed flap. She wanted to rip it open. *Think*, she thought. She was in enough trouble. Opening a sealed envelope would only be a further violation. There was an address handwritten in pencil on the back of the envelope. She examined the writing closely. It looked familiar. The same address was written on a piece of paper she had found in the files. It had been torn from a legal pad. It was in Puerto Montt. She wrote the address down on her notepad.

Emmanuelle slipped the envelope back into the inner pocket of the file, still eyeing it. If Stephan didn't appear today, she would open it. But she would visit the address first. Maybe this was the address of the people Stephan trusted. Could it be a law firm? Or maybe a government office? She felt a small surge of optimism. It was Sunday, so there was a good chance it would be closed, but she would check out the address anyway, and confirm what it was. She would shower and dress nicely just in case.

Her cell phone rang.

"Hello?"

"Emmanuelle? Thank God you answered." It was Maríana Cianti, a colleague from Oliver & Stone. The forty-year-old Argentine lawyer left her job as professor of commercial law at the University of Buenos Aires a year earlier to join the firm. The firm had several corporate clients that had filed suits against the government of Argentina after its economy collapsed. She advised the firm's Arbitration Group on Argentine law. "Where are you? I was worried about you when you didn't show up for work today."

"I'm in Chile taking care of a family matter," she responded, gazing out the window. Another procession of adorned boats was floating down the coast in celebration of Fiesta San Pedro.

"Is everything okay?" Maríana had stopped by Emmanuelle's office frequently after Stephan disappeared.

Emmanuelle was suddenly aware of how desperately she needed a friend. "Everything's fine," she said. "Hey, you know, it's a coincidence you called. I was thinking about you. I was wondering if you might know anything about the Patagonian dam project proposal. Apparently, one of Thorman's clients here won the bid on it. It's a controversial project. Who's working on that case with Thorman?"

"Are you talking about Chile or Argentina?"

"Chile."

"No idea. Should I ask Albert?"

"No, I'll talk to him when I get back. There are major protests against the project here, so I just wondered who was on it. I thought you might know."

"I know nothing about it. There are always protests in South America against foreign investment. Welcome to the continent of protests," Maríana said, laughing. "I'll let you know if I hear anything. When are you coming back?"

"Next week."

"Everything okay?" Her voice was matter-of-fact.

"I'm okay. Thanks. Hey, anything new about Stephan?"

"No."

"Has anyone in the office said anything about it recently?"

"Well, everyone talks about it, but no one knows what happened. Everyone agrees some leftist group with a grudge against foreign investment is behind it. We just hope he's still alive," she said, lowering her voice.

"By any chance, do you know who arranged for Stephan's trip from Buenos Aires to San Miguel?"

"Wait, let me close the door," Maríana said.

Emmanuelle could hear her movements.

"Yes," Maríana said. "I heard something to the effect that it was Leandro Piñeres. His family in Venezuela charters private flights between cities in South America."

"Leandro? I thought Thorman fired him."

"Leandro made the reservations several hours before he was fired." Maríana was still whispering.

"Why would Leandro make plane arrangements for a trip inside Argentina? What contacts does he have there?"

"His brother lives there. They operate a private jet service called La Luciérnaga. He has a lot of contacts there. Why?"

"I'm still trying to sort through what happened to Stephan. It just doesn't make sense." Through the window she suddenly noticed someone was getting out of a black sedan parked on the harbor. Thinking about it, Emmanuelle was certain the car had been there for hours. *Could that man have been sitting in the sedan all that time?*

Another car pulled up and a man got out. The two exchanged a package or something. Both men faced her hotel now. They appeared to be looking up at her. She stepped out of view and drew the curtains. *I'm imagining things,* she convinced herself. *Everyone is starting to look suspicious to me.*

"Are you there?" Maríana asked.

"Yeah. Sorry ... I was distracted for a moment.... How was Leandro after he was fired? Were you there? Did he say anything to you?"

"He was *very* upset." Her voice was halftone.

"Like ... how upset?"

"You mean like was he upset enough to do something crazy? I don't know."

"I didn't mean that. Have you had contact with him since?"

"No. What day are you coming back?" Maríana asked. The question sounded casual.

"I don't know. Next week." She ended their conversation and flipped through her address book wondering if she still had Leandro's cell phone number somewhere. She found it but decided not to call now. Instead she typed *Leandro Beltran Caceres* into an Internet search engine. *Nothing.* She tried the words *La Luciérnaga* and wrote down the information, rebelling against jittery muscles in her fingers. She put her pen down and shut off her computer.

The wind blustered against the window and cold air seeped through cracks in the frame. She was going to have to buy warmer clothes. She got up and searched her suitcase for a cable-knit Irish sweater. Putting it on she caught a glimpse of herself in the mirror. Someone else was staring back at her with a pale face and sunken eyes. She unfastened her pearl necklace and laid it on the dresser.

Her phone lit up and rang again. No number identification registered.

"Hello?" The line went dead. Had Stephan just tried to reach her from God only knew where? It rang again. Camilo's number appeared on the screen. She couldn't talk to her brother now. Not yet. He would object to what she was doing, especially under the circumstances. With a trembling finger, she pressed the ignore button.

She organized the files before putting them into her briefcase. Was Stephan's phone call just a dream? How could one of the world's most famous lawyers just disappear into thin air?

Images on the television caught her eye. Another report about the sunken ship in the Patagonia was running. She turned up the volume.

An international commission has been set up to investigate the sinking of the Antarctic Mist *as reports are emerging about the possibility of an explosion on the ship before it sank. The tragedy took the lives of fifty-seven people, among them some of the most renowned scientists investigating climate change. The ship sank last week in the Northern Patagonian Ice Field. It was on the last leg of a year-long investigation. The Chilean Navy is investigating claims that members of a Chilean NGO heard a blast shortly before sighting the prow of the sinking ship. The NGO, an organization committed to the conservation of whales and their ecosystems, had been whale-watching at the time.*

"A blast?" she said to herself. "Sabotage?"

She showered quickly and dressed in a black, white-trimmed suit. She checked the Internet one last time. *Could this be the address of a law firm handling the Chilean dam project?*

She would go there. Maybe from there she would go to the Chilean authorities, explain why she was here and see if they would help her. Was that safer than calling the US Embassy in Santiago? The parliament in her mind was in session again. Who would she ask to speak to? Doubt skittered through her head. The only certainty was that she would call Camilo in the evening.

She called the front desk. Isauro was her point of reference for nearly every move now.

"Isauro, can you give me directions to Calle Vicente Perez Rosales?"

"Calle Vicente Perez Rosales?" He was surprised.

"Yes," she said. There was silence. Did he know the place or not? "Hello?"

"*Si po, por supuesto.* Of course. If you come to the reception desk, I'll give you a map and show you how to get there. But you have to go by taxi. It's far."

Emmanuelle adjusted her suit in the mirror, slipped her laptop into her briefcase and headed to the lobby.

When the elevator doors opened, she saw Isauro combing his hair behind the reception desk. He tucked the comb into his pocket and straightened his tie as she approached him.

Chapter 23

"ARE YOU SURE you want me to leave you here?" the taxi driver asked. Emmanuelle sat quietly in the back seat of the cab for a moment, examining the commercial building in front of them. A crawling sensation scuttled from her wrists to the nape of her neck.

The building had ugly mud stains and rain streaks. The wood frames were splotched with green and black mold. A window on the second floor appeared to have been punched out. It was hard to believe anyone associated with Oliver & Stone could work in a building that looked like that. It was nothing like the well-heeled Santiago law offices where most of Oliver & Stone's Chilean counterparts worked.

It was nearly four o'clock but dusk appeared to be edging toward an early nightfall. A couple of brightly-painted prostitutes crossing the street slowed their pace to a cocotte stroll in front of the taxi. One of the girls wore a pink wig and walked unsteadily on her five-inch-heels.

The taxi driver repeated the question.

"Yes," she said, resolving to go in. It was her only option.

She entered the building through a rusted steel door and climbed the stairs to the second floor where the supposed office was. The door closest to her was slightly ajar. She walked to it slowly, treading lightly on the mud-stained carpet. It opened to a large abandoned room with dozens of desks lined up, one next to another. Each had a telephone. She glanced behind before walking in.

It was a filthy place that reeked of humidity and mold. The back wall was lined with file cabinets, a few with drawers hanging open. She checked each one. They were empty except for a file and a few crumpled papers that could have easily gone unnoticed at the back of the bottom drawer. Emmanuelle pulled them out. A power of attorney, financial statements, United States Security Commission reporting forms and a few other documents. *Could this have been an accounting firm? This dump couldn't have serviced a multi-million-dollar operation. Who are these guys? Why was their address written on Albert's file?* She stuffed the papers into her briefcase.

She heard what sounded like a door on the floor below closing. She froze, listening for movement. It was quiet. A sense that someone else was in the building, maybe following her, raised hairs on the back of her neck. She needed to get out of there. There was something sinister about the place.

Emmanuelle looked around. What was she doing snooping around in a neighborhood crawling with hookers? A hundred thoughts suddenly took to rioting in her brain. She looked out the window. The last rays of sunshine were sinking below the horizon. There were no cars on the street. No noise. No one. She poked her head out the door, looking left and right down the corridors. *Damn.* She should have asked her cab driver to wait. Daunted by the stillness, she left the room and headed for the stairwell. She suddenly felt again somebody present, and then caught a glimpse of a furtive figure. She ran to the staircase, but she could feel him right behind her now. She bolted down the stairs. He jumped on top of her before she reached the bottom. She screamed as loud as she could. She tried to get up, but he pushed her back down, pulling at her briefcase. Emmanuelle curled her body around it. If he got away with it she would be finished. "*Hijo de puta*," she cursed, fighting back, kicking him. He slammed her against the stairway railing.

"*¡Ayudame! ¡Ayudame!*" she screamed for help, punching back at her assailant as he managed to yank her briefcase free.

Suddenly, someone kicked open the door at the bottom of the stairs. It was a Carabinero. "*¡Alto! ¡Policía!*" he shouted.

Every muscle in her body released. *Thank God.* Tears welled in her eyes.

The Carabinero moved slowly closer, pointing a gun at the assailant and ordering him to raise his hands. Two other uniformed policemen came in behind him.

Chapter 24

A YOUNG CARABINERO escorted Emmanuelle from the building. "What were you doing in there?"

"I guess I was lost," she said, rubbing her head. She felt like both sides of her skull were being pressed together.

The police officer reacted with amused disbelief. "Lost? I would say you were more lost than a seagull in Bolivia."

"Would you like to go to the hospital?" another officer asked.

"No, I'm fine," Emmanuelle insisted. Her hip and her head throbbed, but she wanted to go back to her hotel.

She watched as one of the officers shoved her assailant into a green police van. Wasn't he the same man she'd seen two days earlier on the street in front of the courthouse? Her vision swam.

"You will have to come with us to make a statement," another officer told her as he helped Emmanuelle to the car. "*Adelante*," he said, opening the door for her.

***

As the police car pulled up to the central station of the *Prefectura de Carabineros de Chile*, Emmanuelle's head filled with thoughts about her father. He had often boasted about the Chilean national police force. How it operated under the jurisdiction of the Ministry of Defense. How it had high standards of professionalism and a sense of order and organization that earned it international prestige and respect, distinguishing it from other Latin American police forces. She observed the police as they interacted with each other, hoping that would be the case. Something told her things might not turn out as she hoped. As they walked to the entrance of the police station, an officer in a fitted khaki-green, hip-length jacket with matching trousers and a matching peaked cap opened the door for her.

"*Buenos días*," he said politely, tilting his head. He had apparently been waiting for them. He asked her a few questions to verify the information written in the statement and then led her to a large office with a view of the Amphitheatre. The window was open. Cold, humid air stirred in the room. It was still drizzling outside and straggling beads of moisture dripped slowly down the pane, obscuring her view.

"After the lieutenant takes a statement from you, the Comisario will see you," the officer said. A tall man with thin shoulders, similarly uniformed, rose from his chair as they entered. He looked at Emmanuelle for a minute, examining her expressionlessly from head to toe, and then he looked at the other officers, raising his eyebrows as though expecting more information. One of the police officers handed him a report. The lieutenant took it and extended his hand toward the chair in front of his desk.

"Have a seat, please." He was stern, but polite.

She took a seat, looking at the officers around her. They were well-mannered and neatly dressed in starch-pressed uniforms.

"Welcome to Chile," the lieutenant said dispassionately, pausing for a moment to study her. "Are you okay? Do you need to go to the hospital?" His words were kind but his tone was aloof.

"No, I'm fine. A bit dizzy." She rubbed the back of her head.

"So tell me, why are you in Chile? Vacation? Business? Family?" His tone grew more serious by the second.

She straightened and stared back at him. Where was this going?

"Señorita Solis, why were you in the building on Calle Vicente Perez Rosales?"

Why wasn't he asking about the assault? Didn't he want to know about the man who'd attacked her? How much she should tell him? She tried to read his face as she slowly gave him some of the details about herself, but the stone-faced lieutenant gave nothing away.

She smoothed her skirt out with a sweaty palm. "I found the address on one of our office files and thought it was a firm that my office works with on our Chilean cases." She realized that she was only provoking more questions that she wasn't ready to answer, but she couldn't avoid it without raising suspicion.

He proceeded with all of the obvious questions. *You mean your firm doesn't know who's handling one of its cases? Why were you there investigating that? Are you working on the case? What case is it? Why didn't you call your firm to ask? What exactly are you doing here? Where are the files you are talking about?*

She was caught between a rock and a hard place. Her answers were terse. Several police officers in the room stood around listening intently. Their expressions were serious, concerned maybe, but they remained courteous.

She realized they were all taking a long hard look at her. They must have had good reasons for questioning her. This wasn't about the assault on her. Her attacker was probably just a common criminal. A purse-snatcher at best. Something big had happened at Calle Vicente Perez Rosales and now they wanted to know what she might have to do with it.

"Is there something wrong?" she asked. *Obviously, there is.*

She bit her lip and prayed to maintain her calm "Did I walk into the wrong place at the wrong time?"

No one answered. The lieutenant who'd been questioning her tightened his jaw and she saw suspicion flicker in his eyes.

With a thud, she felt her heart accelerate.

Two of the police officers stepped outside and spoke to each other. She strained to hear what they were saying. She thought she heard one say something about detectives wanting to talk to her. Her heart now pounded like a hammer. What *had* she just walked into? She felt like she was choking. *Breathe,* she told herself.

"You mean to say that you just got up this morning and decided to visit the building? How did you know about it?" the lieutenant asked.

"I told you, the address is written on a file I have." Nausea gripped her abdomen.

"May I see that file?"

"I don't have it with me. It's a legal file from our firm." *I shouldn't have even mentioned it. This could create confidentiality problems,* she thought dreadingly. She had to get out of there. She wasn't thinking clearly. She was about to piss her whole career away. She'd probably already done that.

"What firm is that?"

"Oliver & Stone." Her cheeks flushed, a surge of heat rushed through her body.

The lieutenant stood and left the office, taking the report with the notes he'd written. He returned without it twenty minutes later and told her the Comisario was ready to see her.

It was clear now they hadn't brought her to the police station to file a report about a purse-snatcher. She had some explaining to do.

Chapter 25

COMISARIO MUÑOZ STOOD as she entered the room. He was a tall, broad-shouldered man with a tanned complexion, large gentle eyes, and a thick black mustache that curled at the ends. He bowed slightly and gestured for her to sit down. "May I see your passport," he asked.

With jittery hands she took her US passport out and handed it to him. "I am Chilean. I was just naturalized in the United States this year."

"*Osea*, you're Chilean and you entered Chile on a US passport?" he asked. His eyes held hers.

She wasn't making a good case for herself. Emmanuelle started to explain, but only fumbled for answers, conscious that whatever she answered might appear suspicious at this point.

He handed the passport to an officer standing in the doorway. That officer left the room.

"Where is he going with my passport?" She stood, her legs shaking. She struggled to steady them on her high heels.

"He's just making a copy. He'll return it to you immediately. *Tranquila*," he said, softly. "Sit down." The command was gentle, but stern.

She sat. He asked her questions for what seemed like an eternity. Questions about her background, her family, her father, her employment, the purpose of her visit. She knew he wasn't satisfied with her brief, to-the-point answers. She offered as little as she could get away with.

"A colleague and partner at the law firm I work for contacted me on Monday saying that he was on his way to Chile. He wanted me to meet him here with files. I arrived on Wednesday, and he was supposed to be waiting for me at the El Tepual Airport. He never showed up. I've been waiting here for him. I haven't heard from him since. I was worried. I went to the office on Calle Vicente Perez Rosales, because I found the address in one of the files. I thought it was the law firm he works with here."

"What is your colleague's name?"

"Stephan … Stephan Henri Brent."

"Stephan Henri Brent?" he asked, looking up at her. For a moment, it seemed he might have recognized the name, but then he wrote it down and continued to ask her questions. Had the Chief of Police made the connection?

"May I see your cédula, Señorita?" he asked

"I think my brother still has it. I haven't used my Chilean identification card for over fifteen years." As she answered the Comisario's questions, images of the events before and immediately after the death of her father fifteen years earlier filled her head. She blinked away tears.

"I grew up outside of Chile," she said, after a pause. She felt a heaviness overpowering her.

"I might have guessed from your Spanish. It's not *Chileno*."

"That's what my brother says." Her eyes were fixed on the notes he was taking.

"Does he live in Chile?"

"No. He lives in the United States now. He's my half-brother. His mother is from Aysén. He grew up there."

"What is his name?" the Comisario asked, putting down his pen and tilting his head.

"Camilo Solis Ossandón."

"Is he related to Alejandro Ossandón?"

"Yes. Alejandro is his grandfather." She realized Camilo's grandfather was probably well-known in the south. He bred horses for the rodeo.

The Comisario stared at her as though he were trying to imagine where the woman sitting in front of him might fit into the society in the south of his country.

"My family is also from Puerto Aysén," he told her. "It's famous for rodeo," he added. "I know his family. I go to the rodeo often with my wife and children."

Emmanuelle breathed deeply, relieved that he appeared to be softening up. They shared some common ground, however remote. She'd nearly forgotten how important the rodeo was in the south. The strictly-regulated national sport took second place only to soccer. Every weekend, people from all over the area traveled to watch *huasos* mounted on horses, riding laps around a crescent-shaped corral trying to pin down a calf. It was a society in which everyone knew everyone else. She wondered whether Camilo might possibly know the Comisario. She definitely had to call him.

"I used to get mad at my brother when he came to stay with us in the summers," she said. "He loved to sing and dance. He would wave his handkerchief around and lasso me as though I were a calf at the rodeo. He called me *La Consentida.*"

Comisario Muñoz laughed. He knew the ballad well. "Hah! A real *huaso.*"

She remembered how she'd once felt worlds apart from her then-estranged brother who spent hours dancing in front of the mirror in his spurred-boots, sombrero and poncho. Now, as she sat in a police station in Camilo's part of the world, she appreciated him more than ever.

Emmanuelle smiled at the Comisario, but tension still mounted inside of her. The feeling of familiarity began to unnerve her. He reminded her of her father. And her brother. In fact, all of the Carabineros were starting to remind her of her father and Camilo. She had a sudden urge to divulge her whole life story to them. *That would be insane,* she thought. *Suicide.* She glanced at the door. She needed to get out of there. Her head throbbed and she wasn't thinking straight. She would talk to them after she'd thought things through—especially the confidentiality issue. Was there no oxygen in the room? She felt like getting up and shoving the window open, but she sat cemented to her chair by an unbearable heaviness. *I am in deep shit.*

An officer appeared at the door, catching the attention of the Comisario. He stood and left the room. Emmanuelle stared at the Comisario's desk with its neatly stacked files. She reached into her coat pocket, searching for her mother's rosary. She didn't pray much. In fact, she barely prayed at all. But she kept it with her anyway. She clutched it tightly now as if it might impart some talismanic good luck—which she needed. A dizzying pain pulsed in the back of her head.

She stared blankly at the host of government officials in simple black-rimmed, picture frames hanging on the walls. They all stared back at her. The President of Chile. The General Director of Carabineros. Several others she didn't recognize.

He returned. "I just spoke to *Investigaciones de Chile.* They would like to ask you a few questions. Someone from that office will visit you at your hotel first thing in the morning," the Comisario said, coming back into the room and handing back her passport. "Any incident involving foreign nationals must be reported to them. This officer is going to take you to your hotel," he said, placing a hand on the shoulder of the young officer who'd greeted them at the entrance.

So, I'm free to go? She breathed. "There's no need, but thank you," she said. "I'm fine. My hotel is right up the street." Her relief rapidly transformed into deep fatigue. She stood, feeling—for a fraction of a second—like her ankles were tied together.

"If you have any problems, you can always find me here," the officer said as he opened the door for her.

She stepped out of the police station and into the pouring rain like a ghost happening upon reality. The street was teeming with pedestrians carrying umbrellas and skipping puddles. She was only barely conscious of the traffic, the noise and the rain.

***

As soon as Emmanuelle left the room and was out of hearing range, the lieutenant leaned in close to the Commissioner. "Comisario Muñoz, shall we contact the US Embassy?"

The Commissioner picked up a transparent demitasse, savoring the frothy *café cortado* in it. "No. They'll come to us soon enough. *Tranquilo*. Have Miguel track the girl. Day and night."

"Prefecto Cienfuegos phoned a minute ago. He said he is sending an undercover female detective to the Hotel Interamericano tonight and he will question Solis in the morning."

"*Excelente. Muy bien*. Maybe he should send two or more plain-clothed officers there."

The Comisario tore off a sheet from a pad and handed it to the lieutenant. "Call the Ministry of the Interior and request that these reports be sent to my house." He handed the lieutenant a list. "This evening, if possible. Don't mention anything about Señorita Solis. We don't need Santiago breathing down out necks. Not yet. Let's take it one step at a time."

"What about Interpol?" the lieutenant asked.

"We won't call Interpol yet. Call Prefecto Cienfuegos back.

Ask him to meet me at my house at eight o'clock."

"Tonight?"

"Yes. Tonight. Tell him I will call him in an hour and explain more."

Chapter 26

THE ROOM SERVICE girl placed Emmanuelle's dinner tray on the desk, gently pushing legal pads, files and papers to one side. "*Biftek a lo pobre*," she said, uncovering the Chilean "poor man's steak" served on a heaped pile of French fries, topped with fried eggs and onions. "Can I get you anything else?"

Emmanuelle considered the young girl for a moment. She had a pretty, heart-shaped face, jet-black hair pulled back tightly in a ponytail. Why did she feel like she'd seen her before? *Everyone is starting to look familiar.* "No. Thank you."

She picked up the tray and set it on the bed. She was famished, exhausted and her head throbbed. She unfolded the napkin, picked up her knife and fork and began to eat heartily. It tasted great. She lifted her eyes and realized the room service girl not only wasn't making a move for the door, she appeared to be reading papers on her desk.

The papers from Calle Vicente Perez Rosales. She bolted up, snatched them, put them in a file, pulled two thousand pesos from her wallet and handed it to her, pushing her out the door.

She dropped back onto the bed and reached for her mother's rosary beads. They were dangling from the night table. She fell into deep, dreamless slumber before she could utter a prayer.

Chapter 27

THE OLD-FASHIONED ROTARY dial phone that hadn't made a noise since Emmanuelle first checked into the hotel blasted an earsplitting ring. The room spun around as Emmanuelle opened her eyes. She bolted up in bed and picked up the receiver. "Stephan?"

"*Buenos días*, Señorita Solis," a voice said.

Her heart sank. She felt disoriented for a moment. Pain pulsed in her head. And then it registered. She was still in Puerto Montt, and Isauro, the hotel receptionist, was calling. No, it hadn't all just been a bad dream. She was waking up to an ongoing nightmare.

"There is someone here to see you."

She squinted at the brilliant sunlight pouring in through the window. "Who is it?"

"Prefecto Sebastián Cienfuegos. The Chief of Investigative Police."

Her heart thudded. Her stomach flipped like a fish out of water. *What did he want? What would she tell him?* She looked at the clock on the night table. It was 7:00 A.M.

"I'll be downstairs in … ten, fifteen minutes."

"You mean you want me to ask him to *wait* for fifteen minutes?" he asked, lowering his voice. "You realize who he is, right? *Policía de Investigaciones.* He's the *jefe* of the detectives." His tone was bothered and insistent.

"I'll be down in two minutes," she said.

She stared out the window as reality set in. It was a cloudless day. Puerto Montt looked like a different city. The deep blue waters on the port were beaded with colorful vessels and the snow-peaked Osorno volcano puffed a fine strand of pink smoke. Her room was warm for the first time since she'd arrived. But none of that did anything to dissipate the anxiety and paralyzing fear she felt. She walked slowly to the bathroom, the room stirring around her. *Think. Wake up. Think about what you'll say to him.* The floor was cold. She stared at herself in the mirror as she brushed her teeth. The water ran noisily in the sink and seemed to echo as it drained through the pipes. The dark circles under her eyes were more pronounced than ever. She washed and dressed quickly, pulling her hair back into a bun.

***

EMMANUELLE STEPPED OUT of the elevator and looked around the hotel lobby. A short, thickset man with his pants belted high above his waistline was chatting loudly on a cell phone and leaning against the reception desk. She walked toward him and quickly apologized for making him wait.

He looked surprised.

"Señor Prefecto," Isauro called out to a different man sitting in the lobby. "La Señorita Emmanuelle Solis."

That man closed the newspaper he was reading and stood. He was a tall, striking man in his early forties. He wore jeans, a starch-pressed white shirt, a leather motorcycle jacket, and black boots. His thick brown hair was gelled back neatly.

"*Buenos días,* Señorita." Without the slightest smile the Prefecto shook her hand. For a split second, it seemed as though the sight of her startled him. Did he recognize her? Emmanuelle wasn't sure how to interpret it, but she knew she'd caught something in his expression.

"It's amazing how abruptly the weather changes in Puerto Montt," she said nervously, trying to break the ice.

He took his wallet out and showed her his badge.

"Shall we talk in the restaurant?" she asked, barely glancing at the badge. She studied his handsome, but serious face. His resolution frightened her already.

"As you like." His response was flat. He stepped ahead of her to open the door.

The restaurant was empty. The rising sun poured through the wrap-around windows, warming it. The smell of coffee filled the air. Emmanuelle, dazzled for a moment by the sunlight, chose a table by the window.

"I've been looking at your city through a scrim of fog for the past three days. It's a different world when the sun shines in Puerto Montt." She searched the Prefecto's dark, brown eyes. Would he help her? Could she tell him everything?

"The winters are generally rainy in the south," he offered. There was disinterest in his voice, warning that he wasn't there to engage in idle conversation.

He stared at her. She stared back. His hair, olive complexion, athletic build, large dark eyes and general appearance reminded her of Camilo. Unlike Camilo, however, it seemed the Prefecto rarely smiled. There was a scar over his right eyebrow. She wondered whether it had been from a fight with criminals or a tussle over a woman. She guessed he had a bad temper.

The Prefecto crossed his arms and looked at her, as though waiting for her to talk.

It was already clear the interview wasn't going to be pleasant. Emmanuelle's mind made another calculated guess; the Prefecto was a difficult man with no patience. She ordered coffee, contemplatively straightening out the wrinkles on the napkin on her lap. The waiter would soon bring her breakfast. Homemade bread, avocado spread, cheese and runny eggs. It was included in the price of her hotel room. "Would you like watery eggs?" Emmanuelle asked, still hoping to break the tension.

Humor wasn't going to work. As handsome as he was, the Prefecto seemed brooding and unpleasant. Without shifting his attention from Emmanuelle, he told the waitress he didn't want anything.

Emmanuelle took in a deep breath and, in a hurried sort of way, she repeated a condensed version of what she had told the Carabineros the night before. Then she stared at him for what seemed an eternity, waiting for a response of some sort. But he just sat there, staring back at her. She sensed he knew there was more that she wasn't telling him. She poked nervously at the eggs with her fork, moved them around the plate. She couldn't contemplate eating them.

A ribbon of light refracting from the moving waters on the port shot a multi-colored ray into her glass of water. She ran a finger up and down the glass skittishly.

He reached into his jacket, pulled out a paper and methodically unfolded it. "Is this the man you were supposed to meet in Puerto Montt?" he asked. She detected a hint of anger in his tone. A muscle tightened in his face.

Her eyes dropped to the paper. It was the article from the *Tercero* with Stephan's picture. Her stomach clenched. She tried to keep her gaze focused on the Prefecto, but it traveled everywhere else. She finally said, "So … you know about Stephan Henri Brent? Yes. That's him. I work for him." *Damn it*. What was happening to her? She'd never acted so unprofessionally. Why wasn't she handling this like a lawyer? Wasn't she trained to respond to these situations? *Think*. Her mind drew a blank. She heard herself repeat exactly what the paper said. *Come on. Obviously he knows what the papers say,* she thought. Tension peaked when he kept silent after her brilliant revelation. Her nervous system activated in every direction— her hands trembled, her feet shuffled, she struggled for composure. She wondered if he noticed.

He called the waitress over and ordered coffee. He smiled endearingly at her when she brought it to him.

That's weird, she thought. Did he know her? Emmanuelle watched as he carefully measured the sugar and powdered coffee and spooned it into his cup before the waitress poured the steaming milk over it. He seemed to count the times that he punctiliously stirred the mixture … six, seven, eight, nine, ten times before striking the side of the cup with the spoon. Was he some kind of neurotic with obsessive-compulsive disorder? A short-tempered, obsessive-compulsive cop. *Great.* Just what she needed.

He finally broke the torturous silence. "Why did he call *you*?" His eyes drifted from hers to the waitress who was now on her way back to the kitchen.

Emmanuelle was startled by his directness. A surge of boldness came back to her. It had been the assault. The head injury had her in a state of confusion, unnerved and weakened. "We work together," she said, feeling her dignity and strength returning.

"Why didn't he call a partner at the firm? Oliver & Stone? That's the firm you work for, right? *¿No es cierto?* Why would he call a simple associate like you?"

Simple associate? He was nasty. But it was a good question. She didn't have a good answer. At least not one she was prepared to divulge to the Puerto Montt Chief of Detectives. "We work together," she repeated.

Silence again.

By the time he finished firing a barrage of questions at her—most of which she couldn't answer— her cheeks burned. Had she called the US Embassy? Why had she not told anyone else in the firm? Why would he contact her as opposed to the police, the embassy or the FBI?

"I still don't understand why *you* are here, Ms. Solis."

"He called and asked me to bring the files to him here." She heard her own voice raise a notch.

"Who do you know at Calle Vicente Perez Rosales?"

"I don't know anyone there. I told the police yesterday, I found the address in files I was asked to bring here. He said we would go to the authorities together with some evidence he had discovered."

"Evidence of what?"

"I don't know what he meant. He said he couldn't tell me over the phone." What did he suspect her of? Why was he putting her through this? A sense of apprehension thickened inside of her, restricting airflow to her lungs. She felt dizzy

"Why did he want to meet you here in Chile? Why not Argentina? Wasn't that where he was, *supuestamente*?"

"I can't tell you that. I can't tell you everything I discussed with him."

The more he glared at her, the more it riled her. It was a suspicious sort of stare. A way of displaying his power over her. It seemed like a psychological ploy he was accustomed to using to assert authority over people he interrogated. As though he could peer into their psyche. She was angry.

"You think you have that option? The building you were in was the center of an operation for a big investment scam. We arrested over twenty people connected to it last week. I think you'd better start talking. *What* were you doing there?"

Emmanuelle felt like she'd just received a blow to the stomach. Her brain went into a whirl. That's why the police appeared to be suspicious. The office on Calle Vicente Perez Rosales resembled a boiler room operation. Investment fraud operatives used inexpensive offices in obscure, rundown places like that, employing telemarketers to make thousands of random calls, using high-pressure sales tactics to sell stocks. She knew that. What had she been thinking? But how was that joint connected to what Stephan had uncovered? The documents she found there were securities-related documents. And someone at the office wanted to derail the securities arbitration Stephan was supposed to testify in. It was making more sense now. She had to think carefully before she said another word. The Prefecto was studying her face. Something twisted inside her like a heavy-bodied snake, wrapping around her lungs.

He didn't suspect *her*, did he? "Think about it," she said, groping for a response. "If I were involved with whomever it was you arrested, do you think I would go there knowing a bust had just taken place?"

He ignored her question. "Señorita Solis, there's no record of Señor Brent entering Chile after he disappeared in June. Why did you come here? Why Chile?"

She knew he spoke with authority; *Extranjería* was a division of *Policía de Investigationes Internacionales* and they had jurisdiction over anything related to border control and immigration. He could pull those records in minutes and find out exactly when someone entered and exited the country. But she knew Stephan could have crossed the border in an area with less or no border control. She'd heard it was easier the farther south you traveled. His abductors had his passport and identification documents, so he would probably have tried to avoid border inspection.

"According to Interpol, he disappeared after a meeting in Tucumán. *Your* embassy says he was abducted, and judging from the popularity of the companies he represented in this area of the world, I wouldn't be surprised if he turned up dead."

"What? What do you mean?"

"Your firm represents companies accused of violating human rights in this part of the world." He unfolded the *Mercurio* newspaper he'd been reading in the lobby "This is today's paper." He pointed to an article about a corporation represented by Oliver & Stone. There was a picture of Stephan next to it.

She took the paper and read it. Her cheeks flushed with humiliation. It claimed a mining company Oliver & Stone represented was involved in human rights violations against indigenous groups. She didn't know anything about the company and she'd never heard of the case. There were over thirty-five lawyers in the Arbitration Group. Any one of them could have been handling some transaction for that corporation. "Corporations are always accused of all kinds of things," she said. "Stephan represents corporations in *commercial transactions* with governments. He has absolutely no relationship to any private security company hired by the corporation." She calmed herself, prepared to defend the firm against false accusations.

"The truth of the allegations is of little relevance to me. I don't care what your corporate friends do in Bolivia or Argentina. It has nothing to do with Chile. But if you're wondering why your friend disappeared in South America, his association with corporations that are politically unpopular here is a good enough motive for someone to abduct him." He paused. "The Argentine Air Force has just located the remains of a plane that crashed in the Aconquija Mountains. In fact, they think the plane might have been sabotaged with explosives. They suspect it's the one that was chartered to take him back to Buenos Aires after the meetings. In any case, your friend didn't come to Chile. So once again, Señorita Solis, why are you here?"

He didn't believe her. He thought she was covering something up.

She said, "You don't understand. He *called* me after that plane was sighted. *He's alive.* He never got on that plane. He was abducted. And he escaped and called me on his way here three days ago."

"That may be," he shrugged. "But he didn't enter Chile after his disappearance in Argentina. He was here eight times in the past year. In fact, he was here in Puerto Montt the day before he was abducted in Argentina."

"Eight times? He was here before going to Argentina? I don't think so. He flew to Buenos Aires. I took him to the airport," Emmanuelle stood up. "I ... think you're mistaken."

"*Claro que sí,* Señorita Solis, he *was* here the day before the protests in Argentina. We're certain of that."

That can't be. Was he lying to try to get her to talk? She moved closer to him. "He's alive. I know he is. He's here or he's trying to get here. Please," she insisted, lowering her voice, "I need your help. He's in danger. He said he'd uncovered some kind of a criminal conspiracy involving people in our firm. Maybe the criminals you arrested on Calle Vicente Perez Rosales are connected to what he was talking about. He said we would go to the authorities together when I got here."

The Prefecto looked at her intently. "So, now you admit that you know something about fraud on Calle Vicente Perez Rosales?"

She took stock of her predicament. "I don't have any idea what was going on at Calle Vicente Perez Rosales. I told you that. I only found the address in one of the files he asked me to bring here."

"May I see the files?" he asked. "Do you have them with you?"

"Yes, I have the files. But ... I can't show them to you. I'm a lawyer. They belong to the firm. I could lose my license to practice law if I turn them over to you. It's a confidentiality issue."

"Ms. Solis, you don't seem to understand the gravity of your situation." He leaned closer to her. "I'm in charge of an investigation of a criminal ring that's defrauding investors in Latin America. You were apprehended at the scene of the crime. And you may be in possession of evidence relevant to that investigation." His eyes locked with hers. "Tell me something. Why didn't you contact your embassy and let them know he called you?"

"He asked me not to. Not until he met with me."

"*Claro.*" He nodded condescendingly. "So you do whatever he tells you to do?"

"He's my boss."

"Even if it means violating the law?"

Her cheeks seared. "That's insulting. I've never violated *any* law in all of my life." They were nearly face to face, both searching each other's eyes for more information. "He's an international arbitrator. I assist him in the arbitrations he presides over. I am bound by the confidentiality of proceedings. He was going to explain everything to me when I got here. We planned to go to the authorities together. He's on the run. His life is in danger."

The sun reflected in the Prefecto's eyes. He turned away from her and punched out a text message on his cell phone.

Who is he texting? What is he telling them? She was certain it had something to do with her.

"If you have anything you would like to tell me, you can reach me at my office," he said, taking a card out of his wallet.

Their meeting was ending in disaster. The tables had turned. Suddenly, *she* was the one who was under investigation. *This is absurd.*

She *had* to work with him. He had to believe her. "Señor Prefecto, wait." She didn't want him to leave this way. She touched his arm. Their eyes met but he quickly looked away, as though disturbed by something she couldn't put a finger on. "He called me. He said his life was in danger." *Please believe me.*

The Prefecto didn't say anything, but his eyes did. It terrified her. He was deeply suspicious of her. But there was something else she just couldn't place. Something about her unsettled him. But what was it?

"Is there any way he could have entered the country without passing border control?" she pleaded. "I've heard there are areas where people can cross without inspection."

"I can't tell you that. It's confidential." He gave her a bitter smile.

Emmanuelle watched him walk away.

Chapter 28

AVOIDING THE HOTEL InterAmericano reception desk, Emmanuelle climbed seven flights of stairs to get back to her room, her head still throbbing. She was certain the receptionist had called the police and tipped them off after she'd asked him for directions. Everyone in the country must have known about the bust on Calle Vicente. Everyone except her. It was clear it wasn't merely a coincidence the police had showed up when they did. She needed to pay more attention to Chilean news or soon she would be the headline.

After Prefecto Cienfuegos' visit, the place would certainly buzz with rumors. Their conversation had turned into a nightmare. *She'd* become a suspect. How could this be happening?

As she neared her room, she saw the door was open. Had she left without closing it? She heard water running. She held her breath and pushed it open. The housekeeping cart was parked in the middle of the room. Someone was cleaning her bathroom. She breathed. *I'm paranoid*, she told herself, scanning the room. Something was missing. Her briefcase wasn't where she'd left it. She ran to the bathroom.

"*Señorita. ¿Mi maletín?* My briefcase was on my desk when I left this room ..." She struggled not expose her proximity to meltdown.

The woman, bent over the tub, straightened and turned to

128

her. It was the room service girl. The one with the heart-shaped faced.

"*Está en ese armario*," she said, pointing to the armoire.

Retrieving her briefcase, Emmanuelle observed the room service girl. Now she was cleaning water spots off the showerhead. Vigorously polishing it. She didn't seem to have plans to leave the room anytime soon. A vague uneasiness about the girl swept over her.

Emmanuelle settled back down at her desk and organized the Patagonia Files. She picked up the folder with the handwritten address. *Whose handwriting is this?* She booted her laptop and tried to log onto the Oliver & Stone server to retrieve her emails. An "Access Denied" message blinked. *What the hell?*

She picked up her phone and started dialing the office, but she changed her mind. She looked over at the bathroom. She had to get rid of the girl. "Can you bring me a *café cortado*?" she asked, standing at the bathroom door. "*¿Ahora?*"

"*Al tiro.*" The girl hurried out.

Emmanuelle shoved the cleaning cart out of the room and returned to her desk to call her office.

Lynn answered the phone. "I have no idea why you can't access your account. Where are you? When are you planning to come back?"

Emmanuelle averted the question. "Is Chris in?"

"I don't think the tech staff is in yet, but I'll put you through. Hold on."

She heard Chris' voicemail and hung up.

Her conversation with Prefecto Cienfuegos still swirled like a tornado in her head. Had Stephan been in Puerto Montt the day before he was abducted? It seemed impossible. Maybe the Prefecto was bluffing to get a reaction out of her. Did he really suspect that she was connected to the seedy scam artists he'd busted? Would Stephan ever appear?

The television blinked again with images of the ship that sank in the Patagonia. She jumped up to raise the volume. An officer from the Chilean Armada was being interviewed. *Forty-five scientists and twelve volunteers on board the* Antarctic Mist *are now presumed dead. Some of the bodies have been recovered. Even the ones who were best-equipped for cold couldn't have survived for more than eight hours in the icy water.* The reporter asked the officer if he could confirm rumors of an explosion. *We haven't come to any firm conclusions as to why it went down. We're still gathering evidence. We know it sank quickly. The general suspicion is still that the ship hit an iceberg. Icebergs pose a serious threat to ships and tankers traveling through the Northern Patagonia.*

The room service girl appeared at the door. *"Permiso."*

Back already? Was she some kind of a marathon runner? "Adelante. Come in."

"Cafecito y galletitas." She placed a tray of coffee and cookies on Emmanuelle's desk.

Emmanuelle gestured for silence.

The girl pushed her cart back in the room and watched the news report with her.

The scene switched to a young man with aquiline features wearing a beret. *"This is an exceptionally dark moment for those of us who are concerned about the Patagonia,"* he said. His voice was hoarse and there was distress in his eyes. *"In one day, we lost so many skilled experts—scientists, geologists, hydrologists, environmentalists, human rights activists, students and volunteers—all of whom were dedicated to saving the Patagonia. The team was preparing to release a report on their investigations— the most comprehensive to date on the Patagonia. The team was assessing climate change and its impact on human and wild life populations."* The screen identified him as Miguel Fontana, the Chilean representative of Green Peace. Emmanuelle wrote his name down.

"*Que lástima*," the room service girl said. She took toiletries and towels from her cart and headed back to the bathroom.

Emmanuelle sifted through the files again, pen in hand. She took out the hydrological study, jotting down the name of the firm that authored it. She typed AECCo into a search engine on her computer. *AECCo, the American Engineer Consulting Corporation, an engineering consulting firm specializing in integrated site development services for commercial, energy, government, industrial and transportation clients.*

The corporation was based in Chicago, but there was no indication of any important projects they had undertaken. She glanced through the environmental impact study report in the file. A cover letter addressed to Albert Thorman was attached.

Who are these guys? They'd apparently subcontracted the investigation out to *Grupo Meridional, Avaliação do Ambiente, Engenharia e Consultoriae. Must be a Brazilian engineering company.* She checked online for information on the company and nothing came up. She scanned the UN website on trade that ranked transnational corporations by their assets. The company wasn't listed there either. She checked a few other registries. *Nothing.* She downloaded several articles on the dam projects in the Amazon and the Patagonia and saved them to her computer. She thought of Thorman. *That bastard chose an unknown company to do the environmental assessment for the project.*

She pushed away from her desk, grappling to make sense of it. Albert had pressured Stephan to go to Argentina in his place. After the financial crisis, Thorman seemed to be scrambling for clients, taking bigger and bigger financial risks. *Just how far would he go?*

But right now she had an even more urgent problem. She'd taken Albert's files from the office without his permission. She could be guilty of a whole host of ethical and maybe even criminal violations. She plucked the sealed envelope from the files once again. No matter which way she stacked up the facts, she was in trouble. *The bastard will probably report me to the bar or the State Attorney's office.* It was clear that if Stephan didn't appear, she was in trouble.

With trembling fingers, she broke the seal of the envelope and slid out its contents. A golden seal glimmered in the light of the desk lamp. A chill trickled through her veins. *Stock certificates.* The issuing company's name was Ameriminco. The certificates were issued to Thorman. She examined them carefully. He'd endorsed them over to Paul Saunders. One of the firm's wealthiest partners who'd recently joined from one of Germany's most prominent law firms. *Why did he endorse these over to Saunders?* Did he owe him money? She felt nauseous. Her better judgment was telling her she had better try to talk to Prefecto Cienfuegos again.

If anyone in *her* office were involved in investment fraud, it had to be something more significant than the Calle Vicente Perez Morales operation. It had to involve high yield or there would be no incentive.

She needed to find an angle to work with the Prefecto. She remembered the papers she'd picked up at the abandoned building the night before.

She turned to the room service girl who was gathering her cleaning gear and preparing to leave.

"Have you heard of the *Notario Publico* Bernardo Jara Carcuro?"

"*Si, po.* He has an office on Urmeneta Street." The girl took a brochure from her cart, unfolded it on the desk and drew arrows indicating how to get there from the hotel. "Don Bernardo is a very reputable notary public."

Emmanuelle reached into her purse and handed her several thousand pesos.

She eagerly accepted the tip. *"Gracias."*

The thought that she'd seen the girl somewhere before dangled from Emmanuelle's brain for a long second, like a spider from a thread. She scrutinized the girl's dark hair and facial features wondering, for a split second, what she would look like in a pink wig. Was she a hooker by night?

Chapter 29

THE NOTARY PUBLIC'S office was crammed with people waiting to get papers notarized, emboss-sealed or stamped. A clerk, obviously accustomed to controlled chaos, methodically tended to clients. After forty-five nerve-wracking minutes of waiting in the queue, a middle-aged, light-skinned man with a creamy complexion and a stylish suit emerged from a room at the back of the office. He fluttered back and forth between clients like a bee pollenating flowers. Emmanuelle assumed he was Don Bernardo.

"*Buenos días, señorita.* What can I do for you?" he asked Emmanuelle, bypassing several people in line ahead of her, one of whom muttered his discontent.

"*Buenos días.* I was wondering if you could provide me with some information," Emmanuelle said, nervously removing the documents she'd found at the bust scene from her briefcase. "These stock certificates were sold to me recently." She handed one to him, conscious of her trembling fingers. "The Santiago Stock Exchange now tells me they're not valid. I'm trying to get more information about the corporation that issued them. I want my money back. Your office authenticated the signatures of the original buyer ... so I thought you might be able to give me some information about him as well." *Please let this work,* she prayed.

Don Bernardo held the document up and examined it as

though he were inspecting a wall for termites. "You just bought the certificates without knowing anything about the corporation that issued them?" he asked.

"Well ... it's not exactly that simple. I trusted the person who sold them to me. Corporations can merge with other companies and still be financially successful, but just not operating under the name on the certificate. Or the corporation might have gone bankrupt or dissolved. I am trying to clarify the status of the corporation."

"Come with me," he said, escorting her to his office.

"I'm just a *notario público*. I only certify copies and verify the identification of people signing that kind of documentation. Or I verify that documents contain the requirements under the law." His words were humble, but his attitude wasn't. Don Bernardo stopped at the door. "Very nice watch, by the way," he said, pushing his glasses up higher on his nose to examine it. "Swiss, is it? I went to Switzerland twice. Beautiful place. Beautiful watch. Just like its owner." His lips curled into a smile.

"Your office apparently verified the signatures on the *traspaso de acciones* when the stock was sold from the stock broker to the person who sold it to me. Can you give me their contact information?"

"I can't share that with the public ... generally," he said, pausing to gaze at her again. "But ..." He inspected her clothes pensively. "Maybe I can help you."

He called over to a portly woman busily typing away on an oversized typewriter that clickety-clacked every time she hit a key. "Can you check this document number and bring me the files?" The question sounded more like a command than a request.

She cast an irritated glance at him but complied. Her high-heeled shoes squeaked under her weight as she disappeared into an office beside his. A while later, she returned. "We have no record of any document with that number."

"That's odd. It has our stamp on it," he said.

"It must be from the Aysén or Futaleufú office." She shrugged, walking back to her typewriter, hips swaying with each stride.

"You have offices out where the dams are going to be built?" Emmanuelle asked.

"Yes. My offices will be very busy when the project begins out there. Project executives say they are going to invest 350 million dollars in infrastructure, building a seaport, airport, etcetera. There's practically nothing there now. Just farmland, mountains, rivers and glaciers. And, of course, my office. We set one up there for that reason."

"I have another document here," Emmanuelle said, holding it out to him. "Can you tell me what this is?"

Don Bernardo ignored the document and her question, eyeing her clothes and jewelry again with unconcealed interest. "What do you do for a living?"

"I am an attorney. I work for a law firm in Washington, D.C."

He took the document from her.

"Can I tell you something?" he asked, taking his glasses off and putting his hands on his hips. The document dangled from his left hip. "I *knew* you were a lawyer. I'm also a lawyer. Not just a notary. What is it like to practice law in the United States? Is it like it is portrayed in movies?" He had a silly grin on his face.

"I don't think it's as exciting as they make it seem," she said, gently retrieving the document from his hip and straightening it out in front of him. "Can you tell me anything about this?"

He took it back from her. "*Ah... ya,*" he said, running his finger along the document as he read it. "*Claro.* This document is a mining claim. That's what it is. A mining claim." He handed it back to her.

"A mining claim? Can you tell me anything more?"

"Ehhh … no," he said, shaking his head firmly. He appeared to be thinking about it. After a few seconds, he snatched it back from her hands again. "I guess I can make a few phone calls for you." He put his hand on the small of her back, gently leading her to the window of the front office. "If you want, you can wait for me. There's a small pastry shop with the best cachitos right next door." He pointed to a quaint restaurant with tea tables, lace tablecloths and fresh flowers. "Have you had them before?"

She shook her head. She couldn't think of eating. Emmanuelle looked at the wall clock and wondered how many minutes away from arrest she was.

"You'll love them." He clasped his hands together. "Get a table, order some coffee. I'll make some calls and meet you with the information in a few minutes." He made a copy of the document and handed her back the original.

Emmanuelle noticed him whisper something to his clerk as she walked out. Both of them smiled at her.

***

Fifteen minutes later, Emmanuelle was sitting in the pastry shop nervously sipping a *cortado* when Don Bernardo breezed in waving a paper and smiling. In his long overcoat, he waved his arm and snapped his fingers to get the attention of a waitress he appeared to know. She followed him to Emmanuelle's table and took his order.

"I found some information for you," he said cheerfully, pulling out a chair. A file was tucked under his left arm. "So, I am not *such* an ordinary *notario público, no es cierto*?" He laughed.

Emmanuelle smiled. There was something genuinely

entertaining about the man aside from his self-adoration. She examined his tailored suit and guessed he was from a wealthy family.

"Did you know that Chilean notary publics are more powerful figures than their counterparts in other countries?" There was a sparkle in his eyes.

"No. I didn't know that. Very interesting," she said, making sure there was interest in her tone. "So, what did you find out about the document?" She shifted in her chair. She needed answers. She needed information that would put her in a position to help with the investigation and gain credibility in the eyes of the Prefecto. She stared at the file the Notary had placed on the table. What did it contain? She feared appearing desperate.

"We act like clerks of the court in the United States. And I must admit that I've made a very decent living as a *notario* in spite of the mundanities of my trade."

She wanted to scream. She started to doubt he would ever get to the point.

He picked up the plate of twisted sugared pastries and fruit tartlettes the waitress had just placed on the table and held it out to her. She took one and watched him as he bit into his.

"*Exquisito.*" Powdered sugar from the pastry coated his lips. He licked it away, sipping his *cortado*. "*Que rico.*"

"So ..." she said, eyeing the folder near his elbow.

He opened it finally. "The document was executed by one of my satellite offices and, oddly enough, I don't have very much information about it here." His smile twisted into a grimace. "But I *can* tell you that it is registered in the *Registro de Propiedad del Conservador de Minas*, the registry office for mines and mining claims. Apparently, the mining rights pertain to a land somewhere near the Futaleufú River Valley. A corporation by the name of Ameriminco owns the rights, and I suspect it's a foreign corporation. The company must have a legal representative in the area." His tone brightened.

Emmanuelle's heart thudded. *The stock certificates in the Patagonia Files were issued by that company.* She wrote the information down on a pad. She was one step closer. But the exact connection between the mining claims, the ship, the investment fraud and Thorman was not apparent. "How can we find the legal representative?" she asked.

"His name should be registered in the office where the land is located as well as in the place where the business is based. Any foreign corporation operating in Chile has to designate a legal representative here."

"Can you get me his contact information?"

"Maybe. I'll have to check when I'm in the Futaleufú office. I'll be there next week. I may go whitewater rafting while I'm there. Would you like to join me? Or maybe we can discuss this more over lunch? Today? Or dinner tonight?" he asked, breaking into a smile.

"Thanks, but I've got some work to do this afternoon. Please call me if you find out anything more. I'm staying at the Hotel Interamericano."

The addresses and phone numbers of his Aysén and Futaleufú offices were on a business card he handed to her. "Yes. Yes. My cell phone is on the back of the card."

"How can I get to Aysén?"

"You can take a ferry. Or you can come with me. I leave Thursday morning."

"Thanks. I'll let you know before then," she said, getting up to leave.

Chapter 30

THE THOUGHT OF going to Aysén pressed in Emmanuelle's mind. Cringing against the gusting cold wind, she walked a mile and a half from the notary's office to Angelmó, a picturesque fishing port from which ships departed on voyages into the Patagonia. The port was a tourist hub in the spring and summer. Its restaurants were filled with tourists seeking exotic dishes made with mollusks they couldn't find in the rest of the world. Now only a handful of tourists—identifiable by their fluorescent parkas, enormous backpacks and hiking gear—stood in line to board the Patagonia-bound ferries.

At another time in her life, she would have been exhilarated to be here. But after her conversation with the Prefecto, the darkest possibilities were flooding through her. Her simple plan had gone all wrong. Her decision to get on that plane and come here could end up costing her career, maybe even her liberty. It was the first in a string of catastrophically bad decisions that she would soon have to account for. She had no clue what had happened to Stephan. She couldn't just get on a plane and go back to Washington, D.C. Who could she trust now if she went back? In spite of the cold, she felt beads of sweat forming along her spine.

She stopped on a street corner and looked out at the Pacific Ocean. Her hair and clothes lashed in the wind. She had to find a way to work with the Prefecto. Maybe the notary office in

Aysén had information about Thorman's stock certificates and the company that issued them. But how soon could she get there? She spotted two blonde-haired, college-aged girls waiting in line at the ferry terminal. She approached them and asked about the travel routes of the ferries.

"We've been all over the Patagonia," one said with a smile, her Spanish carrying a distinct accent. European, perhaps German. "But not in the winter. The sea is rough this time of year. I'm having second thoughts ... especially after news about the ship that hit the iceberg and sank a few days ago." She reached into the pocket of her parka, pulled out a hair clip and corralled her wind-swept hair, pinning it back.

The reports about a possible explosion on the ship crossed Emmanuelle's thoughts. They hadn't seen the news.

"But it's an adventure," her friend said. She bit her lip and wrapped her scarf tightly around her neck. "This ship will take you to Chiloé Island, the Puyuhuapi Hot Springs, and the province of Aysén. Best vacation ever."

Vacation? Emmanuelle wiggled her numb toes in her shoes. How many years had it been since she'd taken a vacation? She couldn't remember the last time she'd taken a trip without the burden of a pending memorandum or filing looming over her. Her thoughts momentarily skirted memories of her childhood vacations in Geneva. "How long does it take to get there?" Her teeth were chattering.

"Depends how far you want to go. It's a three-day boat ride from Puerto Montt to Puerto Natales. You'll pass spectacular waterfalls, rapids and white rivers. This place is great in the summer. Motorboats, schooners and sailboats whizz along the Reloncaví Inlet and the archipelago of Chiloé Island. From that point on, a string of islands stretches all the way down into the Patagonia."

"Thanks for the tip."

The girl eyed her. "If you need warm clothes, you should visit the second hand shop on Calle Antonio Varas. They sell everything tourists leave when they're traveling back home. Ski suits, parkas, gloves. Great stuff! Anything you want." She fiddled through her backpack and took out a small card. "Here," she said, offering it to her. "The owner's cell phone number. He delivers anything you need to your hotel. He's great. We called him a few times."

The line was moving now and passengers were boarding. Emmanuelle took the card and waved goodbye as the girls moved forward in the line. She continued along the port, struggling against the wind. She took refuge from the cold an hour later in a tiny pastel-colored restaurant mounted on stilts that, from a distance, looked like a birdhouse. A waitress ushered her to a table. She had been practically living on *café cortados*. She ordered seafood empanadas while examining the documents. Now she knew exactly what they were. One of them was an instrument defining the rights of security holders. She connected to the Internet on her phone and searched the words 'Ameriminco mining project Futaleufú' into a search engine. An article published in 2009 by an environmentalist organization came up. She clicked on it. *Ameriminco, a consortium of companies that purchased mining rights in the Patagonia has filed another controversial claim to exploit gold by tunneling under the Yelcho Glacier in the Futaleufú area of the Patagonia. The mining project will involve digging tunnels under the glaciers to reach the gold trapped in the rock under the glacier. The consortium's stock soared this week when it announced an estimated 17.6 million ounces of gold deposits were discovered under the glacier. In addition, the mining company has filed claims to extract mineral deposits beneath and surrounding the Futaleufú River. These companies need only the infrastructure and power supply brought by the proposed dams to begin capitalizing on their claims.*

Without dams, the claims would be worthless. But what was the connection to the Calle Vicente Perez Rosales scam? A flash of silver illuminated a raincloud in the distance. It would rain soon. She would be drenched before she reached her hotel. Emmanuelle put money on the table and left before the waitress brought out the food.

On the street, she noticed a man on a corner fiddling with something in his hand. She caught his searching eyes. He looked vaguely familiar. She lost it for a moment. Paranoid possibilities crowded her brain. Was he the man who'd assaulted her? Could he be connected to the thugs who abducted Stephan? Pulse pounding, she clutched her briefcase and scanned the streets for a Carabinero. She spotted one a few meters away and quickened her steps to reach him, engaging him in conversation about the ferries. He accompanied her for a few blocks. The man eventually disappeared into the market and the Carabinero went on his way. The muscles in her back released.

A block away from her hotel, the rain started in with large drops. Emmanuelle took cover under the awning of a restaurant and considered going in. She was famished.

She stepped inside and waited for the receptionist at the darkened entrance. The place was hazy with cigarette smoke. The candle-lit tables were filled. A woman with a deep, expressive voice—competing with the cacophony of whistles, applause, laughter and a rumble of conversation—was singing a tango to the rhythm of a bandoneon and a piano. A well-built man and a woman with gel-slicked hair were dancing. They moved in circles through the light and shadows of the room. It was Prefecto Cienfuegos. The Prefecto's companion looked in her direction, as though sensing someone's stare. She had a vulgar, energetic air that Emmanuelle recognized. She was one of the prostitutes from Calle Vicente Perez Rosales. Why was the Prefecto with a prostitute? With a sense of disgust,

Emmanuelle retreated to the door. Music and noise from the restaurant spilled onto the streets as she left. She knew the Prefecto had seen her. She slipped around the corner and down the street. Concealed by the shadows of an alleyway, she looked back to the restaurant and saw the Prefecto open the door and step out into the rain. She held her breath. He looked up and down the street before going back inside.

She sprinted for the hotel.

Chapter 31

SEBASTIÁN CIENFUEGOS STIFFENED at the sound of Detective Pilar Bustamante calling him. He quickened his stride to the conference room, ignoring her. She caught up as he reached the door. "*Señor Prefecto.*" She was out of breath.

"*¿Que pasa Pilar?* What do you want?" he said, pulling open the door and stepping into the room. It was filled with detectives and Carabineros waiting for the Public Prosecutor.

"I want to talk to you about the lawyer who was picked up on Calle Vicente Perez Rosales last night." Pilar's brother had been Sebastián's closest friend on the force until he was shot and killed in a stakeout ten years earlier. After his death, Pilar switched from law school to the *Escuela de Carabineros,* perhaps to honor his memory. Sebastián knew that her brother wouldn't have wanted that, but he couldn't dissuade Pilar. He took her onto his team and into his realm of protection. But now, her born-to-rule-the-world attitude was unnerving him. "Not here, Pilar."

"Why not here?"

"Because I said so."

"*¿Y porque?*"

Ignoring her was easier than arguing with her.

Several of his detectives immediately began asking him about the case.

He explained, "It's called a Ponzi Scheme. A fraudulent investment operation that pays returns to its investors from the investor's own money or from money paid by other investors," he explained.

"How does that work?" a detective asked, jotting down notes.

"Often there is no real corporation, no real investment. They just take your money and pay themselves and someone else who invested before you did. The hook is to entice new investors by claiming higher returns than other investments, usually short-term returns that are either extremely high or unusually consistent."

"So, to keep the scheme going, they need a continuous flow of money from *new* investors?"

"That's exactly how they operate. High-pressure salespeople make calls to thousands of potential investors to peddle unregistered stocks in fraudulent or failing companies. The operation is destined to collapse when they can't keep it up. South America is increasingly susceptible to this kind of fraud."

Sebastián paced the front of the room. "Usually, the scheme is detected by authorities before it collapses. The more investors, the greater likelihood of apprehension by authorities."

"Was the operation shut down entirely, or are they operating elsewhere?" a detective asked.

"We have evidence they're operating in different locations. We suspect they're linked to a Santiago investment firm run by a man by the name of Antonio Carrasco. But, so far, much of his operation appears to be legitimate."

"So now, we're waiting for the public prosecutor to say we can move forward?"

"Yes, and he's already an hour late." Sebastián picked up a folder with information about Emmanuelle Solis, Oliver & Stone, and Stephan Henri Brent. He took a seat and leafed through the documents, removing a picture of Emmanuelle and examining it. He decided not to bring her to the attention of the public prosecutor. That would only slow things down. He was under no obligation. He didn't have any evidence she'd committed a crime in Chile. She'd been the victim of an assault. *That was all,* he told himself. But something about the bust on Calle Vicente Perez Rosales reminded him of the Inverlink Scandal ten years earlier.

That scandal had sent shock waves throughout the world. Chile previously had a spotless reputation for investment until news broke that the country's biggest brokerage firm had laundered one hundred million dollars' worth of stolen certificates of deposit from the government's own business development agency. High-ranking government and banking officials had been arrested.

He shifted in his chair. *So, why had the pretty little lawyer been poking around on the scene? Why was the address in her files?* His conversation with Solis ran through his mind as he looked at pages of the files. *Amazing resemblance,* he thought staring at a picture of her. He chased away a painful memory of his sister. *Emmanuelle…. Beautiful name. Beautiful face. An angel or a rogue?* He tucked the picture back in the file.

Whistling sounds brought him back to the room. Several detectives were harassing Camila, the newest member of his team. "*Oye* Camilita, where's the pink wig?"

More whistling. Laughter.

"You look hot in pink," one detective called out.

Camila's first street assignment had been to be the bait in a sting operation to bust a Puerto Montt prostitution ring.

Her eyes locked with Sebastián's, begging rescue from her colleagues.

"We are planning a sting operation at *La Cage au Folles*." Sebastián called out to the detective harassing her. Everyone in the room knew the place was a discotheque frequented by transsexuals. "Maybe I'll send you to go in drag."

The detective flashed him a defiant look, but said nothing. His manhood was screaming to respond, but he knew the Prefecto could be merciless.

Camila took a seat next to Sebastián.

"What did you find in Solis' hotel room?" His voice dropped to a whisper.

She handed him the file. "Here are pictures."

"No word to those idiots about Solis. They don't need to know we're tracking her. *¿Entendí?*" Prosecutorial involvement often paralyzed their operations. "If we wait for the public prosecutor's office to tell us to act, the evidence and the criminals will be in Brazil before they get off their asses. If you do this right, I'll move you up quickly on my team. You screw up, you're out. *¿Entendí?*"

"*Si, po.* You can count on me."

Comisario Olivares walked in, his eyes scanning the room until they found Sebastián. He headed towards him, the detectives and Carabineros going quiet.

Minutes later, a man in a wrinkled suit and dusty shoes came through the door. He sat his battered attaché on the ground and announced the prosecutor would not be able to attend.

Sebastián shook his head in disgust, eyeing the lawyer with tousled, shoulder-length hair. "More delays. Did you contact the prosecutor about Solis?" he whispered to Comisario Olivares who had taken a seat beside him.

"Of course not. I didn't contact the US embassy either." The Comisario's voice dropped to a whisper. "I did speak to a colleague from Santiago though." The police commissioner paused for a moment, looking around again.

Sebastián leaned closer. "And?"

"Solis' law firm represents Hébère International Energy, S.A. Several of its subsidiaries have operations in Chile and Argentina. Hébère recently threatened to file a claim against Chile for suspending its operations in Hualqui."

"Who is handling that case?"

"The legal department for the Ministry of the Economy. They hired a United States law firm with expertise in international arbitration. Oliver & Stone represents Hébère. They had lawyers here several times this year on that case. If it's not successfully negotiated, the case will end up in the World Bank. It's all here." He handed him the file.

"If Solis insists the missing lawyer is here, the press might start trying to connect his disappearance to that case. The government won't be happy about that. Bad press for investment. A potential political nightmare. Oh, and I checked again with Interpol. Brent never entered Chile after the meeting in Buenos Aires," the Comisario added.

"Which attorney is handling it?"

"Estuardo Gonzalez, for the Ministry of Economy," said the Comisario. "And some lawyers from the Foreign Investment Committee. These cases are complicated. Politically charged. Chile wants to encourage foreign investment. Not scare it away."

Sebastián checked his cell phone to see if he had the attorney's number. He found it.

A young female Carabinero knocked on the door and peeked in. "Señor Prefecto Cienfuegos, your secretary is on the phone. She says the American who was assaulted yesterday is waiting for you in your office. What should she tell her?"

In my office? "Tell her to wait." He turned to the Comisario, whose eyebrows were raised.

"*Y eso?* Did she have an appointment with you?"

"No. I have no idea what she wants." Sebastián stood to

149

leave. "She's Chilean by the way. Her father is from Chile and she does have a RUT. We checked with Civil Registry."

"I know. She told me."

Chapter 32

SEBASTIÁN ENTERED THE offices of the Department of Foreign Affairs and International Police from the back of the building and sprinted up its four flights of stairs. He saw her as soon as the door to the hallway swung open. She must have been there for over an hour. She stood at the opposite end of the hall looking quite elegant in a finely tailored, white-rimmed, charcoal-blue suit, clutching a briefcase and watching detectives file in and out of the offices. The afternoon sunlight streamed through the window and dappled on the floor around her. It was striking how much she resembled his deceased elder sister, Cristina.

His thoughts reeled back twenty-five years to memories of Cristina and her struggle with leukemia in the last year of her life. It discomposed him, but he reminded himself that the association was irrational. Emmanuelle Solis was a potential suspect in a criminal investigation. He regrouped his emotions as he approached her.

Maybe she brought me the files. "*Buenos días,*" he said, motioning expressionlessly for her to follow him into his office.

***

Prefecto Sebastián Cienfuegos' office was a reflection of ordered thinking and a regimented mind. On the wall directly in front of his desk was a brittle, browning portrait of President

Domingo Santa María from the late 1800s. Handwritten on the photograph were the words, *Along the entire coast, as far Cape Horn, Chile stands alone. In other lands you find but the remains of the past vigor and the deep footprint of Spanish power fallen into ruins, which time respects in spite of man. I know not whether to shame or to glorify the name of the Spaniards ...*

He was from a family of uniformed men dating back to the early president who had passed on the belief that the country's long history of orderly progress entitled it to regional preeminence. They were conscious of the disparity between law and order in their country, and chaos and turmoil in neighboring countries. He believed that Chile's tradition of law and order had given rise to its greatness and stability. *We have to work hard to keep it that way,* he thought.

Chile's image of law and order, however, was changing in Sebastián's mind. Carabineros and *Policía de Investigaciones* caught criminals and arrested them, but the Public Prosecutor's office frequently failed to act or was so dilatory in authorizing other law enforcement agencies to proceed with investigations that successful prosecution was very often thwarted. When they managed to get into court, judges with incongruously democratic notions made sure the criminals were back on the streets in no time. It often seemed that the Criminal Reform had only opened revolving doors to crime.

Files were neatly stacked on Sebastián's desk. His books were arranged on shelves in perfect order of descending height. Photos, maps, newspaper clippings, and other evidence were arranged with symmetrical precision on the walls. Documents, small notes, photos of victims and crime scenes and other evidence were neatly arranged on a pin board. His handwriting was careful, small and measured. There was a large map of Chile behind his desk.

Sebastián watched Emmanuelle as she moved through the

room. She was immediately drawn to one of the articles on his pin board. He realized why. There was a picture of Brent next to it. She stopped to read it.

She had a femininely athletic figure and long smooth legs. Her stylish suit was finely tailored to her tiny waist, although, if he was not mistaken, it appeared to be loose on her. Had she recently lost weight? A delicate scent of perfume drifted in the air. Something about her presence altered him today, just as it had the first time he saw her. In his mind, Solis looked exactly the way he imagined his sister would have looked had she lived to be her age. That made him uneasy. He forced himself to block the thought from his mind. They looked alike, but the similarities ended there. The woman in his office was a potential suspect. He took off his leather jacket, hung it carefully over the back of his chair, then spent a moment adjusting his collar and straightening out his sleeves. He sat down at his desk and crossed his arms.

She had her back to him, still examining articles on the pin board. One was about the ship that had sunk in the Patagonia. Another about two indigenous Indians who were murdered in Saltos del Laja. He had just learned from Comisario Munoz that her law firm was defending the company whose security contractors were implicated in that incident. He watched her as she pulled out a pen and scribbled something on a notepad. She was taking a liberty he had not authorized. He cleared his throat loudly. "How can I help you, Ms. Solis?"

She turned around and slid into the chair across from him. "I came to apologize." His eyes wandered over her. She was stunningly beautiful, with delicate facial features and brown, almond–shaped eyes that had a liquid depth to them. They didn't just tell him that she'd been spending sleepless nights; they expressed fear of something or someone.

There was a tap at the door and Pilar appeared at the

threshold. Sebastián's pulse surged. She'd followed him here from the meeting.

He shot her a *get out* glare, but she entered anyway. *"Permiso* Señor Prefecto Cienfuegos. Here's the latest report on the *Antarctic Mist* ..." Her eyes darted to Emmanuelle, traveling all the way down to her black stilettos before meeting Sebastián's eyes.

"I didn't realize you were with someone." She dropped the report on his desk and left.

Sebastián returned his gaze to Emmanuelle. *"Bueno,* you wanted to see me about something?"

Her fingers toyed with the clasp of a gold-braided bracelet. "I came to apologize. I wasn't thinking clearly yesterday. It was the blow to my head, the shock of what you were telling me. My life has turned upside down and ..." Her voice was soft. "I thought about everything you said. I came here to tell you I want to cooperate with you." One of her hands smoothed out her skirt a few times as she spoke. She was nervous.

Her eyes dropped to the report Pilar had just placed in front of him. *Was she trying to read it?* He snatched it from the desk and tossed it into a drawer. He would have to be on guard with her, he told himself.

Another tap on the door. Pilar came in again carrying a tray with two *café cortados* and an assortment of miniature *galletas*.

"Are you my new secretary?" He couldn't contain the sarcasm in his voice. Pilar set the tray on his desk and left the room. He spooned sugar into one of the cups and handed it to Emmanuelle without asking her if she took it.

Emmanuelle was clutching her briefcase tightly. *Did she have the files with her?*

He searched her eyes as she told him more about herself, Oliver & Stone, Stephan Henri Brent, his disappearance, what he had revealed to her about his abductors, his suspicions about his colleagues, and finally why she decided to come see Sebastián.

"So, if what you are saying is true, wasn't it imprudent, even dangerous to come to Chile the way you did? Especially for someone as obviously intelligent as you."

She looked dazed for a moment. "Yes. I realize how strange it appears. I just never imagined it would take the turns it took. I believed he would meet me at the airport, we would take the files to the authorities, and the truth would be exposed. I thought it would be that simple." Her voice trailed off. Surely, she acknowledged how absurd the plan had been.

"That seems a bit...." He stared up at the corner of the ceiling for a moment as if he might find the word he was looking for up there. "Fantastic, don't you think?" *Was she a con artist or just very naïve?* He suspected she was in love with the missing lawyer. He noticed that her perfectly-painted red lips and her creamy complexion paired well together. Her eyes looked tired and sad, though, accentuating her delicate features. He thought of Cristina again. He chased the thought from his mind.

"Look, I'll cooperate in any way I can," she said, pulling a file out of her briefcase. "But I need your help in return."

The red flag rose. Did she think this was a bargaining deal? She was a potential suspect. He resisted the urge to respond sarcastically. This was a woman who made well over two hundred thousand dollars a year. There was still no plausible explanation as to why she went to Calle Vicente Perez Rosales. It was a seedy crime scene, but something in it reeked of high-level crime. Why was the address in her files? He inspected her as she blew softly on the steaming coffee before taking a sip.

The Inverlink scandal crept through his mind again. He would have to be extremely cautious. Perpetrators of high-level fraud were the hardest to identify. Most were sophisticated; no prior convictions and degrees from the best schools. *Like her.*

She was waiting for him to say something. He released a deep breath, calculating his words. She was pretty. In spite of her stature as an international lawyer, she was a delicate-looking woman. He liked her full lips, her perfect teeth. He leaned back against his chair, stretched out his legs and crossed them to the side. "You're still not telling me much more than you told me yesterday." He finished his coffee and set the cup down on the saucer with a loud clank. "Get to the point. Why are you here?"

She held the file out to him. "I found these in the abandoned office, caught between the drawers of a cabinet."

He took it. It contained the documents Camila had taken pictures of in Emmanuelle's hotel room. *A point in her favor.* It was plausible she had found them there. He wondered which lazy-ass Carabinero had not bothered checking behind the drawers when they'd examined the crime scene. He'd make sure his sorry-ass was assigned to the most miserable districts in town, he thought, clenching his jaw.

"They're fraudulent stocks. The companies are not registered on the New York Stock Exchange—as they claim."

"How do you know that?"

"I checked. They aren't registered on the Santiago Stock Exchange either. And this one is a mining lease for a site near the Futaleufú. It's valid. I checked with a notary public's office. A foreign company owns it, but I couldn't get information about its Chilean representative. The notary told me the supporting information should be filed in his Aysén or Futaleufú office. The company is called Ameriminco. It's a subsidiary of Barretta Gold. A company that recently bought a seat on the New York Stock Exchange. I checked them out. I also found these," she said, pulling more documents from the files.

She was definitely smart. He'd seen the documents before,

but he scrutinized them anyway. At length he asked, "Why are you telling me this?"

"Because I want to work with you. I believe I can help you. I thought about what you said yesterday about the boiler room you busted. If someone in my law firm is involved in some kind of criminal conspiracy, I have an interest in seeing to it that he is prosecuted. Stephan told me that he'd come across information during an arbitration. We're both bound by confidentiality rules unless we have clear evidence of a crime. Short of that, we can't divulge information obtained in the course of confidential proceedings. That's why I hesitated to show you the files. I have them here with me."

Sebastián took out a pen and paper. "So, you're sticking to the story that you just stumbled on the address in the files and went to there thinking it might be a legitimate contact?"

"That's the truth. I'll show you the files. I thought Stephan worked with someone there. I was searching for answers." Her eyes glistened, catching him off guard. Was she on the verge of tears? For a moment, he wanted to believe her. But he knew how easy it would be to fall into the lair of a lioness. She could be a master criminal. Skilled at deception.

"Stephan was desperate for help when he called. He believed he'd been abducted to derail FINRA hearings. To prevent him from testifying. FINRA is the agency that regulates investment and protects investors. Apparently, he'd been collecting evidence against one of the partners. Evidence of suspicious wire transfers of large sums of money. There are major disputes between the more recent and older partners over capital investments in the firm. Thorman was soliciting partners from other firms to join on promises of paying them salaries of five million dollars a year. After they joined, they learned that more than a third of the salary promised would be paid to the firm in capital investment. Some believe they'll never get their money back when they retire.

They feel defrauded. Stephan said that when he asked the firm's chief financier about the wire transfers, Albert Thorman became extremely hostile and aggressive with him. Stephan had no one else to turn to. He couldn't trust anyone in the firm. That's why I didn't tell anyone that he called me. I suspect Thorman is involved, but I can't prove it yet." She paused a second, thoughtful.

Sebastián sat up straight and gripped the pen, ready to take notes. "What's the FINRA hearing about?"

"I only wish I knew. That address was all I had to go by and now I am even more certain it's connected to Stephan's disappearance. Maybe he was headed to Puerto Montt because he thought it was a law office. I don't know. But what I can tell you is that if you are trying to bust a securities fraud scam, I can help you. I represented victims of securities fraud while I was in law school. I have a general idea how scams work. Clearly, someone in our office had some connection to the abandoned office. I suspect something bigger is going on. Much bigger, Señor Prefecto Cienfuegos."

Sebastián agreed silently. Something about the case told him it was connected to a more extensive crime network.

"Maybe related to the water or the dam project."

"Did you say the dam project?" *She couldn't seriously believe that.* She just dropped a notch in his ratings.

"Well, last night the news suggested that the *Antarctic Mist* might have been sabotaged. The files Stephan asked me to bring here pertain to the dam project. It may sound crazy, but I wonder if the scientists' report would have jeopardized the project. Is it possible the expedition was sabotaged to prevent them from publishing it?"

"I'm not involved in the *Antarctic Mist* investigation. And I fail to see any connection between the Ponzi operation and the ship. Other than being charged with interviewing a few witnesses, it's out of my jurisdiction. The theory seems wildly far-fetched anyway."

"Don't dismiss the possibility. Albert Thorman hired the company that did the environmental assessment report. That report decided the project could move forward. It's an eleven billion dollar project." She drew in a deep sigh. "Look, I'll provide you with any information I have … but please help me. Give me the benefit of the doubt." She spoke rapidly. Her eyes were excited. They haunted him, reminding him of a distant moment from his past. He wished he could identify the emotion flickering in her eyes as she spoke. Was it grief? Fear? Betrayal? She seemed complicated. Different from most women he had known. Had he wrongfully taken her for a scam artist?

"*Bueno*, I'll to hear you out. Where are the files?"

"I have them here," she said. "Something Stephan said keeps echoing in my mind, making me believe this is bigger than the Calle Vicente Perez Rosales operation."

"What was that?"

"He said, *'Governments rise and fall over these matters.'*"

"And what do you think he was referring to?" He straightened his posture, staring at a blank page in front of him, still gripping the pen as though it were going to start writing on its own.

"I don't know, but I think it's more than a microcap investment scam."

"Microcap?"

"Yes. I checked out the stock certificates from Calle Vicente Perez Rosales and they are for microcap investments. Low-priced stock issued by small companies that are difficult to get information about. The easiest type of fraud. Stephan was talking about large-scale crime. He warned me not to talk with anyone in the office." She set her cup down. "But it's obviously somehow connected to smaller crime in Puerto Montt." She picked up the file with the address handwritten on it and offered it to him.

He took it and examined the writing.

She handed him more files. "I've been through these documents hundreds of time in the past few days. There are some correspondence, preliminary studies, assessments."

"Hmm," he said, flipping through the pages. "Are you going to show me the files?"

"Yes," she said, handing them over. "I could be disbarred for removing them from the office. I can't prove I was instructed to do so unless Stephan appears." There was distress in her voice. "This morning, I discovered something even more damning for me …. There was a sealed envelope in the files. I knew I shouldn't open it. I knew it could make things worse for me. But I couldn't put the pieces of the puzzle together. Nothing made sense. I had to find out what was in it."

"And?"

"I opened the envelope finally yesterday. It contains stock certificates. More than a million dollars' worth of shares in a company called Ameriminco."

"Ameriminco? The company that owns this mining claim?" He shuffled through the documents on his desk and picked up the mining claim.

"Yes, it's the same mining company. The stocks were issued in Albert Thorman's name and endorsed over to a partner in the firm, Paul Saunders. He's a British lawyer who recently became a partner. He's one of the partners disputing the salary agreement with Thorman. Look," she said, pulling certificates out of a manila folder. "Maybe he signed the shares over hoping the partners would accept them instead of suing him for breach of contract. But my question now is how is that connected to the investment fraud."

Sebastián stood. "Now we're getting somewhere. Come. Let's sit over there."

They moved to a round table at the back of the room. A connection between Calle Vicente Perez Rosales and Oliver & Stone now seemed plausible to Sebastián.

He sat beside Emmanuelle, feigning indifference to her presence as she explained the contents of the files. He was keenly aware of her every movement, her expressions, her mannerisms, her gestures, her hands, her choice of words. He caught the slightest falter in her voice, the pauses between sentences as she spoke, moments when she seemed to lose the thread of her sentences. His twenty-plus years of experience as a detective told him she was telling the truth. Her story made sense.

When she'd finished, he pushed his chair away from the table and moved it around so he could face her again. As he watched, she shifted her legs, also turning toward him. Her leg brushed his slightly. Unintentionally. Their eyes locked for a few seconds. His eyes roamed from her face to the double-strand pearl necklace around her neck. It matched her pearl-drop earrings. Then his eyes dropped to her hands. They were wrapped around more files she was taking out of her briefcase. Her fingers were long and elegant, like those of a pianist, and her red fingernails were perfectly polished. He liked that kind of femininity in a woman.

She said, "I believe there is a connection to the dam project because the files pertain to it. Tell me something about it that is not in the news. I need to understand my office's involvement."

Sebastián considered her for a moment. She was exceptionally intelligent and had another perspective. She might provide them with insight. "You know that Hébère International was recently ordered to cease its operations in Chile?"

"No, I didn't know that." She sounded surprised. "I just

saw the article on your wall. Thorman has represented Hébère for years in projects across the world."

Sebastián grew tense, wondering if he'd caught her in a lie. "Señor Brent represented Hébère."

"No, Señor Prefecto Cienfuegos. That was falsely reported in the press. The firm represents Hebérè, but Albert Thorman handles that case. I work with Stephan. I didn't even know about the Patagonian dam project until I read through the files on the plane. I am sure that's why Stephan was here. I keep a calendar of Stephan's cases. I wrote arguments for most of his ICSID cases over the past three years," she told him. "I would know."

"What is ICSID?" Sebastián hated North Americans acronyms.

"The World Bank arbitration court where investors and countries arbitrate their disputes."

"*Ah si, ya. La CIADI.*" he said, using the Spanish acronym. "I just spoke to a colleague in Santiago handling the case. He explained it to me. A representative of Hébère tried to persuade the prosecutor to drop criminal charges against its security contractor for unlawfully detaining and murdering two young Mapuche Indians protesting the construction of the dam in Saltos del Laja."

"Murder?"

"Yes, murder. There were clashes between the company's security contractors and indigenous residents over relocation plans for the local community. To create the reservoir for the dam, ancestral grounds of the Pehuenche-Mapuche Indians had to be flooded, provoking protests from the residents. After the protests, the bodies of two young men were found near the river. Both had been shot in the back of the head at close range. The government was quick to react. Such incidents threaten indigenous support for the government. The institution that financed the project investigated and found the company's security contractors were guilty of using excessive force against protesting residents. The report was supposed to have been confidential. Instead, it was leaked to the press causing more public outrage."

"So, what happened?"

"The government ordered Hébère to cease its operations on the dam until the conflict could be resolved. Companies might get away with that kind of crime in other countries in Latin America. But not in Chile. This is a country of laws. Murder is a serious charge."

"And?"

"The Chilean government ordered Hébère to prohibit its security forces from using violence against protestors. Maintaining public order in Chile is strictly a function of Chilean law enforcement agencies. But the security contractors ignored the orders and took matters into their own hands. Hébère admitted they'd made mistakes by not checking the background of their security contractors. In other words, they conceded they were negligent in hiring them. But the government insisted on stopping the project pending the criminal investigation."

"What happened next?"

"There were more protests. Company trucks were burned by protestors. Hébère sent lawyers here to negotiate. Your friend, Señor Brent, came in for that. Negotiations broke down. Hébère threatened to file suit. They argued that company representatives couldn't be prosecuted for the crimes of its security contractors. Hébère was charged with attempting to bribe officials. It claims it offered money to the government in restitution to the families of victims to settle the claims. That it was in the interest of coexisting with and preserving the culture of the Pehuenche-Mapuche Indians. It insisted it wasn't trying to bribe the prosecutor in exchange for dropping the criminal charges. Hébère representatives were arrested in Santiago and a judge ordered the company to cease operations in Saltos del Laja. Hébère argued that the government was acting on political pressure from its constituents and not on the evidence."

"When did this take place?"

"Over the last few weeks. Hébère is trying to keep it out of the press. The company is now threatening to sue Chile in the World Bank."

She stood and walked to the wall with the articles.

"What a nightmare. I never had even the slightest suspicion that the firm I was giving my life to was so involved in … such corruption."

Sebastián observed her reaction, increasingly convinced of her integrity.

He went to his desk and took a file out of a drawer, offering it to her. "This is about the Bio-Bio killings."

"You said Stephan was here eight times this year. Do you know the dates?"

The question irritated Sebastián. Who was interrogating whom? She was a suspect. Not a colleague. "Señorita Emmanuelle, I'm not here to respond to your questions. You're a potential suspect."

In the unnerving silence that followed, Emmanuelle's cheeks flushed. She backed down, resignation in her eyes. Her acceptance of his contempt made him realize he'd made his point. He almost regretted it.

He broke the silence. "He was in Chile the day before he was abducted in Argentina." He saw doubt in her eyes. Should he tell her more? Should he show her the pictures taken with hotel security cameras of Brent and the woman who had stayed with him in his hotel room? And he had pictures of Brent and a high-class call girl. He leafed through his files and found them.

"You doubt that, *no es cierto?*" He stretched back on his chair, studying her.

She sighed and shook her head. "I don't know what I believe right now."

He put one of the pictures on the table in front of Emmanuelle. "These are security camera shots taken at the hotel where Brent stayed on that trip. Notice the date, time and location in the upper right-hand corner." He placed another next to it. "The woman with him is an Argentine national. A professor from the University of Buenos Aires."

Emmanuelle leaned forward to examine them, then shifted back.

There was a picture of Stephan checking into the Intercontinental Hotel in Santiago. "They checked in as Mr. and Mrs. Brent," he said. In another picture, Stephan was kissing the same woman in the hallway, perhaps near his room.

"Maríana?" Emmanuelle uttered. He heard disgust in her voice.

"You know the woman?"

Emmanuelle nodded.

Sebastián moved the pictures around. "Here they are at the hotel restaurant." In the photo, Stephan and a woman were sitting close together at a table, drinking champagne, smiling, and laughing at something. He watched for her reaction.

Emmanuelle cleared her throat as though she were about to say something. Her lips quivered. Finally, she said nothing. Her face was pale now.

"The woman with Señor Brent in *this* picture," he said, sliding another picture toward her with his finger, "Is a high-class call girl. She's well-known to Santiago Carabineros. She has a long-standing criminal history."

A delicate frown creased her forehead. She looked away from the photograph quickly, seeming offended. She crossed her arms, stretched her legs, and then crossed them too, letting out a deep breath. He'd struck a chord. She was scandalized. She twisted, writhed in her seat, clearly grappling to maintain her composure. She was coming unraveled. Now they would get somewhere. "Would you like more coffee?"

She didn't answer. Her breathing was stressed.

"Water?"

He was coming to some conclusions quickly. She was either very naïve or very dishonest. Although she was exceptionally intelligent, something told him she might be naïve in her relationships with men. For a moment, he wondered about her family background. Whether an over-protective father had sheltered her. Her father died when she was in her teens. He wondered how that had affected her relationship with men.

"*Bueno*, I want to be frank with you. Señor Brent was well aware of the murder and bribery charges," he said. "There's a videotape. It's a very tight case. He came here· to review the evidence against Hébère. I can arrange for you to talk to the person in charge of the case in Santiago. I am sure he would be interested in what you might have to say."

"Yes, I'll talk to him. I'll leave for Santiago today if he'll meet with me." For a long moment, she held his gaze without saying more. She probably wanted to learn more about the Stephan Henri Brent she thought she knew. She'd taken great risks for him. Maybe there had been romantic involvement. People do stupid things for love. She now seemed simple, transparent. He had imagined that her stature as an international lawyer would be accompanied by aggressive behavior or intellectual arrogance, but it proved not to be the case. He resolved to make peace with Emmanuelle. Maybe they could work together. She would be an asset to the investigation.

Her eyes slid back to the pictures. Instinct told him Stephan probably *did* call her and ask her to bring him the files. If so, she had risked her career to bring them to him with no clue about what he was really like. "Would you like more coffee?" He asked again.

"Yes, please. And water."

Unraveling nerves always dry the throat, Sebastián thought, pressing the intercom button and asking his secretary to bring more *café cortados.* In minutes, there was a tap on the door.

"Permiso, Señor Prefecto." His secretary came in, set a tray down and started to arrange its contents before he stopped her.

"Gracias. That will be all."

She smiled sweetly at Emmanuelle, gathered the cups from earlier, and closed the door behind her.

Sebastián spooned sugar into Emmanuelle's coffee again and handed it to her. He liked his coffee sweet, and surely she did too. He poured sparkling water into a glass.

She drank it quickly. "Look, I have a strong feeling the expedition was sabotaged. And I believe my office was involved." Her hands were trembling. "I suspect the report the scientists were planning to publish would have put corporate plans in jeopardy if it reached the public."

He filled her glass with more water, listening.

"The company Albert Thorman hired is the Meridional Group. The full name is *Grupo Meridional, Avaliação do Ambiente, Engenharia e Consultoriae.* It's a Brazilian engineering company. I checked them out. There's barely any information about them anywhere online. Why would Thorman hire an unknown engineering consultancy group to draft an environmental assessment report on a multibillion-dollar project? My guess? Because it's easier to get them to say what you want them to say, instead of the truth. I suspect the scientists were planning to refute the company's findings."

Sebastián's phone rang. He looked at the screen. It was Comisario Olivares. "I have to take this," he said.

On the phone, Olivares said, "Sebastián, an official from the US Embassy just called. Agents from the National Security Branch of the US Embassy in Santiago are on their way to Puerto Montt. They want to question the American lawyer. Is she still in your office?"

"Yes. She's here." His gaze traveled back to Emmanuelle. "But why would they contact you and not *Prefectura Central de Santiago?*"

"I have no idea. I told them I thought she was in your office. I assume they'll go directly there," Olivares said. "The plane arrives at noon."

It was 11:15 A.M.

Emmanuelle stood up and walked over to where he was, running her fingers nervously through her hair. She knew the call was about her.

Sebastián ended the call.

"American authorities are on their way here. They want to interrogate you."

"Me? What do they want from me?"

"It's related to the securities investigation."

"You must be joking. The Calle Vicente Perez Rosales?"

"It's much broader than you know. Authorities just arrested a ring of people in Brazil on securities fraud—from bankers to brokers. They're calling it *Operaçaö Vigarista*. They targeted investors across the Americas." He felt strangely absorbed in her plight now. It almost made every other case he had seem irrelevant, although he knew that was dangerous. He focused for a second on the window behind her. The sky had clouded over and it was beginning to rain.

"What does it have to do with me?"

She seemed to be a person of integrity. He wondered how

had she gotten herself into this mess. "You're a securities arbitration expert, aren't you? You tell me"

"My experience in securities makes me a suspect?" Her tone was sarcastic. She paused, searching his eyes. "You called the embassy, didn't you? You told them I went to Calle Vicente Perez Rosales." Her eyes glinted with suspicion and distrust.

"No. You're wrong. We didn't contact the embassy. Or Interpol. Or any international authorities," he said emphatically. "We decided not to contact them until we had more information. We didn't even contact the public prosecutor's office. They didn't find out through my office." He hesitated before continuing. "I'm afraid I have worse news."

She reached for the water. "Tell me."

He saw her heart rate pulsing in her delicate neck. She was scared. He cleared his throat. "A body was found close to the Argentine-Chile border. In a place called Paso El Leon. Interpol suspects it's Señor Brent's body."

The blood drained from her face.

"It appears you are correct," he continued. "Brent never got on the plane. He probably was abducted. The *Policía Federal Argentina* is working with Interpol for a final identification of the body." He paused. "Preliminary DNA samples match, but it could take months to get a final confirmation." He gave her a moment. "I don't know what he meant to you personally, but legally you have a problem. Your witness is dead."

She reached to put her glass back on the desk, but accidentally toppled it. A trickle of water spread across the surface.

He quickly moved a stack of files from its path.

She reached for a tissue and wiped the spilt water with trembling hands.

"Don't worry about that," he said, placing a hand over hers.

She glanced at him and pulled it free. He'd seen that look

before. It wasn't grief. It was terror. She was afraid for her own life. He wondered if Brent's assassins might come after her next if they thought she had evidence implicating them.

"I should tell you the rest."

"Tell me." Her voice quavered.

"Embassy officials believe he was tortured."

She gasped and brought her hands over her face.

"The body was burned. They think to hide the evidence."

"So how do they know it's Stephan?"

"Apparently a preliminary DNA match."

Her tiny frame was trembling.

"If he's your principal witness, things don't look so good for you."

She looked like a frightened animal. Mascara-stained tears streamed down her pretty face. "This is insane."

"Can I get you more water?"

Her uncontrolled sobbing caught him off-guard again. Every element of her presence now reminded him of his deceased sister.

He wanted to protect her. He took a step closer. "Listen to me. It gets worse. I have something else to tell you. It's important you listen to me now." He put his hand on her shoulder. "The American authorities don't believe your story … that Stephan called you and told you to bring the files. They think you're lying. Apparently, Mr. Thorman thinks you're here for other reasons. He's here as well."

Emmanuelle jerked back. "What? *That* bastard. Why is he here?"

"Maybe because you took off with more than a million dollars' worth of stock certificates from his office?"

"Thorman knows I'm not crazy. What could I possibly do with them? All he would have to do is call the transfer agent and request a stop-transfer. They'd already been transferred to

Paul Saunders. I'd have to be the world's stupidest criminal to take them with the intention of cashing them in. Albert's not here because of the stock certificates." She got up, walked over the table and picked up the files. "Here. They're yours. I am surrendering the evidence to you. At least I *tried* to cooperate with the police."

The urge to help her and all of its implications left Sebastián silent for a moment. The thrum of the rain filled the void.

"Thorman just wants the files," Emmanuelle said. "Something in those files implicates him. That why he's here. I'll find out what he is involved in. I will expose him." She stared right though Sebastián. "I promise you that."

"I need to ask you a few more questions."

"Ask." There was rebellion in the word.

"Were you in Brazil recently?"

"Brazil? Yes. Why?"

"Why did you go to Brazil?"

"For an arbitration conference in São Paulo last September. I spent three days there. I was with Albert, Stephan and a group of lawyers from our office. Everyone who practices international arbitration was there. What does that have to do with anything?"

"Interpol and FBI have pictures of you in Brazil with the man they suspect is running the securities fraud operation."

"What?" she cried, disbelievingly. "With who?"

"Gilberto Pereira."

"Who?"

"Gilberto Pereira. Do you know him?"

"The name doesn't ring a bell. I meet many people at conferences." She shrugged. "Do you have picture of him?"

"I can get one."

"So what is my alleged connection to this person?"

"No idea. Just so you know, this isn't coming from us. We

aren't investigating you. US officials want to interrogate you. As far as my office is concerned, unless we receive something formal from the US embassy, we won't facilitate an investigation."

Emmanuelle looked relieved for a second. "I'm going to call Thorman now," she said, taking her cell phone out. She started dialing. Then she stopped and stared at her phone as if it were an animal about to attack her. She slipped it back into her purse.

"Ms. Solis, listen to me. If American officials want to interrogate you in Chile, they'll have to start with a Letters Rogatory. I don't think they have one."

"How does that work here?" The lawyer in her woke up again.

"They have to go through diplomatic channels—through the Ministry of Foreign Affairs first. Moreover, you are a Chilean national. Even if a U.S. prosecutor or judicial authority makes a request to interrogate you in Chile, they can only conduct a formal interrogation in our presence and with our cooperation. You're in Chile, not the United States. And even if the request is made, you can still refuse to talk to them." He looked at his watch. "They will be here in less than an hour."

"Do I have to wait here?"

"No. I have no reason to detain you. You're free to go."

She picked up her briefcase and walked to the door. She turned around as though she were going to say something, staring at him for a lingering moment with a haunting sort of gaze. A gaze he had seen twenty-five years earlier in the eyes of his dying sister. Agonizing her fate. Begging for deliverance.

Chapter 33

DURING THE FIFTEEN minute walk back to her hotel, heels pounding against the pavement, Emmanuelle barely noticed the mongrels that followed her. Or the taxi that rolled dangerously close as she crossed the street. Or the little boys with torn sweaters and sunbaked faces selling pint-sized cartons of strawberries on the corner. Instead, she heard only a strange buzzing noise in her ears as though a swarm of bees had flown inside her head. Her mind was busy with only one thought—that her entire world was imploding. Collapsing like a house of cards. Stephan was dead. Her career was over. And she was a now suspect in an international criminal investigation.

She was too shocked, too angry, and too numb to feel the grief she might have expected to feel. Images of Stephan and Maríana Chianti only cluttered the wrangle in her brain. Stephan had brought Maríana to the firm from Buenos Aires. He had known her for several years. How long had they been together? Had it been just that once? It was starting to make sense. Maríana had not been in the office when Stephan left on his trip. In fact, she came back a few days after he was abducted. What was that about? Had they been together up to the day of his abduction? When did their relationship start? What about Paris? What about what Stephan told Emmanuelle right before the trip? Why would he have suggested a serious relationship with Emmanuelle when he was with another woman? And the call girl? That was disgusting. Unforgivable. *The bastard sent me here to help him out of a mess. Now I am a suspect in a major criminal investigation and he's dead.* She should *never* have gotten on that plane. She should never have risked her career— worse yet—her life, for him. How had she made so many wrong decisions? Why hadn't Stephan gone to the police immediately? *How could he have been so stupid? Wasn't he the world's top lawyer? Top arbitrator? Sure. I wrote most of his arguments for the past seven years.* The smartest thing she'd done in the last week, no, in the last few years, was to turn the files over to the Prefecto. The more she thought about it, it started to seem the firm had quite a few sleazy, unscrupulous characters. *Like Mariana Chianti. Bitch. Whore. Hypocrite.* She hoped they would all get arrested.

She marched into the hotel lobby and headed straight to the elevator without responding to Isauro's greeting from behind the reception desk. Another two-faced hypocrite.

As soon as the elevator doors opened on the seventh floor, she noticed the door to her room was open again. She scrambled backwards and put her hand on the elevator door to stop it from closing, her heart beating furiously. Shaken and out of breath, she craned her neck to see more. Her belongings were scattered on the floor. Someone had ransacked her room. She could hear her heartbeat in the deadly stillness of the empty corridor. There didn't seem to be any movement or noise in her room. Could Thorman and the embassy official have gotten here already? *Impossible.* The flight should have just landed. She slipped a hand into her handbag and slid out her cell phone and the Prefecto's card. She dialed his number.

"Someone broke into my hotel room and ransacked it." Her words were whispered. "I'm sure they were looking for the files." She edged closer to the room. She could see it was empty.

"Did you see who it was?"

"No, he's gone." She walked around the room in disbelief. Everything was thrown upside down.

"Are you okay?" She heard concern in his voice.

"I … I feel like I'm losing my mind. This can't be happening. Not to me."

"*Mira*, I am on my way there now."

She closed her eyes and clutched the phone to her ear. She could hear his movements. He was rushing. Maybe running down the steps of the *Departamento de Policía de Investigaciones*. She felt relieved for a moment. She wished he were with her right now.

"Señorita Solis, listen to me. I just learned Thorman and the embassy official decided to bypass us. They are going *directly* to your hotel from the airport. They just left the airport now. They could be there in ten to fifteen minutes."

"What?" A wave of nausea rose inside of her. "I won't talk to them. Not without a lawyer. I don't trust them. They might try to kill me. They killed Stephan! You realize that don't you? Tell me you realize that!" Her voice was shrill.

"Emmanuelle, I am on my way now."

She could hear he was running.

"Stay where you are. They don't have authority to take you into custody. They don't even have the authority to question you yet. *Tranquila.*"

She closed her eyes again and took in a deep breath, still clutching the phone to her ear.

"They *can't* do anything to you. They're foreign officials. They *have* to follow Chilean procedures."

Criminals don't follow national procedures, she wanted to say. She wasn't going to wait. She hung up. *Think carefully.* She did a quick assessment of how much trouble she might be in and the cards didn't stack in her favor. She changed into pants and stuffed a few things into a backpack she'd purchased on the way back to the hotel. She wouldn't be around when Thorman showed up. Fully-charged instincts kicked in. *Run. Don't stop. Run. Run for your life. Stephan is dead, and you are being set up for some big-time crime.*

Her beret was lying in the middle of the floor amidst her clothes and other personal items that had been dumped by the intruder. She grabbed it with trembling fingers and put it on. She scanned the room for her mother's rosary. It was on the floor under the night table. She crammed it into her coat pocket, put on her sunglasses, and headed out the door. They would be there in minutes. She looked around.

The stairs at the back of the building were her only option for getting out of the building inconspicuously. She raced down to the first floor. *The door was locked.* She turned the knob back and forth desperately, slammed her body against it. It wouldn't release. She ran back up a flight of stairs. The wooden door leading to the fire escape was swollen from rain and moisture. No force she exerted was going to make *that* door give. What would she do? Beads of sweat formed on her forehead.

By now they might be pulling up to the hotel. She had to get out of here. *The window.* She thrust all of her strength against it. Flakes of white paint and dead insects fell from the half-rotted window frame until finally it opened and a gust of fresh cool air rushed over her. She sucked it into her lungs and crawled out onto the fire escape. The last six feet of stairs on the escape were missing. She looked down. She heard a dog bark somewhere. *Do it! Jump!* she told herself. She closed her eyes and jumped. She landed hard, knees buckling under her, rolling onto the ground. She scrambled to her feet, surprised she hadn't broken anything. She motioned to a taxi parked on the corner and jumped in when it pulled up.

"Take me to the bus terminal."

"Adelante."

Her heart pounded wildly in her chest as they sped down Salvador Allende Street toward the port a few kilometers down the road. The taxi swerved through traffic and rolled down the hilly road. She stared out at the tiny island with the prominent crucifix over the sanctuary. It was straight across the narrow channel. She pressed her eyes shut, stinging tears streamed down her face. Everything she had just learned had left her with a cold, clutching emptiness inside. It made her question everything and everyone she had worked with. Everything she had worked for was going up in smoke. She'd spent a week desperately trying to find Stephan, praying he was safe somewhere. Now all she wanted to do was strangle him. That, however, wasn't an option because he was dead. And now, someone was trying to pass her off as the likely suspect in a very significant crime that she knew little about. There was no one to answer the thousands of questions that clamored through her head.

The taxi rolled close to the craft market. She could cut through it to get to the bus station, rather than walk on the street in plain view. *"Acá!"* she told the driver. "I want to get out here." She handed him ten thousand pesos and jumped out. She had to go someplace where she could think and sort things out. *This is madness.* She pushed past a small crowd of tourists milling through the stands, jumped over handmade fur boots, skipped over copper work, piles of ponchos, woolen sweaters, hats and gloves, and finally made her way to the doors of the crowded bus station.

The terminal was filled with what seemed to be hundreds of people, some appearing to have been there for days. She scanned the schedules posted on the walls, desperate to make a decision. *Santiago.* That was where she would go. She would call the Prefecto and go see his colleague. She would use cash to buy a ticket so they couldn't trace her. She could buy herself some time, if the agents from the U.S. Embassy were still looking for her. She weaved through a labyrinth of luggage and people leaning or sitting on mountains of suitcases, boxes, and backpacks and got in line behind a woman with three small children.

Minutes later, Emmanuelle felt someone watching her. She instinctively glanced behind her and saw two Carabineros staring at her. After a whispered conversation, one started toward her. She turned her back to him, a chill tightening her spine.

A second later, she felt a light tap on her shoulder. *"Señorita."*

She held her breath, turned. *"Si?"*

"Be careful with your bag. Purse-snatchers are everywhere." He flashed a smile.

"Thank you," she said, forcing a smile in return.

He lingered a bit. "You are not from here, are you?"

"No." She offered no more, praying he would leave her alone.

"Be careful, *ya?*" he said, inclining his head forward politely and walking away.

She exhaled. *Think this through.* What the hell would she do in Santiago? Where would she go? She would be apprehended if she checked into a hotel. She had no guarantee the Prefecto's colleague would see her, and if he did, he might not believe her. She stuffed the money back into her purse and took out a credit card. A bus was scheduled to leave for Santiago in twenty minutes. She could buy herself some time if Thorman and the embassy official *thought* she was headed to Santiago. They could trace her moves through her credit cards. She had about three thousand dollars in cash in her purse. She searched for an automatic teller and took out another thousand. She wouldn't be able to use the card again on the run. She paid for a one-way ticket to Santiago with a credit card and hurried out of the bus station.

Quickening her pace, she advanced toward the marina in front of the terminal, ran down the stairs and followed a path along the channel. Several times she'd seen a man take passengers in a rowboat across the channel to Tenglo Island. She prayed he was there now. She felt relieved sunlight was now breaking through the clouds; maybe she could get to the island before the rain started up again. She raced along the banks, her backpack pounding against her shoulders, until she found the man resting against an apple tree. His rowboat was turned upside down near a thicket of brambles.

"Can you take me across the channel?" she asked, pointing to the chapel on the hill. "To the *Santuario*." Her mouth was dry, her voice cracking. She tried to catch her breath.

He stood up, but didn't say anything. Light dappled through the leaves and reflected her silhouette in his grey eyes.

She realized she looked like a crazed woman. A rush of self-consciousness came over her. She straightened out her jacket, pulled back her hair. In a more collected voice she asked him again.

The man flashed a nearly toothless smile and nodded, handing her a bright orange life jacket and motioning for her to put it on.

She looked back towards the port nervously as the man dragged the boat to the water's edge. He helped her into the boat and then got in. Wrapping his large hands around the oars, he started rowing. As they pulled out across the channel, Emmanuelle breathed in the wet, salty air.

She had made the right decision, she decided. She had read newspaper articles about a priest from Tenglo Island who worked with indigenous communities in the Patagonia. She would talk to him. Get more information. Any possible source was better than surrendering to Thorman and the embassy official.

She relaxed slightly. The boatman looked like a gentle-soul. She studied his leathery, deeply wrinkled face. It occurred to her that the silent oarsman was mute. She wondered how he had managed through life, not simply poor, but voiceless as well. Did he feel disconnected, severed from the rest of world? The way she felt right now? She tried to fight it, but tears streamed down her cheeks.

The magnificence of the Osorno and Calbuco volcanoes and the snow-capped Andean Cordillera seemed to shrink the rest of the world. She felt a sudden belonging. A surge of childhood memories whirled in her head.

Emmanuelle felt her fear lifting as they pushed closer to the island. There, she would collect her thoughts. The man put down an oar and pointed to the little chapel on the hill next to the sanctuary. She nodded, smiled through tears.

From the middle of the channel, she could see the road that ran from the marina up to her hotel. She wondered whether any of the cars racing along it was an embassy vehicle carrying Albert Thorman. If he were here looking for her, it was because of something he thought she had on him. *"You bastard. I will find out what it is and expose you."*

The sound of the rowboat scraping shore broke her thoughts.

Chapter 34

IT WAS A TWENTY-minute walk up the dusty, shrub-lined path to the little wooden chapel on top of the hill. Emmanuelle wondered whether she would be able to find her way back after dark. The cold wind stung her eyes, blew open her jacket, and bit through her gloves.

Her nervous energy drained away as she tugged on the chapel's door. It was a tiny rustic structure with exposed beam ceilings. From the outside, it might have easily been mistaken for a barn had it not been for the large crucifix perched on top. Fortunately, the door was unlocked. Exhausted, she went inside. A small, gabled window illuminated the altar, but the rest of the place was darkened by afternoon shadows.

Despite the warmth of the sanctuary, her insides felt cold.

The altar was unadorned except for a wooden crucifix hanging above it. An indigenous-looking Jesus was nailed to it. She crossed herself and went to the pulpit. She sat in front of a battered, meter-high wooden statue of a bearded man, perhaps a saint that appeared to have suffered some sort of punishment or vandalism.

Her cell phone hummed in her handbag, startling her. She dug it out. It was Prefecto Sebastián Cienfuegos. She stared at the screen until the ringing stopped. Should she have listened to him? Should she have stayed in the hotel and waited for him?

She turned her phone off and took her laptop out of her

backpack. She slid the latch, lifted the screen and her laptop quickly came back to life. Before it had time to boot, she heard men talking loudly outside the chapel. The voices grew closer. They seemed to be approaching the chapel. She couldn't make out what they were saying. She quietly placed her laptop on the pew. Could Thorman have caught up with her so fast? Blood pounded in her ears.

Silhouettes of two men moved across the stained-glass windows towards the entrance. She held her breath, crouching between the pews. She heard the rumbling and clanking of iron and a loud click. The men were walking away.

She ran to the door and tried to open it. Someone had locked her in. She had read that clergymen lived in the house annexed to the chapel. *La Casa Tenglo,* it was called. Had they locked the chapel for the evening? Would she have to sleep there? Should she call after them? *No. Wait out the night. Go through your files. Collect your thoughts.*

Glancing around, she tried to convince herself she could sleep here if she had to. A thought crossed her mind that left her uncomfortable. It would be dark in an hour or two. She'd heard something about deadly spiders in the area. Especially in damp, dark places. She started to feel itchy. There were candles on the altar. She would light them before it got dark so she could spot anything that crawled. Hurrying to the altar, she tripped on a step and lunged forward, knocking over the table with the sanctuary lamps. A loud crash shattered the silence. She froze and heard movement coming from the house next door. Above the thunderous pounding of her heart in her ears, she could hear someone approaching, uttering a long string of obscenities.

She crawled toward the confessional and hid inside. Panic-provoked thoughts seized her mind as she sat in the dark, musty confessional holding her breath. With her luck, there were probably thousands of tiny spiders crawling in the corners. She wanted to scream.

The lights came on and she heard a man's voice. "*Cabro de mierda!* Shitty goat! Little son of a bitch, you are."

She pressed her face against the door of the confessional, trying to peer through a crack. She heard the man's shoes clicking loudly on the stone floor as he walked to the pile of shattered glass. "You demonic shitter," he shouted. "Come out and face me. *Entendí?* Come *out*."

She held her breath and felt like her heart would explode. With her face pressed against the door, she watched him. Could things get any worse? *Yes.* He was walking to the pew with her laptop. She had a resolve to confront him, but her brain was not sending the signal to her legs. A second later, the confessional door swung open under her weight and she fell to the ground at the man's feet.

"*Demonios!* What the hell are you doing here?" he shouted. His eyes were haggard, as though he had just seen a ghost. He had an unhinged look, unruly hair, and thick glasses that magnified the size of his eyes.

"I ..." She struggled to her feet.

"You what?" He was clutching a stick that he apparently was ready to use as a weapon. "What is this? Are you one of those vandals? An activist? Is that what this is about?"

She opened her mouth, but nothing came out. Beads of cold sweat formed on her upper lip.

"What's your name?" he demanded.

"Emmanuelle Solis," she said. "No ... I'm not an activist." Her knees felt weak.

"So what are you doing in here?"

She eyed the stick in his hand.

He put it down and straightened up. "Why were you hiding in the confessional?"

The buzzing started again in her ears. *Is this really happening?*

"Why are you here?" he said, impatiently. "What do you want?"

A young boy in a hoodie and sweats, carrying a soccer ball, appeared at the open door to the chapel. "Padre Javier. Everyone is waiting for you."

Her eyes dropped to his muddy soccer cleats. "You're a priest?" Emmanuelle asked in disbelief. "Can I talk to you for a minute?" She looked at the young man with the soccer ball. "Privately."

The priest told the boy, "*Vaya.* I'll be there in a few minutes."

The boy ran back outside.

"*Ya y*? Why are you here?" He asked, keeping his hands in the pockets of his jacket.

She started explaining, beginning with Stephan's abduction.

Halfway through her story the man's eyes traveled to the ceiling, then dropped to his fingernails. He took a deep breath and sighed heavily, interrupting. "*Lo siento.* I am sorry … but can you be quick about this?" He tapped his watch. "I'm late."

Everything she wanted to say got all jumbled up.

"Are you in trouble with the law?" His tone was matter-of-fact. Slightly impatient.

"No. Officials from the U.S. embassy and Interpol want to *talk* to me."

"*Ya y*?" He put his hands behind his back and stared down at his muddy cleats.

"I can't talk to them. Not now. Not yet. I'm being framed for a crime I didn't commit." Her voice dropped to a whisper. "The Chilean police might also be looking for me."

He looked at his watch again. She thought she heard him utter a swear word.

"And?" He gave an exacerbated sigh and then looked towards the door as though he contemplated springing out. "So how can I help you?"

"I read about a priest who was mediating disputes between the government and protestors in the Patagonia. I need to speak to him. Would that be you?"

"No." He kneeled to tie a shoelace. "That would be Padre Cristóbal Dionisio. He runs a mission in the Patagonia. He stays here often. Most of the people who come to see him are running from the law. Just like you," he added.

She didn't like the way that sounded.

"He should come back this evening, depending on the weather."

To her great misfortune or good luck, he was absolutely disinterested in her state of affairs. Emmanuelle felt relief. At least, he would not be calling the authorities.

"I have to go." He started to the door.

"Wait! *Padre*, please," she said, one step behind him. "I need a place to stay. Just for a day or so."

"Go to Casa de Tenglo. Talk to María." He pointed to the house. "*Que Dios te bendiga.*"

She watched as he caught up with a dozen or more young boys kicking a soccer ball around a field. Cheers and laughter went up as he broke into the game.

Chapter 35

SHE FOLLOWED A narrow path from the chapel to the entrance of Casa de Tenglo. Several hundred meters to the west stood a small, rickety wooden house with a yard full of chickens. Beside it, there was a lush vegetable garden with a fence around it. A scraggly-looking brown and white goat with a bloated belly stood in the middle of the patch chomping on leafy greens.

Emmanuelle picked up the doorknocker and tapped on the door. She waited, then banged loudly.

Seconds later, a middle-aged, broad-shouldered woman opened the door. "*Buenos días…*" Her Indian features were offset by her sparkling blue eyes, which shifted from Emmanuelle to the gated patch. "*El chivo!*" The woman screamed. "The blasted goat."

The demonic goat? Emmanuelle wondered.

The woman gasped, throwing her arms up in the air. "Lita!" she yelled in the direction of the rickety house. The goat stopped chewing and looked at her as though he understood he was about to be implicated.

"*Santa María del Carmelo!*" The housekeeper hollered louder. "Lita! The goat's eating everything in the vegetable patch again."

The goat bleated something in her direction.

In seconds, another middle-aged woman bolted out the door with a broom. She opened the gate and chased the creature around the patch, her hair blowing wildly in the wind. She was a squat, caramel-colored lady with a flat face, high cheekbones, a flowered dress, brown lace-up shoes and hair chopped straight across at the back. She finally shoved it out the gate. "*Cabra de mierda!*" she cursed, slapping it on the tail. An older, wrinkled man watched expressionlessly from the weather-beaten porch.

"*Santa María del Carmelo*," the housekeeper repeated. "Come in, *hija*," She let her in to a small drawing room paneled in dark wood.

The place was furnished with four high-backed chestnut chairs, a tatty, tan-colored sofa and a faded ottoman-styled footstool with an embroidered floral design on its cushion. A pot-bellied woodstove hissed loudly in the corner. A stack of wood piled neatly beside it. A large wooden crucifix hung from the wall behind the sofa.

Emmanuelle followed her through the corridors.

Chapter 36

A YOUNG MAN by the name of Martín Araya staggered through the north-side door of the wooden-pillared, copula-topped Cathedral of Puerto Montt. It had taken him two days to get there from Puerto Edén—two days during which he drank himself into a profound stupor after learning that the *Antarctic Mist* sank and everyone aboard, including his brother Belisario, had perished. How could he have worked for the criminals who had sabotaged the ship? The question tormented him.

"Padre Felipe," he shouted, his voice sounding like a drumroll in his own ears.

An elderly man with white hair, bushy eyebrows and an oversized overcoat was seated on a front pew with two women praying the rosary. The trio craned their necks, staring at Martín as he staggered to the back of the church. One of the women, plump with cold eyes and a black lace veil, whispered something to the woman beside her and both clutched their handbags tightly.

Martín saw condemnation in their eyes. "I'm worse than you imagine. I am a monster," he said, stumbling toward them. He heard people on the pews gasping, but their faces were a blur. He didn't care. He leaned against one of the columns dividing the nave from the side aisles of the church. It was all slipping away from him. Except for anger, he was numb. Horses were galloping in his head. His brain felt like it would explode. The unthinkable had happened. It was as though someone had opened a wound in him and everything was rushing out. Every conviction, belief, hypothesis and structure that his religion, culture and education had formed in him was rapidly escaping.

He felt he could murder Bruno with his own two hands. That thug had gotten him into one miserable mess. Why had he not gone to the Carabineros and told them he suspected the men had poisoned Karl Gustav? He never imagined they would sabotage the ship. He would not have left Puerto Edén if he had known they would do that. He would have fought them, informed the authorities, and warned Nils and the rest of the team that they were spying on the scientists. Martín had been secretly turning their investigative findings over to Lucas Braga, but he never realized he was working for cold-blooded murderers. His brother had been aboard the ship when it sank. *Hijo de puta! He made me an accomplice to the murder of my own brother.* Tears seared his cheeks. His ears burned.

Everything spun. In the tympanum, the painting of Jesus encircled by the winged angels came to life. Were angels floating about him? Was it an optical illusion caused by light reflecting through the stained-glass windows? Martín tripped, fell face down and broke into sobs.

A tall priest in a cassock appeared. His clean-shaven, bronze-colored face expressed unpleasant surprise.

"Martín?"

"Rodrigo." Martín rose and struggled to balance himself. He felt a rush of relief. Rodrigo had managed the shelter where Martín and his brothers spent most of their childhood. "I've come to confess something terrible." His tongue faltered and the words came out thick and slurred.

Rodrigo hurried to his side. "*¿Que esta pasando aqui?* What's going on?"

Even in his drunken state, Martín could recognize disappointment in Rodrigo's eyes. Rodrigo took hold of his arm and tried to pull him away from the crowd that now gathered around him. He wrapped an arm around Martín's shoulders and asked quietly, "Why are you here shouting like a madman?"

"I *killed* my brother."

Gasps followed by strained whispers came from the small crowd.

"Come with me," the priest said, tugging hard on him. He led him through the side aisles to the front of the church. They passed a series of large paintings of Christ's life illuminated by the afternoon sunlight, which now streamed through the lunette windows. *"Tranquilo,"* Rodrigo whispered. "What's all this drama about?"

"Belisario was on the ship. He's dead now. It was my fault."

"Tranquilo. You can't blame yourself for that. The ship hit an iceberg. It sank. It wasn't your fault." His words were hushed. "I know how terrible you feel. You were a good brother. You did what you could for them. That's been your cross and it will be your salvation."

Martín turned to face him. "No, you don't understand. I *am* responsible," he said through gritted teeth, tears staining his dirty face.

"Give yourself a break, *hijo.* Belisario died doing what God called on him to do. He's with God now." Rodrigo looked at the swarm of people following them, straining to hear the conversation. He opened the door to the vestry and pulled Martín inside.

"Shall I call the police?" the old man called after them before the door shut.

Rodrigo gestured a plea for privacy. "No. He'll be fine."

"Rodrigo, I killed my brother," Martín cried, sinking into a chair.

"I killed them all. It was my fault. I gave them the information."

Rodrigo pushed a candelabro away from the center of the table. "Gave who what information? What are you talking about, Martín?"

Martín could see how perplexed Rodrigo was. He felt a million kilometers away. He realized how bizarre he must now seem. How far he had strayed from the days when he lived in Padre Felipe's shelter. He pulled himself forward on the chair and explained how he had worked for a Brazilian company. He told him how he had been giving the company representative information about the scientists' investigations.

"You were spying on the scientists?"

It wasn't condemnation in Rodrigo's eyes. It was sorrow. It only made Martín feel worse. "Well, *si po*. But I thought they would just use the information to refute the claims the scientists would make. I had no idea they would hurt anyone."

"What do you mean? Who did they hurt?" A shadow passed over Rodrigo's face.

"They sabotaged the ship with the scientists."

"Sabotage?" Rodrigo was horrified. "I'm listening."

"The day before the ship left port, two strange men came to Wellington Island. They weren't with the team. We all knew each other and everyone was getting ready to head out on the last trip of the expedition. One of the men had a Brazilian accent, so I immediately thought Lucas Braga sent them to me."

"Lucas Braga?"

"He is the representative of the company I worked for. The men were looking for Karl Gustav, a Brazilian scientist who worked with the team. One of them said he was a friend of his."

"Continue," the priest said grimly.

"I didn't like the looks of the men. From a distance, I could see that one of them had something under his coat. I thought … maybe a gun. Karl Gustav had been staying in a house that the Kawésqar owns. I took them to him and then I went on to the meeting. But … I had a bad feeling about the men."

Martín paused and studied Rodrigo's face. It was clean-shaven and his hair neatly trimmed. His eyes reflected deep serenity—something far removed from the torrential rains pouring inside of Martín right now. Guilt welled in him. How had he strayed so far? Sunlight filtered through the rectangular blocks of stained glass, casting a violet hue on the walls around them, warming the sanctuary. He felt safe. Safe from himself. He wanted to never set foot in the world outside again.

"Finish the story, Martín."

"There was something evil about those men. Really evil. *Algo … malvado, perverso.*"

"So what happened?"

"I went to the expedition team meeting in the Armada building and I started to feel like something was terribly wrong. Everyone asked for Karl. It was an important meeting. The team members were supposed to be there to discuss the plans before the ship left port. When Karl didn't show up, I knew something bad had happened to him. By the time I got back to his bungalow, Karl was nearly dead. I think they poisoned him. A Norwegian scientist got there right after I did. He told me to stay with Karl while he went for help. Then the Kawésqar showed up and I told him everything. Who I was working for, how I'd been spying on them. I confessed it all."

"Why didn't you go to the police?"

"I planned to. I wanted to talk to Lucas Braga first and see what he knew about the men before I went to the Carabineros. So I took the first ferry back to Puerto Montt. But a few hours after we left, the captain told me he'd just learned that the *Antarctic Mist* sank near the Pope Pius XI Glacier. I kept praying they would rescue the team members. The captain knows me. He let me stay with him in the communications room. Little by little, news trickled in. Messages were coming in from different vessels. From the *Fuerza Aérea* and the *Armada*. I heard the captain of a vessel say he and his crew heard explosions … and flames had engulfed the *Antarctic Mist* just before it sank. At that point, I knew it had been sabotaged. As time passed, hope of anyone surviving was shrinking. *My little brother was on that ship.*" Martín broke down "And there were other brothers on board. Brothers from the mission."

Rodrigo reached out for his arms and shook him. "How did you get involved with these people?"

"I couldn't find a job. Bruno told me about the work."

The last vestige of serenity vanished from Rodrigo's eyes. "Bruno Barilla Perez?"

"Yes." If Rodrigo had been capable of hatred, he would have hated Bruno. For years, he had urged Padre Felipe to throw him out of the shelter. He was beyond salvation, even in his early years, and bent on corrupting everyone else in the shelter.

Rodrigo cursed under his breath. "What did the men look like?"

"One of them was tall, thin, fair-skinned, light-brown thinning hair. Cold eyes. You know, like a bird ready to swoop down and make a kill. He seemed to be the one giving orders. Argentine maybe. Or *Uruguaya*. Spoke with that kind of accent. Fancy leather boots. The other was Brazilian. He spoke just like Lucas Braga. Dark-skinned, curly hair, heavy-set. He looked like a cross between a pimp and a boxer. Broken nose. Heavy jacket with fur lining."

"Are you going to tell Carabineros?"

"I'll tell them everything."

"When?" He didn't trust Martín anymore.

"I'll go to my place, pick up some documents I have about the company… and I'll go. Now."

"I'll go with you. Meet me in front of the police station in an hour. I want to be there when you talk to them."

Martín reluctantly agreed. "*Bueno.*" Rodrigo clearly didn't trust him anymore.

"I have to do something first." Rodrigo adjusted his clerical collar. "Don't let me down. In front of the *Prefectura de Investigaciones* in an hour."

"*Listo,*" Martín agreed.

"We'll go to Tenglo Island after. You have to warn Padre Felipe. They may be in danger."

Chapter 37

PREFECTO SEBASTIÁN CIENFUEGOS pulled his Hyundai into the driveway of the Hotel Interamericano, parking behind two Mercedes Benz luxury sedans with diplomatic plates. He jumped out and sprang to the door. Intuition was telling him Emmanuelle had already fled.

The lobby was empty except for a girl mopping the floors. "They're on the seventh floor," she told him.

He unfastened the holster around his waist and pulled out his Glock pistol. He pressed the elevator button but didn't wait. He pulled open the door to the stairwell and bolted up the stairs.

"*Hijo de su puta madre,*" he cursed. *Who does he think he is bypassing Chilean authorities?*

From the end of the hall, he saw the open door to Emmanuelle's room. Two men walked around, stepping on and picking through clothes and personal belongings strewn about. The mattress was off the bedsprings, pillows on the floor, desk drawers hanging open. The place looked like it had been ransacked by criminals. Sebastián recognized John Byrns from a picture the Comisario had sent him. The man had thin lips, small shoulders and wore a grey, bureaucratic suit that matched his reputation. According to the Comisario, he was an arrogant, phlegmatic sort of man. He'd held a few positions at different American embassies in Latin America, but nothing prominent. He was rumored to work for the American CIA. He was reading something written on a notepad on the desk.

Sebastián tucked his gun back into the holster and stepped into the room. *"Buenos días,"* he said loudly.

Byrns looked up. *"Buenos días* …uhh … Mister … You are?"

"Prefecto Sebastián Cienfuegos. *Policía de Investigaciones.*" He opened his jacket for his identification badge, exposing the Glock.

"Delighted to meet you, Sebastián." The man lips curled in a disingenuous smile.

"What you are doing here?" Sebastián looked at a man by the window. He fitted Emmanuelle's description of Albert Thorman. The buttons securing his jacket appeared ready to burst.

"We came to chat with Emmanuelle Solis. She's not here. Someone obviously combed the place."

"Mr. Byrns, we're always willing to collaborate with North American authorities in investigations, but there is a protocol. You can't break into someone's hotel room and conduct a search."

"We didn't do this. Someone else was here before us."

"Even if that's true, you have no authority to search the room. You have to act in accord with Chilean procedure."

"It's not necessary to call on the Minister of the Exterior for this. We just want to talk to her. Where is she?" Bryns asked. His eyes roved about the room.

Sebastián didn't answer.

"It looks like someone is after the girl, Sebastián. Don't you think? Now, what kind of mess do you think she's involved in that would make someone want to turn her room upside down this way? She was in your office about an hour ago, wasn't she? So where'd she go?"

Everything about Byrns already irritated Sebastián. "Show

me a document that establishes you are here in an official capacity, or get out of this room."

Byrns yawned lazily and turned his back, still checking items strewn about.

Sebastián glanced over at Thorman, who had been keeping his distance. Byrns might employ his political connections to avoid the consequences of violating Chilean criminal procedure, but Thorman was simply a civilian of foreign nationality. "Your name?"

"Albert Thorman, I...."

"If you don't leave this room immediately, I'll have to arrest you."

Thorman shifted his weight and cast a nervous glance at Byrns, as though waiting for instructions.

Byrns continued with his inspection, stopping in front of the bed. It had been pulled away from the wall and the sheets ripped off the mattress.

Sebastián stepped in front of him. His back stiffened. "I can't allow you to search this room. You need to contact the Directorate of Juridical Affairs of the Chilean Ministry of Foreign Affairs if you want to be involved in an investigation in Chile. They'll forward it to the Unit for International Cooperation and Extraditions of the Chilean Public Prosecutors. They forward to me. Then we talk."

"I don't want to extradite the girl, for Christ sakes. I just want to talk to her. She left the United States under very suspicious circumstances. We believe she has evidence relating to the disappearance and death of Stephan Henri Brent." Byrns picked up a cosmetic bag, pulled out a vial of medicine and reached into his shirt pocket for reading glasses.

Sebastián snatched the vial and case from his hands. "You have to leave this room." He shut the drawer and stood in front of it. "You're violating Chilean law. Get out. Now."

"Prefecto Cienfuegos, we're working on information provided to us by the Judicial Division of the United States Securities Commission. An American lawyer was killed in Argentina, I'm sure you know. He was a partner at Oliver & Stone, the firm Ms. Solis worked at. A prominent U.S. citizen. Left wing anti-democratic activists spurred protests against a water privatization deal he was negotiating with the government. They abducted him, sought a ransom for him, tortured and killed him. We have reason to believe his abductors are associated with a ring of Bolivian and Colombian activists funded by the Venezuelan government to stir up problems and generate hatred against the United States and its operations. We believe the group funds its operations through securities fraud."

"And what does that have to do with Ms. Solis?" Sebastián asked, shifting his attention to a large man who'd just walked into the room. He was stone-jawed with a crew cut, bulging muscles and a tight-fitting suit.

"She stole files with more than a million dollars' worth of stock from my office and fled to Chile after Brent disappeared," Thorman added, apparently emboldened by the newcomer.

Comisario Olivares came into the room with three Carabineros. More were in the hall. He took charge saying, "There are procedures to follow if you want to question a suspect."

"There's a sophisticated international securities fraud organization working this area. Many of the firm's wealthy clients were scammed. It was a multimillion dollar operation," Byrns replied.

Sebastián took Thorman firmly by the arm and pushed him to the door. Carabineros ushered the men outside.

Chapter 38

"DON'T WORRY SO much, *compadre*. Who would suspect the *famoso* Renato Vinicius Almeida from the São Paulo Chamber of Commerce of investment fraud?" the voice on the other end of the phone said. It was dense. Words tightly compressed. Then, laughter. Arrogant laughter. Maybe even a little bitter. The message vectored like an arrow, piercing Gilberto Pereira's conscience. Was the bastard mocking him?

Gilberto was silent. Garlands of cigarette smoke rose in whorls around him. The Cristofle ashtray on his leather-topped writing table overflowed with stubs and ashes. Still clutching the phone, he ground out the cigarette, and emptied the ashtray into the wastebasket. He dusted off his desk with his silk handkerchief. As much as he smoked, he hated ashes.

He ran a hand nervously through his fine, golden brown hair and cleared his throat. If his profession didn't kill him— that is, being a co-conspirator in a massive investment fraud operation—the cigarettes would. He was dying from the inside out. And he was only thirty-two years old.

This was the first time he had spoken directly to the mastermind. He had always communicated with Gilberto through Antonio Carrasco or Sean Michael Epstein. But now, hearing his voice, Gilberto had a disturbing feeling they'd met before. He sounded familiar. Gilberto driftingly wondered what he looked like. What his real name was. Definitely *gringo*. He called himself *el Artista*.

"Are you there?" the voice asked impatiently.

"Yes," Gilberto said. He reached for his unfiltered Gitanes and put one between his lips without lighting it. "I am listening." He played nervously with his gold lighter, flipping the lid open, closing it, fiddling with the flint roll bar.

"You got the paperwork, right?" the voice asked.

Gilberto looked at the pile of fraudulent documents on the writing table. Certified financial statements, balance sheets, statements of income, statements of cash flows, and reports on internal control. "*Sim. Belíssimas*. Beautiful. The clients will love them," he answered flatly. The fancy gold seals on the stock certificates glittered in the light of the Tiffany lamp near the credenza.

More laughter. Arrogant, bitter laughter. Cold terror spilt through his veins. But what was Gilberto expecting? Did he think the mastermind of an intercontinental securities scam would be a nice guy? He struck the flint, lighting the flame on his lighter. "*Os certificados de ações são belíssimas.*" He groped for the words in English, "Yes … beautiful, the certificates." He wondered whether *el Artista* could hear the skepticism and fear in his voice.

"We're wrapping it up for a while. The heat's on. Those are the last ones for now. Then we'll talk details. Antonio gave you instructions, eh? You know where we are meeting?"

Gilberto's lighter slipped from his fingers, skittered across the surface of his desk and fell onto his rosette-styled Persian carpet. He bent down and picked it up, lit his cigarette, and drew deeply on it, still clutching the phone. He wondered why the leader of the South American investment fraud scam wanted to meet with him. He'd worked for him for two years, never talked to him directly. Why now? Why couldn't they just go their own way? Was the gringo planning to kill him? Get rid of any potential witness against him? What would happen if he didn't show? Would he chase him down? Kill him? "Yes. Yes. Okay. We meet in Chile. At your orders," he said, in faltering English. "*Às suas ordens.*"

As much as Gilberto grappled to mask his distrust, he doubted that ability now. He thought about Gabriela. She was pregnant with his baby. She was the only person from his childhood who had discovered his fraudulent life. He thought of how she had pleaded with him to abandon it. He thought back on his life. No one could arrest his conscience like she could. She didn't even have to say a word. It was her entire being that made him want to be a better person. Each untruth he had embraced led to a greater untruth, and an even greater hazard of detection and disgrace. And here he was. *This* was where he found himself. Had it been worth it?

Gilberto's thoughts sank into the recesses of his conscience. He had worked his way into the well-heeled social circles of Rio de Janeiro and São Paulo from a small town in the north-eastern state of Bahia. He was now a prominent member of the São Paulo and Rio de Janeiro chambers of commerce. But very few people in those circles knew that he wasn't really Renato Almeida. He was, plain and simply, Gilberto Pereira.

Eight years earlier, when Gilberto was working as a clerk in a bank in Salvador de Bahia, he'd funneled money out of the account of Francisco Almeida, an old lawyer then on his death bed. Many years earlier, when Gilberto was a child, his father had tended the delicate orchid garden of Almeida's gated, upper-class residence on the outskirts of the city. It was there, amidst a sea of magenta orchid blossoms, that Gilberto, peering in from the outside, came to know a life far different from that of his home in the *favelas*—the shantytowns of Bahia.

He'd accompanied his father as often as he could to the estate, cajoling the servants into letting him into the house for a drink of water or a bite to eat—something much tastier than the beans and rice he ate every day at home. The charming little boy would offer to help the housekeepers, dusting in places where only he could reach or carrying a stack of freshly pressed-linens and towels to the rooms upstairs.

He would wander about, daydreaming, stopping often in the spacious, high-ceilinged bedroom at the far end of the stucco house where Renato, the lawyer's only child, slept. He had an enormous bed with a mountain of pillows, wide windows, and French doors that opened out to a balustrade terrace above the orchid garden.

If no one were around, Renato would play with Gilberto. He was only a few months older, but he was a book of knowledge. He talked to Gilberto about faraway places and showed him his collection of the newest electronic toys and games. He lent Gilberto books that he took back to his tiny home in the slums. There—in spite of the sweltering heat, the noise from his oversized family, the deafening volume of their fuzzy television, the radio booming with Samba, Djembe, Conga drums and gourd percussions, and the noise of car horns screaming in the streets—he would read books about a world to which he yearned to belong.

In spite of his squalid poverty, Gilberto was endowed with several attributes that helped him get where he was now. He was tall, strikingly handsome, elegant of posture, cunning, and theatrically imaginative. He was also relatively fair-skinned compared to the majority of people who lived in the Brazilian favelas who were descendants of African slaves brought over by Dutch colonialists. He learned that he if walked, talked and dressed differently he could pass himself off as the son of an upper-class man.

When Renato died in a car crash after a night of celebrating passing the bar examination of the *Ordem dos Advogados do Brasil*, his mother blamed her husband for buying their son an English sports car right before the ill-fated trip. The couple fought like demons, each accusing the other of causing their son's death, neither able to be consoled by the large quantities of alcohol and Valium they ingested.

Gilberto was working as a clerk in a bank when he learned of Renato's death. He visited Renato's aging father, telling him he was Renato's companion from the prestigious *Universidade Federal da Bahia*. The old lawyer, despairing over his son's death, clung on to Gilberto like a drowning man, never discovering he was merely the son of his former gardener.

Eventually, Gilberto got his hands on Renato's law books, diplomas, and identity documents and moved to São Paulo. In no time, he became known as Advogado Renato Almeida, a specialist in Brazilian business and banking laws.

He then spent all his time trying to teach himself what a prestigious university and an upper-class lifestyle had taught his dead friend. With money in his bank account, a new name and a law degree, Gilberto began to find his way into the social circles of fine-feathered South Americans, faltering every so often with a *faux pas* or expression that drew silence or a condescending glare from his five-star colleagues, threatening to expose the whole sham, briefly reminding him of how ephemeral this act might prove to be.

He made contacts in big law firms and attended conferences where lawyers came from across the world to discuss international business transactions.

Four years later, he met Sean Michael Epstein at the São Paulo conference on international arbitration. The man was a fast-talking Canadian securities broker who'd set up a brokerage firm in Santiago, Chile selling microcap stocks in what he claimed were "North American oil companies with Brazilian concessions sitting on several billion dollars' worth of oil." Sean was eager for a Brazilian partner. He later introduced him to Antonio Carrasco, a Chilean stockbroker whom he would put in charge of the Santiago operation.

In no time, Gilberto was incorporated into Sean's scheme to sell fraudulent Brazilian micro-cap stocks throughout the Americas and was making more money than he ever dreamed of.

Gilberto loosened the starched collar of his shirt and patted the vest of his pinstriped Italian suit searching for more cigarettes as he recalled the day he met Sean at the conference. The banquet table behind Sean had silver trays stacked with slices of the finest meats, seafood, exquisite dishes, delicious pastries, and cakes. All his life he had wanted to belong to that world. He had run out of money. He had been telling people he had clients abroad, but the only thing he had been working on was keeping up his act. So when Sean took the bottle of champagne from the waiter that day, filled Gilberto's glass until it bubbled over and offered him the deal, all Gilberto could do was nod.

Gilberto didn't like Sean. Who would? He was slicker than a boar from the *campo*, but he needed him at that moment in his life. At the time, it seemed like the only option he had to keep up with the act. Had it all been worth it? The cash holdings and real estate properties had been a consolation, but he had spent every waking minute of his life fearing exposure. He had climbed higher and higher—up a stack of lies that was destined to come crumbling down. It now seemed to cause more suffering than pleasure.

Was he repentant? Well, maybe he felt a bit guilty about some of the people they cheated. Now, in retrospect, he felt remorse for the way he had treated old man Almeida. At the time, it seemed like poetic justice. But the man had taken him in like a son. Yes, it bothered him that he had betrayed his trust. Stolen from him. Enjoyed life on ill-gotten gains. Was he just a weak man taken to crime because of his circumstances? His parents always seemed contented with their meager earnings and scant lifestyle in the slums. He had never understood that. He did not delight in crime. Not the way *el Artista* did. He just wanted the wealth and the lifestyle. He never intended to hurt anyone. Was it remorse? Or just fear of detection? Fear of punishment? That too, certainly, but his conscience truly arrested him when Gabriela told him about the baby. Things were different now. He needed to find a way out. He needed to rectify his past before his first child was born.

Chapter 39

ANTONIO CARRASCO WOKE up in his sumptuous, marble-floored Vittacura apartment. A strange feeling was in his stomach. He'd pressed his luck too far. Maybe it was just paranoia, he thought, as he slipped his feet into his red leather slippers and reached for his silk bathrobe. He hadn't calculated the paranoia factor into the equation when he'd embarked on this lifestyle. For a moment, he stared out at the Andean Mountain range through the immense French windows of his bedroom.

Paranoia was a vicious demon that plagued fraudulent tricksters. Not that *he* was a trickster or criminal. He wasn't. He was Antonio Carrasco. The proud son of an upper middle-class businessman from Santiago. He'd gone to the best schools and graduated from the University of Santiago. Although he had never been a good student, with the help of a friend of his father, he defended his thesis and became a lawyer.

Chilean investors were convinced he was a legitimate securities broker. If he *was* a scoundrel, he was a very refined and sophisticated one. He had an extravagant office in Vittacura with a trilingual staff ready to entice any potential North or South American investor—in Spanish, Portuguese or English—into the latest investment scheme. He was enamored with expensive colognes, trendsetting business suits, silk ties, silk socks, shirts with gold cuff links, modish cell phones, iPads, laptops. He spent all of his free time in vogue Santiago restaurants and clubs impressing colleagues with his knowledge of the New York and Tokyo Stock Exchange.

Perhaps he should have stopped while he was ahead. But how could anyone resist the temptation? More and more money rolled in every day. Easy money.

They had created a state-of-the art website. His team targeted owners of sports teams, heads of corporations, and charitable foundations throughout the Americas. They told investors they would get returns of more than twenty five percent on their investments. They traded shares on the OTC Bulletin Board, the Pink Sheets, or the Pink Sheets Electronic Quotation Service. Most were too small to be traded on the big stock exchanges or NASDAQ. It was easy because they were not subject to the listing standards and reporting requirements.

They engaged in all kinds of tricks. They purchased stock from company promoters for pennies per share and then resold them to unsuspecting investors for several dollars per share. They hired people to promote the stock through web sites, bulletin boards, chat rooms, or on-line investment newsletters. They drew up false press releases indicating something fantastic about a company—like an incredible new product that just hit the market or precious minerals found in some remote part of South America. After the price skyrocketed on the stocks, they would sell to unsuspecting investors and pocket the large profit. The stock price would eventually collapse after the hype ceased. Investors ended up holding worthless shares, but they were told to hold on to them. "Once these hit the NASDAQ, they will be priceless," he told them.

Antonio controlled a group that worked telephones in

Santiago and Puerto Montt and Gilberto worked stations in Brazil. Their teams made thousands of unsolicited telephone calls a day. They ran boiler room operations with hundreds of telephones manned by salespeople who engaged in high-pressure tactics and worked off scripted sales pitches, brazenly soliciting purchasers for stocks with outrageous promises.

Sean sent them the prospectus and financial statements. He occasionally stole the identity of well-known North American brokers who worked for established firms and drafted letters in their names. They used investors' money simply to keep the doors open and to fund their lavish lifestyle. Sean drew up fraudulent certified financial statements, balance sheets, statements of income, statements of cash flows, and reports on internal control. And Gilberto and Antonio mailed them to their clients. They even printed out stock certificates with fancy gold seals that looked beautiful.

Antonio finished law school several years earlier and he was already a partner of one of the most sophisticated international securities fraud organizations in the world.

There's an art to this, he told himself. It was in the misrepresentation of fact. It took work to deceive a party, to give them a justifiable reason to believe in and rely on a misrepresentation. To lure qualified investors, he had to promise the moon. If they were dumb enough to believe it, that was their fault. He didn't lie outright. He just *misrepresented* the facts. Hey, wasn't that what the saying was all about? *En pedir, no hay engaño.* If you accept what I offer, there's no fraud. You took it. You swallowed the hook. The blame falls on the victim. They accepted the deal. *Cagaron no mas, por we'on.* He was so good at lying that every word came out believable. And he could argue his way out of anything. Everyone always believed him. The firm had become one of the biggest securities firms in South America—with offices in Argentina, Brazil, and now

Chile. Some of its operatives were members of the most prominent chambers of commerce. Lawyers, arbitrators, and businessmen from North and South America.

But busts had taken place in Miami and Puerto Montt recently and several people on the lower echelons of the scheme had been arrested. His North American and Brazilian partners told him to be cool. No one could trace anything to them. The only person who could possibly identify him was dead. They managed it all cryptically, through a complicated maze of bank accounts that hid money sent in by the victims.

But paranoia agonized him. PARANOIA. *Un demonio.* Maybe it was the cocaine. The ugly-headed demon.

A few of the boiler rooms *had* gone down like dominoes. There were busts throughout the Americas. The Brazilian Federal Police were on to them. They were wiping out some of their operations. Antonio Carrasco wondered if he would live to regret having gone to that fateful international arbitration conference in Buenos Aires four years ago....

Chapter 40

DETECTIVE PILAR BUSTAMANTE pressed on the accelerator. The *Policía de Investigaciones* van ripped through the long-shadowed backstreets of the shantytowns. She came to a skidding halt in front of a ramshackle building with crumbling walls and peeling paint.

A light rain fell. Carabineros dressed in olive-colored rain capes waited for her on the street. A few were taking statements from people she assumed were neighbors or witnesses of the victim.

It was the fourth time that week that Prefecto Sebastián Cienfuegos put her on the nightshift for homicide investigations. He was acting like a tyrant to keep her out of his way so he could trail that North American lawyer without her asking questions. She knew Sebastián better than anyone else on the force. She called him Señor Prefecto in public, out of respect. But in private she called him by his first name. They were family friends. They went back years. She had a right to tell him what she thought. *And a duty to protect him,* Pilar thought. *He is coming unraveled by that lawyer's presence. That woman is a danger. She will cost him his career if he's not careful.*

To add to it all, she had her own problems. Her husband and kids were fed up with her work hours. As she turned off the engine and pulled the key from the ignition, she asked herself whether she had made the right career choice for herself.

Sebastián sometimes bragged she was the best on his team, which didn't do much to abate hostility from male officers. They resented women encroaching on what, until recently, had exclusively been their territory. The job was too dangerous, too physically demanding for a woman, they claimed. Moreover, working the streets was to experience the absolute worst side of humanity. There were encounters with dangerously angry, drunk, drugged or violent people. Or dead ones.

She jumped out of the van and slammed the door.

"It looks like a suicide. A pretty young fellow, too," one of the Carabineros said to her.

"Do we have a name?" she asked, pulling a notepad out of her jacket.

"Martín Araya."

She had dressed quickly. Her hair was still wet from the shower. Icy beads of water trickled down her back.

She listened as the Carabinero surmised what had happened. Suicide, just another faceless kid from the ghetto. Drugs were probably involved. She moved towards the dimly-lit room where the body lay on the cement floor, a white cloth draped over it.

"Get the body out of the apartment," another Carabinero called to two men standing near an ambulance. They picked up a gurney and headed to the room.

"*Espera*. Wait a minute," Pilar called out, walking briskly toward the building. "Has anyone shown up from the Public Prosecutor's Office?"

"No one's coming. We spoke to them earlier."

That figures. She slackened her pace as she got closer to the boy's dingy make-shift apartment. "What is this place? Was he living in a storage room?" It was dark and cold. A musty smell prickled her nostrils.

She braced herself as she went close to the body. She had never gotten used to this part of her job, no matter how many stiffs she examined. Facing death always made her uncomfortably conscious of life's brevity, abruptly summoning her back to life.

She snapped on gloves and lifted the sheet covering the corpse. She flinched when she saw the boy's grey face, open eyes and parted lips. She clicked on her flashlight and checked his face and neck. There was a distinct mark of a ligature. It was depressed and bruised. *Had he hung himself or was he strangled?* A crucifix glimmered. *Did someone give it to him? Did he steal it?*

"This is a pretty refined piece of gold for someone from a shabby neighborhood, *no es cierto?*" she asked the Carabinero. "Who is this kid?"

"A street kid, I guess. *Un pobre, no más …*" He shrugged with disinterest. "A simple mendicant. A vagrant. A nobody."

"No suicide note?"

"No."

The eyes of the corpse haunted her. Even in death, they reflected suffering. Maybe even terror. She was still debating whether the hanging was self-inflicted or the work of a killer. There were some signs of asphyxiation. His lips and tongue seemed bluish, his eyes dilated. It was too dark to be sure if the coloring suggested strangulation or hanging. In the latter, the victim died from the lack of blood to the brain, not necessarily the lack of oxygen. She studied the wounds around the neck again. "Hmm."

"*¿Suicidio? ¿Si o no?*" the Carabinero asked, impatiently.

She felt a twinge of annoyance. He was just looking for confirmation. The Carabineros were eager to write this off as a suicide without investigating. He had called her here to rubberstamp his conclusions so they could go home. "I don't know." She pointed to the bruises on his neck "What does this look like to you?"

"I don't know. Maybe dirt." The officer scratched an eyebrow and shrugged again. "*Permiso*," he excused himself and turned to leave.

She called after him, "An inverted v-shaped furrow around the neck is usually what you expect to see with a suicide hanging. *Mira*, the groove completely encircles the neck. It looks like he *was* strangled."

The officer looked back at her. He said nothing, but his expression said, *Who cares if he took his own life or if someone else took it for him? He was probably just another* roto de mierda *who the world will never miss anyway.*

He didn't like responding to crime in the ghettos. No one liked investigations in these neighborhoods.

"I wouldn't be surprised if his trachea were crushed. If it is, then we *know* it was murder. He would have jumped from this chair if it were suicide, right?" she said, looking at a filthy plastic chair. "There's nothing else he could have jumped from. The impact of this hanging alone couldn't have crushed his trachea or even damaged it. Let's see what forensics says." Pilar's voice trailed. The Carabinero was gone. She was talking to herself. She got up, scrutinizing the corpse for a few more moments.

Carabineros outside were taking a statement from a young woman who had called them. Pilar immediately knew she wasn't from Puerto Montt. Within hearing range, her distinctly accented Spanish confirmed that she was from the countryside, somewhere south of Puerto Montt where poverty didn't necessarily rob you of your self-respect and dignity.

Pilar slipped in between two of the Carabineros to hear what she was saying.

With impassioned facial expressions, teary eyes, fluttering

hands, and vivid description, the country girl told them she was the deceased's cousin and she lived on the southernmost tip of Chiloé Island—the first and largest of a string of islands comprising the archipelago that led into the Patagonia. In her sing-song Chilote accent, the neatly-dressed, perfectly-coiffed, sweetly-perfumed young lady said she'd taken a ferry across the sea-lion and dolphin-filled Chacao Channel from the sparsely-populated town of Castro, and then a half-hour bus ride to Puerto Montt to visit him. She'd heard that his brother had perished with the *Antarctic Mist* in the Patagonia.

"*Perdoneme.*" Pilar's brain whirled. "Did you just say the deceased had a brother who died on the *Antarctic Mist*?"

"*Si po.* His brother, Belissario Araya, was a volunteer for the expedition team."

"Was he a scientist?"

"*No, po.* He was a volunteer for the Patagonia Environmental Conservation Project. As I was saying, I came here to console Martín for Belisario's passing, and I found him dangling from a cord in his apartment." She held a hand to her chest.

"What did Martín do for a living?" Pilar pressed.

"He was a marine biologist. He just started working for a company a few months ago. He sometimes visited me in Castro on his way down to the Patagonia. He would spend a night or two at my house. In fact, he came to visit so frequently that I fixed a little room for him there. *Si, po. Asi es el asunto.* Only a week ago, I cooked *milcao* potato fritters for him and we had them with tea. If there's one thing my mother taught me to do well, it was how to cook. I am the only relative the boys were in contact with after their mother, Tia Rosa, disappeared." She spoke with a provincial, non-stop, story-telling style. The emotionless eyes of her audience projected their disinterest clearly.

Pilar's attention was drawn to a tall, slender figure moving through the shadows of the alley next to the building. She recognized him when he got closer. He was a well-known priest, Padre Felipe Montero. A hush fell over the crowd of bystanders as he approached.

For years, the priest had dedicated his life to the poor, espousing the causes of indigenous groups—something that rubbed coarsely against the grain of the elite circle in which he was born. His father was a wealthy fruit exporter in Santiago who maintained sprawling orchards in the central region of the country where the climate was so favorable and land so fertile that the *campesinos* swore that they just dropped seeds and stepped aside to watch them grow. His parents had sent him to an all-boys, Jesuit *colegio* for the privileged where men were taught to be gentlemen, Catholics and conservatives. He went on to study law at the Pontifical Catholic University in Santiago.

Despite his birth into fortune, he was disinterested in the moneyed-aristocracy that typified his social class. After he graduated, he told his family that he wanted to walk in the footsteps of Padre Alberto Hurtado, the renowned Jesuit, lawyer, social worker, and controversial-in-his-day author who had established the Hogar de Cristo shelter for the poor and was canonized by Pope Benedict XVI in 2005.

Like the renowned Padre Hurtado, Felipe became very involved in the labor movements of Chile, arguing for the improvement of labor conditions and higher salaries for workers. Felipe's focus was the south of Chile, a place where many who lived there felt largely abandoned by their government in Santiago.

The crowd parted to let him through. The priest wasn't wearing a coat and his rain-drenched shirt clung to his chest.

Pilar greeted him with a kiss on the cheek. The police offered handshakes and embraces.

"What's going on?" he asked them. Rain dripped from his face.

Pilar saw apprehension in his eyes.

"Do you know the young man who lived here?" one of the Carabineros asked.

"Yes. His name is Martín Araya. Is something wrong?"

"I am afraid he's committed suicide."

"Suicide?" The look in his eyes changed to shock. Maybe even disbelief. He turned away from them and headed for the apartment.

Pilar wondered how well he knew the victim. She followed him, stopping in the threshold of the door to watch.

The priest was born to a small class of people who had come upon their wealth either through inheritance or the fortunes of trade in their mineral-rich country, with its desert in the north and temperate rainforests in the south. *What would have made him want to work with people from the darkest corners of life like this one?*

He knelt down beside the shrouded body and lifted the cloth, uncovering the corpse's face. "Martín," he whispered, as though the corpse could hear him. Were they tears she saw? There was something intangibly mysterious about the man. *Who could reject scintillating riches to dedicate his life to the dregs of society?*

The idea of life after death was appealing. Pilar clicked her flashlight on again and pointed it in the dead boy's face. *But who can have faith in anything when all you see day in and day out is the dark and sleazy side of life?* She bent down and placed a hand on the priest's arm. "Was he from your shelter, Padre?"

He nodded.

She waited, but he offered no more information. She looked over at the Carabineros standing outside the room. Were they going to try to elicit more information? No one made a move.

What was it he sought in the suffering of the poor? Wasn't it just another way of romanticizing poverty? She understood why the poor needed him. But why did he need them? Her eyes searched the filthy room with mold pullulating in the corners. There was no aura of mystique in the filthy, grinding poverty of Puerto Montt. She envied the priest's faith. She would wait to ask questions when they were alone.

The inappropriate curiosity of the neighbors who were creeping closer was getting to Pilar. She got up and walked to the door. *"¿Que stai sapiando, mierda?"* she cursed them. They recoiled.

For what may have been an hour, the priest stayed beside the body, murmuring prayers as the night dripped in rain. Carabineros scoured out the room more diligently this time and questioned neighbors, seemingly animated by the priest's presence.

When they were finished, Pilar gently put a hand on his shoulder. *"Padre, lo siento.* I'm sorry, but we need to take him down to forensics. Can you come with us? Can you give us more information about the boy?"

Chapter 41

THIS MAY HAVE been the worst day of Padre Felipe Montero's life, but as he headed up the hill in the direction of the Casa de Tenglo, something told him the worst was yet to come. The feeling that Martín Araya might not be the only one to die tonight haunted him.

The night was dark, but he could have made his way up to the sanctuary blindfolded. He knew the trail so well. He instinctively followed the hazy glow of the hand-hammered, wrought iron sconce at the entrance.

Nothing made any sense to him. Rodrigo had left him a message at the rectory a few hours earlier saying that he was going to accompany Martín to the *Prefectura de Investigaciones*. He had not explained why. What happened? An hour later, Martín was dead. The Carabineros were calling it a suicide. He reached for the iron doorknocker of Casa Tenglo and banged heavily. He wondered if anyone could hear him over the noise of the whipping night winds.

After several minutes, Javier Salas opened the door. "Felipe! What a surprise. *Que t'al?*" The priest was wearing soccer cleats and sweating profusely.

"Back from a game?"

"*Si, po.* The little bastards beat us again."

Felipe had taken Javier under his wing ten years earlier after he abruptly abandoned his national soccer career with

Deportes Puerto Montt and joined the seminary. Newspapers bore pictures of Javier's fans with tears streaming down their faces, holding lit candles at his last game. The press questioned his motives and veracity. Soccer players were like rock stars. How could a young man abandon such a promising career for a life of religion and celibacy? Were his parents pressuring him? Was he gay? He spent the next six years studying philosophy and theology in a seminary. There he met Felipe, who had already been ordained as a Roman Catholic priest and was setting up a shelter for street children.

"*¿Que pasa hermano?* What brings you here?"

"Is Rodrigo here?"

"Rodrigo? No. Why?"

"He left me a note at the rectory asking me to meet him here," Felipe said, pausing for a moment in front of the open door. "Listen, I've come with very bad news. He stepped inside. "Martín's dead." The icy wind whirled around the room like a spirit on the loose.

Javier shut the door firmly. "*¿Cómo?*" He stood frozen, as though the news had not yet processed in his mind.

"Carabineros are saying it was suicide."

Color drained from his cheeks. "*¿Qué? ¿Suicidio?* I can't believe that."

Felipe realized that the news would strike where Javier was weakest. Maybe even carry him back to the days just before he had joined the seminary, when his young girlfriend had tried to take her own life, spinning him into an existential crisis. He wrapped an arm around his friend's shoulders. "Let's talk in your office."

Chapter 42

EMMANUELLE SOLIS HAD been waiting for hours on a bench in the dimly lit corridors of the Casa Tenglo when Padre Javier reappeared, sweating and still in his filthy cleats. He failed to notice her as he walked by with a slender, elegant looking priest in a trim-fitting cassock.

He opened a door to an office and closed it behind them. They were despondently engaged in hushed conversation. Her eyes followed them before fixing back on the rain-spattered window.

She realized that a mild frenzy was breaking out in the little house. The young men dressed in black with Roman collars who had been eating in the dining room when the tall priest arrived were now abandoning the table, their bowls half-filled with stew. A few paced up and down the halls, talking to each other in low, anxious voices. One knocked on the door to the office. He went inside for a few minutes and then emerged again. He appeared to be crying. Emmanuelle sat upright, wondering what was going on.

There was a crack in the wall that separated her from the priests. She felt a flush of embarrassment as she contemplated eavesdropping, but it passed as survival instincts kicked in again. She inched along the bench, straining to hear their conversation.

The priest was talking.

***

"Isabella found Martín dead in his apartment today," he said.

"I just can't believe it. How did he die?"

"He was hanging from a cord."

"That's ... that's just ... insane. Why would he commit suicide?"

"Carabineros suspect suicide, but...."

"But what? Don't tell me you think he was murdered?" A mix of incredulity and horror was in his voice.

"I don't know what to believe. Where's Rodrigo? He said he'd be here." He sighed grimly.

Emmanuelle made sure no one was watching as she moved closer. She could now see the men through the crack.

"I haven't heard from him. Why?" Javier asked, brushing aside a tear with a dirty hand.

"He left me this message at the rectory a few hours ago."

Emmanuelle inched closer. The tall priest was taking something out of his pocket.

"Martín had gotten into some kind of trouble and they were going to the *Prefectura de Investigaciones*. Apparently, Martín had something urgent to tell us and Rodrigo wanted to meet here."

"What kind of trouble was he in?"

"I have no idea."

"The note also said the mission in the Patagonia could be in danger." He handed Javier the note.

He looked down at it. "What could that mean?"

"I have no idea. I went to Martín's apartment to catch him before they went to PDI. When I got there, Carabineros and PDI were there, but Rodrigo wasn't." He was silent for a long while. His hands were clasped, resting on his lap. His chin, on his chest as though he was deep in prayer. "God rest his soul."

Javier got up. "Where could Rodrigo be? What could this

be about? He wanted to meet here at six?"

It was nearly eight. Emmanuelle saw movement at the end of the halls where seminarians were clustered. She straightened and sat back on the bench.

Over the noise down the hall, she thought she heard the tall priest ask about Cristóbal. Were they talking about the priest she was waiting for?

"He was in Temuco when the protests started last week," Javier said. "I heard he went to Aysén after that. He's supposed to be back tonight or tomorrow. Why? Do you think he might know something about this?"

"*Bueno* … he always seems to be wherever trouble is. Carabineros showed up at the Curia a few days ago, looking for him. They said they wanted to question him again about the Victoria incident. *Osea* … they think he knows more about who was responsible for the Klingemann killing."

Emmanuelle had read about the incident. A group of hooded men had torched the home of a wealthy ranch owner in a town near Temuco. The ranch owner died. Carabineros arrested several suspects including a Mapuche machi. There were protests and violent clashes with the police for several days after.

"Why would they think he knows something about it?"

"I don't know. He needs to disassociate himself entirely from those who are actively engaged in rebellion and unrest."

For years, the Mapuches had been fighting for repatriation of traditional lands in courts and in the streets. The government entered agreements to return some of the land, but the repatriation process was drawn out and marred by conflict.

"*Sí, se*. Rodrigo had an argument with him about that last week. But it's complicated. They trust the old man."

"Priests shouldn't be involved in armed rebellion. He has been treading a thin line for years."

"Padre Cristóbal would agree that the solution isn't violence. But he will tell you that the people feel like justice will never happen and they have to take things into their own hands."

"Priests are intercessors between God and men. Not between governments and rebels."

"Felipe, you don't need to convince *me* of that."

"I know. And I may be jumping to conclusions. Maybe there's no connection, but the fact that Martín was working in the Patagonia and with Cristóbal's presence there …" He sighed with frustration. "*O sea*, Padre Cristóbal is always tangled up in some conflict. I thought he might know something."

Emmanuelle strained to peer through the crack again.

"I sometimes wonder if the old man is all there, you know. *O sea*, it's one thing to support the causes of the indigenous and another to be as involved … the way he is," the tall priest said. "I just have this strange feeling." His voice trailed off again. "Martín's place was ravaged, the panels ripped from the walls, what little he had thrown upside down. *O sea* … as if someone were looking for something. I think he never made it to the *Prefectura de Investigaciones*."

"So, you think someone was looking for something in Martín's apartment? And then they killed him?"

"Yes. That's my instinct. I saw the body. There was a look in his eyes. I think it was terror. *Pobre Martín*."

"But what would anyone be looking for at Martín's place? It was a hellhole. He couldn't have been making much money working for that water company. What would anyone want from Martín?"

Emmanuelle held her breath. The water company in Aysén? She stood up, glancing down the foyer where a few seminarians were gathering. One looked her way. She sat back down and put the laptop back on her lap, feigning interest in what was on the screen.

"Yes … and he didn't seem very happy either. When I spoke to him last month, I expected he would be happy to be employed. But he was acting strange. *Nervioso.* Distracted. Like he wasn't at peace with something. Listen, there's more. The deacons said he showed up at the cathedral today hysterical, looking for me. Just an hour or so before his death."

"What was it about?"

"They said he was crying, screaming like a wild man. Rodrigo ushered him into the vestry. Apparently they talked for a long time."

"Martín drunk? He's never touched alcohol in all the years I've known him. You weren't there?"

"No, I was with the Archbishop all day. Rumors have it Martín kept saying something about having killed his brother."

"That's insane. Emilio's interned at the rehab center. Jaime saw him today."

"Apparently he wasn't talking about Emilio." He hesitated. "He said he'd killed Belisario."

"But Belisario died on the *Antarctic Mist.*"

Emmanuelle was startled. Her laptop nearly fell from her lap. Had she heard correctly? The *Antarctic Mist?* She wanted to knock on their door.

Two seminarians appeared at the end of the corridor, now walking toward her. One nodded his head solemnly as they passed. Teary-eyed, they continued down the hall. Emmanuelle fixed her eyes on the rain pelting against the window, straining even harder to hear the conversation of the priests above the noise of the footsteps and the wood floors creaking.

"Martín felt somehow responsible. People were crowded outside the vestry trying to listen to what they were saying. By now Rodrigo must know Martín's dead." There was the noise of rustling, as though both were standing, maybe coming to the door.

Emmanuelle began typing nothing on her computer. The door would open at any moment.

"I'm going to the rectory. Maybe he's there," the tall priest said.

"Did you talk to Carabineros?"

"No. I haven't said anything to them yet. I agreed to go to the station in the morning. I have to talk to Rodrigo first. We know he won't talk to them if he learned something in a confession."

"Shall I meet you at the rectory in the morning?"

"*Bueno.* Let me know if Rodrigo shows up here tonight."

The door opened. Emmanuelle struggled to keep her eyes on the computer screen as the men emerged. Her eyes then followed them down the hall.

A few minutes later, Javier reappeared. "You're still here?" he asked as though just noticing her there.

"I'm still waiting for Padre Cristóbal," she told him. "I understand he's on his way."

"*Ah, ya,*" he said, gazing vacuously at her. "He may be late. Weather's been bad. Slows down the ferries. Get something to eat in the dining room. María will help you." He leaned against the wall and pulled off his cleats. Drying mud crumbled as he dropped them to the floor. He disappeared down the hall.

Rivulets of the raindrops streamed down the panes. What the hell was she doing here?

Chapter 43

PADRE FELIPE MONTERO searched for the boat keeper as he neared the edge of the channel. He walked toward a shadowy outline in the mist, his cassock fluttering in the wind, until he came upon El Indio. He took his arm and climbed into his boat.

He felt linked to the old man and his hushed existence in an indefinable way. Now more than ever. He was a reaffirmation that his work with indigenous communities had been worth the effort. He wondered where his home was. The old man seemed to live on the banks of the channel. Machis claimed he had been there for hundreds of years. He was part of the landscape for as long as he could remember. He wished he could communicate with him. Had he heard about Martín's death?

His thoughts shifted to Padre Cristóbal. Would he return tonight? It was time they had a serious conversation. The seventy-five-year-old priest belonged to the Salesian order of Don Bosco that had established missions throughout Latin America. For more than half a century, he had been involved the tribulations of indigenous people. The decades-old land rights conflict in the southern part of the country occupied most his time.

Year round, he traveled to the farthest reaches of the Patagonia to visit those communities that considered him one of their own, in spite of his European features and translucent white skin that exposed every blue vein in his head. He spoke their language, dispensed native medicines, baptized their children, buried their dead, prayed with them and participated in their hunger strikes when they protested against the government. He'd partaken in their activities so often that a group of conservative priests in the Santiago Archdiocese fifty years earlier, fearful that Cristóbal was organizing his own cult, urged the Cardinal to expel him for heresy.

They were outraged that he was invited to participate in *ngillatun* and other indigenous rituals where natives made offerings to the spirits to ensure the continued blessings of Ngünechen, one of their gods. He even baptized the Machis who practiced a mix of native medicine, biomedicine and Catholicism to cure their ill, incorporating images of *Jesús, la Virgen María, and San Francisco* into their ceremonies.

After a five-year witch-hunt, the commission assembled to investigate Cristóbal concluded it was politically risky to excommunicate the popular priest although he confounded Catholic and indigenous rituals. His popularity and high number of conversions made it beneficial to keep him within the institution. So the church established a mission and financed the construction of several schools, deciding that educating the Indians would correct any thinking among them that wasn't entirely Catholic.

Felipe concluded he hadn't been paying enough attention to what was going on at Tenglo Island. Years ago, he had authorized Padre Cristóbal to stay at Casa Tenglo whenever he was in town. However, it seemed to have become Padre Cristóbal's base and the recent visits from Carabineros were disturbing. Javier was in charge of the parish now, but he was more interested in soccer than evangelizing, and although Padre Felipe hated to admit it, he knew it was Javier's retreat from life rather than his mission.

Javier joined the seminary in response to a personal struggle. Seventeen years earlier, after he had risen to fame as a soccer player, his family tried to remove his beautiful, but impoverished girlfriend from his life. The shantytown girl's dreams of marrying him had shielded her adolescent mind from the thought that her neglected existence in the miserable *barrio bajo* would be her reality for life. Javier eventually succumbed to family pressure and ended the relationship. Crushed by the weight of impossible dreams, the girl recoiled to her wooden, corrugated-metal dwelling in the depressed settlement and slit her wrists. She survived, but the wounds of social injustice were harder to redress.

Equally, Felipe thought, *in Javier.*

The young girl vanished. When Javier entered the seminary, Felipe knew Javier was searching for her among the slum children. *The children with the lights turned out in their eyes*, he called them.

Felipe devoted his energy to working with Mapuche Indians and obtained the approval of the Vatican to establish a mission seminary on Tenglo Island premised on the role of Mary in the salvation of mankind. It was accepted well in the predominantly indigenous south of the country. The majority of Indians incorporated Mary into their spiritual world after Catholicism was introduced. First, peaceably by Jesuit missionaries from German provinces in the 1500s and later more violently by the Spanish *Conquistadores* who never completely succeeded in conquering them.

Conflict between landowners and Mapuches increasingly led to deep-seated hatred and outbreaks of violence. Poor Martín was an example of how that evangelization was failing. Felipe put his head in his hands. He wondered how Rodrigo would shed light on the mystery unfolding in their world.

The boat scraped against the shore. El Indio rose to help him disembark.

Chapter 44

EMMANUELLE WATCHED AS Padre Javier disappeared down the dark hall. She closed her laptop and peered out the window. Across the channel, a string of headlights streamed along the coastline. She wondered whether Thorman was still out there somewhere. She pulled out the detective's card and stared at his handwriting, debating again whether or not to call him. Would he turn her in if she did? She studied the trajectory of the windblown raindrops moving across the pane in front of her as her mind tried to process everything she had heard the priests say. Who was the boy they were talking about? Which water company had he worked for? Was he murdered? If so, what had his assassins been looking for? Was it related to the *Antarctic Mist*? Why had he claimed responsibility for his brother's death? Had he been involved in some kind of sabotage of the ship? Could those events somehow connect to the Patagonia Files and Stephan's abduction and murder?

She closed her eyes. For a fraction of a second, her mind defaulted back to a comforting thought of Stephan and life before he disappeared. Then the horror came back. He was dead. The pictures the Prefecto had shown her resurfaced in mind like long fingernails clawing at the window. Stephan had lied, cheated on her, and gotten her into a monumental mess before he was killed. And that was why she was sitting there, eavesdropping on priests and trying to build a defense for herself before Interpol and the FBI caught up with her.

She had to keep moving forward. She glanced towards the dining hall. Housekeepers were a great source of information. She picked up her things and headed there.

***

Emmanuelle peered through the door. María was clearing the table. Emmanuelle hesitated, wondering whether she should just leave the island. But where could she go? If she waited for Padre Cristóbal, she might learn more about what was happening in the south. She wondered whether he was in danger, as the priests' conversation suggested, and whether he really did harbor men wanted by the authorities.

A large-boned man in a high-neck fisherman's sweater and grey jacket sat at the table. He looked more like a Mexican revolutionary than someone connected to the church. He had a large handlebar moustache, kohl-rimmed eyes, and thick black hair tied back into a ponytail.

"*Buenas noches*," he called out, startling her. He stood. "*Adelante.* Come in."

"You're still here?" The housekeeper turned to face her. In spite of her indigenous traits, she had a porcelain complexion and blue eyes like many of the mestizo of the south whose ancestors had mixed with German settlers several hundred years earlier. "Would you like something to eat?"

Emmanuelle sank into a chair.

"You're still waiting for Padre Cristóbal?"

"Yes. I'm still waiting for him."

"He might be late. We never know when he'll show up." She lifted a tray of plates and bowls and carried them to the open kitchen.

The man with the moustache held his hand out to her. "Nahuel Carrillanca." He had a hyper-masculine stance and the countenance of the leader of a peasant movement.

She took it. "Emmanuelle Solis."

"*Encantado.*" He examined the dark liquid in his cup before drinking it. "Any friend of Padre Cristóbal is a friend of mine."

Emmanuelle focused on the housekeeper, avoiding his eyes.

"Nahuel is waiting for Padre Lautaro as well," the housekeeper said, opening the oven. She pulled out a tray of fresh baked bread.

"Who?"

"Padre Cristóbal. We call him Padre Lautaro. Lautaro was a Mapuche military leader who led the Indians in the War of Arauco, defeating the troops of Pedro de Valdivia. He nearly succeeded in expelling the Spanish from Chile. But they caught him and killed him." She set the bread on the countertop. The aroma swirled through the room. Emmanuelle was famished.

"Thank you."

María lifted the lid of an enormous pot. Syrupy liquids dripped down its sides. The fire under it crackled and spit. She stirred the mixture and lowered the flames. Her eyes were puffy. A single tear ran down her cheek. "He might not get back until late tonight."

"I'll wait," Emmanuelle said gently.

The woman seemed close to breaking down and crying.

"Are … are you okay?" Emmanuelle asked. "I just overheard … something about a young man who took his life."

"That's what the Carabineros are saying."

"Never believe anything a *paco* tells you," Nahuel said, stroking his moustache.

Emmanuelle knew *paco* was a diminutive for Carabinero. She asked María, "Was the boy who died close to you?" *Please talk to me.*

"Yes," she said quietly. "His name was Martín Araya."

"His real name was Huenchullán," the man with the

moustache broke in again. "Kids these days don't use Mapuche names. They don't want to be different. They don't want to be called an *indio*. Martín was like that. But he learned that you can't change who you are."

María gave Nahuel a look of disapproval. Did she disagree with what he was saying or that he was saying it to Emmanuelle?

"Padre Felipe raised him and his brothers."

"Their mother abandoned them on the steps of his shelter twenty years ago. The youngest one, Belisario, was only a few weeks old at the time." María set cups down on the table and reached for a teapot. "They brought me into the shelter to take care of him and his brothers. The kids were a mystery. We didn't know anything about them until their cousin from Chiloe showed up a few years later. She told us the story. Martín's mother ran off with a sailor when she was sixteen. He got her pregnant and left her. Martín and his mother were on the streets for a while. His brothers are from a different father who wasn't any better. No one knows where the mother is. Martín always believed he would find her." She poured stew into a bowl and set it down in front of Emmanuelle.

Emmanuelle thanked her again.

"He could never deal with that abandonment. He made excuses for her, always saying she was coming back for them. When Martín came to the shelter, he told the priests that the *Chonchonyi* had taken his mother away."

Nahuel said, "The *chonchonyi* is an evil creature with massive ears from Araucano folk tales. It lures victims to isolated places and sucks the life out of them. We figured out that the *chonchonyi* Martín was talking about was a well-known pimp with big ears who traffics girls from shantytown neighborhoods."

María said, "Martín was very special for Padre Felipe. He and his brothers were the first children ever to stay in the shelter. Rodrigo thought they were too young. The baby was only a few weeks old. Emilio was two. Martín was five. But Padre Felipe called me and I agreed to move in and take care of them. When they grew up, I came here to keep house for the priests in residence. I have been here since. I remember Belisario that day … a wrinkled, blue-faced creature with black hair. Two of them are dead now." She mopped up tears with her apron.

"Did you say *two* of the boys are dead now?"

She nodded. "Yes. Belisario died a few days ago. He was on the *Antarctic Mist* when it sank in the Patagonia. Belisario was an angel—a true angel. Always optimistic. Full of hope. Full of love. Saw the best in every situation. My mind still can't accept this tragedy. It seems impossible."

"I'm so sorry."

"Martín was more complicated," Nahuel said, filling his cup.

"Why Martín would take his own life? Was he having problems?" She blew on the stew before tasting it. It was a delicious and colorful mix of meat, carrots, potatoes, peas and cilantro.

María said, "I don't know. He went away a few years ago to study marine biology at the University of Concepcion. When he graduated, he had a hard time finding a job. He was upset about that." She paused for a moment. "He came here a few months ago. Said he'd found a job out in the Patagonia. Didn't seem very happy though. Came back looking for Padre Felipe, but he was in Santiago. He didn't come around again after that. I saw him a few times at the clinic, visiting his brother."

"The youngest brother, Emilio, is a drug addict," Nahuel said.

"Who did Martín work for?"

"I don't know. A foreign company in Aysén. His cousin probably knows."

Emmanuelle had heard the priests talking about her. "His cousin, Isabella?"

"*Sí, hijita.* Do you know her?" María looked at her, surprised.

"Yes … well, I mean … no, I don't know her. I've heard about her. I haven't met her yet," she answered, flustered.

"She's staying at the Albergue Monte Carmen until the funeral."

Her heart skipped a beat. "Where?"

"A retreat home run by nuns from Cunco. That's where I'm from." Cunco was a predominantly Mapuche city several hours north of Puerto Montt.

"Why are you so interested in Martín?" Nahuel asked. The question came like an arrow projected from a bow. A question she was dreading. She had avoided his eyes for most of the conversation, but now they locked with hers.

Emmanuelle decided that nothing she told this man was going to be relayed to authorities or anyone else she was worried about. She leaned closer, dropping her voice a notch. "I am an investigative journalist. I want to write about the dam project in the Patagonia. Not many people in the United States have heard about the proposal to build dams on the Patagonian rivers. I understand there are plans to displace the local communities out there. Flood the land. Environmentalists say it will threaten the Patagonia. You know … dams alter the environment. It affects the whole world. With climate change and the rapidly melting glaciers, these are the kinds of decisions that the world continues to pay for centuries later. Corporate decisions ultimately affect the rest of the planet." She worried about how easy the lie came out. *What next?* "I heard that Martín worked for the water company. I'm planning to go out to Aysén this week.".

"That's what you wanted to see Padre Cristóbal about?"

"Exactly. I assumed the mission could put me in touch with good sources for a story."

"I can give you names of people out there who can help you."

She reached into her bag for a notepad.

For the next hour, over the meal and many cups of tea, the three talked about the conflicts between indigenous communities and the water and forestry companies. Emmanuelle learned nothing new. Most of it had been reported in the press. But now she had some names, although she wondered whether some of the man's contacts might be in worse trouble with authorities than she was.

Emmanuelle realized that their words were echoing. Their voices became more distant by the second. Was her mind playing tricks on her? Was this just a bad dream?

"You look exhausted," María said. "Padre Cristóbal probably won't be back until the morning. I'll take you to the guest room. You can sleep there tonight. I'll clean this up after."

María led her to a small room at the end of the hall.

Emmanuelle put her bag down and sat on a wooden chair. The walls were bare but for a crucifix over the bed. There was a large statue of the Madonna with mestizo features in a corner next to a *kultrun* drum. "To keep evil spirits away," María told her.

The guest bed had a hand-embroidered bedspread and a dark blue pillow with a white moon and fleet of stars sewn onto it.

"Did you make these?" Emmanuelle asked, running her fingers over the stars.

"Yes," she said softly. María explained how she associated

Mary with the full moon; she was the symbol of birth, life, and abundance.

Emmanuelle laid her head on the pillow, listening to María's voice fading in and out. After a long recitation of prayers for Martín and Belisario, in which María called on the powers of *Virgen María*, the moon, and Old Woman Ngünechén, María blew out the light in the oil lamp by the bed and left the room.

For hours, Emmanuelle hung in a dreamlike state wondering how, in just a matter of days, her life could have fallen into such chaos and confusion. In the fog of her exhaustion, the chill of what she had learned in the past twenty-four hours lingered. Two months earlier, she would have considered herself one of the luckiest women in the world. Then Stephan was abducted and murdered and she was discovering things about him she never would have imagined. And now she was on the run from the authorities. She wondered if she was losing her mind. Tears streamed down her face. She felt like her entire being was floating, spinning, and whirling around like a speck of dust caught in the light.

Chapter 45

PADRE FELIPE MONTERO walked through the parking lot behind the cathedral, lost in the echo of his thoughts. He noticed a car he had never seen before. A deadly cold stirred over him. This wasn't a public parking lot. It was reserved for those who worked in the cathedral. The car was rolling slowly through the driveway with no headlights. With blinding brightness, the lights came on and the car sped toward him. Its windows were tinted. He couldn't see the driver. He jumped out of its way, tumbling on the wet asphalt. He turned back, straining to see the license plate. It had none. He scrambled to his feet, still watching the car as it tore down the street.

He pulled his cloak tighter and ran to the back entrance of the cathedral. Something told him Rodrigo was inside. He reached into his pocket for the key and grabbed the doorknob. It jiggled loosely. It was unlocked. His heart thudded. Thieves and vandals were plentiful in the inner cities. *No one would leave the door open in the evening.*

He stepped into the kitchen. The rectory was generally empty at this hour. There was no noise other than the humming of the refrigerator. The housekeepers had cleaned up and left early, taking advantage of the fact that everyone was out. He passed through the dining room. No one. He was the only one that slept in the building. Occasionally, celebrants lingered, reading in the library or meditating in the drawing room. Empty as well. He walked through the hall into the corridor. There was an eerie stillness about the place.

The moonlight sifted through the curtains in the drawing room. In a few minutes, he had searched the whole floor but for his office. Something told him Rodrigo would be there. From several meters away, he noticed the door open, the room in semi-darkness. The office's curtains were usually drawn in the evening, but now Puerto Montt street lights flickered in the fogged up-window. Rodrigo was there, sitting at his desk in the dark facing the window.

"Rodrigo? Why are you in the dark? What's going on?" He tried flipping the light switch, but the light didn't come on. A dim glow reflected from outside. He froze for a second, his mind whirled to the thought of the car he had seen leaving the parking lot. The room felt icy. Colder than the air outside.

"Rodrigo?" He felt like his feet were glued to the floor.

"Rodrigo?" He whispered this time, moving closer. He felt glass crunching under his shoes. He looked down. The desk lamp was on the ground. His eyes strained against the darkness as he instinctively bent down to pick it up. He noticed a shiny, dark brown patch on the rug near the desk. Reluctantly, he touched it. It was warm, viscous. It was dripping from Rodrigo's chair. *Blood.*

Felipe let out a cry of horror. Rodrigo's throat was slashed, his head resting back against the chair. His clothes were soaked in blood.

Frantically, Felipe grabbed Rodrigo's arm and felt for a pulse. There was none. His cries echoed through the cathedral.

Chapter 46

The bang on the door sounded like the blast of a shotgun. Emmanuelle scrambled in the dark.

She heard someone cry, "*Santa María del Carmelo!*"

Emmanuelle was on her feet in seconds, one hand on her chest to calm the jackhammering. She searched the shadowed room and groped for the brass candelabra on the dresser. Clutching it like a weapon, she blinked hard to adjust to the darkness. Where the hell was she? It took a few seconds to orient herself. She would swing at the first person to enter the room.

The banging grew louder. She heard frantic movement in the house. Someone yelled, "*¿Qué pasa?* What's going on?" She relaxed a bit and peered out into the halls.

Padre Javier was shuffling along in his slippers towards the front door. A long woolen robe hung loose around his pajamas. "*¿Qué pasa? ¿Quién es?*" he shouted, clutching the doorknob and turning the iron key.

Two wide-eyed, young men in fishermen sweaters and jeans were at the door. They were out of breath.

"Rodrigo was murdered!" one of them uttered, his face twisted in fear. He clutched the frame of the door as though hanging on for his life. "His throat was slit. Padre Felipe wants you to go to the Cathedral. You must come with us immediately."

Padre Javier stared dumbfounded at the two men.

Cries and exclamations of horror rang out as the news quickly traveled through the house.

"El Indio is waiting in his boat to take us across the channel," one of the men said.

Chapter 47

PREFECTO SEBASTIÁN CIENFUEGOS stood in Padre Felipe Montero's office, two meters away from Rodrigo Pacheco's corpse, studying the crime scene. The smell of copper and burnt candles hung in the air.

It was 1:00 A.M. and police cruisers and vans blocked the street in front of the cathedral. Carabineros and investigative police filled the rectory. Their uniforms and shoes were covered with protective clothing and plastic bags. They communicated with hushed voices, strenuous whispers and gestures, perhaps in keeping with the atmosphere of the cathedral.

Sebastián paced nervously. The news of the murder of the priest was going to generate explosive controversy. The investigation would have to be dealt with carefully. "Get me everything you can find on Rodrigo Pacheco. All of his background. Childhood to present," he told the two homicide detectives standing at his side. "Search police records, school records, hospital records. Everything. Take statements from anyone who'll talk," he said. "Find out where he was yesterday. Retrace his footsteps to the moment he entered this room. Talk to the housekeepers. Ask about his habits, his friends, any strange or unusual behavior." His voice trailed off to a whisper. "He was obviously wrestling in the mud just before this happened. Find out with whom and why."

"He wasn't just wrestling either," a forensic photographer said, snapping close-up pictures of the corpse, still upright in the chair. A pool of blood stained the carpet beneath it.

"His knuckles are bruised and he has abrasions on his face," Pilar said as she watched the forensic photographer shoot a close-up of a bruise on Rodrigo's right cheek. "It looks like he was in a fist-fight."

Click. Click. Click.

"He must have landed a few good blows on whoever did this." She scribbled something on a notepad and looked up at Sebastián. "Weird, *no es cierto, Señor Prefecto?*"

Sebastián eyed the mud on the dead priest's clothes and shoes.

"A *priest* in a fight? Who was he fighting with?" Pilar asked. Attacks on religious workers were extremely uncommon in Chile.

Forensic police dressed in white suits had cordoned off the room and were collecting samples of blood, body fluids, hairs, and fibers, placing them in vials, plastic bags, and containers. Others were examining the windows, the curtains, and the furniture.

"Where's Marco?" Sebastián asked the fingerprint technician as he dusted for prints, applying black fingerprint powder with a fiberglass brush.

The technician shrugged. "He said he was on his way thirty minutes ago."

Sebastián watched as he carefully applied clear tape to the prints, lifted them, and then applied them to the print card, making a few notations on the card. "If he doesn't get here soon, he won't have a job tomorrow. I want the scene videotaped before the body is moved."

"Videotaped?" Pilar asked, squatting to inspect the victim's mud-caked shoes.

Sebastián's attention was drawn to a young police officer standing by the corpse. The officer appeared about to retch. Sebastián grabbed him by the arm. "What are you doing, *huevón*? Vomit here and your neck will look like *his*," he said between clenched teeth, pointing to the corpse. "*¿Estamos claro?*" He shoved the officer out of the room.

He had everyone's attention now. "When word gets out that a priest was murdered in the cathedral, fear will ripple through this city. Do you understand? This investigation has to be handled carefully. No screw ups."

"Keep an eye on these imbeciles," he grunted under his breath to Pilar. She watched over new detectives and police on crime scenes like a hawk. He could rely on her and he needed her now. He wasn't thinking clearly. His mind was elsewhere and he knew it. He motioned for her to follow him into the hall.

"What's the story with Emmanuelle Solis?" he asked. "Has anyone located her yet?"

"I was just about to tell you ..." She was studying his eyes, reading his mind. Or *thinking* she could—which was equally irritating. "Adriana's still following her. Solis fled before the Americans got to the hotel. She went to the bus terminal, bought a ticket to Santiago with her credit card, then slipped away to Isla Tenglo." She watched for his reaction.

He avoided her eyes for a moment, glancing down the hall. A reporter was talking to Carabineros near the front entrance.

"Isla Tenglo?"

"Yes. Coincidence or what?"

"Mmmm." He crossed his arms.

"Why would she have gone there?"

"I don't know, but I'll find out."

They exchanged stares.

A homicide detective approached them. "Señor Prefecto,

Padre Felipe is coming out of the meeting now." His voice was hushed. "None of them said very much. It's like they're afraid to talk."

A cluster of priests and clergymen in purple and white silk robes and capes were whispering amongst themselves. A group of brothers from the Mount Carmel Order with no sartorial elegance to match also waited patiently in front of a door leading to the drawing room. Sebastián headed towards them.

A thin, youthful-looking priest dressed in a cream-colored chasuble adorned with an elaborate band of gold embroidery stopped him. "I'm sorry. There's a private meeting in this room. May I help you?" The man was calm, amiable, but evidently firm on keeping the police out.

Was he serious? Sebastián took out his badge. "I have to speak to Padre Felipe Montero and Padre Javier."

"*Si, Señor Prefecto.* We understand, but you'll have to wait a little. The Archbishop is meeting with them now. They are preparing to hold a mass now for Rodrigo. Perhaps you'll be able to talk to them after," the priest said, shrugging that he wasn't in charge. "May I get you some water or tea?"

"Are you saying I have to wait to speak to witnesses?" His blood pressure pulsed in his ears.

The priest looked startled, as though he'd never contemplated that police authority superseded sacerdotal priorities. He looked to the clergymen behind him for rescue. Padre Patricio Silva hurried to the task. He had been Sebastián's teacher twenty-five years earlier.

"Sebastián Cienfuegos. *Prefecto* Cienfuegos." The priest said, offering a handshake. "Congratulations on your promotion to Prefecto."

"Thank you. That was six years ago."

"Has it been that long? I remember when you were just a child."

Sebastián wondered if he heard a hint of amusement in the old man's voice. The two of them had argued often. In contrast with his invective nature, Padre Patricio had the soft, friendly gaze of a llama. Lips permanently curved upward in contrived complacency, particularly long eyelashes, a few wisps of hair that curled softly around his eyes, sprouting from the top of his head and bushy eyebrows. Sebastián was sure he practiced the gaze in the mirror to give himself the air of innocence that priesthood required.

"So, what can you tell me?" Sebastián said.

"We don't know yet. Monsignor Montero found him dead in his office. The only thing like this that ever happened before was the unforgettable murder in Santiago ten years ago by that … satanist." It sounded more like a stifled cough than a word. A puzzled, fearful look drew his face.

"Did Rodrigo have any enemies? Was he in any kind of dispute with anyone?"

"We don't know. *Osea*, there are some who had their differences with him, but I am not sure how significant those differences were," the priest said quietly.

"What does that mean?"

He shrugged.

"Are you saying there was some kind of conflict between priests?"

Padre Patricio stared at him blankly. He wasn't going to offer more. Not now, at least.

"I need to speak to Padre Felipe Montero."

"Yes. I am sure he will talk to you but he's with the Archbishop now."

"Later won't do. Now."

"*Tranquilo*, Prefecto. You won't resolve anything by being angry and impatient."

The archbishop and several prelates emerged from a

backroom. They spoke in low voices, ignoring the police, looking around to verify that no one uninvited to their circle was within hearing range. More clergymen gathered around them as they moved into the drawing room, some were crying. A very fat bishop whose cassock fit him like sausage-casing appeared to be consoling them as they gathered for a prayer.

Sebastián heaved a sigh. The air was humid and dense. News of the priest's death was no doubt traveling quickly. People were already gathering on the main street outside of the church. Maybe as many as a hundred or more. The sirens of police cars and ambulances would surely alert the town.

"*Por Dios Santo*. Mercy of God," a voice cried out in the night.

Sebastián spotted Javier among the clergymen at the Archbishop's side. He felt a surge of relief to see someone he knew. He felt certain Javier would talk to him. He and Javier had been inseparable throughout high school until suddenly, without explanation, Javier made a decision to enter the seminary.

Javier acknowledged him, raking a hand through his thick, shabbily cut hair and slipping away from the crowd to greet Sebastián. They had barely spoken for years.

Sebastián tried not to stare, but Javier looked odd dressed in a clergy shirt with a clerical collar.

"*¿Cómo estai?*" They embraced. Sebastián patted Javier loudly on the back.

"Sebastián, how have you been?" They regarded each other for a moment.

"It's good to see you."

Javier looked nervous, disheveled and very self-conscious.

"The question is, how are *you*, Javier? A priest murdered in the rectory office of the cathedral? *¿Qué cresta está pasando?* What the hell is going on?" Sebastián's eyes fixed on the clerical collar.

Javier ran a finger along the inside of it, trying to straighten it out. It looked worse when he finished. Sebastián guessed that putting it on had been an afterthought, something that occurred to him after he was out the door.

"I don't know," Javier said, in a low voice. He squirmed in his collar. "We aren't sure what happened or why."

"Do you have any idea who might have done this? Were there threats against him or anyone in the church? Why would someone harm him?"

Javier blinked twice before answering. "I don't know... I don't know what to say."

"You can start by giving me some background information on Rodrigo Pacheco."

"I'll have to wait."

"Wait for what, Javier?"

Javier just stood there, looking defenseless.

"Talk to me. What are you afraid of? What's going on?" Sebastián caught movement outside a window. The fat priest was outside now, lighting up a cigarette.

"We are seeking the assistance of the Cardinal. I think they've decided we should wait until he arrives before we talk to any authorities. He's on his way from Santiago. I am sure there'll be a communication from the church soon."

"*¿En serio?* A communication from the church? What's going on? Is there some kind of conflict within the church? A priest was murdered and you expect Carabineros and PDI to wait for an official communication from the church before interviewing witnesses?"

Javier didn't answer. The fat priest was blowing smoke rings.

"Tell me something, Javier. Why is Emmanuelle Solis staying at Casa de Tenglo?"

He looked genuinely confounded. "Who?"

"Emmanuelle Solis. A lawyer. Long brown hair, heart-shaped face, running from American authorities. Does that jar your memory?"

"Oh," he replied, shifting his weight from one foot to another and glancing nervously at his colleagues still in the antechamber. "I'm sorry, Sebastián. I have to get back to the others."

"Where was Rodrigo yesterday?"

Javier shrugged.

"Did you see him yesterday?"

"No."

"Today?"

"No."

"What about the others? Did any of them see him or talk to him today? Everyone's talking over *there*." He jutted his chin in the direction of the clergymen gathered in the antechamber. "What are they saying?"

"I don't know. I am here with you." He avoided eye contact.

"Did Rodrigo Pacheco have any enemies?"

"The church always has its enemies."

"Did *Rodrigo Pacheco* have enemies? Do you know any reason why anyone would want him dead?"

"No, Rodrigo was a good man. Spiritually devoted to God."

"Spiritual? He was in a fistfight right before this happened. Judging from the bruises on his fists, he probably broke someone's jaw right before he was murdered. How spiritual is that? Do you know where he was right before this happened?"

It suddenly went silent. Sebastián hadn't intended to raise his voice so loud. Several of the priests stopped talking and were staring at him.

He leaned closer to Javier and lowered his voice. "There was mud on his clothes. He'd obviously been in a brawl. Is there anyone you are aware of that he might have had a conflict with?"

"I just told you. I don't know." He wrung his hands. His voice sank to a whisper. "Sebastián, I would like to help with your investigation, but there is nothing I can say that will help you."

"Just tell me what you know. I can help you. You can trust me, Javier." His eyes searched Javier's for the connection they'd shared years ago, but Javier was different now. He reflected a silent repose that Sebastián didn't understand.

"You'll have to excuse me. We're preparing for a special service." His eyes implored patience.

Sebastián watched his friend walk away. Outside, the fat priest was staring at him now. He must have been blowing his third cigarette in fifteen minutes. He blew a smoke ring in Sebastián's direction. It floated and hit the window.

Chapter 48

SEBASTIÁN LEFT THE rectory on foot and headed to the office of the *Comisario de Carabineros.* The sun would rise over Puerto Montt in just a few hours. When it did, the murder of the priest would throw the entire city into panic. Even the smell of rain-washed grass could not mask the stench of death still stinging his nostrils. It bothered him profoundly. Like everything else about the case. His men had thoroughly probed the crime scene. They had talked to every potential witness in the rectory. Right now, they had nothing to even remotely explain why a well-regarded priest had his throat cut in the cathedral.

His thoughts, though, kept shifting to another matter. Emmanuelle Solis' insistence on a link between the *Antarctic Mist* incident and the disappearance of Stephan Henri Brent. Connections between Calle Vicente Perez Rosales and projects in the Patagonia *were* surfacing.

The press was demanding answers. It was already formulating theories about the *Antarctic Mist.* There was pressure on the Chilean government from Norway, Germany and Sweden to resolve what happened to the ship. Their nationals had been aboard. Soon business interests and politicians would steer the investigations. *Mierda.* Rodrigo Pacheco's murder had just lit a new fire under his ass.

Chapter 49

A Carabinero on duty in front of the Comisario's office opened the door for Sebastián before he reached the steps of the building "*Buenos días, Señor Prefecto.*"

More officers stood up to greet him as he walked in. "*Buenos días, Señor Prefecto.*" Their faces said they believed he had the answers everyone was waiting for.

He hurried past them and marched up the three flights of stairs to Comisario Olivares office, knocking on the door.

The police commissioner was expecting him. "*Adelante Sebastián.* Come in."

Sebastián opened the door. "*Permiso.*"

He felt the Commissioner's eyes rummaging his for information. They picked up on it immediately. He knew the answer even before Sebastián uttered a word.

"What have we got?"

"We've got squat."

"You weren't able to get any information from the priests?"

"No, the priests aren't talking. Padre Patricio suggested there might have been some disagreement or conflict between the priests, but he wouldn't say what it was about. I thought Javier Salas would talk to me, but he didn't. Andrea and Tonio took statements from the staff. Let's see what forensics comes up with. They took enough samples to clone the priest."

"A disagreement between the priests about what?"

"I have no idea. *Ni idea.*"

The Comisario pressed the button on his intercom system and called the *mayordomo*—a middle-aged, thin man of minor ranking in the Carabineros' hierarchy who slept at the Comisaría at night and did any kind of task he was called to do by officials, including preparing food and fetching things. "Bring us two cortados and something to eat."

Sebastián contemplated sitting down. "They seem to have a pact of silence. They're waiting for orders from the Cardinal, they say." He decided to stand. "One more thing, it may just be coincidence, but that kid from the *barrio bajo* was murdered."

The Commissioner looked puzzled.

"The kid from the slums who your men wrote off as a suicide, Martín Araya. He was with Rodrigo Pacheco less than a half hour before he was killed."

"What makes you believe it was murder?"

The mayordomo came in with a tray of cortados, empanadas—still smoking from a microwave blitz—and a tray of assorted cookies. Comisario Olivares put sugar in his coffee, picked up an empanada and bit into it. "Sit down, Sebastián. Eat something." He pointed to the chair with his spoon and then used it to stir his coffee.

Sebastián looked at the tray and shook his head. He needed to wash his hands. Take a shower. Change his clothes. He felt grimy. The way he always felt after investigating a bloody crime scene.

Comisario Olivares sipped his coffee.

Sebastián waited for the Mayordomo to leave. "Pilar identified signs of strangulation—bruises on his neck and indications of blunt force that weren't consistent with a suicide by hanging. She returned with a few of my men after yours left yesterday. They conducted a detailed investigation of the scene. She was there when the coroner examined the body. They determined the type of ligature used, the knot, how it was tied, the number of times it was wrapped around his neck, bruises on his neck, the method of ligature application—it adds up to murder. The coroner's report now confirms it."

"Why the thorough investigation? He's just a street kid."

"Pilar is convinced someone wanted it to look like a suicide. Padre Felipe Montero showed up during the investigation. Martín lived in his shelter. That's his connection to Rodrigo Pacheco. He was strangled and then he was hanged. Whoever did it tore the panels off the walls as though they were looking for something. They ravaged the place. I know it's possibly sheer coincidence, but the timing ..."

The Comisario nodded. "Sheer coincidence, I'm sure."

"Less than an hour later, Rodrigo was murdered."

The Comisario dusted a few crumbs from his uniform before moving on to the sweets. He alternated between a flaking sugar wafer and sipping his coffee. "You think there's a connection?" Flakes fell on his uniform.

"I don't know. We have information that Martín was at the Cathedral with Rodrigo right before he was murdered. I tried to talk to Javier, but it was impossible. He said the priests wanted to speak to the Cardinal before they talked to authorities. I sensed, though, that Patricio would talk soon."

The Comisario licked sugared pastry flakes from his lips.

"Your men took a statement from Martín's cousin, Isabella Riquelme. Do they know where she is?"

Comisario Olivares summoned an officer into the room and asked him a few questions about the interview.

The officer took a notepad from his jacket pocket. "We have a home address for her in Chiloe. She didn't know where she'd be staying while she's in Puerto Montt." He looked at the pad. "I'll have someone check on it, but I would imagine she'd stay here for the funeral. I'll find out when it is."

Sebastián waited for the officer to leave before speaking again. "Padre Felipe Montero went to Tenglo Island last night—right after he learned that Martín was dead. We know because we have Emmanuelle Solis under surveillance. She's been there since yesterday."

"*¿Qué?*" Comisario Olivares said, looking astounded. "She's staying at Casa de Tenglo? *Interestante.* What's *her* connection to these priests?"

"*Ni idéa.* But I'll find out soon. I know she's running from Byrns and Thorman. She left my office very distressed. *Osea,* she has this … crazy theory. She thinks there's a connection between the *Antarctic Mist* case and the disappearance of that lawyer, Stephan Henri Brent. She thinks Thorman is involved in some criminal conspiracy related to the Patagonia." He leaned against the ledge of the window. He debated telling the Commissioner about the stock certificates that were now in his office.

"Have you talked to Solis since yesterday?"

"No. She was convinced Brent's abduction in Argentina had something to do with corporate projects in the Patagonia." He thought for a moment. "Martín Araya had a brother who was on the *Antarctic Mist*. He was a volunteer for the scientific expedition team. You have to wonder if these events could possibly be connected. There are so many coincidences surfacing."

"I don't know," the Commissioner said. "You could be shooting at hens if you try to go down that path. Sometimes these absurd coincidences lead to nowhere but a waste of everyone's time."

"Have you heard more from Byrns?"

"No. They still haven't formally requested our assistance."

"Don't provide them with any information unless they do."

"I don't plan to. Byrns doesn't work for the United States Embassy anymore."

"*¿En serio?* There's your answer to why he isn't following the protocol for criminal interrogations. How do you know that?"

"A colleague in Santiago. The administration eliminated Byrn's position from the Embassy a year ago. But I'm confused. He *was* riding around in a car with diplomatic plates."

"That doesn't mean anything. So, he still has connections. Friends, maybe. But that doesn't make it a visit from the U.S. government. I'm going to request information about him from the United States State Department."

"He's rumored to be CIA."

"Rumored. Maybe he's just a son of a bitch criminal who wants everyone to think he's CIA. Maybe that's why they got rid of him."

"*Interesante…*"

"I'll call a few colleagues at Interpol also. Maybe someone will know. As far as I am concerned, he has no right to be investigating her on Chilean soil without a Letters Rogatory request."

"I agree." The Comisario bit at a hangnail. "So, why do you think she is running? I mean, innocent people don't usually run."

"According to her, Brent came across information implicating lawyers in their firm in some criminal activity, possibly related to the Calle Vicente Perez Rosales operation. She claims he was about to go to the authorities when he disappeared. She says he called her the night before she came here and said he'd escaped and was on the run. According to her, he asked her to bring files that supposedly had some kind of evidence. They were going to turn them over to authorities here. She brought the files, but he never showed up. She thinks he was murdered because he was going to blow the whistle on them. The one thing I can say in her defense is that her story is consistent. She left the files in my office."

"What's in them?"

"Mostly documents relating to projects in the Patagonia. *Estraño.*" He wondered again whether he should mention the stock certificates. Maybe her law firm was hurting. Maybe some of the partners *were* involved in investment fraud.

"What else is in the files?" the Commissioner asked.

He gazed at the traffic below. "I'm not sure. Most of the documents are in English. We have to get them translated." Mist was billowing about on the streets below. "I am going to send them to the attorney for the Ministry of the Economy. Oh … and there are satellite images in the files, too."

"Of what?"

"I don't know. Santiago should be able to confirm the location."

Comisario Olivares opened a drawer and pulled out a file. "I guess you haven't seen this yet. Interpol sent this in to both of us. It's more background on Solis. Everything she said checks out except the phone call from Brent."

Sebastián glanced back at the Comisario. "What do you mean?"

"Apparently, she *did* get a call from Argentina early in the morning the day before she came here. But it wasn't from Brent. The call was traced to Gilberto Pereira."

"Gilberto Pereira?" Anger pulsed through Sebastián's veins.

"Yes, Gilberto Pereira. Brazilian authorities believe he runs a major transcontinental investment fraud operation, possibly linked to Calle Vicente Perez Rosales."

"I know. We are on them." It hit a raw nerve. "So, he's her connection to Calle Vicente Perez Rosales," he said grimly. He pictured her face. He had fallen for her lies.

"Interpol must be tracing her phone."

Rage churned on Sebastián's insides. He stood by the

window, unzipped his jacket and shoved the pane open. Winter swirled into the room in cold, moist gusts. Heat rose from his chest. He breathed the cool air in deeply and watched the traffic roll on the wet street below. It rained gently, but endlessly outside. He had the sudden urge to be alone. He wanted to walk in the rain. It might cleanse him of all the filth he felt around him.

"The Argentines confirmed Brent's identity even though the body was pretty charred. North American newspapers today are claiming he was tortured and killed by a group protesting South American water takeovers. They suspect a small leftist group connected to an Argentine socialist organization. They asked for a ransom. Interpol believes they get support from Venezuelan and Colombian rebel groups. They claim the organization instigates protests and rallies people against the US and its operations in Latin America."

"Which organization is it?" Sebastián's voice couldn't conceal his skepticism.

"EPA. Ejercito del Pueblo de Argentina."

"EPA? How is it that I've never heard of EPA before?"

"I don't know. I guess it's a very small group. Relatively new. Supposedly opposed to the political influence of the United States and foreign monopolization of the region's natural resources."

"Those theories reflect North American short-sightedness. They don't understand the realities of those groups. They usually put little bombs in empty buildings. That's their *modus operandi* for attacking international businesses, banks, and political groups. They never do anything this big or drastic. I haven't heard of them kidnapping and torturing foreign executives before. They have no money and very little popular support in the region."

"The United States claims they use kidnapping and ransom

to fund their operations. And there's a good possibility that Brent's family was contacted for a ransom."

"What makes you believe that?"

"Because Interpol traced calls made from Pereira's number—the same number he used to call Emmanuelle—to a Canadian who is Brent's only living relative." Olivares said, handing him the report.

Sebastián snatched it from him. "Really?" He scanned it, aware of the Commissioner's scrutinizing eyes. He felt self-conscious.

"Yes. Apparently Brent has a brother in Canada who is the CEO of a mineral exploration company. US investigators believe that Pereira might have called him for ransom. The family might have chosen *not* to contact the police if Brent's abductors threatened to kill him in retaliation. They are tracing bank activity on his accounts to see if any big amounts of money were transferred over the last few weeks. If they didn't pay the ransom and Brent was murdered, they might not want to go to the police now either. They might be afraid of the press running with the story. *Osea*, that the press might claim Brent was killed because the family refused to pay the ransom."

"I don't know. Something is missing from the equation. There could be thousands of suspects for kidnapping and ransom in Argentina. Even government officials and members of the police force are involved in that kind of crime. What's the name of the company?"

"I don't know. The report doesn't say."

Sebastián turned around and faced the Commissioner. "I need to talk to her. Is there anything else? Did you find out anything else about her?"

"Not much. As for the rest, it's all just as she said. Her father was a Chilean-born economist who worked for the OAS. He was well connected to diplomatic and social circles in D.C. Her mother was an environmentalist who worked for a

Geneva-based scientific institute. She lived a fairly privileged life, traveled all over the world, went to the best schools, on to law school, worked for a prominent law firm in the United States. Her half-brother is Camilo Solis Ossandón, Alejandro Ossandón's grandson."

"You mean, Alejandro Ossandón—the horse-breeder from Puerto Aysén?"

"Yes. The girl's from a good family. Good people from the south." In the Comisario's mind, there were only two types of men in Chile. *Huasos*, or cowboys, and *rotos*, vulgar city people. "The Ossandon's are southern gentlemen. Courteous countrymen, educated, though not terribly wealthy, but they know how to ride a horse," he said, straightening his posture. "She doesn't exactly fit the profile of a Latin American left wing activist, does she?"

Sebastián had been pretending to scribble notes. He shut his notebook and looked up at the Comisario. It was as though he had read his thoughts. "No. She doesn't. It's perplexing."

"And there is one more theory," the Commissioner continued. "She was angry with the firm when she was told she wouldn't make partner. So she might have had an axe to grind."

Sebastián stared unblinkingly out the window. "Who told you that?" The lack of sleep burned in his eyes.

"It's in the report Olivares replied. "That's what Byrns told them. I guess the ... *guatón,* the fat lawyer told Byrns."

"We can't rely on those thugs for information. You just said that Byrns doesn't work for the embassy and it's possible he's lying about his representation of the U.S. government."

"I know, but he insists the U.S. government is processing a request to conduct an interrogation of her here. If so, we will have to cooperate. Any update on the men who broke into Solis' hotel room?" Olivares asked.

"We have a picture of two suspects—men who entered the

building just before her room was ransacked. Isauro confirmed they aren't hotel clients." Sebastián showed the Comisario the photo.

"Who took the pictures?"

"The hotel had surveillance cameras installed because of all of the protests and vandalism taking place."

"That's what I thought." The Comisario nodded approvingly. "Isauro informed us Solis was headed to Calle Vicente Perez Rosales. Seems like our training was effective." He put his reading glasses on and took a better look at the picture. "Do you have any idea who these men are?"

"Interpol is trying to identify them. Isauro said one had a foreign accent. The housekeeper and cook gave us a description of two men who entered the rectory right before the murder. They were dressed like priests. The cook said one of them was talking on a big cell phone. Based on the description, I assume it was a satellite phone. She said he wore fancy boots. She also said he had an accent."

"Venezuelan? Colombian? Argentine?"

"Couldn't distinguish."

There was a loud knock on the door. Pilar appeared. "*Permiso*, Comisario Olivares, Prefecto Cienfuegos."

"*Adelante*, Pilar. Come in."

She was out of breath.

"*¿Que pasa*, Pilar? What did you find out?"

She opened a file and took out a picture. "We have a witness. He was walking down the plaza when he saw Rodrigo Pacheco in a fist-fight with this man. He took pictures with his cell phone. Look."

The three huddled around the picture.

"I have seen him before." Sebastián took it from Pilar and examined it closely. "I know the little bastard," he said. "Isn't that Bruno Barilla Perez?"

Chapter 50

THE ANNOUNCEMENT OF Rodrigo Pacheco's murder turned Emmanuelle's blood to ice. The instinct that had led her to Tenglo Island now paralyzed her with terror. A connection between the recent murders and Stephan's abduction and murder now seemed very real. What were the killers after? What did the victims know that got them killed? No doubt the Prefecto was at the crime scene. She wondered what he had found out. Would he share it with her? She wanted to call him but she knew that might backfire miserably on her now.

She strained her ears for sounds from the shadowed hallway. For one impulsive moment, she wanted to run as fast as she could. To escape to someplace far away and hide. But *where* didn't occur to her. She knew she needed information that maybe only someone in this house could give her. María was bordering hysteria so she wasn't an option. She probably didn't know more anyway. Nahuel seemed nervous and agitated, constantly stepping outside for phone calls. If he had such a close relationship to the priests, why had he not gone to the cathedral with the rest of the men after learning of the murder?

In her opinion, whoever was responsible wasn't likely to stop now. Would they come after her next, like Stephan had warned? Emmanuelle crumpled on a sofa in the front room, searching the shadows for the faceless monster that she felt was lurking somewhere. Every shadow seemed to have a human form. She had turned on every light in the house. Only the kitchen had an overhead light in this damn place. The few battered table lamps and sconces in the house seemed to cast more shadows than light. She fed logs into the woodstove, hoping the fire would keep her from trembling like a heroin addict. Flinching at the creaking floor, she decided she'd wait for Padre Cristóbal to appear. She tried to imagine what he would be like. Was he some kind of a saint? Or a renegade? Had he left the church for the class struggle? Did he really harbor criminals? What was that all about?

Shortly after midnight, a clanking noise outside sent a crawling feeling over Emmanuelle's body. She reached for the fire iron and stepped into the shadowed hallway, evaluating her options. Someone outside slid a key into the keyhole. It twisted, clicked. The door swung open letting in a blast of cold air.

A strange figure entered the house. A thin, frail-looking old man jousting with the wind to close the door. His long, white hair was a wind-blown mess. The light from the sconce on the wall behind him illuminated it. He had pale blue eyes, crepe paper skin and the veins on his temples looked like they'd been inked in. He was either Padre Cristóbal or an escapee from a mental institution.

María emerged from the halls, puffy-eyed. "Padre Cristóbal. I heard noises at the door. Thank God, it's you. *Por Dios*, we have terrible news." Nahuel was one step behind her.

"I heard," Padre Cristóbal said mournfully. "I saw the PDI and Carabinero vans in front of the cathedral from the port. I knew something dreadful had happened. I went straight there."

Emmanuelle watched the men from the shadows.

The priest took a few staggering steps into the room, dropped his battered travel bag on the pedestal table and collapsed on the sofa. Nahuel, with the care of a son for his father, lifted his feet and slid a footstool beneath them.

María disappeared to the kitchen.

"Nahuel, maybe you should leave."

Nahuel appeared startled. "Padre, you couldn't think that I…."

He dismissed it with a feeble wave. "Word is out that you and Rodrigo had an argument last week. He told other priests he intended to keep you from coming around Tenglo again. Carabineros will figure you or someone connected to you took revenge. You need to be careful. They'll be pressed to make an arrest."

"Do Carabineros know we argued?"

"The clergy hasn't spoken to authorities yet. They're waiting for the Cardinal to arrive from Santiago. We both know the divisions in our church. And I can't protect you here. They are divided about me. Most of them would ex-communicate me if it they had the opportunity. This might just be it. They've been trying to pressure Felipe to kick me out of here."

"Padre, I understood Rodrigo's position. I respected it. I wasn't angry at him."

"I know that, but it doesn't matter now. Carabineros will come looking for you and arrest you anyway as soon as they find out. They will, you know. Padre Patricio, *tu sabí po*, you know how he feels."

Emmanuelle edged closer to the drawing room, peering at them from the shadows. What had Nahuel and Rodrigo argued about?

"Padre, do they have any idea who killed Rodrigo and why?"

"Nahuel, the only suspect at this point is you in the eyes of some of the other priests. I sometimes wonder if God is listening to my prayers," the old priest said. His voice was sad, his eyes closed.

María appeared holding a tray with a teapot and cups. She

placed the tray on the table and left again.

Nahuel covered the priest's legs with a blanket. The priest rested his head back on the sofa while Nahuel poured him a cup of tea.

"All of our brothers know how opposed Rodrigo was to priests getting involved with Mapuche activists." His hands were cupped around the mug as if he were trying to dispel the chill. It was the kind of chill Emmanuelle felt for the last few days.

"Last week, after the protests in Cunco," he continued, "Rodrigo delivered an angry sermon to me in front of Padre Patricio and several others. He said that love for the poor shouldn't be exclusive. That the notion that getting people to Heaven is more important than providing them with tolerable living conditions. He said I was bent on getting the church to refocus on *this* life. But I ask, how are we to be Christians in a world of injustice and destruction? Poverty and injustice are difficult to accept. They claim, and very wrongfully, that my primary concern is this world, not the next. I can't change their perspective. Eventually it will become known to the Carabineros that these divisions exist among us. They will probably start gathering up the usual suspects from your community and accuse one of them of taking revenge on Rodrigo. I only pray that…."

"Padre … that's absurd. No one in our community would hurt Rodrigo or any other priest. I always knew how he felt. But he wasn't our enemy. He was our brother. Rodrigo did so much for the Mapuche community. No one expects priests to be involved in our politics." He leaned forward, staring into the fire.

Emmanuelle, still watching from the shadows, knew she had to tell them what she knew.

"Rodrigo has bruises on his face and body. He fought with someone before he was killed. Rodrigo always had a temper.

But for him to get into a fight … that would require someone attack him," the old priest said.

Nahuel sat in stunned silence. His eyes were two dark pools. "My God. What could have happened?"

Padre Cristóbal seemed to be examining his face, searching it for answers.

Emmanuelle suddenly understood just how easily innocent people could be arrested for crimes they had nothing to do with. She *had* to talk to them. "*Permiso* Padre Cristóbal," she broke in.

The priest was startled. "Who are *you*?"

"Señorita Solis, not now." Nahuel gave her an irritated look. "I need a few minutes alone with Padre."

"Nahuel, I was listening to your conversation. I have to confess something to you. I lied; I'm not a journalist. I am an attorney. I need to tell you both why I am here. I think I have information that you need to know. It could be related to Rodrigo's murder."

Nahuel eyed her with new interest. Cristóbal looked baffled.

"I don't think Martín committed suicide. I think he was murdered." Both men exchanged glances. "Martín was going to go to PDI right before he was killed. He was supposed to go with Rodrigo. And Rodrigo was murdered right after Martín died. I believe they were both killed because of what they were about to tell the police."

"What was he about to tell the police and how would you know?"

She took a deep breath, hesitating.

"What are you talking about?" the priest asked.

"I apologize," she approached him, putting a hand on his before sitting on the arm of the sofa. "I'm not making sense to you. Let me explain from the beginning."

They listened as she told the whole story.

Nahuel said, "So, you're not a journalist?" He poured tea

into another cup and handed it to her.

She accepted it. "No, I'm a lawyer. A lawyer on the run."

"Why did you come to me? What did you think I can I do for you?" the priest asked.

"I read news articles about your mediating disputes between indigenous groups and the government. I was hoping you could help me to understand the conflict related to the dam project. I thought there might be some connection to Stephan's abduction. But everything I learn keeps pointing in the same direction. I'm certain the *Antarctic Mist* was sabotaged, and I am afraid someone in my office is involved."

"You say that Padre Felipe suspected Martín was murdered?" Cristóbal said, inhaling the word. He sat up. "I didn't see Felipe at the cathedral. He would have shared that with me even though the others keep me at bay."

She nodded and told him what she had heard him say. "A short while later, Rodrigo was murdered. Padre Felipe said he suspected they never made it to PDI."

"So, maybe Martín confessed something to Rodrigo," Nahuel said.

The tension eased and Emmanuelle felt she could breathe again. Nahuel clearly preferred a theory that would clear Mapuche activism.

"Yes. The interesting thing is Martín was working for some company out in Aysén. News reports today suggest the *Antarctic Mist* was sabotaged. A possible explosion on board. If it was sabotaged and Martín was somehow involved, that would explain why Martín was crying in the church saying he'd killed his brother, right? His brother was aboard. He may have confessed to Rodrigo and then they decided to go to authorities."

"That's absurd. Martín would never have been involved in sabotage," Cristóbal protested. "He wouldn't sabotage a ship his brother was on."

Nahuel opened the door to the woodstove and fed it another log. "Maybe he didn't know Belisario would be on the ship."

The priest waved his hand dismissively.

"Do you know who he worked for?" Emmanuelle asked.

"No. I only know he worked for a foreign company," the priest said. "I don't recall the name."

"If it turns out he worked for the company that my firm is connected with, maybe my instincts are right." There were so many issues she needed to resolve. Judging from what Cristóbal and Nahuel had discussed, it seemed it would only be a matter of time before the authorities came around to Casa Tenglo to try to talk to Nahuel about Rodrigo. She didn't want to be there when they arrived.

"Do you think the police will come here tonight? Do you think they will come around and ask questions?"

"Probably not tonight. But I don't have a doubt they'll be here tomorrow." He shook his head in dismay. "It's already an investigative frenzy. I implore you both to leave before they get here" the priest said, staring at the flames.

"Does my theory seem plausible or do you think I'm wrong?"

The priest shrugged. "I don't know. There are so many foreign companies in the south now." His tone was dry. "Their mining, hydroelectric, aquatic, forestry and even nuclear waste projects threaten to destroy the area. They will irreversibly change life there forever. The Patagonia is the life reserve of the planet."

Bishops on both sides of the Patagonia had written letters to the United Nations Secretary-General, top U.N. climate officials, and other politicians. She knew that kind of letter always fell on deaf ears. She understood his frustration.

Cristóbal adjusted the blanket on his legs.

Emmanuelle continued, "If scientific reports would have jeopardized projects, it's plausible that someone with a vested interest in the projects could have been involved in the sabotage. Sinking the ship was the perfect crime. The report will never be published now. The evidence is irretrievable. There were no surviving witnesses. The entire expedition team perished."

"Not the entire team," Cristóbal said.

"What do you mean? The press reported that the entire team perished. Were there survivors?" Hope surged in her for a moment.

"The Kawésqar didn't die."

"Who?"

"Juan Carlos Messier. The scientist who put the team together."

"He wasn't aboard when it sank?"

"No."

"Do you know him?"

"Well, of course I do. He stayed behind because one of the scientists got sick before the ship left port."

"So, there are two survivors?"

"I'm not sure. Apparently, the scientist was … very sick."

"Did he die?"

"I don't know. I heard about him from one of the brothers from the Misión Don Bosco."

"Someone tried to kill him *before* the ship left," Nahuel said.

"We don't know that for a fact," Cristóbal protested with a flick of his wrist. "There are rumors to that effect. However, you have to understand. There are *always* conspiracy theories circulating whenever anything happens out there. You can't be sure."

"They say the Kawésqar is hiding the scientist. He believes someone tried to kill him," Nahuel insisted. "Just about everyone who lives in the area would agree with your theory."

"If the Kawésqar believes the scientist was poisoned and he is hiding him, that confirms or at least supports my theory. Do you know where he is?"

"He's in Puerto Edén. He has a little *palafito*, you know, one of those stilted houses on the edge of the water."

Emmanuelle had to find him. The thought of calling Prefecto Cienfuegos crossed her mind again. She wanted to tell him what she knew. But that would be risky. She had no idea what had transpired since she fled. They could be fixing to arrest her for all she knew. "Do you think I could talk to Martín's cousin, Isabella?"

"She's staying at the Albergue Monte Carmen until the funeral. Padre Felipe authorized it because she is Martín's cousin. He always favored Martín. I can have someone take you there in the morning. But both of you must be gone by the break of dawn or you'll be in for an encounter with Carabineros." The priest's voice was forlorn. He sounded defeated. It was the voice of a man who was wondering whether his life-long struggle had been an exercise in futility. He stood and walked down the hall.

Chapter 51

"SANTIAGO WILL BE up my ass with a microscope if this investigation doesn't draw conclusions quickly about Rodrigo Pacheco's murder," Prefecto Sebastián Cienfuegos said. Detectives and police had gathered in his office around a conference table. News of the murdered priest was sounding off alarms and Puerto Montt authorities were spinning into a frenzy. "News reporters connect the murder of Rodrigo Pacheco to the death of Martín Araya and a series of other incidents that we have little information about. I don't want to be firing detectives and hiring news reporters because they are better at investigative work than you. *Estamos claro?*" His voice was husky with aggravation and fatigue.

A few detectives nodded in acknowledgement, afraid to speak.

"This kid was fighting with Rodrigo Pacheco right before Rodrigo was murdered. A witness is giving us a statement right now." He held up the picture. "The suspect's name is Bruno Barilla Perez. He has a long criminal record. I want him arrested." He dropped a report on the table.

All eyes went to it. No one touched it.

"Shortly before Pacheco's murder, two men entered the rectory from the back of the building. The only people in the building were staff. The cook overheard one of the men talking on a cell phone in the parking lot. Foreign accent. She assumed they were visiting priests. One had an oversized cell phone and, based on her description, I am guessing it was a satellite phone that functions in places where cellular ground-based systems are non-existent or destroyed." His mind drifted for a second to Emmanuelle's theory. He said, "Like, for example, the ice fields of the Patagonia."

"Rectory staff gave us a detailed description of the men—which seems to match the description of suspects of a break-in at the Hotel Interamericano. Take the pictures, revisit witnesses. See if anyone can identify them."

As Sebastián spoke, someone gave out photos of the men suspected of breaking into Emmanuelle's hotel room. The enlarged shots zoomed in on the men's faces.

"The curia says they weren't expecting visiting priests this week. We are running searches on the men through our photo-ID databases. Interpol and FBI are doing the same. Bruno Barilla Perez must be connected to these men. Find him."

He decided it was time to head over to Tenglo Island to have a talk with Emmanuelle Solis.

Pilar came barreling in. "Prefecto Cienfuegos, he'll be in the interrogation room in five minutes. They got him! They're bringing up Bruno Barilla Perez."

***

Sebastián opened the door to the Interrogation Room as officers ushered Bruno in. It was the smallest room in the precinct. A place that emitted the sensation that the walls were closing in on you. It had no furniture other than a tiny table with a dirty ashtray and three chairs in the center of the room.

Pilar unlocked Bruno's handcuffs and shoved him into a chair. She sat across from him. Sebastián grabbed hold of the pendant lamp and projected its light onto Bruno's face. His bottom lip was swollen and cracked. Sebastián scanned his dark copper-colored face. After examining a bruise on Bruno's left cheek, Sebastián sat down. Bruno's black eyes followed him.

"So, *huevón*, you must have missed me," Sebastián smirked. "Is that why you're back here? It's been … what? Two years now? I thought you might have straightened out."

"I don't know what the hell you want from me. You got no business arresting me." He scratched his head, fumbled through the pocket of his sweat pants and dug out a pack of cigarettes. With jittering fingers, he pulled one out.

Sebastián plucked it from his fingers and broke it in half. "If you light a *pucho* while I'm in this room, I am going to make you eat it." He dropped the broken cigarette in the ashtray. "Where were you last night, *huevón?*"

"Didn't she tell you? I was with your mother, *sapo quico.*"

"Keep pulling out the rope, *cabrito.* You can use it hang yourself when we book you with double-murder." Sebastián stared coldly at Bruno.

"*Double-murder?* You're crazy! What the devil are you talking about, psycho cop?"

"Why were you fighting with Rodrigo Pacheco? Why did you kill him?"

"You're crazy. I didn't kill Rodrigo. I don't know what you're talking about."

"Really? *Mira, huevón* … we have witnesses. And we have pictures of you and Rodrigo fighting right before he was killed." He took the pictures out of a folder and placed them in front of Bruno.

Bruno swallowed and looked away.

"*Now* do you remember what you were doing last night?"

Bruno clutched the pack of cigarettes, squeezing it into his fist. "Look, I didn't kill Rodrigo. He started attacking me." He squirmed in his chair. Sebastián liked it when suspects squirmed. It meant they felt powerless and isolated.

"*Pucha.* That's lame, you little scum. I thought even *you* were capable of coming up with a better story." He paused and stretched the silence out.

Sweat had broken out on Bruno's upper lip and forehead.

"We have your prints all over the crime scene."

"What? That's bullshit. You lying *hijo de puta!* I didn't go near the cathedral. I didn't kill him. He came to *my* house and starting hitting me. He just went crazy. I don't know what the hell he was talking about. *¿Cachaí?* I don't care if you believe me, *sapo quico.*"

"You'd better start talking. We have fingerprints, witnesses, photographs. It's a tight case and, *créame,* the whole country will want to see a little *resentido-conche-su-madre* scum like you fry for this."

"You don't have my prints because I wasn't anywhere near him when he was killed. I didn't do it." He went silent.

Pilar was taking notes. "Talk or we book you now."

At length he said, "Look, my boss, Lucas Braga called me yesterday."

Pilar looked up. "Who?"

"Lucas Braga. I work for GM. I've been working for GM for a year now."

"What's GM?" Pilar asked, writing it down.

"Grupo Meridional. I'm a driver for the company. Look, I cleaned up. That's why you haven't seen me in two years. I work a real job now … I got a kid. My girlfriend had a baby. It changed me, *po'hombre.* I swear. I take care of them. I work for real now."

"*Ya y*? So what does a little *pastel* like you do for GM?" Sebastián asked.

"I take their workers around. Anywhere they need to go. That's it. Most of their workers aren't from here. I help them get oriented. I take them to government offices. Or anywhere they need to go. Like to get their paperwork done. You know. *Trámites.* A new worker comes in. I take him to *Registro Civil* so he can get his cédula, work permits, licenses. That's it, man."

"Aahh. *Ya. Claro.* Of course." Sebastián crossed his arms. "So, why did you kill Martín and Rodrigo?"

"Like I said, I didn't kill nobody. *Cachai?* Why would I do that?"

"Because you're a low-class, *resentido conche-su-madre.*"

"You're crazy! Fucking pyscho cop!"

"Tranquilo," Pilar stepped in. Her voice was calm, soothing. "Tell us what happened."

Bruno's eyes shifted to Pilar. They pleaded for mercy. Maybe he would talk to her.

Sebastián sat back in his chair and waited.

"So, yesterday I got a call from Lucas Braga. He said some guys came looking for Martín."

"How do you know Martín?"

"We lived together when we were young."

Pilar and Sebastián exchanged glances. "You mean in the San Paolo Shelter?"

"Yeah."

"So you knew Rodrigo Pacheco well?"

"Sí, po, huevón. Of course, I knew him well. He ran the shelter when Padre Felipe left."

"So?"

"So, it's like this, man. I helped Martín get the job with GM."

"And how did you do that, *huevón?*"

"I told him they needed a biologist. I took Martín to meet Braga."

"So what did Lucas Braga say to you when he called you yesterday?

"That two men came around saying they wanted to know

where he was. They wanted to know, like, now. Like, immediately, *cachai? Urgente.*"

"Why did he call you?"

"Because I know Martín, *huevón.*"

"Walk me through it. What happened?"

"It's like this, I got my kid with me at my house and these guys show up. So, one of the guys, he says, 'Where's Martín Araya?' I say, How do I know, *huevón?* I'm not his mother. So, *como que,* like, one of the guys, the bigger guy, he grabs me by the neck. So, I say hey, *que chucha stai haciendo, huevón?* I tell him, I haven't seen Martín for weeks. I tell him where Martín lives, but I don't know if he's there. So they start getting rough, *cachai?* Threatening me, and one of the guys says he wants me to take them to Martín's place. Personally—like, *I* drive them there. So I'm scared, and I agree to take them."

"What did they look like?"

"They weren't from here. You know like … they talked funny. One of them had a nose like a boxer. Flat and ugly. He talked just like Lucas Braga. Same accent."

"Brazilian?"

"Yeah. The other guy was skinny. Fancy boots. Tattoo on his neck. Weird accent. He spoke Spanish, but he wasn't from here."

"And so what happened next, *pastelito?*" Sebastián straightened up. "Finish your story, *huevón.*"

"So, like I said, I told them where he lived, but they wanted me to take them there. And we got on the street, *cachai?* They wanted me to get into their car. They're pushing and shoving me. And suddenly, out of nowhere Rodrigo Pacheco shows up on the street outside of my house. Clerical collar and all, standing there, yelling over at me, saying he wants to talk to me. Then he started screaming at the guys, the foreigners, saying he knew what they'd done. Saying he was going to call out the *pacos* on them. People start coming out to see what's going on. The guys get into their car and take off, *cachai*?"

"*Ya y?*"

"So, then Rodrigo, who I thought was coming to save my ass, comes up to me, grabs me by my ear, like I'm some kid or something, and asks me who they were. He wanted their names. I say I don't know. He says we're going to the *pacos* now. He starts blaming me. Then, he hits me. Starts attacking me. So I punched the son-of-a-bitch back. Crazy son-of-bitch priest. Can you understand that? *¿Que cucha es esta we'a?* Then I left. I went home. To my girlfriend and my kid."

"What was Rodrigo Pacheco yelling at you about?"

"I don't know, *po'hombre.* I have no idea what his problem was."

"*Ahh … ya.* So … let me see if I understand. All of the sudden, out of nowhere, for no reason, a priest saves you from two ugly men and then he attacks you?"

"Believe what you want, *sapo quiko.*"

Pilar said, "Bruno, what was Rodrigo saying when he was screaming?"

"He was saying something about Martín getting into trouble."

"In trouble how?"

"I don't know. Look, that's all I know. I don't know nothing else. You want more, talk to my lawyer."

Sebastián stood up and headed for the door. He glanced back at Pilar. "Charge him with double-murder." He motioned to the officers on the other side of the mirrored glass.

A second later, the door swung open. Two undercover PDI agents stepped in and Sebastián walked out.

Bruno screamed after him, "*Maricón*, psycho cop. I didn't do anything!"

The door slammed shut.

"So, what do you think?" a PDI agent who had been watching the interview through the glass pane asked Sebastián.

"I think he knows a lot more than he is telling."

"*Do* we have his prints?"

"I hope so. The priest is coming in this morning to give us a statement. Felipe Montero."

"Yes, Padre Felipe."

"Let's see if he's interested in talking to Bruno."

"You mean, like, we'll ask Padre Felipe to talk to Bruno? You know priests won't tell us what a suspect confesses to them."

"Film it. Just like this interview."

"And not tell the priest we're filming it?"

"*¿Eris huevón o qué?* Of course, you don't tell the priest. After I take the statement from Felipe Montero, I'll ask him if he wants to talk to Bruno before he leaves." He lifted his shoulders. Stretched out his neck. "And he will. He's always trying to save the scum of the world. That's what priests do. *We* try to keep them off the street. *They* try to save them. Keep Bruno in that room all morning. No food. Give him all the cigarettes he wants. Get him a carton. Hopefully he'll smoke himself to death. Keep the cameras on. And give him back his cell phone."

Chapter 52

It was 7:00 a.m. Sebastián Cienfuegos had showered and changed into jeans, a button-down shirt and his blue PDI bomber jacket. He sat on the veranda of his home with a cup of coffee in his hand, reading the *Mercurio* newspaper. There were pictures of the cathedral and Rodrigo Pacheco on the front page. Half of the paper was dedicated to the slain priest. A small article on the inside of the paper was headlined, North American Lawyer's Corpse is Found in the Slums Outside of Barriloche; Argentine Government Confirms Identification.

Despite the evidence Interpol appeared to be gathering against Emmanuelle, her story still held up in Sebastián's mind. Stephan Henri Brent's body had been found near Barriloche. Maybe Brent *had* in fact been trying to get to Puerto Montt like she said. Barriloche was only a few hours away from Puerto Montt. Maybe he *had* been planning to go to the authorities with her. He read the article and put down the paper. Connections to the *Antarctic Mist* kept surfacing. He dialed on his cell phone.

"Andrea. Where are you?" he asked when she picked up.

"I just left the marina. Antonio took over. I'm headed home."

"No, you're not. I need you to collect the witness

278

statements and put them into a report. We need it today. This morning."

"Prefecto, I haven't slept yet. My children are waiting for me at home." She groaned.

"No one slept last night, Andrea. Do you understand how imperative this is? This is the biggest crime this city has seen and people want answers. It's not a time to go home and go to sleep. Go back to the office."

Andrea groaned again.

"If you don't like it, turn your badge into PDI and then go home and go to sleep," Sebastián said coldly. "Is Solis still at Tenglo?"

"Yes," she said. "She was there all night."

He hung up on her and dialed Antonio.

"Is she still there?"

"No boats have left Tenglo since I've been here."

"I'm heading over now."

Fifteen minutes later, Sebastián pulled up to the waterfront and turned off the engine. He sat in his car staring at the island across the channel. Antonio was supposed to be tracking Solis. He was nowhere in sight. The darkened streets near the marina were empty. The lights from the Tenglo House sifted through the gauzy fog. He glanced around for El Indio. No sign of him. An abandoned rowboat was anchored at the edge of the water. He yanked the anchor out of the water and shoved the boat into the channel.

Chapter 53

SEBASTIÁN BANGED ON the door to Casa Tenglo. After a considerable wait, he banged again. A small boy peered at him from behind a fence that enclosed a vegetable patch. The boy wore a torn sweater, dirty jeans cut to his knees, and rain boots sunk deep in the mud.

"A detective is here," the little boy said in a hushed voice, but loud enough for Sebastián to hear. The boy motioned others to join him. "Come quickly. He's come to take the goat away." In seconds, a group of runny-nosed children joined him, staring wide-eyed through the fence.

Sebastián ignored them and knocked louder on the door.

"Shut up, Pancho," a little girl whispered loudly, her hands planted firmly on her hips. She was the tallest of five kids now straining—tiptoed or tilted—to see Sebastián through the planks of the gate. "Detectives don't arrest goats," she said, rolling her eyes. "See?" She pointed to Sebastián. "He has a gun. He's going to shoot the dumb goat to smithereens. *Frito el cabro!*"

The door to Casa de Tenglo finally opened.

"*Buenos días,*" Sebastián said, taking off his sunglasses. "*Policía de la Investigaciones.* I'm here to see Padre Javier."

"*Por supuesto*, Señor Prefecto. *Adelante.* Please come in." She opened the door and stepped aside.

"*Permiso.*" He took off his gloves and looked around. He

kept his jacket on in defiance of the pot-bellied stove in the corner of the room. "Is Padre Javier awake?" He glanced about and spotted a small laptop on the pedestal table by the woodstove, assuming it belonged to Emmanuelle. He wrestled with the temptation to pick it up and slip it in his jacket. "Tell him I'm here, *por favor.*"

"*Por supuesto.* Of course. He's in the dining room. I doubt he slept last night. Follow me."

Sebastián had never been in Casa Tenglo before. It was a rustic house tucked between drizzling woods. It smelled like freshly waxed floors. He knew Javier lived there. For a time after Javier joined the seminary, every time Sebastián saw Tenglo Island amidst the brume, he sadly recalled that his friend had withdrawn from the world with no explanation and isolated himself there. Over the past few years, Sebastián had practically forgotten about him.

Following the housekeeper, he peered down the hallways, conscious that the thud of his boots was announcing his presence to whomever might want to avoid him. As they passed a dimly lit passageway lined with closed doors, perhaps bedrooms, he picked up the scent of Emmanuelle's perfume. She was definitely nearby. He took in a deep breath. He needed to find her. She was haunting him, drawing near to a place inside of him he'd long sworn never to revisit.

The housekeeper led him to a small dining room that connected to an open kitchen. An assortment of wrought iron pots and old-fashioned appliances hung on racks. A crudely handcrafted door opened from the kitchen to a little garden. It was slightly ajar now, letting in fresh air for which Sebastián was very grateful.

The sun was rising above the channel, carving out an outline of the city's buildings in the fog. Javier was seated at the table staring blankly out at the city's blurred skyline.

"Padre Javier, Señor Prefecto Cienfuegos is here to see you," the housekeeper announced softly.

Javier turned, looking startled. He was disheveled, and his eyes reflected a familiar sorrow—an unease that Sebastián recognized from the past. Sebastián imagined, with the death of his friend, Rodrigo Pacheco, Javier's understanding of the world would shift radically to make room for all of the new factors entering into the equation.

"*Buenos días* Javier. *¿Como estai, amigo?*" he asked sincerely.

Javier stood to shake his hand. "I wasn't expecting anyone this early," he said, running his hand along his unshaven cheeks. "What can I do for you, Sebastián?"

Javier appeared to have been crying. He looked uncomfortable, perhaps embarrassed, by Sebastián's presence as though he assumed Sebastián was here to try to figure him out—above and beyond his interest in solving a murder.

"I hope you didn't come here thinking I could tell you more. I don't know more than what I already told you. The church is under siege." Javier ran a hand through his hair. It only made it worse. Large tufts of his thick hair stood up defiantly. "The seminarians are afraid. I often tell people that death is a reunion with God so we shouldn't fear it. But the brutality of Rodrigo's murder ... that was the work of the devil."

Sebastián considered his long, lost friend for a moment. Seeing Javier this way raised ambivalent feelings in him. On the one hand, he wanted to press him for questions. On the other, it made him more certain than ever that priesthood, for Javier, was a refuge from life. A self-imposed penance. He suddenly felt sad, but not just for Javier. Something about everything that happened in the past week made him revisit moments of his own life that he wanted to forget.

"We need to talk about Rodrigo, but I'm also here to speak to Emmanuelle Solis."

María came into the room holding a tray with plates of ham, manchego cheese, bread and quince jam. They both waited for her to leave before talking. She arranged it all on the table and left.

"I feel devastated beyond explanation," he said, letting out a sigh of exasperation. "This past week was a nightmare. First Belisario, then Martín, and now Rodrigo. Rodrigo was my best friend. Three lives gone in a matter of days."

"I understand how you must feel. But we need to talk. Martín didn't commit suicide. He was murdered. It's been confirmed. Witnesses saw Bruno Barilla Perez fighting with Rodrigo Pacheco shortly after that. Right before Rodrigo was murdered."

"What? Bruno?" He was visibly shocked. "Are you sure?"

Sebastián pulled out his cell phone and showed him the pictures.

"*Dios mio*. You believe *Bruno* killed Rodrigo?"

"It's seems very likely. Why do you seem surprised? The kid has a criminal record longer than the distance to Antarctica. They were fighting right before. Do you know why?"

"I haven't a clue. Why would Bruno want to kill Rodrigo? I can't even believe they were fighting."

"Javier, the church's cooperation with the investigation is critical. Other people could be in danger. I know you realize that." Sebastián gave him some space. "What did Felipe tell you when he came here last night? I know he talked to you after Martín was murdered."

María came in again and poured orange juice into Javier's glass. She asked Sebastián if he would stay for breakfast. He declined. She left again.

He waited for an answer, but Javier just sat there, looking helplessly distressed.

"Tell me what's going on. Padre Patricio mentioned some

kind of disagreement between priests. What was that about? I can't help you if you don't tell me what you know."

"Talk to Padre Felipe."

"*Bueno.*" He couldn't force him to talk. "I need to speak to Emmanuelle Solis. I know she's here. It's about another criminal matter. Maybe related." He blinked against the sunrise breaking over the channel and into the room. He felt exhaustion from a night without sleep.

Javier said nothing.

"We've identified two additional suspects in the Pacheco murder. They are the same men who broke into Solis' hotel room. We want to clarify the connection between these two crimes. I need to speak to her."

Sebastián caught movement down the hall. He stood up and walked to the door, seeing Padre Cristóbal Dionisio. *Mierda.* He knew things would take a bad turn. The man was a walking plague. A scourge. It would be impossible to make any progress in the investigation in his presence.

The priest padded toward him, then he turned back and whispered something to María before entering the room.

What had he told her? Sebastián geared himself for a renewal of warfare.

The old priest, wearing a ragged cassock and worn slippers, trudged toward him. "What do you want, Sebastián?" the old man asked dryly.

"I'm here to ask Emmanuelle Solis questions regarding a criminal investigation."

"A criminal investigation into what?"

A sickly smell prickled Sebastián's nostrils as the priest neared him. He guessed he'd spent the night smoking salmon in the woods with some very bad people. Probably planning some act of rebellion.

The priest stepped closer. His clothes reeked.

Sebastián took a step backward. "It's none of your business what I'm investigating." Sebastián had a mental image of himself lunging forward and wringing the old man's neck. The priest was a renegade with no respect for police authority. He was a liberation theologian deeply hated by the right in the country. Even the church rejected his theology, but it feared that placing restrictions on him would cause a backlash from the indigenous groups he supported.

Cristóbal pointed a boney finger at his face. "Sit down, Sebastián. I want to have a talk with you."

"Address me appropriately. *Prefecto de Policía de Investigaciones.* I didn't come here to talk to *you.* Nor do I require your permission to interrogate a witness in a—"

"*Pendejo*, sit down," the priest cut him short, his finger now stabbing in the air close to Sebastián's chest.

"I can charge with you obstructing an investigation."

"Ha! Don't make me laugh. Shut up and sit down as I said."

Sebastián crossed his arms. He didn't want to evoke official authority. That would require him to file a report and be answerable to his superiors. The public prosecutor could take a decade to authorize the interrogation. With Interpol and the FBI involved it could become even more complicated. He glanced over at Javier. "Why are you allowing her to stay here? It's in her interest to cooperate with me if she's innocent. You're hurting her more than you're helping her."

Javier stared back at him with an apologetic look, shrugging.

"Why aren't you investigating Rodrigo's murder?" Cristóbal asked.

"We *are* investigating Rodrigo's murder. You people aren't cooperating."

"Well, who wants to cooperate with a bunch of dimwits who aren't capable of organizing a parade?" Cristóbal said. He turned to Javier and placed a hand on his shoulder. "*Hijito,* how are you?" He pulled out a chair and sat down next to him. He gave Sebastián a defiant look while spooning powdered coffee into a cup.

Sebastián yanked off his wool cap and unzipped his aviator jacket.

"Aren't you supposed to be at the protests in the Magallanes? Or in Chiloe? Don't they need a seventy-five-year-old priest there encouraging civil strife?"

Cristóbal pointed his long finger at Sebastián's face. "Do you know what the cost of living is in the Magallanes? Do you have any idea how cold it is there? Three hundred days out of the year, it is unpardonably cold. The government can't just cut off their subsidy of natural gas. You let salmon farmers dump several thousand tons of dead, rotting salmon into the sea, contaminating fishing waters. Then you haul away anyone who speaks out against injustice. You label them terrorists. Set up hearings with secret evidence."

"I don't make the laws in this country. I enforce them. Where is she?" Sebastián turned to Javier.

Javier took his hands off the table, nervously adjusted the napkin on the table, and picked up his cup of coffee.

"She's not here," Cristóbal said.

"I know she's here. My men have been tracking her." He looked at Javier again. "Why are you protecting her? You don't know anything about her or what she might be involved in."

"She's not here anymore," Javier said.

Cristóbal turned his attention to the food, ignoring Sebastián.

Javier nervously swallowed a piece of bread with cheese. Chewing slowly, he watched Sebastián.

"Impossible."

Cristóbal shrugged. "Search the place if you want."

Sebastián made his way down the halls, opening all of the

doors, heels pounding against the floors. The laptop that he'd seen on the pedestal table at the entrance of the house was gone. The room at the end of the hall looked like a guest room. It was empty but fragrant with Emmanuelle's perfume.

"Where is she?" He put his hands on his hips.

Sebastián walked over to the window. The sun was now blazing over the horizon. The Tenglo rowboat was making its way back to the marina. A man was rowing quickly toward the port. A woman in a flowing habit accompanied him, wimples fluttering in the wind. "Is that her?" He glanced back at Javier and Cristóbal. Javier shrugged.

Sebastián pulled his cell phone out and dialed Antonio. "She's getting away. She's in a boat, headed back to the marina. Dressed like a nun. Follow her."

"I'm not at the marina. I went back to headquarters because *you're* there."

"Well, *get* there. Move it, immediately. And send the rowboat back here." He hung up and watched the rowboat pull up to the stony shore. The rower threw aside the oars and rose, helping the woman out.

She was at least four inches taller than the man. It *had* to be her.

He turned to Cristóbal. "You can go to jail for this." He punched the wall of the dining room. The whole place rumbled.

Chapter 54

TWENTY MINUTES LATER, Sebastián was back at the port running to his car. They were nowhere in sight. "Where are they?" he shouted into his cell phone. Morning traffic was beginning to clog the streets.

"A van just picked her up, Señor Prefecto. They're heading west. I think they're about to turn onto Salvador Allende," Pilar said. "I'm right behind them. Sirens?"

He slid into the driver's seat. "No! No sirens. Don't lose them." In a matter of seconds he'd spun the car around and was out on the road.

"Can I arrest her?"

"No. I'll do that. Where are you now?" He pulled out onto Avenida Diego Portales.

"They're heading up Camino Monasterio."

"To Albergue Monte Carmen?" He swung across two left lanes.

"Yeah. It looks like it."

"I'll be there in ten minutes. Don't let her out of your sight." Another call was coming in. It was Juan Bravo, the Prefecto of PDI in Aysén. He hung up on Pilar and took the call. "*Buenos días Señor Prefecto*," Sebastián said. He blasted his horn and swerved past a minibus that stopped to pick up passengers. PDI in Puerto Montt had been collaborating with PDI in Aysén on the *Antarctic Mist* expedition incident.

"Sebastián, there's been a strange twist to the investigation." His voice was tense. The way it was when he had bad news. "They've taken the matter out of our hands."

"Which investigation?"

"The *Antarctic Mist* investigation. They don't want us interviewing more witnesses yet. They're sending someone here from Santiago who will be working with us from now on."

"But the witnesses are here in Puerto Montt. That's our jurisdiction."

"They are going to be calling you soon. I understand that Santiago is taking over several investigations or at least they want greater control over certain investigations that are international by nature. They say Santiago is directly in charge now."

"Why?" He swerved onto Salvador Allende and stopped at the light. A group of teens in school uniforms was crossing the street. "What's going on?" He knew what it meant. The investigation into the securities fraud would be next. Anything related to Emmanuelle Solis certainly would be on the list.

"So, did they confirm there was an explosion on the ship? Are they saying it was sabotage?" The kids had crossed, but the light was still red. He pressed hard on the accelerator anyway.

"I don't know. Someone in the Ministry of Interior called to say that Santiago's handling the investigation. They want us to coordinate *all* of our investigations with them. They didn't mention other ones yet, but I think that means the Calle Vicente Perez Rosales case and maybe even the Pacheco murder case. It's political. I don't know what they have. They aren't going to let us know."

Sebastián hit the steering wheel in frustration. This would bring departmental and jurisdictional rivalry from every direction. Santiago would have the last word on every move they made. He had to get to Solis. Especially before Santiago

PDI found out about her and brought her in. Byrns and Thorman would be sure to play Santiago against her. With big business interests pressing, they would find supporters.

"Let me know when they get in touch with you. Maybe you'll find out more than I could."

Sebastián hung up and dialed Pilar again.

"She just went inside the building. Do you want me to follow her inside?"

"No." He saw Pilar's SUV parked up the hill next to a stone wall. He drove up behind it and parked. The hill overlooked the port and from that position, he had a clear view of the building below. A small dirt path twisted through the pines trees, falling out of sight at the back entrance to the grounds. "Get out of here."

"What?"

"I'm behind you. You can leave now."

"Why?"

"Go! Goodbye. Go back to the station."

"What? And miss out on this? I can't wait to see her arrested."

"Get out of here, Pilar. *Now.*"

"Wait. The meeting with Padre Felipe was postponed until after the mass. The mass for Rodrigo will be at ten o'clock. He said he would go to the station with you after the mass."

"After the mass? I won't be there."

"I think he expects you will."

It was 9:15 A.M. now. He would get there as it ended.

***

Sebastián Cienfuegos sat in his car and reflected on what he should do. He watched as more and more people left the building below. Most, he assumed, were going to the mass for Rodrigo. He had to be back in his office to interview Padre

Felipe Montero in less than two hours. So, now what was he going to do? He didn't have grounds to arrest her. Technically, he couldn't even question her without letting Santiago know. Until Santiago contacted him directly, he quickly decided, he was going to run with this as far as he could. He feared that when they caught onto her, they would certainly have her arrested and sent to Santiago. That would end his involvement in the investigation. He drew a deep breath. Something about Emmanuelle kept pulling him in.

It was clear he couldn't enter the retreat home through the general entrance. He would be recognized and that would spin further questions. He took off his PDI jacket and reached for his fleece-lined leather bomber on the back seat. He couldn't take any risks with the likelihood of press coming around because of Pacheco's murder. His conversations with Solis churned through his mind again. The truth was that he had serious doubts about her involvement in any fraud, although PDI might not agree with him now, especially if Thorman and Byrns were using their influence to get the U.S. Department of Justice to issue a request for authorities to question her in Chile. He had to question her first. Maybe she could explain her alleged relationship with Gilberto Pereira. He had to get her alone.

He got out of his car, leaned against the door, watching several nuns leave the building and head down the street. He would wait a bit.

His cell phone rang.

"Mr. Cienfuegos?"

It was Byrns.

"Prefecto Cienfuegos, we want to know whether you can confirm Solis' location at this moment? We've had some interesting developments in our investigation. More evidence that she's involved with international thugs."

"Did you apply for the judicial order to question her?"

"We have one in the pipeline. You'll see it soon."

"Well, call me once it gets *through* the pipeline."

"Sebastián, do you know where she is?"

"Who do you work for Mr. Byrns? I understand you aren't at the embassy anymore."

"Are you in touch with her or not?" His tone was insistent, authoritative. "We think she's still in the south. If your men pick up on where she is, you'll let us know won't you?"

"That depends on who you work for."

"We can trace her cell phone. We'll know where she is soon enough."

"My guess? You were hired by a law firm managed by a very fat lawyer with lots of money. Am I right?"

"I spoke to the commissioner today. He knows where our orders come from."

"I can't hear you. I am passing through the mountains …" Sebastián said, hanging up the call. *Hijo de puta.*

There was no one in the garden now except for an overweight nun circling the grounds, exercising probably, with the inertia of a planet in orbit.

Chapter 55

A YOUNG NUN led Emmanuelle through the corridor and up a winding staircase to the second floor where many closed doors lined a narrow hallway. She guessed the nun could not have been more than twenty years old. "You will stay here," the woman said opening a door. The room had a slanted ceiling and a single bed pushed up against the bare wall. The room was sparse, nothing more than a place to sleep and hang your clothes. Emmanuelle put her things down on the bed as the nun politely told her the schedule for meals and the general rules. It was clear that if she stayed long enough, which Emmanuelle had no intention of doing; she would soon learn how the religious community that ran the place established its spheres and boundaries. She turned to thank her.

"Will you be down for breakfast?"

"Yes. I guess I will. Thank you."

The nun turned to leave.

"By any chance, do you know Isabella Riquelme?"

"Yes," she said, from the door. "She stayed here last night. She's having breakfast now. She'll be leaving soon for the funeral though. If you want to catch her, you should go now. Will you be needing anything else?"

"No, thank you."

When the door closed, Emmanuelle changed into slacks and an Irish wool turtleneck sweater. Her legs were shaking.

The conversation between Cristóbal and Prefecto Cienfuegos left her fearing the Prefecto had turned against her. She had to talk to Isabella Riquelme and get out of here. From here, she would go to the port and travel to Puerto Edén. She would find the Kawésqar. The place had less than two hundred inhabitants and only a few Kawésqars. It couldn't be that hard to find him. If he were hiding a scientist, it would prove her theory. From Puerto Edén, she would go to the notary's office in Aysén for information about Ameriminco.

The sooner, the better. Being here made Emmanuelle nervous. She knew the murder of Rodrigo Pacheco would attract law enforcement and press to any buildings related to the church. Her presence would appear suspicious. She walked down the stairs to the dining room. Above the soft sounds of birds outside and the rustle of wind in the trees, she could hear her own heart pounding.

Two men dressed in black shirts and dress pants were in the drawing room talking to a man in a tweed jacket. A reporter, she decided. She headed in the other direction.

She caught a glimpse of a girl who fitted Isabella's description. She disappeared at the end of a corridor leading to the dining room. Emmanuelle quickened her pace, but found the dining room empty. Where had she gone? The sun sifted softly through the lace curtains. She walked down a hall leading to the kitchen. Also empty. She searched the adjacent rooms. The girl reappeared in front of a set of French doors leading out to the garden. In a second, she was outside. A chilly draft of rose-scented air swirled through the room.

Emmanuelle followed her. Wearing a flowered dress, flat shoes, a blue crocheted hat, and a matching long sweater coat, the girl walked down a winding stone path lined on either side with rose bushes and fruit trees. The path coiled around to a five-foot statue of the Madonna. Someone had left fresh-cut roses at her feet. Emmanuelle peered through the rose bushes. The girl was now seated on a stone bench in front of the statue.

Emmanuelle hurried to her. "May I join you?"

The girl was startled. "Certainly."

"Isabella Riquelme?"

"*Si, po,* have we met before?"

"No, I am a friend of Padre Cristóbal. I heard about your cousins, and I just wanted to tell you how sorry I am."

"Thank you," Isabella said.

Emmanuelle sat beside her. The bench was cold.

Before she could utter a word, Isabella began talking and it seemed she would never stop. Emmanuelle glanced nervously around as the girl recounted the entire history of her life, lingering tenderly over certain moments in her childhood, her relationship to the boys, how she'd reconnected with them after her aunt died, where she lived, how Martín often visited her. It all came out in long run-on sentences, leaving little time or opportunity for Emmanuelle to ask questions. Anxiety took over Emmanuelle again. Isabella's lips moved endlessly, but little was registering in Emmanuelle's mind. Her thoughts shifted to her next move and her fear of being taken into custody by the authorities. She recalled what the Prefecto said to Padre Cristóbal about Thorman and Byrns seeking authority from the Chilean government to question her. *Was it true? On what basis?*

"You're not a religious worker, are you?" Isabella asked, jolting her back.

"No, I'm a lawyer."

"Oh, so maybe you can answer a question for me."

"Sure. Go ahead. Ask."

"Well, you see, I came here to see Martín ... to keep him company when I heard Belisario died. I brought some of his things. He had his mail sent to my house. He was afraid someone would steal it if it went to his Puerto Montt apartment and he wasn't there. His paychecks have been coming to my house for months now. One came last week and I knew he would need it, so I brought it with me. I was wondering…." She wrung her hands on her lap. "Can I cash the check myself and use it to pay for his burial?"

Emmanuelle froze. "You have it with you?"

She spotted Carabineros in front of the building. Why were they there? Would they burst in and arrest her? She had to calm down. They were there because of Padre Rodrigo's murder. *Calm down. Get the information and run.*

"Yes, I have it right here." Isabella began fumbling through her large handbag. It seemed like an eternity before the girl finally pulled out an envelope and opened it. "Here it is."

Emmanuelle took it from her. Her eyes dropped to the check. *GM.* It was exactly as she suspected. "Martín worked for Grupo Meridional de la Patagonia." The check had an address and phone number at the top. She took out her cell phone. She had to take a picture of the check. "I thought he worked for the water company."

"He worked for Grupo Meridional de la Patagonia. It's an engineering company."

"What kind of work did he do?"

"Research on the environment."

"Do you have any of his work?"

"Yes, I have lots of his files and documents at my house. I haven't read them, but I have them there."

"You know, I'm thinking about writing an article about all of this. I would like to publish it in the United States. Do you think I could come to your house and interview you? Maybe see the documents? I wouldn't take them from you. I would just talk to you some more. Would you mind?"

"No, not at all." She jumped up. "I have to be on my way to the mass. I can't be late."

"Where can I find you?" Emmanuelle pulled out a notepad. "Write down your address and phone number for me."

As Isabella began writing, Emmanuelle discretely photographed the check with her cell phone. She looked at the address again and tried to memorize it before handing the check back to Isabella.

"I'm grateful you're interested in Martín. The police and the press don't seem to care. No one cares when poor people die."

Emmanuelle placed a hand on the girl's. "I am very interested in their lives. Listen, I wouldn't try to cash the check. I'm not licensed as a lawyer in Chile, but I would say don't try. It would probably be considered theft."

Isabella stood and adjusted her hat, looking disappointed.

Emmanuelle realized the girl needed money. She took money out of her wallet and told her, "Here ... take this for the funeral services ... or whatever you need."

The girl looked surprised. "Thank you ... *que Dios te bendiga.*" She smiled. They both stood.

"When will you be returning to Quellon?"

"Sunday night."

"I'll call you and let you know when I will visit."

Isabella disappeared behind the rose bushes.

Chapter 56

SEBASTIÁN KNEW THIS was his last chance. He had to talk to Emmanuelle before she vanished or before foreign authorities caught up with her. He drove up the steep hill and parked his car on the side of the road near a cluster of small plum trees. He took binoculars from his glove compartment and got out of the car.

Within minutes, the French doors of the mansion's terrace opened and a young girl came out, walking along a winding trail in the garden. A few moments later, Emmanuelle came out, following her. *What is she doing?* More people were leaving the building and heading out the gates onto the main street. Some in cars, some on foot. Probably for the cathedral. He watched with curiosity as Emmanuelle approached the girl and sat down next to her.

It was time to move in. He drove down the hill to the back of the garden and parked alongside a high terrace wall surrounding the mansion. Climbing and clinging to a balustrade at the top of the wall, he saw a rambler rose lining the entire length of the inner wall. A mature rambler made a formidable barrier for unwelcome intruders. This one was exceptionally thick with threatening thorns. *That's a problem,* he thought peering down. The menacing plant seemed to crowd every space of the wall surrounding the property. It climbed the trellises and porch-rails, encircled windows, and arched around the French doors. Clearly, the landscaping was conceived with the notion of keeping intruders out.

Sebastián didn't have a choice. He jumped, suppressing a groan as he landed. There was no one in sight. He walked along the path and found Emmanuelle at the opposite end of the trail. The young woman with her was preparing to leave. He waited until she left. Emmanuelle sat on the bench with her back to him, her laptop open in front of her.

Chapter 57

EMMANUELLE SHIVERED AS she waited for the computer screen to boot. She glanced around, sensing someone watching her. Nothing but the wind rustling through the leaves of the garden. *Come on. Boot.* She had downloaded information about Puerto Edén and the ferry routes. She had to check it before heading to the port.

She heard the sound of leaves crunching under someone's foot. She twisted around. The Prefecto was approaching in quick strides. He looked angry. He was here to arrest her. She shut her computer and turned to run, but he caught hold of her arm.

He pulled her close. "You are not going to run again. We're going to talk." His voice was a harsh whisper.

He looked towards the Carabineros at the entrance of the building. He seemed to be trying to pull her away from their sight. As if worried they might see them. Why would that be? She wondered how he had gotten into the garden. "Why did you sneak up on me like that?" She struggled to get free from his grip.

"I suggest you not make a scene. The papers are calling you a fugitive of the law."

Her heart thudded and the bushes seemed to spin past her. "That can't be." *Breathe*, she told herself. *Think and breathe.*

"I will let go of you, but I suggest you don't run. Byrns and

Thorman know you are still here and they're looking for you. They claim a Letters Rogatory request is being processed."

She opened her mouth to say something, but nothing came out. If that was true, she was in grave trouble. Letters Rogatory meant that a serious investigation was underway in the United States and it was focused on her.

"They claim to have more evidence against you. That's what I need to talk to you about." He was standing in front of her now. "If you run from me again, I'll never help you again. You're on your own."

Help me? Did he plan to protect her? Some of the tension drained. She took in a deep breath of crisp air. It was quiet. It seemed the building was empty now. No one was in the garden and the Carabineros at the entrance were gone.

His reflector sunglasses obscured his eyes.

"What do you mean you won't help me again? Are you cooperating with Byrns and Thorman or not?"

"I'm still giving you the benefit of the doubt." He scanned the grounds. He seemed nervous, as though he weren't supposed to be there. Was he not there in some official capacity?

"You have one last chance to cooperate with me. *Entendí?*"

"I *want* to cooperate with you," she whispered. "I found out so much in the last twenty-four hours."

"Go back inside, get your things together and wait. At exactly 12:30 P.M., be waiting for me on the street," he said, indicating to her where he expected her to be. "If I drive by and you're not there, it's over. You're on your own."

That was the last thing she wanted.

"*¿Estamos claro?*" he said.

She nodded her agreement.

Chapter 58

THE FUNERAL MASS for Padre Rodrigo Pacheco wouldn't be for another nine days, but more than a thousand worshippers crowded the cathedral for the first of nine masses mourning the death of the beloved priest. More filled the streets outside the cathedral. The Bishop of Puerto Montt was officiating, and priests from around the area came to attend. Carabineros lined the streets and entrance. In an expression of unity, priests were concelebrating the liturgy. Padre Felipe was among them.

Few priests meant anything to Sebastián, but Padre Felipe was the exception. He had been close to his family when Cristina had fallen ill with leukemia. Sebastián felt that the priest's integrity was reflected in everything about him, from his physical presence to his words and manner of speech.

When mass was over, Sebastián headed to the sacristy to meet with him. There were several clergymen with him when he opened the door. As Sebastián entered, a thought pressed its way into his mind, bringing the past into the present. Padre Felipe's presence had always been soothing for young Sebastián. A sweep of emotion suddenly overcame him and he was speechless.

Padre Felipe embraced him and held him at arm's length for a moment, considering him. "*Cómo estás, hijo?*" His voice was a solemn whisper.

"I am sorry about Rodrigo, Padre...." For the first time,

Rodrigo's death became real to Sebastián. Human. It suddenly occurred to him that he and Padre Felipe were men who had chosen professions requiring them to deal intimately with death. For the priest, death was surrounded by a great sense of mystery and sacredness. It represented the passage into eternity. It required care and reverence for the body that remained, consolation of the living. From Sebastián's perspective, death merely represented a question that needed to be examined methodically and in detail. A cold, analytic process of expounding evidence at the end of which a conclusion would be drawn, reports written and eventually filed away in a cabinet. He asked himself, when had he started treating the loss of a human life so emotionlessly? Sometime after the death of his sister, he knew.

He watched as the priest slipped off his gold-embroidered stole and chasuble. A lifetime of memories compressed into a few seconds of thought and the twenty-five years that had passed since his sister's death shrank. He noticed the priest's hair was grey at the sides and he saw aging around his eyes. Both men were somber.

They left the building and made their way through the crowds of mourners to Sebastián's car. A reporter and an overweight cameraman shoved their way through the crowd, trying catch up to them. "Señor Prefecto! Padre Felipe Montero! May I ask a few questions? Sir? Sir? May I ask you just a few questions?"

"Not now," Sebastián shouted, shielding Padre Felipe.

"Señor Prefecto, is the priest a suspect? Is that why you're taking him away?"

"No, he is *not* a suspect," Sebastián shouted again. "*¡Retírate!* Get back. Have some respect."

In the car, he apologized for not having thought of a more discreet way to drive away. On the way to the station, the priest asked Sebastián a few questions about his life. They were simple questions. Nothing prying. But coming from Padre Felipe, given all he knew about Sebastián's family, his sister's illness and death, and his pain-filled adolescence, the questions pressed into the deepest recesses of his mind. A place he systematically had avoided. His answers were laconic and followed by silence.

When they got to the *Prefecturia*, they took the elevator to a floor reserved for top-level officials. It was the place where important meetings were held and special guests were entertained. The priest declined offers of coffee and something to eat. They sat face-to-face. He wore black clerical garb and a Roman collar. His eyes were sad but tranquil. Didn't he question whether horrible tragedies were part of God's universal plan? He had to ask.

"When someone dies ... when death comes, however it comes, it signifies the end of the earthly pilgrimage and a movement toward God. He will judge in truth and in love. For those of us who remain behind, the journey is different—more difficult even. The journey of separation from a loved one, the raw confrontation with death, challenges our existence, our confidence in ourselves, our lives, our purpose, and sometimes our faith. Don't confuse God's plan with the free will of man. The role of free will should always be carefully examined before attributing acts of human suffering and evil deeds with God's plan."

"Padre, I am sorry to make you come here. I don't want to keep you away from your other obligations now, but...." He sighed.

"Don't apologize. I understand." His hands were clasped as though in prayer or reflection, his fingers pressed close to his mouth.

"Do you have any idea who could have done this and why?"

"Someone who doesn't believe in God. Someone with no understanding of morality or ethics. There are those who are drawn to the light and those who are drawn to darkness. Almost without exception, all forms of life follow that rule."

"Speaking of those drawn to darkness ... we arrested Bruno Barilla Perez last night. Witnesses saw him fighting with Rodrigo shortly before Rodrigo was murdered."

Blood drained from the priest's face. "Are you certain?" His hand passed over his jaw.

"More than certain." Sebastián picked a manila envelope out from the file. He laid the photos of Bruno and Rodrigo fighting in front of the priest.

"*Dios Santo*," Felipe exclaimed shaking his head sorrowfully. "I thought he'd changed."

"I know he was in and out of your shelter for years. That's how they knew each other, right?"

He nodded.

"Tell me about their relationship."

"I don't imagine they'd seen each other much in the past ten or fifteen years. I don't think they *had* a relationship since Bruno left the shelter."

"When was that?"

"I don't know. More than fifteen years ago."

"Did they get along in the shelter?"

"They weren't fond of each other. Rodrigo felt Bruno didn't deserve to be there. He felt he was trying to corrupt kids in the shelter. But that was years ago."

"Have you been in touch with Bruno since then?"

"Yes. In fact, I saw him a few times this past year. It seemed...."

"Yes?"

"It seemed he was trying to change."

"*¿Y como?* He's been in trouble with the law so many times.

305

Why would you think he might change?"

"He came to see me right after he was released from prison. The last time. His girlfriend had a baby while he was in jail. Seeing the baby affected him. It seemed he was rethinking his life. He said he wanted to change. For the baby's sake, I imagine. I believed he didn't want the baby to suffer the way he'd suffered."

"Bruno suffered?"

"Certainly. No one is immune to human suffering. The human condition alone causes suffering in all of us. His parents abandoned Bruno entirely. Not a soul in the world would claim him."

"He had the good fortune of being in your shelter."

The priest shrugged. "God puts people where they are supposed to be. What one does with the situation in which he or she finds himself is another matter. Those choices are our own."

"And you believed him when he said he wanted to change?"

"We try to teach men like Bruno that only with the armor of God can men withstand the schemes of the devil. I thought that he finally understood. It is not my business to judge. I try to help them find the way. More, importantly I pray. That's all I can do."

"So I take it you don't know why he was fighting with Rodrigo."

"I have no clue."

"Listen Padre, Bruno is here. I don't know if you want to talk to him. But you can see him, if you want to."

"*Claro que sí.* I'd like to see him."

There was something soothing about this noble man's simplicity, his lack of pretention, his humility, his serenity. It almost made Sebastián feel guilty for what he was about to do.

He escorted the priest to the interrogation room.

Chapter 59

"PADRE! YOU HAVE to help me get out of here. I swear I didn't kill Rodrigo," Bruno said, pushing aside an overflowing ashtray.

The priest stared at Bruno, skepticism on his face. "How are you, Bruno?"

"Please tell them you believe I didn't do it."

"Bruno, they showed me pictures of you … fighting with Rodrigo." His voice faltered.

"Padre, Rodrigo came after me like a madman."

"Bruno, I would like to believe you, but … Padre Rodrigo, why would he do that?"

"Padre, I don't understand what happened, *cachai*? Like I told the Prefecto, I'm home with my girlfriend and kid, and these two sickos show up at my house. Foreigners. They're looking for Martín. *Lívidos. Furiosos.* They mean business. They start threatening me, trying to get me to tell them where Martín was."

"Who were they and why did they want Martín?"

"I never saw them before. They said Martín stole a hard-drive and they wanted it back."

Sebastián and Pilar, observing from behind the Plexiglas window of the interrogation room, looked at each other.

"One of the *chu*…." Bruno stopped himself. He had enough respect for the priest to control his profanity in front of him.

"One of the guys, he grabbed my throat … like he was going to kill me. He said he wanted Martín and the hard-drive now."

"*Osea*, hard-drive as in an external hard-drive?" the priest asked, appearing transfixed.

"*Supongo*. They said Martín stole if from a scientist in Puerto Edén. One of the expedition team scientists. *¿Cachai?* And then he took off and fled. They came looking for him at my place."

"*Pero* … why would they look for him at your place?"

"My boss probably told him I would know where he is."

"Your boss?"

"Martín and I worked for the same company. Aguas Meridionales de la Patagonia. It's an engineering company. Everyone calls them Grupo Meridional. It's a Brazilian company. They are doing some kind of environmental study. I'm a driver for the company. When they needed biologists a few months ago, I helped Martín get the job. *¿Cachai?* The guys, the foreigners, they said that Martín fled Puerto Edén the night the ship left. You know, the Antarctic Mist. The ship with the scientists. He said Martín took off with some hard-drive that same night and fled."

"*Osea* … Martín was working for the same company you work for?"

"Yes."

"What exactly was Martín doing?"

"He was … uh … gathering reports."

"Gathering reports? What do you mean?"

Bruno's gaze traveled around the room. "He was kind of … spying on the scientists for the expedition team. He was pretending to be a volunteer, but he was getting their reports and turning them over to Grupo Meridional."

"*Dios Santo*. Bruno, please tell me that this has nothing to do with the sinking of the ship," the priest said.

Pilar leaned forward in her chair.

"Was that why Rodrigo and Martín were supposed to go to PDI? Was that what Martín had come to the cathedral to confess? Bruno, please tell me Martín was not involved in that. Tell me *you* weren't involved in that." Felipe's face was pale, his hands clasped.

"Padre, I swear on my son's life, I didn't have nothing to do with the ship or Rodrigo's murder."

Behind the glass, Sebastián and Pilar were both furiously taking notes.

"I hadn't seen Martín in weeks. I don't know what he was up to, but I don't think he was involved in sabotaging the ship. All I did was tell the men where Martín lived." He paused for a second, teary-eyed. "But that wasn't good enough. They wanted me to go with them. They started trying to shove me in the car with them. Then, out of nowhere, Rodrigo shows up, screaming like a madman."

"What was he saying to you?"

"He starts shouting, *cachai*, telling the men he knew who they were, saying he knew what they'd done, that they'd sabotaged the ship, telling them he was going to PDI to report them. They took off and Rodrigo came after me. He was yelling, calling me a *sin-verguenza de mierda*, accusing me of corrupting Martín. Then we started fighting."

"And then?"

"He punched me in the face and told me he was going to take Martín over to PDI to tell them everything and that I was going with them. I punched him back and ran. He left. I never saw him again. Next I know, he's dead."

Chapter 60

EMMANUELLE WAITED FOR Prefecto Cienfuegos on the street in front of the Albergue Monte Carmen. She looked up and down the street nervously. Traffic was cluttered on the main street. She watched each passing car and fought the instinct to run. That would only make things worse. She sensed she stood a chance with the Prefecto. There had to be a reason why he had chosen to talk to her. She wondered if there was turmoil in the investigation. Maybe he needed information from her. Maybe he would help her if he were convinced of her innocence. She had to tell him everything she knew. Then, she would head to the port and take a ferry to Puerto Edén.

It seemed like an excruciatingly long time before the Prefecto's Hyundai appeared and pulled up to the curb. He jumped out of the car. "Get in quickly," he ordered, looking up and down the street as he approached her.

"Am I under arrest?" She stepped back.

He took hold of her arm and hustled her into the car.

"What's going on?"

"Give me your cell phone."

She reluctantly took it out of her purse and handed it to him. He put it in the pocket of his leather jacket.

"Hey, what are you doing?" she asked, reaching for it.

He pushed her arm away.

They were facing each other. The smell of his leather jacket and the scent of his cologne filled the car.

"Byrns said they're tracking you through your cell phone. If they get the authorization to do it, he'll know exactly where you are."

She recoiled and sank into the front seat.

He started the engine and drove past the Hotel Interamericano, down the hill, and pulled into the driveway of the police station. He took her phone out of his pocket. "Back your phone up to your computer, then clear all the information. I'll give you another phone."

She plugged the phone into her computer. They waited for few minutes as the information transferred, then she handed it back. He got out of the car and then turned back to her. "If you aren't here when I get back...."

Trust in him welled inside of her. "I won't go anywhere." She looked down the street at the hotel. "I promise."

He got out of the car, slammed the door, and walked to the entrance of the police station.

Emmanuelle craned her neck to see what he was doing.

He was talking to a Carabinero outside of the building. He handed him her phone.

Seconds later, a second Carabinero came out with a cardboard box and a bag that he loaded into the trunk of the car. Then the Prefecto got back into the car and they sped towards the marina.

"Can we pick up my things from the hotel?"

"They aren't there anymore. We have your things."

Emmanuelle decided not to say another word until she figured out what was going on. She watched the buildings, traffic, and pedestrians who lined the sidewalks and crossed the wet streets. As they headed south, the landscape changed to large stretches of jade-colored plains scattered with clusters of poplars, fire trees and wildflowers.

Fifteen kilometers south, they turned onto a gravel road and headed east on a heavily tree-lined road toward the Andes. The jagged snow-peaked mountains grew more towering the farther he drove. The silence became stony, peaking her frustration and anxiety.

Emmanuelle pulled off her beret and looked at herself in the sun visor mirror. She had dark circles under her eyes from too many sleepless nights. She wanted to brush her hair, but she felt awkward doing it in the Prefecto's presence. "Where are you taking me?"

Not so much as a muscle twitched in his face. She felt a wave of nausea. Maybe he was some kind of psycho taking her some place to kill her. Or maybe her fears were running away with her ability to reason. She sensed, however, that he could turn against her at any moment if he didn't believe her.

"So, do you want to talk?"

"Sure. Talk."

She told him everything that had happened since she left his office and all that she had learned. "I'm sure Martín was murdered."

"Yes. It was confirmed. We know Martín worked for Grupo Meridional."

"I have a copy of his last pay check in my phone files."

"How did you get it?"

"I took a picture of it while I was talking to Isabella. It has an address for the company. That's the company that Thorman hired to do the environmental assessment report."

"I remember you telling me that."

"The contract is in the files." Emmanuelle breathed a sigh of relief. At least, he wasn't hostile.

"This is my residence," he said, as they pulled up to a house tucked between clusters of towering cypresses. "If you try to run away here, pumas and mountain cats will eat you alive."

"I'm not going to run away." She looked around wondering why he had taken her here as opposed to his office. She was growing more certain something was going wrong in the investigation. Maybe he didn't want anyone to know he was talking to her.

He unlocked the front door and led her through a glassed-in hallway filled with potted-plants and ferns leading into the living room. It had terracotta tiles and modern-style leather furniture. His house, like his office, was impeccably neat. It was beautiful but miserably cold. He set the box from the police station next to a large picture window overlooking the backyard, then he took off his jacket and picked up logs for the woodstove. His biceps hugged the short sleeves of his black button down shirt. The Prefecto was a well-built and very attractive man.

Emmanuelle dragged a chair over to where he was, praying the fire would warm the place quickly. The extensive flatlands and plains leading up to the magnificent snow-covered Andes Mountains were a splendid green with young grass. Patches of wild flowers were splattered everywhere. Spring would soon be here.

"Nice place," she said, picking up a log and offering it to Sebastián. It was a gesture of peace. *Peace, please, peace.*

He took the log but didn't talk. He scrunched up a newspaper and set it under the log before lighting it. She guessed it would blaze before he gave her any attention. When it blazed, he shifted his focus to the box, pulling out files and organizing documents on the table in neat little piles. He was making her nervous. She could feel the dampness of her palms. She rubbed them against the sides of her pants. He brought her here for a reason. He had to have some faith in her if he brought her to his home.

Finally, he showed her a picture. "Do you recognize this man?"

"Yes. He spoke at a conference I went to in São Paulo. An international arbitration conference. I told you about it. He was on my panel."

"Gilberto Pereira spoke at a conference on international arbitration?" He moved his chair around to face her.

"That's Gilberto Pereira? It can't be."

"Yes, it is. Interpol sent us this picture."

"That's not his name," she insisted. "I know the man in the picture. He had dinner with us at the conference in São Paulo. His name *isn't* Gilberto Pereira. I have his business card in my office. Stephan and Thomas seemed to know him well. They introduced me to him. They said he was an attorney, and, if I remember correctly, a member of some executive board at the São Paulo Chamber of Commerce. If he's your man, you're after a pretty high-powered, well-connected Brazilian lawyer. Everyone seemed to know him."

"Interpol confirmed that the call you claim to have received from Stephan the night before you came here was made from Gilberto Pereira's phone."

There was silence as she tried to grasp the point. She took her laptop out and searched for the backed up phone files and scrolled through the numbers. "Here it is. Stephan called from this number."

The Prefecto went to the table and sifted through files in the box from the police station and then showed her a document. "That number is registered under Gilberto Pereira's name."

Her mind raced.

"That's why you came to Chile, isn't it? To meet with Gilberto, right? And that's why you went to Calle Vicente Perez Rosales?" the Prefecto asked.

Emmanuelle stood. "That's absurd. I never spoke to the person in that picture except for that one time. He never called me. Stephan called me from that number."

The Prefecto studied her.

She could tell he didn't believe her. "Maybe he was involved in Stephan's abduction. Maybe the guys who held Stephan worked for Gilberto Pereira or maybe they had his phone. Or a phone registered to his name. Maybe Stephan stole the phone from his abductors and ran with it. How do I know?"

He just stared at her, forearms on his knees, appearing to evaluate her trustworthiness.

"I don't know whose phone it was, but when he called, he told me he recognized one of his abductors. He thought he'd been our driver in Brazil."

"Who arranged for that driver?"

"I would guess Hébère or Thorman's contacts maybe. He was there for them. We have an office manager who makes travel arrangements for partners, but ... in this case, I'm guessing someone with closer contacts to Brazil." Her mind shifted to Donaldo and then to Leandro Caceres. "Stephan wanted me to bring him files and a USB drive that I found in his car the day I dropped him off at the airport. It must have fallen from his briefcase. I tried to open it to see if any of the files could answer some of the questions, but it's locked with a password. He said he thought it might have pictures of the driver on the USB drive."

"You didn't ask him for the password?"

"No. At the time, I didn't imagine it was locked and I didn't expect to need to view its contents. I thought I would see Stephan in Puerto Montt."

He walked over to where she was and stopped in front of her, hands on his hips.

"I only vaguely remember the driver. There may be a picture of him in my own files. Maybe in the background of one of the pictures we took."

"What do you remember about him?" He sat down next to

her as she clicked through pictures.

"One thing I remember is he had this black mark or something on his right hand. He was kind of heavy-set. He wore sunglasses all the time. Crocked nose, maybe broken at some point in his life."

Sebastián picked up his iPad and swiped through pictures. "Is this him?"

She took the iPad and expanded the photo. "It looks like him. How did you get this picture?"

"He was caught on video camera at your hotel when your room was ransacked. We suspect he was involved." He swiped through more pictures. "He also fits the description the housekeepers gave of one of the men suspected of killing Rodrigo Pacheco."

"My God. How frightening." Her stomach twisted.

"What do you think they were looking for in your hotel room?"

Her mind raked through the alternatives. "Maybe the stock certificates? The files?"

"What about the USB drive?"

She shrugged. "The only person who knew I had it was Stephan."

"If the phone was tapped, whoever was tapping it would know you had it. Obviously, if he wanted you to bring it here, it has evidence on it."

"Yes. Wire transfers and what he'd been collecting about someone at Oliver & Stone." She clicked through more picture files. One of Gilberto Pereira, Albert and Stephan came to the screen.

"If this man is Gilberto Pereira, he operates under a different name in legal circles."

Sebastián ran his hand over his cheek and stared at the screen. She couldn't tell if he believed her or not.

"Look, I can prove it. I'll show you." She searched through her files for the conference agenda. "See." He moved closer to her. She pointed to the screen. "This is the conference brochure. He's listed as a speaker on the same panel I spoke on. That's his name. Renato Vinicius Almeida. He spoke about Brazilian banking laws. His presentation was brief and largely uninformative. The bios and pictures of all the speakers were published in the conference program. I should have a picture of him here in these files." She rubbed her cold hands, cupped them together and blew on them before searching through the pictures again. "Hold on. It has to be here. They requested bios and pictures from all of the speakers. Wait a minute…." She searched through the files again, clicking on each of the speaker profiles. "Almeida. That's odd. His bio is here without a photo."

Sebastián was now sitting very close to her. She could feel warmth radiating from his body.

He stared at her pensively. He picked up his cell and dialed. "Antonio, do a search for a person by the name of Almeida. The international database. Renato Vinicius Almeida. See if the ID matches Gilberto Pereira. Maybe he's operating under two different names." He hung up.

"I never spoke to him after the conference." She thought it through for a moment. "Could you have the wrong person? Almeida didn't seem like a big-time criminal to me. Although … come to think of it … he was a bit strange."

"How so?" the Prefecto stretched his arm across the back of the sofa. His arm was behind her now. She leaned back and looked at him. The flames from the fireplace highlighted the angles of his chin and cheekbones.

"Nothing major, but it seemed as though he read his presentation with difficulty. He was nervous and uncomfortable. I found that a bit unusual. When I talked to him later about his presentation, he ducked the issues. Like he wasn't an expert in the field. He was definitely uneasy. When he talked to me, he would glance over my shoulder at the same time." Emmanuelle typed on the keyboard. "At the same time, he seemed like a nice person. A chain smoker, but he definitely didn't come off as a criminal."

Sebastián's phone rang. He stood up and paced the room as he listened, glancing at Emmanuelle occasionally.

He hung up and walked back to the sofa. "You're right. Gilberto Pereira is using Renato Almeida's identification. Renato Almeida was a lawyer from Salvador de Bahia who died in a car crash. My team is checking with authorities in Brazil for more information. Apparently, Gilberto is originally from the shantytowns in Bahia."

Optimism surged. She was gaining ground with the Prefecto. "The shantytowns in Bahia? That's incredible. It's hard to believe that someone from the shantytowns could climb so high in Brazilian society. He definitely doesn't look like he's from the slums."

"Interpol confirmed wire transfers between Brazil, Canada and France that were part of a sham to convince clients that the transactions were generated from the investments they promised. The money just went back and forth between accounts and it was used for their personal enrichment. There were no European or Canadian investments. The FBI traced the transfers back to Oliver & Stone and Pereira. Pereira convinced some of Oliver & Stone's clients to invest in South American companies. He sold securities, and some of them were fraudulent."

"Thorman must have been involved. Maybe the certificates in the Patagonia Files are part of a scam. Pereira was probably in contact with Thorman. Thorman's assistant is a Brazilian lawyer."

"What's his name?"

"Donaldo Moreno. His father is partner in a big São Paulo law firm."

Sebastián punched out a text. Probably to the same person he had just spoken to. Maybe he was checking out Donaldo. She felt relief.

"I'm sure Thorman is involved. That has to be why Stephan warned me not to talk to him or to anyone in the office. He probably figured they would have me eliminated as well. I am sure that's why Thorman is here."

"He's told authorities here that he was being defrauded. He claims he was a victim. Why would a powerful, wealthy lawyer like Thorman need to commit that kind of fraud?"

"The firm has been in trouble financially since the 2008 crisis. One of the banks that provided the firm's revenue collapsed because of bad oil-patch investments and the effects were staggering. The firm let go of eighty associates that year. It doesn't have enough big-money clients to match Oliver & Stone's big billers. That's why Thorman was desperate to keep Hébère as a client. The firm runs on the point system. Partners are paid depending on the number of points they make over the year. A management committee decides who gets how many points. Thorman heads that committee. The dollar-amount of the points depreciated by more than thirty per cent over the last two years. So, partners are taking home thirty percent less than they were seven years ago. Some of the partners were incensed that Thorman gave himself a bonus each of the last six years to make himself whole. Especially since the bonus hardly corresponds to his productivity. He also brought in partners from competing firms—thinking the firm would benefit because of the clients they brought with them—promising them big salaries. The newest partners have been in a nasty dispute with Thorman. They claim he tricked them and didn't tell them that a large part of their salary would be invested in the firm and not paid to them directly."

Sebastián was silent for a long stretch. "I still can't connect the dots." He was looking at the pictures of the suspects. "Why would the same thugs who abducted Brent, kill Rodrigo Pacheco and Martín Araya?"

"There is a connection. Martín worked for GM and Albert Thorman contracted GM to do the environmental assessment for Hébère. The question is what did Martín confess to Rodrigo?"

"He was spying on the scientists. He pretended to be a volunteer, but he was transmitting all of the information to AMP."

"How do you know that, Prefecto?"

"Sebastián." He told her about Bruno Barilla Perez.

"So, they *were* tracking the scientists? I'm so sure they were afraid the scientists would publish something that would jeopardize plans to build the dam. That's what I've been saying all along. Isabella has some of their documents at her house. Martín left them there."

The Prefecto shook his head. "It still seems too absurd that they would go so far as to plot the murder of a team of scientists. Something is missing from the equation." There was something in his eyes. The same distance she had seen before, as though recalling some past sadness. "Something tells me they could come after you next."

Was it concern? Was he worried about her?

He got up and walked to the kitchen.

She followed.

"Are you hungry?" he asked, opening a cupboard.

She was famished. She couldn't remember her last meal. "Yes."

"I don't cook, but I know how to grill meat." He handed

her a bottle of wine and two glasses, took a bag from the refrigerator and motioned her to follow him. She followed him through French doors to the back of the house, feeling tension in her neck ease. She suddenly felt safe with him. Something she hadn't felt since she'd landed in Chile.

They chatted as he emptied wood chips and ashes from a stone grill and started a fire. For a while, she almost forgot the events of the previous week. She almost forgot that he was the chief of detectives and she was a suspect in an international crime.

She leaned closer to the fire and wriggled her toes inside her boots. Could she get frostbite and lose a limb? How much exposure did it take? She rubbed her hands together near the crackling fire. Her body trembled. The chilling wind was stirring again.

Sebastián took his jacket off and draped it on her shoulders.

"Thanks," she said through chattering teeth.

A moment later, Sebastián pulled off his wool sweater and gently removed his jacket from her shoulders. "Here," he said. "Put this on first." He helped her pull his sweater over her head, and then eased her arms into his jacket, brushing aside a wisp of her hair from her cheek. They exchanged smiles. She felt warmer. She finally felt he trusted her.

"Not used to this weather?"

"It gets cold in D.C., but it's so humid and cold here. And the wind sounds like there's a cat screaming somewhere."

He laughed and poked at the fire. "There probably is one out there." This was the first time she had seen him laugh. He had a beautiful smile that displayed his perfect, white teeth. He reminded her of Camilo. "Aren't you cold?" she asked.

"No." He blinked as smoke rose near his eyes. "Look, I'm sorry I was a bit rough with you earlier today," he said, rubbing his cheek against his own shoulder. He opened a bag, forked out sausage and meat, and placed it on the grill. "If Byrns is tracking your phone, he must be headed to Santiago by now."

"Why Santiago?"

"Your phone is there. If they're tracing it, they should be pulling up to PDI Headquarters in Santiago soon."

"I don't understand."

"I sent it there."

"You mean … like, on purpose? To mislead Byrns?" Emmanuelle felt a surge of relief. He would help her, maybe even protect her.

"I hate that arrogant *hijo de puta*," Sebastián said, under his breath.

They both laughed.

"Thanks," she said. "But … can that cause problems for you?"

"Not really. Byrns isn't an embassy official. At least, not anymore. We don't know who he works for now. I don't take orders from him, anyway. My orders come from Santiago." His face changed. She saw concern in his eyes. She sensed something wasn't right with the investigation. Would he tell her?

Emmanuelle suddenly felt light-headed. The wine was hitting her.

She reached for support.

Sebastián noticed and caught her by the hand.

Now she felt self-conscious and wondered what she looked like. Her hair felt wet and clumped together in bunches from the humidity. She tried to smooth it out.

"Are you alright?" he asked, catching her by the arm as she lost balance again. He pulled her close. She felt the warmth of his body again next to hers. She wanted to drown in it. She wanted to close her eyes and stay there forever. *Wait, what?* Was she losing her mind? She froze for a second.

"Too much wine on an empty stomach. I've never been one for alcohol."

"Here," he wrapped an arm tightly around her. "I'm almost done. We'll go inside in a minute."

She watched as he poked the meat and sausages on the *parrilla*. Juices dripped into the fire. She blinked her eyes several times with the strange sensation that she was dreaming again. She looked up at his face and he smiled again. "You okay?"

The tremendous walls around the Prefecto were coming down. She wanted to cry again. He was a real gentleman. Well-mannered in spite of the seeming inflexibility in his ways and thinking. There was something soothing about the man behind the façade. She felt safe with him.

"It's ready. Let's go in and eat."

Chapter 61

EMMANUELLE SAT ACROSS the table from Sebastián. Light from the flames of the *caldera* shone softly from her eyes. He liked her delicate features. Her hair was pulled back into a bun, accentuating her high cheekbones. He wanted to reach out and touch her. Instead, he sipped his wine. The more he thought about what she was involved in, the more anxiety it caused. He was now convinced she was innocent, a victim of some conspiracy, but could he save her? Could he protect her from the assassins if they caught up with her? He knew this case reached far beyond his jurisdiction and control. Moreover, it dripped in politics. If he was caught assisting her, he could lose his job. Risking things as he was lately, it was beginning to seem like a possibility. However, something about her made all of that less important. He almost didn't care.

He considered her as she ate, sipping more wine. She was eating as if she hadn't eaten in weeks.

"This is so tender. What kind of meat is this?"

He put his glass down. "*Interiores*. You know, *chunchules, mollejas, panitas*."

"What's that?" She stopped chewing.

"Insides … you know glands, lungs, intestines. The insides of the cow."

For a moment, she looked as though she had a ball or something caught in her throat and she might choke. She swallowed repeatedly.

. "Seriously?" she asked, when she was finally able to talk.

"Yes. More hot sauce?"

"No, thanks." She pushed her plate away and picked a piece of bread from the basket.

"I thought you liked it."

"I mean … sure. I did. I'm full. I'm not a big meat eater."

He poured more wine into her glass. She picked it up and moved to the far end of the room, near the enormous stone fireplace. His eyes followed. She let her hair loose and sank into his leather sofa, drawing her legs under her. The fire softly carved her out in the surrounding darkness.

He liked everything about her from her looks to her mind. Maybe they could work together on the case. She certainly had knowledge and expertise they could use. But how would he convince PDI headquarters not to heed to the pressure that would swiftly be upon them? He had tried every different way to catch her in lies, but she was consistent in her version of events. It all matched up. Even the phone call now. He believed that Brent *had* made that call to her. He picked up his glass and went over to the fireplace. He threw in more logs and poked them with the iron. He glanced over at her. She was an amazing replica of his sister.

"Tell me about yourself," she said. "Tell me where you grew up. What your life was like."

"I grew up here. In Puerto Montt. No big story."

"Do you have brothers and sisters?"

"I had a sister. She died when I was twelve."

"I'm sorry."

"It's okay. It's been so many years." He sat down next to her. "She looked exactly like you."

"Seriously?"

"Very seriously. An incredible resemblance." They held gazes. "She had leukemia. Back then, treatment options were limited.

She suffered so much. The disease was painful. Treatment was painful. We all suffered watching her. My parents passed a few years ago. My father went first. My mother, shortly after. And that's it."

"I can relate to what you are saying. I lost my mother when I was in my early teens. Less than a year later, I lost my father. We have so much in common."

"We have more in common than you know. When Cristina passed, I lost my parents as well, in a sense. It was as if their commitment to life had been broken. There was nothing to celebrate anymore. Our house was a dreary place. I was happy to leave it after high school. When I moved to Santiago to study at the *Escuela de Detectives*, I felt like I had escaped from prison." He poured more wine into their glasses. "I drowned myself in my studies, and later, in my work." He felt like he was drowning now. Drowning in Emmanuelle. But he *wanted* to drown.

The fire crackled. He regarded her, noticing the rhythmic rise and fall of her breathing. She tilted her head back and rested it against a pillow, exposing the curve of her neck. He knew the alcohol was starting to have an effect on her. She was gazing out the window somberly. As though some distant object on the other side had reached out from some world she once belonged to and had caught her. It was now holding her captive.

He wondered where she was.

Chapter 62

SEBASTIÁN'S CELL PHONE rang. He was at the dining table in front of his laptop, reviewing the files he had picked up from the station. A long trail of documents stretched the length of the table.

Emmanuelle was asleep on the couch. She opened her eyes briefly, gathered the blanket Sebastián had draped over her more tightly around her, and closed her eyes again.

He picked up the phone and checked the number. It was Tonio. He would ignore him for now. A few seconds later, a text blinked on the screen: Assault at Tenglo.

He jabbed the call back button, gathering his jacket and keys at the same time. "Get up," he called to Emmanuelle. "Pick up, *mierda!*" he shouted into the phone.

Emmanuelle looked at him fearfully and clambered off the sofa. "What's wrong?"

"You can't stay here. Someone was assaulted at Tenglo. I have to go."

"What?"

He had his back to Emmanuelle. "Tonio, what's going on?" he said, when the detective finally picked up.

"Some girl was attacked at Casa de Tenglo. I'm just pulling up to the pier. Carabineros are already on the scene."

"I'll be there in fifteen minutes."

Emmanuelle put her hand gently on Sebastián's forearm. "What happened?"

He brushed a wisp of her hair from her face and placed his hands on her shoulders. He felt the urge to hold her tightly. To protect her. "A woman was assaulted with a knife at the Casa de Tenglo. Someone broke in. I fear the assailants mistook her for you."

"Is she dead?"

"She's still alive. I have to get over there. Let's go. Get your things."

"Where are you taking me?" Panic hitched her voice.

Good question. Where would he take her? She wasn't safe here. His home was isolated in the woods. If anyone had followed them here, she would be easy prey. He dialed Tonio again.

"I need you to send Carabineros to Albergue Monte Carmen to guard the place."

"Why? Is there something happening there?"

"Just do it."

He took a cell phone out of the box from the station and handed it to her. "Keep this with you. Answer when I call you."

She took the phone and stared at it.

"What are you thinking?"

She didn't answer, but he knew. She was calculating her next move.

"Stay put until I come for you. You'll be safe there. It's probably the safest place you could be right now."

"Sebastián, I'm going to Puerto Edén in the morning. I'm going to follow up on the leads. I am sure that the answers to my questions are there. The Kawésqar has the answers. I can't stay here. I'm a sitting duck here. You know that." Her eyes pleaded with him.

"You're not going anywhere. What the hell is wrong with you? Don't you understand the trouble you're in? You are up to your ass in piranhas. Interpol is after you. US agents want to question you about a criminal conspiracy that could put you behind bars for years. Someone is trying to kill you. Do what I tell you to do. *¿Entendí?* Get your things. Let's go. *Ahora.* " He wasn't going to give her the choice. He knew what was best for her and that was that.

Chapter 63

THE WIND WHISTLED through the cracks of the ill-fitting frame of the window of Emmanuelle's room at the Albergue Monte Carmen. The place was dank and cold. She got up, pulled the blanket off the bed, wrapped it around her body, and peered out the window. Carabineros were at the entrance. It was quiet. She guessed no one else in the building was awake although occasionally a creaking noise shot adrenaline through her veins. She prayed the sun would soon rise.

She retrieved the USB drive from her purse and plugged it into her laptop. She racked her brain trying to guess the password until she finally gave up. She scrolled through picture files on her computer. She had photographs she had copied from Stephan's office computer after Lynn told her that the FBI would be coming to take his computer away. There were pictures they had taken in Paris just before Christmas. The trees along the Champs-Elysées were strung with twinkling lights. The windows of the Galleries Lafayette department stores were adorned with shimmering decorations. They had stayed at the Intercontinental Hotel. There was a picture of her standing on the hotel balcony overlooking the Opéra National de Paris, smiling, arms stretched out to the sky. It had just started to snow. She couldn't remember ever feeling happier in her life. How did she skydive from that moment to this one? The events of the past week had reduced her to a mere shadow of the person she once was. How illusory it had all been. She scrolled on. There were pictures of Stephan and her at the Alain Ducasse restaurant—one of the finest in Paris. They were smiling and embracing. One big lying illusion. To her, it now looked very similar to the pictures of him and Maríana. She quickly scrolled past it.

There were many pictures of a much younger Stephan. She lingered over them. He'd said so little to her about his past. There was one of Stephan and a boy who looked vaguely familiar. Who was he? They were maybe high school age in the picture. Both wore black helmets and red hockey jerseys, holding hockey sticks in the air and smiling. Stephan had his arm around the other boy's shoulder. Emmanuelle struggled to remember where she might have seen him. He would have to be in his forties or fifties now. She scrolled on to photographs of Stephan and a middle-aged woman with reddish hair. She saw Stephan in the woman's eyes and guessed she was his mother. She had the eyes of a woman worn by a difficult life. They were standing in front of a brick apartment house built between two wood-framed homes. She wondered if Stephan had lived there in his childhood. It looked like a working-class neighborhood. Emmanuelle came upon several more pictures of Stephan, the same woman, and the same young man. Was he a relative? A cousin maybe? She stared at them for a moment before moving on to conference pictures. Others of Stephan and a different, very attractive woman on a white sandy beach, a sparkling azure sea behind him. She guessed it was Brazil.

She came upon one that made her heart miss a beat. It was Stephan, Thorman and another man at a table in an elegant restaurant with a soaring, vaulted ceiling. She immediately recognized it; the Galvin La Chapelle in London. She had been there many times with Stephan. She reached for her reading glasses and brought the laptop closer, expanding the image.

The third person was Gilberto Pereira. The three men were smiling with champagne-filled crystal glasses lifted to the air. What were they celebrating in London with the Brazilian con artist?

Chapter 64

SEBASTIÁN DROVE FAST, heading north on the coastal road. He cut off the lights and sirens as he neared the pier. Carabinero vehicles lined the road. The area was not generally a safe one, especially at night. There were incidents of tourists being mugged there. More recently, there were a few cases of rape. He wondered if the assault at Tenglo was mere coincidence. Nearing the pier, he noticed a dark car in the shadows farther down the road. He drove toward it slowly, reaching beneath his jacket for his Glock.

Carabineros on the shore below were shepherding a handcuffed man off a boat. A PDI van waited for them on the street. Investigative police were all over.

The suspicious car moved slowly, inching closer in the shadow of the street. It had no plates.

"*¡Atento!*" Sebastián shouted into the VHF radio of his car. He flicked his lights and siren on. It had become clear whoever was in the car was preparing to attack as Carabineros moved the assailant into the van. Sebastián aimed his pistol at the car. Other officers saw the car now, reaching for their weapons as it accelerated toward them.

The passenger-side tinted glass window of the car opened. The tip of a rifle barrel emerged. The explosion of gunfire cracked through the air. PDI and Carabineros fired back. The handcuffed man fell to the ground, pummeled by lead. The car gunned its engine and headed south of the marina. Several PDI ran to a Carabinero struck down by the gunfire.

Sebastián spun the car around in pursuit, tires screeching against the pavement. Police sirens filled the air. The bastards were getting away.

Chapter 65

EMMANUELLE SAT FOR hours in the room at the Albergue Monte Carmen, lights off, waiting for Sebastián to call. The wind seemed to have grown long, sharp nails that were clawing the window and her anxiety was crawling the walls like a black insect. She told herself that this was just a hellish nightmare. *Wake up now*, her sleep-starved mind urged.

As hours ticked away, she grew more paranoid. She needed to know who had been assaulted at Tenglo. She wasn't going to just wait there like a sitting duck. A few hours earlier, she'd overheard people in the vestibule downstairs talking about a shootout at the pier. Had the Prefecto been hurt? Why hadn't he called? Self-doubt and insecurity were marching in goosestep in her brain. How was she going to pull this off?

At 4:00 A.M., the cell phone Sebastián gave her finally rang. She picked it up on the first ring. It was Sebastián, telling her one of his officers had been shot and he'd been with him all night. Assailants in a car on the pier gunned down the suspect as police were escorting him to a van.

"They got away," he said. "So, for the moment there's no one to question." She heard defeat in his tone.

"And the girl?" *Please say she isn't dead.*

"She's alive. Intensive care. Lost a lot of blood. Same hospital."

"Who is she?"

"Isabella Riquelme."

Emmanuelle's heart flipped. "Oh my God. Martín's cousin."

"I don't know if they were after her, or if they were after you. It doesn't seem they would have any reason to be after her."

"Don't be so sure. She has Martín's paycheck. It proves he worked for GM. She told me Martín left documents at her house. They probably have evidence that explains why the ship was sabotaged."

"Well," he hesitated. "I'm not sure." His voice dropped. "Listen, I'm going to pick you up at 8:00 A.M." He sighed grimly. "I have to bring you into the station. Apparently the Letters Rogatory request was processed. It's nothing like an arrest. It's simply permission to question you. There was some kind of motion heard by a judge in Santiago. I don't know details. We're going to have to cooperate with the foreign authorities in the case. I haven't seen the paperwork yet, but Pilar told me Santiago has been calling. I've put off responding to those calls, but orders are orders."

Orders are orders? She squeezed her eyes shut. "Question me about what? What are the grounds for questioning me?"

"I don't know. I'm going into the station now. Wait for me where you are. Don't do anything crazy. You can't escape this. It will only get worse if you run now."

She opened her mouth to say something, but nothing came out. A shudder of dread swept her spine. Was he going to turn her in?

"Are you there?"

"Yes." The freezing wind whipped and whirled outside. "I'm listening."

"I'll know more when I get into the station ... before I bring you in. Listen, Emmanuelle, I know you don't know who to trust, but I want to help you. I believe you're innocent. Whatever you do ... wait for me. I'll pick you up from the Albergue Monte Carmen at eight." He hung up.

Of all of his words, three rang most loudly in her head. *Orders are orders.* And she knew they summed up the situation for him. Every bone in her body was telling her to run before the four hours were up. She splashed cold water on her face in the bathroom and gathered her things. She wasn't sure whether running or waiting implied a greater risk at this point.

Her thoughts froze at the sound of an approaching vehicle on the street. She held her breath, stepped lightly on the cold floor and peered out the window at the darkened city. Carabineros were still at the entrance. A van marked *Diario Llanquihue* had pulled up and a boy bracing a stack of newspapers got out. A Carabinero exchanged a few words with him before taking the newspapers. She heard the front door open, then noise in the vestibule. It went quiet.

She wondered what the papers were saying. Maybe she should get one. She left her bag on the bed, opened the door to her room and peered down the hallway. It was empty. From the top of the stairs, she could see that someone had stacked the newspapers on the coffee table in the drawing room.

She crept down the stairs, careful not to draw the attention of the Carabineros outside.

A large picture of the murdered Puerto Montt priest was on the front page, under the headline Church Under Siege. She snatched a copy and bolted back up the stairs to her room.

She skimmed the paper. It was filled with stories related to Rodrigo's murder and the assault at Casa de Tenglo. The front-page article cited a special investigative report that had aired on television the night before suggesting a connection between the sinking of the *Antarctic Mist* and the string of attacks on individuals associated with the church in the south, arguing that the church was under siege. It quoted an anonymous clergyperson as saying that an altercation between Rodrigo Pacheco and Cristóbal Dionisio had taken place only a week earlier related to Cristóbal's association with Mapuche activists. The article claimed that the murders might have been revenge killings by activists who resented the opposition of clergymen. The information was terribly wrong. These crimes weren't related to any indigenous conflict. They were about corporate greed and fraud. Emmanuelle wondered if Nahuel or people he knew would be arrested.

She was about to put the paper down when a small picture on the opposite page caught her eye. It was a picture of her. Her heart slammed against her ribs. The headline read: Chilean American Lawyer Sought In Investment Fraud Investigation.

The blood drained from her face. After she got past the headline, the words jumped all over the page. *Focus.* She smoothed out the paper with trembling hands and continued reading. *Emmanuelle Solis, a Chilean-American lawyer, is sought in an investment fraud investigation. The attorney is believed to be a member of a ring that spans North and South America according to the International Crime Division of the United States Embassy in Santiago. The lawyer appears to have fled after multiple attempts were made by United States authorities to question her in Puerto Montt this week.*

"That's a lie!" she gasped. No authorities from the United States embassy tried to question her. Byrns was a *former* official, according to the Prefecto. And Thorman was no official of the embassy. She felt like her heart would explode in her chest.

She read on. *Solis is believed to be in Chile. The FBI and Interpol suspect she will attempt to cross the border into Argentina. A former embassy official told Associated Press that a United States District Court initiated service on Solis by means of Letters Rogatory. On Tuesday July 5, 2016 federal prosecutors will present evidence to the Federal Court for the District of Columbia seeking an indictment of Solis for purposes of requesting her extradition from Chile. Solis is suspected of stealing over a million dollars' worth of stock certificates. The United States federal court has meanwhile requested judicial assistance from Chilean courts to enable US authorities to formally interrogate her in Chile. The Chilean Prefecto de Policía de Investigaciones, Sebastián Cienfuegos, has declined to comment on the case.*

"Extradition?" Her heart lodged in her trachea. She was a formal suspect now. She read on. *The attorney is an associate attorney at Oliver & Stone. In a potentially related matter, Stephan Henri Brent, a partner from the same firm disappeared in Argentina last month amidst protests against a water privatization. According to an attorney for the firm who prefers to remain anonymous, prior to Brent's departure to Argentina, Solis was given notice that she would be laid off.*

Emmanuelle felt a weight drop inside of her. That was a blatant lie. *Apparently, Solis believed she was positioned to be partner and was disgruntled by the notice. The firm has laid off more than eighty-five associates since the 2008 financial crisis. Although the firm intended to keep Brent's meetings with the Argentine municipality confidential due to the volatility of privatizations, authorities now say that a fax was sent from Oliver & Stone's Washington DC office to* Clarin Newspaper *in Buenos Aires the night before the meetings. Massive protests broke out prior to the meetings. Brent was abducted amidst the chaos. Solis is expected be questioned in that connection as well. Brent was unaccounted for until last week when his body was discovered on the Argentine/Chilean border.*

"Oh dear God," she gasped. Someone was deliberately trying to frame her. Not just for the investment fraud, but even linking her to Stephan's abduction and murder.

Emmanuelle reached for her bag. She had to get out of here.

Through the dense mass of confusion billowing in her brain, a short list of five alternatives was becoming apparent. Two of which required she obtain a gun and learn how to use it quickly. One: She would commit suicide. Her life was crumbling. Her career was over. And she was being framed for a crime that implied many years in prison. She had severely miscalculated the enemy. What was there to live for? Two: She would wait for Thorman in Puerto Montt and shoot him instead. Three: She would take the ferry to Puerto Edén and find out why the Kawésqar was hiding the scientist and why he'd been poisoned. Four: She would retrieve the information from the notary about the corporate representatives of the gold mining firm. And Five: She would break into Isabella Riquelme's home and collect all of Martín's files.

Prioritizing the list, she decided Three, Four, and Five would be the first steps. What did she have to lose? The thought, however, of obtaining a gun was becoming more and more attractive.

Chapter 66

UNITED STATES PROSECUTORS would be requesting Emmanuelle's extradition in court in Washington, D.C. on Tuesday. Theoretically, if they were successful, the orders could come from the State Department that same day or shortly thereafter. That gave her three days at best, to come up with the evidence she needed to exonerate herself—and three and a half hours to disappear before the Prefecto came to pick her up. When he returned to his office without her, certainly the wheels would start spinning. She guessed he hadn't known about all the details when he spoke to her earlier. He'd told her he'd been avoiding Santiago's calls. But he was heading into the office now. He would know soon.

When he received orders to surrender her, he would comply. Even if he substantively disagreed, she knew he would comply with procedural requirements. He would tell her she *had* to cooperate. He believed in the system. He was part of it, after all. Moreover, the case was drawing international attention so he would be pressured to surrender her.

The ferry to Puerto Edén left port every morning at 7:00 A.M. If she managed to make it, she would be an hour out to sea before authorities realized she'd run again. But temperatures in the Patagonia often dropped to sub-zero. She didn't have clothes for that trip. She searched her wallet for the card the tourist had given her days ago on the port. It had the cell phone number of the owner of a secondhand clothing shop. Carlos Sevilla. It was now 4:30 A.M. He'd be sleeping. She dialed the number. *Please, please answer.* It went to voicemail. She dialed again. Voicemail. She'd have to make do with what she had. She folded up the paper, stuffed it in her bag and cracked the door. No one was in the halls.

Her cell phone buzzed in her pocket. She pulled it out and looked at the screen. He was calling her back.

"Carlos?"

"*Si, soy Carlos.* Who is this?" The voice was groggy, annoyed, but curious.

"*Perdon,* I know it's crazy to be calling you at this hour, but a friend gave me your phone number. I'm leaving for the Patagonia this morning and my luggage is lost. It didn't make my connection flight. She said you might be able to help me get clothes suitable for the Patagonia."

"*Ya.* I have a store in Angelmó. My store, it opens at 9:00 A.M."

"But my ferry leaves at 7:00 A.M. I'm desperate. My team leaves this morning and I have only one week of vacation. I am afraid I'll miss the opportunity. *Por favor,* I'll pay you extra if you help me."

"*Ya?*" The suggestion of extra money woke him up.

"Will you?"

He agreed to pick her up. Fifteen minutes later, Emmanuelle saw the headlights of a car driving up the hill. She knew it was him. She met him on the backstreet. He took her to a store on the pier, which, fortunately for her, was only a few minutes away from the Ferry Terminal in Angelmó. She selected a parka, wind pants, a lighter fleece jacket, a water-resistant jacket, hiking boots, gloves, scarves, a few sweaters and a waterproof duffel bag. She changed in the shop's dressing room and he dropped her off after she paid him one hundred thousand pesos.

She wore a lime green parka and hid her face behind a colorful Andean alpaca ski hat with earflaps and sunglasses. If a hunt were on for her, she guessed they wouldn't be looking for someone who looked the way she did right now. An icy wind blew off the port. She wrapped her scarf tightly around her neck and walked down the wet quay to the terminal. The morning was grey and the artisan shops along the way were all closed.

The ticket office was also closed, but the waiting room was open. She stepped inside and took a seat, growing more nervous as minutes ticked away. She saw a police car pass slowly on the street outside and tried not to flinch with paranoia.

Fifteen or so other people loaded with winter gear waited with her. Athletic types, maybe mountain climbers or white water rafters. Finally, a woman appeared at 7:30 A.M. and began attending customers for the ferry that was supposed to have left half an hour earlier. She needed to get inside and put her bag down. Her legs felt like she'd just stepped on livewire. She purchased the least expensive ticket and boarded.

A woman with a German accent, an athletic figure, and a trendy parka was blocking the door to cabin fifty-six. "I smell cows," the woman said. She had a camcorder dangling from her neck, and Emmanuelle feared the woman was planning on filming a documentary-style reality clip about the trip. She dropped her bags and checked the number on her ticket.

"Uh, I think you're in my room."

"*Our* room," the woman said, hand on hip. "Four of us share this room." She eyed Emmanuelle up and down and pointed to the hall.

Two younger girls—college-aged, also sporty and able-bodied—stood in the hall behind her, waiting to come in. They were loaded with backpacks and cold weather equipment. She hadn't planned on sharing a room with anyone. The woman moved aside to let Emmanuelle into the cabin. It had four berths. Emmanuelle threw her bag on one of the beds and reached for the latch to the window. The smell was making her want to retch.

"I think we're traveling right above the cows."

Cows? The ticket agent hadn't mentioned cows.

"I'm Birgit," the woman said, her face breaking into a toothy smile.

Emmanuelle managed a smile and gave up on the window latch. Birgit went to the task, fumbling with the latch on the other window, prying it open.

"I think the cows have a better arrangement."

One of the girls in the halls called out.

"Hey, we can't all stand at the same time in that room. Hello? Could you sit down, please?" the other girl said.

Emmanuelle sat down on her berth.

"The ships they use in the winter are smaller than the ones in the summer. They pack people in like sardines," Birgit said. "You know what that means right?"

Emmanuelle looked at her blankly.

"It means the choppy water will throw the ship around more." She was breaking out alcohol and little glasses.

"Try it. Pisco Sour, they call it," Birgit said, offering a small glass.

Alcohol in the morning?

"It will help. I've done this trip many times. Very violent waves."

What the hell? It couldn't make things worse. She took the glass from Birgit and swallowed its contents in one gulp. She closed her eyes again. The liquor burned its way down. Her brain fought sleep, struggling to process what was happening and calculate her next steps. In her foggy mind, it was clear that the United States District Court would probably rule in favor of prosecutors and request her extradition. They didn't have to prove she was guilty *beyond a reasonable doubt*. They just had to establish *probable cause*; enough evidence to warrant her arrest. They certainly had that much. The fact that she'd fled with the files and the stock certificates was plenty.

How utterly, utterly stupid she'd been. She'd blindly trusted Stephan and made the worst mistake of her life. Another thought drum-rolled in her mind. They could ask for her "provisional arrest" in Chile because of the urgency of the situation. She was a flight risk, so that would warrant her being held in custody. Emmanuelle *couldn't* get caught before she had the evidence or that would be the end. She wondered what was going on in the Prefecto's office.

She breathed a sigh of relief when the ferry pushed away from the quay. The ship would travel south between the fjords of the Northern Patagonian Ice Field for thirty-six hours before stopping in Puerto Edén for a few hours. Passengers could go ashore for a brief visit before the ship continued on to Puerto Natales. Emmanuelle planned to get off in Puerto Edén and simply not come back. She wasn't sure what she would do when she got there, but the weight of that thought was dissipating. The rocking of the ship made her conscious of just how thoroughly debilitated she'd become.

Sleep fell over her like a curtain ending a show.

Chapter 67

AT 8:00 A.M. Sebastián got into his car with a sinking feeling that Emmanuelle had fled again. Ambivalence better characterized what he felt. Secretly, he hoped she'd fled. There were orders from Santiago to bring her in for questioning by American authorities. The evidence they had—the stolen files with the stock certificates and her links to Pereira—would probably be sufficient to warrant her extradition to the United States. They just suspected she'd taken the files. A witness told authorities he'd seen her leave the documents room with files. If Sebastián revealed she'd given the files to him, that would *prove* she'd taken them and probably be enough to warrant a quick extradition. He didn't want to be a witness against her. It would all come out eventually. He would have to comply. But he just needed a few days.

They were closing in on her and he had doubts he would be able to protect her now. At least, not until they had proof to establish her innocence. It was clear in his mind that her story was consistent. There was one issue he wanted to check out immediately. Whether one of the men had a black mark on his hand as Emmanuelle described. If one of them had been Stephan Henri Brent's driver in Brazil, it closed a very improbable link—that the Brent case was even more closely connected to the recent crimes in Chile. They didn't have a motive yet, but at least they could establish the link.

He parked on the street and rang the front door bell to the Albergue Monte Carmen. A young girl opened. She recognized him immediately. "Señor Prefecto Cienfuegos. Good morning."

"I am here to speak to Emmanuelle Solis."

"I'll let her know," the girl said, letting him into the vestibule and pointing to a sofa near the fireplace. "Please, have a seat."

He followed her instead, waiting at the foot of the staircase.

The girl climbed the winding stairs. He heard her knock at the door. A few seconds later, she reappeared. "She's not answering."

Sebastián bolted up the stairs. He knocked loudly on the door and waited before twisting the knob. The room was vacant.

He called the phone he'd given her. It went to voicemail. He suspected she'd taken the ferry to Puerto Edén. That had been her plan all along.

He bolted back down the stairs, dialing Pilar on the way down. He was out the door by the time she picked up.

"Prefecto? Where are you?"

"I need you to confirm something urgently."

"*Por supuesto.* What is it?"

"Did any of the witnesses mention anything unusual about the hands of the suspect in the Pacheco case? Any distinguishing traits?"

"Interpol just ID'd him. His name is Rodrigo Silva de Souza. Forty-two years old. From Salvador de Bahia. And yes, Bruno said he had a black mark on his right hand. Either an oval-shaped tattoo or a birthmark."

Exactly as Emmanuelle said. He stopped in front of his car, looking around. His stomach clutched. She was in grave danger. They would go after her next.

"Hey, are you still there?"

"*Ya.*" He slid into the front seat.

"Are you bringing her into the office?"

"No. She's gone." He opened the glove compartment and removed his iPad.

"What do you mean she's gone? Where could she have gone?"

"No idea." He turned it on and waited for it to boot. "*Ni idéa.*"

"What are you going to do?"

"I'm going to take a few days off. Maybe go see a friend. Or go skiing." He touched the GPS tracking page. He'd installed a mini GPS tracking chip in the phone he'd given her. If she'd taken it with her, he'd know exactly where she was.

"What? Are you crazy? Right now? With everything going on? Have you lost your mind?"

The page came up and the arrow was spinning. He said, "What's going on? We've been taken off nearly every case we've been working on. Santiago has taken over everything. Until the Prosecutor's office clears us to continue with any of our investigations, our hands are tied. I don't think that will happen anytime soon. They're all preparing for the weekend. I'll be back Monday morning."

"You have orders to bring her in."

"*Cadajo.* I *can't* bring her in if I don't know where she is.*"

"Sebastián, I know you're up to something. You're smarter than to let that woman ruin your life. I hope you are not taking risks for her...."

He hung up. The arrow stopped spinning. The GPS had pinpointed her. She was just outside the port. She *was* on the ferry.

Puerto Edén was only accessible by ferry. He googled the ferry schedule. Hers must have just left. The next would leave at 9:00 P.M. That was too late. But if he caught a plane to Puerto Natales and caught the ferry from there, he could make it to Puerto Edén just a little after she did.

He sped down the road towards El Tepual Airport.

Chapter 68

TWENTY-FOUR HOURS after the ferry left port, screams and cries woke Emmanuelle. *The ship is capsizing.* She tried to stand, but the contents of the cabin—reclining chairs, passengers and their possessions—slid across the floor and slammed against the steel walls of the ship. Her stomach convulsed. She fought to suppress the urge to vomit.

The ship had sailed past Calbuco, the Reloncaví Bay and the Gulf of Ancud, and now it was entering the Gulf of Corcovado—an area notorious for storms. Huge waves rose up and crashed against the ship, slapping and tossing it about.

"Relax," one of her roommates told her. "You're not going to die. It's always like this crossing the Golfo de Corcovado. Right before we get to Puerto Edén, we'll pass the Gulf of Sorrows. *There* we might die." She laughed and threw her arms up in the air as their chairs slid across the room. "It's like being on a rollercoaster ride. Enjoy it."

Emmanuelle put her hands over her ears and curled into a fetal position, praying she could block out the screeching noise of buckling metal. Would the ship shatter to pieces? She questioned whether the *Antarctic Mist* had been sabotaged. Under these conditions, human intervention wouldn't be necessary to make a ship go down. Images of the sinking ship, real and invented, filled her head. She saw herself dropping into the dark, icy water.

Emmanuelle muffled a terrified scream.

***

"Come on. Get up," Birgit said to Emmanuelle. "You're still alive. Let's go up to the deck. You need fresh air."

Emmanuelle strained to focus on Birgit's face. Eight hours of misery had passed before the ship entered calmer water. The seasickness pills hadn't worked. They'd only succeeded in sedating her. "I don't want to go anywhere."

"Come on. You'll feel better if you do."

"Yeah, we'll help you up." Her three roommates were standing by her bed, inspecting her.

They helped her up to the deck and into one of the reclining chairs that now lined the sundeck. She took deep, gulping breaths of the fresh cold air. It soothed the queasiness in her stomach. On the deck, life on board seemed to be returning to normal. Passengers were playing cards, listening to music, smoking cigarettes.

Several hours passed before Emmanuelle opened her eyes again and lifted her head. She was still on the deck. Someone had draped a thick blanket over her. She tried to sit up, but her throbbing head felt larger and heavier than the rest of her body. Every bone and muscle in her body ached. Agonizing glimpses, memories and random flashbacks of the events of the past weeks were on replay in her mind. She rested her head back in resignation, dread coming over her again. She thought of saying the rosary, but the last time she'd done that—right before her mother died—it hadn't worked. She missed her mother. She decided she wouldn't move a muscle other than the ones that blinked her eyelids, unless she absolutely had to. She'd try to focus on something other than the tragedies that had become her life. Night had fallen and swirling winds were pushing white clouds rapidly across the sky, unveiling a tapestry of brilliant stars. The light reflecting off the surface of the moon created a lunar rainbow. The world seemed a beautiful and terrible place.

Then the thought came to her. A memory crystalized. She knew who the boy in the picture was—the boy with Stephan and the woman she believed was his mother. It was Sean Michael Epstein. She sat up. She'd seen him at a conference. He'd been with Gilberto Pereira. How long had Stephan known him? Was he a family member? She made her way back to the cabin, praying the ship's Wi-Fi worked. She opened her laptop and waited for it to boot. She googled "Sean Michael Epstein" and it came up with more than two million hits. She typed in "Sean Michael Epstein & Calgary" and he was her first hit. Executive Vice President And Chief Operating Officer, Barretta Gold. She wondered if he was related to Stephan. She remembered that Stephan had talked to her about his stepfather running a mine in Calgary that had ultimately failed. Stephan's mother had recently passed away. She brought up the website for the *Calgary Herald* and searched its archives. Her heart stopped when the hit came up. She clicked on the first. The obituary of Sybil Francis Epstein appeared.

Sybil Francis Epstein passed away on Friday, March 21, 2016 in Calgary, Ab at the age of sixty-six years. The loving mother of Stephan Henri Brent, Sybil was born in Bield, Mb on May 5, 1947. Son, Stephan Henri Brent, and a stepson survive her. Sybil was cremated and a celebration of her life will be held in May. Expressions of sympathy may be forwarded to the family via the website www.Fostersgardenchapel.Ca. Foster's Garden Chapel Funeral Home & Crematorium. Telephone: 403-297-0888. Honoured Provider Of Dignity Memorial.

She took her notepad out and wrote the information down. A stepson? No name was mentioned. Sean Michael Epstein must be his stepbrother.

The ship was passing through a labyrinth of channels filled with seals and sea lions and weaving its way through the fjords and islands of the Northern Patagonia Ice Sheet. The white, snow-covered crests of the Andes Mountains glistened against the night sky in the distance. Why hadn't he talked about Sean? She'd met him in Brazil, but Stephan never mentioned he was his stepbrother.

She scrolled to the pictures of Stephan, his mother and Sean. She understood how Stephan had come up from his roots and become a famous lawyer. He'd studied and struggled his way to the top. *But how did someone from Sean Michael Epstein's background become the Chief Operating Officer of a gold company?* She stared at the carcass of a rusted ship rocking with the waves in the billowing brume outside her window.

***

A few hours later, passengers were swallowing seasickness pills again in anticipation of the crossing of the Gulf of Sorrows. For eight hours, the boat rolled violently in ice-laden water. After being tossed through the treacherous English Narrows for hours, the calm finally came. The clouds lifted, unveiling the forested mountain range and its cascading waterfalls. They'd arrived at Puerto Edén. The ship anchored several hundred meters off the port.

Emmanuelle climbed to the deck. People from the chain of stilted, tin-roof houses on the port waved at them. Some of the passengers waved back. An orange-colored motorcraft raced ahead of a handful of small, wooden boats making their way to the ship. Passengers began boarding these, eager to visit the town and its unusual inhabitants.

"Keep your life jacket on," the captain yelled over to Emmanuelle.

"Sure thing." She wanted to rip it off. It was suffocating

her. She could barely fasten it around her enormous parka and everything under it itched. She grabbed hold of the ladder and looked down. A sensation that she might jump froze her for a second. What it would be like if she slipped and fell? From that height, she could die. Could that be worse than the hell she was living? She took a deep breath and continued down the ladder.

A blanket of mist covered most of the town. The impoverished fishing village seemed otherworldly. She wondered what Juan Carlos looked like and how the hell she would find him.

Chapter 69

Juan Carlos Messier sat at a rickety table cluttered with papers, reports, and graphs. He ground out another cigarette in the ashtray. For hours, the wind had shrieked like a demon, whirling rain against the pane. Now suddenly the rain stopped and it was deafeningly quiet.

He glanced out the dirty, rain-bleared window of his two-room stilted shack. Time seemed to be suspended. He prayed for the gift of clarity that sometimes came after the rain. He wondered whether anyone would believe his theory. Could he convince law enforcement that the expedition had been sabotaged? He was certain the killers were still out there. Would justice ever be done even if he did? He was wrestling with skepticism about going to the authorities. He lit another cigarette. He felt heavy. Outweighed by the consciousness of what lay before him. He was piecing together the research and findings of his colleagues. Even if it couldn't be compiled into a final report and presented to the State of the Antarctic Conference, he had the names and contact information of several of Nils' colleagues who would help him get it circulated at environmental conferences and maybe even in journals. But he had a more immediate problem to consider right now: Karl Gustav. Someone wanted him dead and Juan Carlos needed to protect him.

The wooden walkway connecting the port's stilted-houses rattled. *The wind is picking up again*, he thought. He stubbed his cigarette in the ashtray and blew out a jet of smoke.

He was afraid he wasn't going to be able to arrange the reports in any sensible order. There were too many things missing. Two years earlier, when Nils Giaever had finally responded to his plea to recruit members for an expedition in the Patagonia, Juan Carlos had been hopeful that their efforts would help stop the proliferation of damaging projects in the region. But now those prospects looked grim. It seemed, in fact, their efforts had been criminally sabotaged.

The gold mining and dam projects would move forward. Companies would clear the land, build the dams, flood farmland, and detonate glaciers to exploit gold. What remained of indigenous life, culture, traditions would eventually yield to industrial plans.

The environment would eventually transmute in response to man's impact. He'd dedicated all of his life to rescuing his ancestors from the shadows of history, but he now felt their spirits would perpetually drift the encroaching darkness. Faith was something they had indoctrinated in him, but it was slipping away. Maybe he should just give up. He had to accept that he was part of a moribund tribe—a thing of the past. He closed his eyes. His head filled with childhood memories of rafting the channels between the fjords and glaciers, diving with his father into the icy waters to hunt for giant mollusks. That was before the government had forced them to resettle in Puerto Edén and abandon their nomadic ways. Before his father sank into alcoholism and abandoned his ancestors and his people.

Twenty years earlier, with a government grant, he'd been able to leave Puerto Edén and study glaciology in Santiago. He'd been driven to return to help his people and protect the environment, which in his belief was an extension of his family. He converted his childhood fascination with the glaciers into a lifelong career. It had spawned from the Alacaluf folktales of mythological creatures whose spirits were trapped in the glaciers. He now felt *he* was that mythological creature.

He rubbed his temples with his large weathered hands and stared at the reports. So many bits of information were missing. Would he be able to do this? Something was going to have to fall out of the sky and land in his lap to make his luck change.

The wooden walkway shook again. This time, he was certain, with the weight of a visitor. People had come calling earlier to tell him some girl was looking for him. *Probably interested in interviewing someone from a moribund tribe.* He studied her through the window. She was wearing an enormous green jacket, struggling along the walkway, up the steep wooden stairs, lugging a duffel bag the size of a body bag. *What the devil could she have in it?* He listened to the rhythmic clanking of the wooden planks as she got closer and finally knocked at the door. He ignored her.

She pounded heavily. *Stubborn, that woman. Obstinate.* Finally she left. *What could she want?* Something told him it wasn't just a photo opportunity. He would follow her.

Chapter 70

"YOUR SHIP JUST left port," a voice called from behind Emmanuelle.

She turned and stared at the immensely tall man who seemed to have emerged from a cloud of vapor. His sketchy outline was partly veiled by the fog, giving him a mystical aura. He might well have been seven feet tall.

"I decided to stay here." Water spurted from her rain-drenched lips. She was soaked. She walked toward him, her feet sloshing around in her boots.

His narrow eyes surveyed her with curiosity. He had a dark, leathery complexion and high cheekbones. He was wearing a long raincoat and no hat. The full mane of thick black hair that fell to his shoulders appeared to be waterproof. Rain rolled right off his head.

The wild, whipping wind blew the rain in every direction. Emmanuelle put a hand over her eyes to shield them. "I am looking for Juan Carlos Messier."

"What do you want him for?"

Her instincts said she was talking to him. She would lose her mind if not. He was her only hope. "I need to talk to him." The words sputtered from her mouth as she tried to get control over her shivering body. In the six or so hours that she had been there it had showered, rained, drizzled, poured—constantly drenching her.

"Bout what?"

"The *Antarctic Mist.*"

"How can I help you?"

"Are you Juan Carlos Messier? The Kawésqar?"

"*Si po.* Why do you look so surprised? Were you expecting to find me naked, oiled up with sea lion blubber? Riding around in a little canoe with a fire lit on the inside?" He crinkled his face and cocked his head to the other side, still studying her.

Emmanuelle put her duffel bag down and pulled off her cap. "Is there any place where we can go and talk? In private?"

"Can't get any more private than this," he said, waving a hand. "We are fifteen thousand kilometers away from nowhere."

She looked around. No one in sight. Smoke rose from the chimney of a stilted home down the walkway where she'd been a few minutes earlier.

He lifted her duffel bag, turned around and started toward it.

She ran after him, the planks of the walkway clanking under her feet. Was this his way of agreeing to speak to her?

"This is my little Puerto Edén chalet," he announced as he opened the door of the shack. It had an iron woodstove, a tiny wooden table piled up with stacks of yellowing, crinkly-edged papers and two old high-backed chairs. "Come in," he said. She headed straight to the woodstove and shed the outer layers of her wet clothing.

There were two doors that she assumed led to a bedroom and, hopefully, a bathroom. A pot of something was bubbling on top of the stove. It smelled smoky. There was a sink and a cabinet with a flowered cloth tacked up for a door. She wondered if he lived there yearlong. It was desolate, and there was no sign he was caring for any sick scientist.

"I can't stop shivering," she said through chattering teeth.

After a long silence, he said, "Shivering is good for you. It's a hypothalamic response to initiate metabolic processes to increase heat production. Mammals have several different ways of producing heat to regulate body temperature and conserve heat. Shivering generates heat quickly because of the muscular activity. In mammals, it increases metabolic heat for about twenty minutes. Then it begins to decline again." His face bore no expression.

"Really?" she mumbled, rubbing her hands together. He was a scientist. She wondered if all of their conversations would be like this. After all, it took a certain type of character to be willing to spend endless swaths of time studying the infinitesimal world of microbial clusters.

"I've been shivering for about three days now non-stop," she said.

"You need to change your clothes. You won't stop shivering until you do. You can change in there," he said, pointing to the door at the other end of the room.

She opened her duffel bag. Fortunately, it proved waterproof. Her laptop, iPad, phone and clothes were still dry. She pulled out jeans and a sweater and opened the door to a closet-sized room with a cot and a window. Nothing else.

She wondered where Sebastián was. What had happened at the police station after they discovered she'd fled? The rain was starting in again. A trickle of icy water leaked through the corrugated metal roof and landed on her head. She brushed it away. She changed and returned to the living room.

Juan Carlos filled a copper kettle and set it down on the stove. The shack had no electricity and the room was illuminated only by the fire and a small kerosene lamp on the table. He placed a chair close to the stove and motioned for her to sit.

"Where are you from?" he asked, bringing another chair over and setting it down by hers.

"Washington, D.C.," she said, running a hand through her wet hair. She sat down and took a deep breath, feeling some of the tension draining from her muscles. "My father was from Chile. My mother was Swiss. Both died when I was a teenager." She stared at the flames. She was beginning feel warm again.

"You're the girl in the papers, right?" He was staring at the back of his hands. "The one the authorities are looking for?"

A wave of paranoia rippled through her. She hadn't seen today's papers. But could it possibly have been worse than yesterday's papers? And how had he seen the papers on this desolate island? She guessed he had Internet access somewhere nearby. She realized the rain had stopped. It was quiet enough for him to hear the jackhammering in her chest. She'd rehearsed what she would say to him when they met, but adrenaline was wiping out information from her brain. Did she just imagine a connection? Was she clinging to the most remotely plausible of possibilities in her despair? Would he help her? Maybe he'd think she was a criminal. What could he do for her anyway?

"I came here because I'm being framed for a crime, and I think the people who are responsible are the same people who sabotaged the *Antarctic Mist*." She could hear water running under his little house. It felt soothing.

"I'm listening," Juan Carlos said.

"I don't know where to start, but this is my story. I'm an attorney and I was working for a law firm in Washington, D.C. called Oliver & Stone." He picked up a pack of cigarettes and plucked one from the box and offered it to her. She hadn't had a cigarette since law school, but she accepted.

"About two weeks ago, Stephan Henri Brent, a partner from my firm disappeared in Argentina. It's been all over the papers." He lit a match and held it out to her. She lit the cigarette.

"I heard about his abduction."

Her sleep-deprived mind began to spin with a nicotine rush. "After he disappeared, there was nothing but speculation about what happened to him. Then, about a week later, out of the blue, he called me. He said he'd escaped." She looked at the cigarette in her hand and considered stubbing it out, but instead took another drag. "He said that his abduction was related to his having uncovered illegal activities of some attorneys in the firm. He didn't name them. He just said that it had to do with securities or financial fraud. He told me that when he questioned the managing partner about some strange bank transfers, all of the sudden the partner became viciously hostile. He didn't have time for more details." Her blood was racing. She tried to steady the hand with the cigarette. "He was on the run and scared. He asked me to bring files with me so we could take them to the authorities here. So I brought them. They are all documents connected to the dam projects in the Patagonia. I don't know where he called from or how he got a phone, but it turned out that he called me from the phone of a high-level investment fraud suspect, Gilberto Pereira. FBI and Interpol traced the call and now have linked me to Pereira. I suspect Pereira was involved in his abduction. Maybe Stephan got hold of his phone and fled with it."

The kettle steamed. "*Sigue.* Continue." He stood and walked to the cabinet, taking out a little sack and a spoon.

"We were to meet in Puerto Montt. Information in the files supposedly proved who was behind his abduction and the criminal activities linked to the firm. We were supposed to go to the authorities after I got here. I trusted him." She watched as he fixed an infusion, dropping dried herbs and flowers into the water. "He was my boss ... and I was sort of in love with him. I'd just started getting involved with him about a month or so earlier. So ... I did the stupidest thing I've ever done in my life. I took the files from the office and came here to meet him."

He poured the infusion into a mug and handed it to her. Something told her that this gentle man was going to be her friend.

"Thank you." She wrapped her hands around it, stretching her back against the chair. "I took the files from the office and left the next night. I was elated that he was still alive. I'm thinking ... everything's under control. I land. I meet him. Give him the files. We go to the authorities and whoever-it-is is busted." He was utterly silent. "I should never have gotten on the plane." She searched his face for an expression. There was none. "A few days after I landed, I realized that the files had stock certificates in them. Over a million dollars' worth issued by a mining company out here somewhere. But I'd have to be the stupidest criminal in the world to steal stock certificates from a partner in my office. All he would have to do is put a stop transfer request in and they would be worthless."

He poured more infusion from the kettle into her mug. She sipped it. It had a citrusy tang.

"The day I arrived in Chile, the *Antarctic Mist* sank. I just can't believe that there isn't some relationship between Patagonia Files and the *Antarctic Mist*. I believe the ship was sabotaged because there are some very high-powered people who have a big stake in the eleven-billion-dollar project and they don't want to see your report published. One of those high-powered people is a partner in Oliver & Stone. And he's here in Chile now, riding around with someone who *claims* to be an agent for the U.S. Embassy but isn't, and is trying to work authorities against me. You see, I have something they want. But I haven't got a clue what it is."

She sipped the steaming infusion.

"Where are the files?"

"I turned them in to the Puerto Montt Prefecto." The thought of Sebastián gave her a rush of sadness. He'd taken risks for her and she'd fled again. She prayed he would understand. "But I took pictures of every page in the files. I have them here in my laptop." She turned it on, brought up the files, but the page went black.

"It's out of battery. Is there somewhere I can charge it?" She wrung her hands.

"Yes," he said. "We can charge it at the Navy Building," he said, lighting another cigarette, but not moving.

Then reality checked in again. The naval officers had to be aware of the lookout for her. They probably had a description of her. They would recognize her. Her stomach dropped to her feet.

She'd talked herself to exhaustion. Was he hiding the scientist or not? Panic was beginning to set in. If he didn't talk soon, she was in serious trouble. Finished.

She stirred in her chair. She had to get him to talk. It was Saturday night. On Tuesday morning prosecutors would be arguing for her extradition. If the trip to Puerto Edén proved fruitless, she was finished. "A few days after I arrived here, Stephan's body was found. He'd been tortured and killed. I believe his murder is related to the *Antarctic Mist*, even though they are seemingly unrelated events." She paused. "I know another scientist, Karl Gustav, survived and I know you know where he is. I believe the men who tried to kill him are the same ones who are after me."

Silence.

"Where is Karl Gustav?" she asked. "Is he dead? Is he alive?" she added gently. "I know you are taking care of him."

More silence. The rain started in again, pelting the roof.

He opened the pot that had been boiling since she arrived. "You look like you need some nutrition. Are you hungry?"

She was famished.

He served her smoked mussel and potato soup. The mussels were about as big as size six flip-flops and rubbery, but they tasted delicious. She cut them with a knife and devoured everything in her bowl. He offered her more and she accepted.

He finally began talking after they finished eating. "I'm what the museums call an 'Urban Kawésqar.' I studied science in Santiago on a government grant and came back to help my people." The rain fell on the zinc rooftop in a rhythmic staccato. He lit another cigarette. Like many of the indigenous Indians of Chile who'd moved to the bigger cities for economic and other reasons, he was schooled in Spanish and used his native language infrequently. "We were once the largest tribe of the Tierra del Fuego. My people lived north and south of the Strait of Magellan and throughout the Brunswick Peninsula, on the Santa Inés and Desolación Islands until the government of Chile forced us to abandon our nomadic culture and settle in Puerto Edén."

"How did you get a French name?"

"Messier's not my real name," he said. "My Kawésqar name is C'oukol. In the 1940's the government passed the Kawésqar Protection Law that forced us to settle in Puerto Edén. Being sedentary made us dependent on the government. It took away who we were. I guess the government thought they were protecting us. They had a big ceremony. A Salesian priest baptized us and gave us Christian names mostly after explorers like Wellington, Edén, Baker, and Messier."

For a moment, she thought of Padre Cristóbal.

"The *Registro Civil* later issued formal registration documents that guessed our ages."

"So you don't know how old you are?"

"No, but it doesn't make a difference to me."

The rain now pounded on the tin roof.

"For thousands of years no white man endured the journey to the Magallanes. They couldn't survive the katabatic windstorms, the subzero temperatures, the violent waters. The seas bubble like a witch's cauldron, devouring their ships. It wasn't until the 1500s that western explorers finally survived the journey. Three hundred years later, greater numbers of explorers and colonialists arrived, bringing conflict and infectious diseases to the land of fire and ice. By the end of early 1900s, there were only one hundred and fifty of my people left. Today, there are only fifteen of us left."

Emmanuelle studied his face in the light of the kerosene lamp. There was something calming about being with him on one of the farthest reaches of the earth. Something that shrank the importance of everything she'd known about the world before she came here. She sipped the infusion, huddling close to the woodstove. She wondered where Karl Gustav was. But now that the Kawésqar was finally talking she was sure he would tell her. For the first time in days she felt some reassurance. Some clouds were lifting. There was some hope that the false accusations against her would be disproved.

"I was always fascinated with the glaciers as a child. We're situated on a jagged cliff that once stood high above sea level, but with the rising sea level, each year it's become more submerged. Soon it will entirely cover this island," said Juan Carlos.

"What happened to Karl before the ship left port? Why didn't you and Karl Gustav get on board the *Antarctic Mist?*" She waited while he decided whether or not to trust her.

"He was poisoned," he said. "Johan Bahr found him in his bungalow nearly dead."

"Do you *know* that he was poisoned?" she asked, nervously tapping cigarette ash into the ashtray.

"Yes. He told me."

"So ... he's well now? He can talk?"

"He's not well. But he can talk. He told me what happened."

"Tell me." She waved away some of the drifting cigarette smoke. "Please."

"He left the ship to find papers the *Armada* was asking for to clear the expedition to proceed. When he got back to his bungalow, two men were in the room. They were going through his things. They started fighting. One of them held him down, and the other injected him with curare."

"What's that?"

"It's extremely potent arrow poison. Indigenous people along the Amazon use it. They shoot their victims with arrows or blowgun darts dipped in curare. It causes asphyxiation and paralyzes the victim's respiratory muscles so they can't breathe. It's more common in the Amazon than in Chile. It's reversible if you can keep the victim breathing. I think they chose it so they could drop him in the water and make it look like an accident. Like he'd been drinking and drowned. But it didn't work out that way."

He told her that a colleague had gone looking for Karl when he didn't show up at the Armada Building for the final expedition team meeting. "He found two men in the bungalow with Karl. One claimed he was a friend of Karl's from São Paulo. Karl was close to cardiac arrest by that time. The men insisted Karl had gotten sick from seafood. Redtide poisoning. *Marea roja* poisoning. They'd turned the place upside down. He thought they looked suspicious although he couldn't think of any reason why anyone would want to hurt Karl. When he went to the ship for medicine, I rushed to the bungalow and got Karl out of there. I knew what the men wanted."

"What did they want? Why did they try to kill him?"

He ignored the question. "Martín was there when I got there. He was crying, trying to keep Karl breathing. He told me he suspected that the men had done something to Karl. He helped me get Karl onto a boat and I took him back to Aysén. It was the only way I knew how to protect him. I figured the men would come back for him and finish him off. On the way, Martín told me that he'd been working for Aguas Meriodionales de la Patagonia. Grupo Meridional. Everyone here calls them GM. They were hired by Hébère to do the environmental assessment analysis for the dams."

"I know. My firm was involved in setting that up."

"Martín told me GM had been spying on our activities, and he'd been turning our reports over to them. He said he didn't know who the two men were. He said he'd never seen them before, but he took them to Karl because Lucas told him to."

"Who?"

"His name is Lucas Braga. He was the general manager of the office here in Chile. The one that Martín reported to. Martín didn't realize they planned to kill Karl. He was distraught when he found him. A commercial ship was leaving, going back to Puerto Montt at dawn. Martín went back on it. He said he was going to confront Lucas Braga and then go to the Carabineros. I'm sure he never suspected they would sabotage the ship. His brother was on board. I am sure that's why he committed suicide … when he found out the ship went down."

"Martín didn't commit suicide. He also never made it to the police."

"What?" His eyebrows rose. "The papers said he was found hanging."

She told him about what she knew. "The police confirmed he was murdered."

"Murdered?"

"I was at Casa de Tenglo the night that Martín's body was discovered. I overheard the conversations of the priests. They didn't believe it was a suicide. In fact, they're certain it wasn't. I later found out from the Prefecto of PDI in Puerto Montt that they confirmed murder. Martín confessed to a priest by the name of Rodrigo Pacheco right before he was found hanged. Shortly after Martín was killed, someone broke into the rectory of the cathedral and slit the priest's throat." Then she told him how Martín's sister was assaulted the next evening. "She told me Martín kept many of his documents and reports at her house. Maybe that's why they went after her."

He shook his head. "No. No. They have all of those documents."

"Look, I know you know more about this than I do. Help me to understand what they were after. They're after me as well. Maybe we can help each other."

Juan Carlos didn't answer.

"The priests said it looked as though someone had been searching for something. There were planks ripped off the walls in Martín's room as though something might have hidden there. What would they have been looking for?"

Juan Carlos stood up. "The external hard-drive," he muttered.

"What external hard-drive? What are you talking about?"

He went to the back room, coming back a minute later with a long, thick woolen jacket which he handed to her.

"Put this on. You'll need it. We're going to Caleta Tortel. Karl Gustav is staying there at my house. It's at the mouth of the Baker River, close to where some dams projects were being assessed. We'll have to take a boat there."

The thought of trekking out on the wild ocean again made Emmanuelle's stomach clench. Caleta Tortel was located between two ice fields at the point of convergence between the river and the sea. The ship that brought her to Puerto Edén headed there after it left. It was several hours away. Could her nervous system withstand another ride across that water?

Juan Carlos picked up her duffel bag and opened the door.

If anyone knew how to survive on that water, it was a Kawésqar. Emmanuelle put the jacket on and followed him out the door. She had little more than a day to come up with a defense. She drew in a deep breath.

Chapter 71

The journey from Puerto Edén to Caleta Tortel was much calmer than Emmanuelle had expected. The motorboat hummed through the labyrinth of narrow channels and fjords, passing scores of seals, sea lions, otters and wildlife along the way to the Baker Channel. She wondered whether the herbal infusion had calmed her jittery nerves.

The squalls of the night before had subsided and the rain was a vaporous mist. The sleepless night and faintness of dawn made it hard to distinguish the sensation of dreaming of being in a strange place from reality. Maybe she was awake and afflicted with madness. She heard the echoing of hushed voices. A distant, but endless howling. "What's that noise?" Emmanuelle asked. A fog enveloped the motorboat.

"It's coming from over there," he said as they passed a tiny island lined with cypress crosses. The Island of the Dead." His voice was hushed. "Over a century ago, more than a hundred laborers were found dead on the island. They were working for a lumber company felling cypresses for export. Patagonian cypress is practically extinct today. The company said the workers died from an epidemic. Rumor had it the company poisoned them so it wouldn't have to pay them. People around here say that their ghosts roam the island at night." He glanced back at Emmanuelle and smiled. "*Tranquila.* The noise, it's probably just the wind."

Caleta Tortel, like Puerto Edén, appeared to have no conventional streets. Instead, it had a maze of steep wooden steps and walkways that began at the pier, wrapped around the port, weaved through the town and connected the wooden houses.

As the motorboat neared the pier, the rising sun illuminated blossoms of clouds on the horizon. The temperate North Patagonia Rainforest rimmed the outer edges of the town. Juan Carlos helped Emmanuelle out of the boat and onto the town's wooden labyrinth. A cluster of children in uniforms crossed a section of the walkway heading to school. They waved at her as they passed. She waved back. They were singing a song that rang through the air. *La madre estaba serena, serena estaba la madre....* The waterway was lined with sprawling ferns and enormous water lilies.

They walked for what seemed like miles along the walkway until finally they arrived at a cottage. The Baker River glistened in the distance. Several *arriero*-cowboys in bombachos, boots, and sombreros stood outside. A guitar was propped against the rail of the walkway. One of the men sipped mate from a silver bombillo straw.

"*Buenos días,*" Juan Carlos called out as they approached.

The men tilted their sombreros.

He spoke to them briefly out of Emmanuelle's hearing range. They appeared to be guarding the place. She looked around, wondering if there had been more attempts on the scientist's life.

It was a beautiful place. A group of tethered horses grazed nearby. She walked over to them and stroked the mane of one. The men talking to Juan Carlos obviously spent a good part of their lives in a saddle. After a few minutes, one of them smiled at her and said, "Welcome to Caleta Tortel." Juan Carlos motioned her to follow him. He walked toward the cottage and opened the door, letting her in to a small sitting room with wide-planked cypress floors, rustic furniture, a stone fireplace and a sheepskin rug on the floor.

This, she was certain, was the Kawésqar's real home. In the far corner, next to a window with a stunning view of the massive turquoise-blue river, was a large desk stacked with magazines, newspapers, papers, charts, maps, a globe, and books. Fat books with crinkled pages warped by the humidity. Jars lined one of the bookshelves. She took a step back. What on earth was in them? Were they specimen jars? What did the Kawésqar collect? Stacked by the desk were crates and wooden boxes filled with what appeared to be monitoring equipment. In another corner, a bookshelf was laden with books of all sizes, and appeared ready to collapse under the weight.

A woman in a rocking chair next to the stove stood as they entered. She'd been knitting from a large spool of white yarn, which she tucked into a bag. "Just in time. I have to go. Will you be needing me later?"

"I'll let you know," Juan Carlos said. He followed her to the kitchen. Emmanuelle stayed close behind. The woman turned out the fire under a pot gently boiling on the stove. It smelled familiar.

Juan lifted the lid. "Smoked mussel stew," he said. Obviously a dish he liked. There was freshly baked bread stacked on the counter.

Two doors were at the far end of the hall. One of them had to be the room where Karl Gustav was staying. Juan Carlos pulled his gloves off and went inside one, closing the door behind him. After a few minutes he came out again.

"Are you hungry?" he asked.

"What about Karl?"

"Let him rest."

The sun was falling in golden rays on the sitting room. She blinked a few times to focus on him. *Smoked mussels for breakfast?* "Sure, why not? I guess I *am* hungry."

He unhooked a copper ladle from a chain and scooped mussels, potatoes and broth into two bowls.

Chapter 72

"COME IN," JUAN Carlos said. He had a kettle of steamed water in one hand and cups in another. Emmanuelle stepped gently onto the creaking floor of the room where Karl Gustav lay in bed, propped with pillows. The room reeked of disease and medicines. His eyes were closed, and it looked like he had gone weeks without bathing. His blond hair was greasy, his forehead pink and shiny. His crystal blue eyes flashed when Juan Carlos opened the curtain next to his bed, letting in the sunlight.

"He's regaining his speech and movement," Juan Carlos said. Karl Gustav lifted his head. Emmanuelle moved closer. He smelled like a goat.

Juan Carlos removed a small sack from a basket with a handle woven from long, reedy grass and poured its contents into the kettle.

After a minute of brewing, he handed a cup of the brew to Karl. "Martín was murdered," he said.

Karl opened his eyes wide. "What?"

"The men who tried to kill you went after him thinking he had the external hard-drive."

"Christ," Karl said.

Juan Carlos looked at Emmanuelle. "Two months ago, a geologist, Guilherme Lisboa, was gunned down in Rio de Janeiro."

Emmanuelle looked shocked.

"What is it?" Juan Carlos said.

"A few days before Stephan left to Argentina someone sent a fax to his home address. It had no phone or fax number on it." She paused to recall. "It was an article about a geologist who'd been killed in Rio de Janeiro. I asked him about it and he said it had probably been sent to him by mistake. It wasn't a mistake, was it?"

Karl and Juan exchanged glances. "When was that?"

"Maybe two weeks ago."

"That's when Guilherme was killed. He and Karl worked together."

"But why would someone send that article to Stephan?" Emmanuelle asked. "What did he have to do with the geologist?"

"*Who* was it sent to?" Karl asked, looking baffled.

"Stephan was a partner at my firm. He was abducted and murdered. His body was found last week close to the border." Emmanuelle briefly explained her story.

"Maybe he's the one." Karl said to Juan.

"What do you mean? What are you talking about?"

"Karl was Guilherme's supervisor at a remote sensing station in Brazil for a year before his murder."

"What's a remote sensing station?"

"Remote sensing is technology developed to acquire information through satellite imaging about objects on the surface of the earth observed from space. It's used for many purposes, like tracking changes in the environment, or assessing and managing natural resources. Our station was monitoring the retreat of the glaciers, seismic and volcanic activity and a wide range of factors in the Northern and Southern Patagonian Ice Fields."

"And? What is this all about? Do you think the geologist was killed because of the studies you were doing? Because if you published those studies, projects might not move forward?" She searched their faces. "That's why they sabotaged the ship, right?"

"I doubt it's that simple," Karl strained with the words. He laid his head back against the pillows.

Juan Carlos shook his head. "I thought about it, but…."

"If they believed your study threatened their industrial plans, don't you think they would kill to make sure it didn't get published? How is that so complicated? It's an eleven billion dollar project. People kill for much less."

"I'm not sure anything in the report we've been putting together would have had a substantial influence on any project, even if it were published. Everyone is aware of climate change and the dangers of building those dams in a seismic region. I just don't think those studies would have been enough for anyone to hunt us down."

"So what are they after?"

"Guilherme was targeted for a reason. A gunman chased him through downtown Rio and right through a mall before finally killing him. A few days before Karl left for the expedition, he came across some emails that had been sent by Guilherme right before he was killed. They were still on the station's server. He found out Guilherme had been blackmailing someone."

"Who was he trying to blackmail?"

"Someone with an email address sisyphus@gmail.com. He signs his emails "El Chefe.""

"Sisyphus?"

"Yes? Do you know who it is?"

"No, but…." The information sent her mind into a brief spin. "I've seen the address somewhere before. Maybe in the office." It occurred to her that it had appeared several times as an autocomplete on a computer she used. "Who was he blackmailing and for what reason?"

"We don't know. Or maybe we do now. About six months ago, Guilherme was sending satellite images to that same email address."

"Images of the Baker River?"

"No, of the Futaleufú region."

"Where's that?"

"North of here. It's famous for its whitewater rapids. Lots of tourists go rafting there."

"Are you certain the images aren't of the glaciers? Depicting the glacial retreat?" she looked at Juan Carlos.

"No one would kill for that," Karl explained. "There are images and studies of the glacial retreat everywhere in the world. It hasn't fazed society yet. It hasn't sent countries into action to make changes. No one would kill to prevent pictures of glacial retreat from being published. It's highly unlikely the blackmail had anything to do with glacial retreat or global warming."

"In an email, Guilherme agreed to surrender the external hard-drive in exchange for blackmail money. He never got it out of the station. Karl brought it here when he came on the trip."

"The external hard-drive has the Institute's archives stored on it. Only I had access to it. We have security cameras everywhere. Whatever the case, I think they killed him, because he showed up *without* it."

"Where is it now?"

"I have it. Karl brought it with him to Puerto Edén. The assassins somehow knew Karl was here and they came here to get the external hard-drive. Karl was poisoned before he ever got on board. They just wanted to kill him and get it."

"And you don't know what's on it?"

"They are images of the Futaleufú, but exactly why those images are so important to someone is not apparent to either of us."

"But what about the other geologists who came here with you? Couldn't they tell you any more about those images?"

"They're all dead now. But I never told them that I knew Guillermo was caught up in blackmail. I needed to be sure no one else in the office was involved." Karl blinked. He seemed to be in pain.

Juan Carlos lifted Karl's head and brought the cup to his lips.

"So the men just showed up at your bungalow?"

He swallowed in loud gulps. "Martín brought them over to my place. As soon as he left, they held a gun to my head and demanded I surrender the external hard-drive. I pretended I didn't know what they were talking about. I'd already given it to Juan Carlos to keep safe. One of them held me down, and the other stabbed me with a syringe. It felt like fire running through my blood. They tore my room apart looking for it. Then Johan showed up when they were still there. I could tell he was suspicious of the men. But I couldn't talk. Paralysis had already set in. I was afraid they would kill Johan, but the men took off."

"I never expected anyone would come here looking for it," Juan Carlos said. "Karl had asked me to keep it in a safe place. But he was more worried about the rain than criminals chasing it down."

"When they couldn't find it, I'm guessing they figured that Karl and Martín had gotten back on the ship and headed out. Maybe they figured it was safer to blow the whole ship up and ensure they'd destroyed the evidence and killed all potential witnesses. But whatever it has on it, it must be worth a lot to someone."

"So the external hard drive was what they were looking for at Martín's?"

"I have no doubt. After the ship went down, word got out

that Karl, Martín and I weren't aboard. They knew Karl and Martín could identify them, but I think they figured Karl would die. They probably thought Martín ran off with it to testify against them. He was a witness. He could have identified them."

Emmanuelle asked him for a list of the names of all of the scientists on board the *Antarctic Mist*. She would try to find more information about them online. "But what kind of evidence could be on it? And why are they killing so many people for it?"

"Maybe the answer to that question is another question. Why were images sent to your lawyer friend? Why was he killed?" Karl asked.

"That's why she's here," Juan Carlos said gently. "That's what she is trying to find out."

They heard voices outside. Someone banged loudly on the door. *"Policía de Investigaciones,"* a voice called. Emmanuelle recognized it. *Sebastián.*

Outside, the *arrieros* surrounded him, ready for a fight. She wondered whether he had come alone. Had he informed his superiors that he had gone looking for her? That he knew where she was? She doubted it.

She opened the door and stepped out.

"I have orders to arrest you," he said, breathing heavily. He paused as though he were trying to overcome a barrier inside himself. "The U.S. government has gone through the diplomatic channels. They have formally requested PDI turn you over for questioning."

Chapter 73

SEBASTIÁN LEANED AGAINST the door to the cottage, listening to Emmanuelle as she related all that she'd just learned from Juan Carlos and Karl Gustav. He knew any decision he made in the next few minutes would change the rest of his life. A warrant had already been issued for her arrest. No one knew he had gone looking for her and he had no law enforcement authority *per se* in the XI Region. Santiago was in charge now, swiftly undermining his authority. Soon there would be nationwide orders out for her arrest. He would have to bring her back to Puerto Montt and turn her over to Interpol. She would undoubtedly be questioned by the American authorities in the presence of a judge in a Chilean court. He stared at her as she spoke. The breeze gently lifting strands of her hair. He knew she was innocent. This wasn't just about running to save herself. This wasn't simply about her. It was about bringing those responsible to justice. And she was willing to fight for it.

She was now armed with a Kawésqar and *arrieros* whose respect for authority in their country was waning because, in their perspective, the government neglected them. Everything he was learning was consistent with information revealed in the investigations and information they'd been given by the *Fuerzas Aéreas* and the *Armada de Chile*. It was clear in his mind now that the ship had been sabotaged and it probably did have something to do with the disappearance of Stephan Henri

Brent. But how could they prove that? They needed a motive and they still had nothing concrete to prove the relationship. They had to find out what the blackmail images actually represented.

The papers ran with a different version of the facts. Mapuche activists were suspects in the murder of Rodrigo. And no connection was being drawn to Martín's murder. According to the papers, Emmanuelle was implicated in stealing stock certificates to fund leftist dissidents who wanted to expel foreign corporations from the region. The government would be pressured to act. Punishment would have to be swift and severe to send a clear message to foreign investors guaranteeing their protection in Chile. Political cases were resolved politically; not based on justice. How the investigation would be handled had become a political and diplomatic matter. The case could have widespread effects on investment and the economy. By the day, the facts revealed generated more international attention and controversy.

The thought of Emmanuelle being arrested and prosecuted unnerved him. He felt drawn in by something beyond his control. On some level, he was measuring up his life experiences with his dreams and he was coming up feeling quite empty inside.

"We need to know why those images on the hard-drive are so important to the assassins. If we don't, we have no proof of anything, just unsupported allegations."

The desperation in her voice rang in his mind. "I know."

They both understood the urgency.

He wanted answers as much as she did, but he wrestled with the thought of the consequences for his career if he chose to help her. Orders were orders. They would soon come, if he continued down this road. But his oath to his duty meant more to him than blindly following orders. This was his country. The integrity of which depended greatly on its ability to deliver justice to all within its borders. He'd never before hesitated to take orders. Somehow, now, the thought of risking his career hardly mattered in light of the fact that he knew she was innocent and he had to help her prove it.

She told him about the fax Stephan had received and about the email address of the person the geologist was blackmailing and how she was certain she had seen it before somewhere.

"Let's go inside, Sebastián. Talk to them." She placed a hand on his arm.

He looked at her hand. At moments he felt his relationship with her was dangerous. She looked amazingly like his sister. There was something in her eyes that made him believe everything she said. Maybe he was just seeing her through memory's eye and confusing her with Cristina. He was sometimes seized by an overpowering sensation that he knew her. In the way you know people from your childhood. A subtle, but overwhelming feeling. Only he didn't really know her. Was he about to abandon all of the rigid rules of his world? All that had gotten him this far in his career? And for what? To run with a mere instinct?

"Let's go inside," she said again, tugging lightly on his arm.

It was that easy. A few words and the world fell away.

He followed her inside.

Chapter 74

THE ARRIEROS WHO had been watching from a short distance followed them into the cottage. After an awkward silence, the men began speaking. Juan Carlos told Sebastián that he knew a scientist who lived close by who might be able to read satellite imagery.

"His name is Luis Bargas."

"Luis Bargas?" Sebastián said credulously.

"You know him?" Emmanuelle asked.

"His father owns an *estancia* close to the river. He's a rodeo champion. How can he possibly help us?"

"He studied astrophysics in the United States," Juan Carlos said. "He does compete in the rodeo, but for four months of the year he's stationed in Antarctica at a remote sensing station that receives satellite images. He knows this region better than Karl. I am sure he can read the images. Yesterday, I learned that he's back at the *estancia* for a few weeks. I was planning to take it to him. We can go together," he said, looking at Emmanuelle. "But we have to go on horses."

Sebastián seemed hesitant. "I know someone who worked for a private satellite company in Santiago who might be able to interpret the images, too."

"But it's urgent. If there is any possibility this man could help, we must go," Emmanuelle said. "I'm running out of time."

Sebastián thought for a moment. "I guess there's no

guarantee I could get an answer from my contact quickly. But after we see Bargas, I *have* to contact my office. We can have a helicopter flown in to transport Karl to Punta Arenas for medical treatment. He will have police protection."

Emmanuelle relaxed. She felt certain that they would have the evidence they needed after Luis Bargas read the images. She agreed to return to Puerto Montt with Sebastián afterwards and turn herself in to PDI. The evidence would clear her. She was certain. It would all be over soon. Justice would soon be had.

In less than an hour, they'd mounted horses and were on their way.

Chapter 75

Under the volcanoes, beside the snow-capped mountains, among the huge lakes, the fragrant, the silent, the tangled Chilean forest…. Anyone who hasn't been in the Chilean forest doesn't know this planet. I have come out of that landscape, that mud, that silence, to roam, to go singing through the world. Pablo Neruda

IN A LIGHT veil of rain, they rode through the valleys of Aysén. They passed over hills peppered with wood-shingled homes, century-old farmhouses, and ranches. All of Juan Carlos's conversations with Emmanuelle about the Patagonia echoed in her mind. It was a land of snow-capped volcanoes, sheer-sided fjords, glacial melt rivers, thunderous waterfalls, pristine lakes, temperate rain forests and an extensive ice field. Yet, looming on the periphery of that paradise were industrial projects that threatened to change it all.

They came to the tremendous waterfalls where companies had proposed building a hydroelectric plant and followed the turquoise river to a calmer point where they were able to cross.

***

Emmanuelle's horse suddenly reared in protest as they descended the path leading into the village where Luis Bargas lived. The cold and the lack of sleep had affected Emmanuelle's coordination and reflexes, and weakened her to the point where she could no longer control the horse. She slid to the ground, her frozen hands still grasping the reins. "I can't go on," she cried. Her legs were numb.

"It's no more than two kilometers," Juan Carlos called back. He pointed to the fresh-water ice fields extending across the horizon, "Look! Those are the last remnants of the Patagonian Ice Sheet. During the period of Llanquihue Glaciation, ice covered nearly half a million square kilometers—from Puerto Montt to Antarctica." She glanced up through watering eyes, still pulling on the reins of her horse. *Was he trying to motivate her to continue?* It took a few seconds, but it did. She realized that Juan Carlos's lifelong struggle had been exactly about this. This was one of the last places on earth with pristine lakes and forests, but that paradise was changing as quickly as its glaciers retreated.

Sebastián turned back and jumped off his horse. He unfastened his horse's saddle. "You can ride with me. It's only a short ride." He helped her up and they rode bareback through the valley. Juan Carlos reined in the irritated horse, keeping him in step alongside them.

They descended into a temperate rainforest. Shafts of sunlight filtered through the dense canopy of leaves above them. Emmanuelle fought the urge, but she was falling forward on the horse. Sebastián caught her, pulling her back against his chest and holding her tightly for the rest of the journey.

It was midday when they finally reached the large stone house that belonged to the Bargas family. It sat in the middle of a sprawling estancia and was the only house on the horizon. Dozens of sheep and llamas with heavy-wool coats grazed the land around it. *Huasos* with sheepskin chaps and immensely thick jackets were gathered at the entrance of the estancia. Beside them, horses with double-hair coats were tethered to the wooden gate.

Emmanuelle was conscious of Sebastián's tight grip on her. She felt safe. She wished she could stretch that moment into eternity.

Sebastián got down from the horse and caught her as she slid off.

A *huaso* appeared from behind the estancia. He was riding an agitated, bucking black horse. The animal's hooves crunched against the frosted ground. The man pulled tightly on the horse's reins, cursing it. He jumped off the horse and tethered it to the fence before heading to them, walking as though he were still riding.

Juan Carlos and the man shook hands and slapped each other heartily on the back. He led them into the house. "Don Luis is home ... preparing for the rodeo," he said, calling out for Luis.

Luis was a slender man, perhaps, in his fifties. He was wearing a Córdoba-style hat, and a short Andalusian-style jacket closely tailored to his body.

"Prefecto Cienfuegos. *Que sorpresa.*"

More hearty handshakes and he kissed Emmanuelle on her cheek.

"So what brings you here?"

"I've come to ask a favor."

Luis looked at Emmanuelle. "The poor girl is frozen. *Adelante*, let's go into the *estar*. It's warmer there." He led them into the sitting room. The spurs of his boots made a slight clinking noise. He had a proud sort of walk—the walk of a man conscious of the attention he drew.

"You look familiar," he said to Emmanuelle. "Have we met before?"

Emmanuelle blushed, glancing over at Sebastián, who made no move to introduce her. Luis ushered them into a rustic living room with a stone fireplace and large upholstered chairs over which his *manta*, poncho, and elaborately woven *chamanto*—which, no doubt, he used in his competitions—were draped. The walls were adorned with still-life oil paintings, framed photographs, and medals of his rodeo competitions. Silver spurs and other rodeo paraphernalia decorated the room.

"I'm afraid not. My name is Emmanuelle—"

"Are you on your way to the rodeo?" Sebastián interrupted, forcing a smile.

Everything about Luis and the rodeo made Emmanuelle's mind skip again to her brother, Camilo. Somewhere in this region his grandfather bred horses for the rodeo. She felt he was very close by. She debated asking Luis Bargas if he knew him. Surely he did. That impulse quickly fell away with the realization he might recognize her as the one from the papers who was sought by authorities. The warmth of the fire revived her. Her mind reengaged and her thoughts were beginning to spin again. Only now her life again seemed like a recurring nightmare. She already sensed that the meeting with Luis Bargas wasn't going to go as she'd hoped.

"*Entonces*, Seba, what's the favor?"

"*Bueno* ... I have a question requiring expertise in satellite imagery."

Luis looked at him as though he were awaiting a punch line.

Juan Carlos took the external hard-drive from his jacket.

"I am told that this contains evidence relevant to a PDI investigation. But PDI is limited in personnel capable of interpreting satellite imagery. By the time it's passed on to the right department ... well, I am sure you understand how slow the process can become."

"Yes, science is always way ahead of the law," Luis flashed him a smile that drew quickly into a look of concern. "What kind of information are you looking for?"

"We aren't sure. But we have reason to believe two assassins

389

have been going to great lengths to get their hands on it," Sebastián said.

"They tried to murder a colleague of mine for it. We believe they killed others for it as well," Juan Carlos added.

"Good God. You're not referring to the rumors about the Brazilian scientist?" he looked at Juan Carlos and then Sebastián. "*Es cierto*? Why on earth would someone have tried to kill him?"

"They want the external hard drive." He told him about the geologist who was murdered in Rio and how he had worked for Karl. "I don't expect you to write a report or do anything extensive. Perhaps just guide us. Informal. Anything you can tell us about what this contains will be appreciated. I am afraid once it gets to headquarters it will be filed in someone's desk drawer and forgotten," Sebastián said.

The *huaso* who'd led them into the house entered carrying a tray with a steaming thermos, cups and metal bombilla straws. "Matte?" he asked, offering Emmanuelle first. She accepted and sat by the fireplace.

Luis hesitated for a moment. "Let me get my computer."

He returned with a large laptop. He opened it and waited for it to boot. Sebastián handed the external hard-drive to him and he connected it to his laptop. With a few clicks and keystrokes, the images appeared on the screen. He flicked through them. "*Osea* ... these are images are from TierraSat. They are images of the Futaleufú region."

"Yes. We know from the longitude and latitude," Juan Carlos said dryly.

Sebastián stepped behind Luis.

Luis explained, "Tierra Sat is a new satellite with one of the most advanced sensors. It identifies different materials by distinguishing their spectral properties. These sensors use infrared and short wave technology to collect the data. They are increasingly used by private companies to collect data indicating areas likely to contain minerals."

"Minerals?" Emmanuelle said.

"Yes. Satellites have undergone rapid advancement in the last twenty years. Their optical sensors measure the spectral data of sunlight reflected from the Earth's surface, and the sensors measure electromagnetic data by transmitting microwaves and receiving backscatter waves from the Earth's surface. Minerals can be identified by the amount or type of wavelengths the materials absorb."

"So they can identify what's *under* the ground?"

"Yes. Now they can more or less identify what is underground by surface rock alteration. The absorption and reflection qualities help us to identify materials *on* the ground that in turn indicate the likelihood of other materials underneath."

"So what do these images tell us?"

He shrugged. "I have no idea. What specifically this reveals is beyond my knowledge and understanding. There are people trained in classifying the information and translating the data into something useful for exploration. These images have already been altered by someone who knew how to read and interpret them. See these colors?" He pointed to the screen. "They indicate different classifications of the materials. They've been classified by someone according to their differences in absorption and reflection. Maybe identifying certain minerals of interest—such as clays and sulfides."

"What about gold?" Emmanuelle asked.

"It's possible. Gold often occurs in sulfides. It can be identified based on absorption and reflection qualities. Geologists also seek surface clues such as alteration and other signs of mineralization to discover subsurface deposits of ore minerals, oil and gas, and even groundwater."

"So what you are saying is that these images probably indicate the presence of some mineral in that area. Possibly gold?" Juan Carlos asked.

Sebastián and Emmanuelle exchanged glances again.

"Yes, it's possible those images indicate gold. Satellite imagery can pick up geological features that are like footprints leading to minerals. In the Patagonia, where volcanoes and hydrothermal vents are abundant, high-sulfidation epithermal gold deposits have been shown to occur. After the satellite stage, geologists are sent to the field to do stream sediment sampling. They can collect and analyze hundreds or even thousands of samples in the identified region. This is much more cost-effective. Today, no company would drill in an area where gold hasn't already been identified by other means."

"So, can't you tell us more about this finding?"

"No. I can't tell you more than that. You need someone specialized in interpreting this kind of data to be able to tell you what exactly these images reveal."

Emmanuelle's heart thudded with disappointment. She reflected for a moment. The revelation that the information related to minerals and not climate change connected her thoughts to many other factors that had been hanging on the periphery of this mystery. For instance, the mining claims found in the building on Calle Vicente Perez Rosales. Albert's stock certificates. The Ameriminco Mining Company. But what would be the great revelation if the images revealed gold? There *was* a gold mine there. So the presence of gold couldn't be cause for blackmail. It would have been known. The stocks weren't fraudulent. They were listed on the New York Stock Exchange. Everything was pointing to the mines, but why? What could Martín possibly have to do with the mine? The associations she'd previously drawn seemed more tenuous. How did the water company factor in? Thorman had been a major stockholder in the gold company and was selling off to partners. Why was he selling off a company with rising stock value? Was he selling because he owed partners money? Was there nothing more Luis Navarro could tell them? He *had* to be able to tell them something more. Where would they go from here? They were running out of time.

An hour later, Juan Carlos was on his way back to Caleta Tortel alone. The images were too large to be to emailed so Luis loaded them onto a private internet site accessible only to those with the password so that Sebastián's friend in Santiago could view them. All they could do was hope he would see the email and get to work quickly. Sebastián had contacted the Prefecto of PDI in Aysén who agreed to dispatch a helicopter to take Karl to a hospital and assign police protection to his room.

Two PDI SUVs pulled up to the *estancia*. One of the drivers gave keys to Sebastián and left in the one of the vehicles. Sebastián would drive with Emmanuelle to Puerto Aysén. From there they would take a ferry back to Puerto Montt. He was turning her over to his superiors.

Chapter 76

THEY DROVE NORTH along a dirt road that wound around mountain villages and towns to the Carretera Austral—the main highway. The only traffic on the sparsely-populated country road consisted of a few oxen-drawn, two-wheeled carts filled with vegetables and a handful of men either on horseback or walking.

"The ferry will get us back to Puerto Montt in under a day," Sebastián said. Emmanuelle's face was turned to the window. She was crying. "I don't want to go back to Puerto Montt. I want to go to Isabella's house. We need those documents. We can't stop now. We know it was all about gold. Martín's documents are the missing link to everything. If I'm arrested, I can't get what I need to expose them. You know that's why they're so desperate to have me arrested."

"Pilar is at Isabella's house now. She's collecting the documents. Trust me, you don't want to run into her. She's convinced you're not innocent."

She turned to face him. "I didn't realize detectives from Puerto Montt could investigate in Castro."

"Technically, we can't. It's outside our jurisdiction but I sent her to get the documents anyway. I haven't been given explicit orders to stop investigating. Until then, I'll do what I can do."

"And what happens after you get those orders?" she protested. "Will you turn me in?"

"You can't keep running. And ..." he hesitated. "I can't run with you." He sighed grimly. "You have to turn yourself in. You have to cooperate. The more you hold out, the less likely it will be that authorities are going to be sympathetic. You can hire an attorney. You don't have a choice. You have to face it and hope for justice." He reached out and took her hand but she refused to look at him. "I'll do everything I can to help you." He pulled to the side of the road. The rain was tapping loudly on the window. There were tears streaking down her cheeks now.

"What about the bank. The bank has to have an address for the holder of the bank account."

"It's Sunday afternoon. Banks are closed." He turned the engine off. "I promise I'll follow those leads next week."

"I only have until Tuesday."

"What do you mean?"

"The US Federal District Court will be hearing a complaint filed by the prosecutor's office. It was in the papers. That's why I took the ferry to Puerto Edén. I knew there was so little time. They're asking for extradition now. It's won't just be a Letters Rogatory request to question me in Chile. They want me extradited. If the US federal court decides in favor of my extradition, the orders could be sent to Chile as early as Tuesday." Her voice was choked with tears. "I was framed. You know that, right? You believe me? They want me put away so I can't expose them. They needed a scapegoat to explain their fraudulent activities. I took the bait," she confessed.

"I believe you. But we don't have the evidence to prove it."

She turned to him. "This is my last chance. Please help me." He felt trapped in her supplicating gaze again. He reached out and pulled her close to him.

She turned her face into his shoulder and wept.

"We're getting closer to solving this. We have to have faith in the process."

His mind skipped to Santiago. Did *he* even have faith in the process? Undoubtedly it was going to be one of the most political, criminal cases the country had known that involved foreigners. But he was determined to help her, through thick and thin. "You have to have faith in me." He stroked her hair. She wept like a child. For a long while he held her tightly, the silence broken only by the rhythmic drumming of the rain on the roof of the car. Alone in their separate thoughts, separate worlds.

"We can't sit here forever," he said finally, kissing her forehead and turning the key. "Let's get something to eat." He let the engine run, the windshield wipers giving no more than a few seconds of clarity to the foggy, rain-soaked landscape with each movement.

"You must be hungry."

She shrugged. "What time does the ferry leave?"

"At eight this evening. We still have a few hours. We can come up with a strategy. Think this through. Let's plan it. Let's talk it through. *De acuerdo?*"

"Can't we keep driving and take a ferry farther north? I don't want to get on a boat yet."

He thought for a minute. He knew he should bring her back. He was risking his job and all that he had fought for throughout his career. But none of that seemed important now. He wanted to help her and they had little more than a day to try to clear her. He knew he could do more to help her by staying away from Puerto Montt. "Yes. We can drive to Caleta Gonzalo and take the ferry from there. It's about three hundred kilometers from here. Let's do that and think through a strategy. *Listo?*"

She nodded, far away in her thoughts.

***

They drove for several hours and pulled up to what resembled a farmhouse with a large sign that said *Rincon Campesino*, Countryman's Corner. It looked like the many farmhouses they'd passed along the way. Emmanuelle, clutching her backpack and laptop, let him help her out of the car. The puddles in the unpaved parking were like small ponds. Water streamed along the gutters. They ran through the rain to the entrance.

The place was vibrant with country life. The aroma of meat grilling on the *asado parado* filled the air. Decorative hand-hammered copper kitchenware and rodeo paraphernalia hung on the walls. A waiter in a traditional folkloric outfit seated them, at Sebastián's request, in a more secluded corner of the restaurant and then disappeared to the bar. Many of the restaurant's customers were dressed in traditional outfits as well. A trio of folk musicians played ballads.

Their waiter was back in a few minutes with wine. He took Sebastián's order—an assortment of grilled meats and avocado salad.

Emmanuelle pulled out her laptop, glancing around self-consciously, aware it was uncommon for someone to take out a laptop at a restaurant in Chile.

Sebastián didn't protest.

She waited for it to boot. "You know … I have been racking my brain for answers and I keep thinking of this painting at Oliver & Stone. It's in the sitting room behind Albert Thorman's office. It's a private sitting room. Associates aren't allowed to use it. A handful of the partners use it to receive the firm's biggest clients or to entertain special people." Her voice trailed off. She gazed at several couples dancing the *Queca* as others clapped to the guitarist. "I think it's a painting by the Italian renaissance painter Titian. Tiziano Vecelli."

"I'm not following you at all."

"The geologist who worked with Karl—the one who was gunned down in Rio—he was blackmailing someone with an email address c.sisyphus@gmail.com. Juan Carlos connected me to Internet in Aysén and we downloaded some information and discovered that there is a painting that used to be at the Prado Museum in Madrid."

"Where are you going with this?"

She leaned toward him. "When the economic crisis hit in 2009, some of Spain's national museums allowed their paintings to be borrowed for exhibition in other countries around the world for a fee so that the museums could continue to support themselves through the crisis. A few of the paintings were sold about a year ago in some kind of murky, under-the-table deal. The articles didn't say which paintings were sold off, so I can't be one hundred per cent certain, but I am pretty sure that one of them is at Oliver & Stone." She turned her computer toward him and showed him a picture of Brent and Thorman. "Look at this. Do you see the painting behind Stephan and Albert? It's either a copy or an original Titian painting."

Sebastián leaned toward the computer. It was a painting of a man pushing a boulder up a hill.

"When the painting arrived, I was in Albert's office with Stephan. I asked him about it. I think I asked whether it was an original. Stephan laughed without answering the question, and Thorman seemed upset. I never knew why." She pointed at the screen. "This painting, if it is the original, is worth something in the range of sixty million euros, but I understand it was sold for a fraction of the price."

"So what are you saying?"

"It's Sisyphus. It's a man pushing a boulder up the hill."

"The Greek myth?" He picked up his wine glass and held it against his lips.

"Yes. The Greek myth about a man who is condemned to perpetually repeat the meaningless task of pushing a boulder up a mountain, only to see it roll down again. That man is Sisyphus. I think Sisyphus is Thorman's secret email address." She looked up at him thoughtfully. "I need coffee." She was coming to life again.

He admired that in her. "Don't you want your wine?" He pulled her chair closer to him and wrapped his arm around her.

"No. I'll fall asleep. Can you please ask the waiter to bring me coffee?"

He signaled the waiter.

Chapter 77

EMMANUELLE'S SURVIVAL INSTINCTS had kicked in again and her adrenaline was flowing. She couldn't accept her predicament. She knew she was swiftly running out of time. She considered Sebastián for a long moment, his handsome face chiseled in the lights of the restaurant. There was stubble on his cheeks. He was probably as physically exhausted as she was. He was risking it all by just being with her. She felt swept by emotion and so deeply grateful for his presence. She wanted to drown in his arms.

"We're going to resolve this," he told her. "*Tranquila.* Everything is going to be okay."

His kind words were reassuring.

There'd been a pause in the music and now a woman took the microphone and began singing "Gracias a la Vida." They both gazed at her as she sang. At that moment, she wanted him to hold her, as he had in the car, close her eyes, press her face against his chest, and breath in that delicate smell of his leather and cologne and feel safe. But she knew she wasn't safe. There was one thing that gnawed at her, even frightened her terribly about Sebastián, as she realized how desperately she depended on him now. He would obey orders. As that reality dawned on her, a cold shiver snaked down her spine. Her mind shifted again to the painting and what they had just learned from Luis Bargas. She knew she could find the connection to the gold mine and the email address.

Then, a thought came to her. She remembered something she'd nearly forgotten. She reached into her backpack and felt around the bottom.

"What are you looking for? What's wrong?"

She found it and pulled it out. "The USB drive. This is the one that fell out of Stephan's briefcase on the way to the airport. I haven't been able to open it because it's protected with a password."

She plugged it into the computer and held her breath. She typed in 'c.sisyphus.' An invalid password message blinked on the screen. She heaved out a sigh. She typed c.sisyphys@gmail.com. The same message. Then she tried 'Sisyphus' alone.

"Dear God! It opened."

***

There must have been several thousand emails and hundreds of attachments on the USB drive. Sebastián shifted his chair closer to Emmanuelle as she scrolled through the files. They studied the screen as the waiter brought their food and arranged it on the table.

"This has to be the information Stephan was talking about. This must be what we were supposed to turn over to the authorities. It has to be." She started reading one of the emails, but her mind couldn't process the information. "Could this be Albert?" she said. She skimmed more emails, but her brain was too accelerated to process the information. Many were signed Sisyphus. The oldest dated four years earlier.

"We need to go a place where I can access the Internet. I need a few hours." She pleaded, determined to convince him. "Just a few more hours. We can take the ferry to Puerto Montt in the morning. Please trust me. These files *have* the evidence. I know I can make sense of the information. I just need time to put them in order. And an Internet connection. Just give me a few hours and I can face Interpol tomorrow."

Sebastián picked up an empanada and took a bite. He was calculating something in his mind. He looked at his watch.

"Please," she said. "Trust me. I can figure it all out."

He signaled the waiter, but he didn't say that he would give her more time.

"Can you bring me the bill?"

The waiter looked stunned. "You didn't like it?"

"She isn't feeling well."

"I need to use the restroom," Emmanuelle said, picking up her purse and standing.

"*Por supuesto*, Señorita. Over there." The waiter pointed to a door next to the kitchen.

Inside the restroom, she glanced around the stalls to be sure no one was there. She took out her phone. If Sebastián decided they were headed to Puerto Montt immediately she wouldn't have the chance to go through the documents before he turned her in. She might never make sense of the information before it left her hands. This was her only chance. With trembling hands, she pulled out her address book and flipped through the pages. She needed a backup plan just in case. Sebastián would never let her investigate on her own. She had two phone calls to make. The first was to the notary public. He'd given her his personal cell phone number. *He said he would be in the south all weekend. Close to the Futaleufú. Please, please pick up.* The line went to voicemail. *Damn!* She tried again. He picked up.

"Bernardo?"

"*Si. ¿Quién habla?*" Who's speaking?"

"Emmanuelle Solis."

"Señorita Solis. *¿Como estas?*"

"I'm well, thank you," *Actually I'm running from authorities and not so well.* She swallowed hard. "How are you?"

"Excellent. I spent the last four days hiking and whitewater rafting far away from the rest of the world. I feel wonderful."

"Excellent … I'm so glad to hear that." *Because it means you probably haven't been reading the newspapers and don't realize that I'm wanted by the authorities.* She glanced back at the door again.

"Did you ever get the chance to look into the stock certificates that I brought you? Did you find out who the local attorney is?"

"Yes. *Claro que sí.* My secretary, she looked into it. I tried to reach you at the number you gave me, but your phone has been off for days. I thought you left Chile."

"I've had problems with my phone here. I have a local number now." She pulled out a pen. "Can you give me the information?"

"Well, I left you a message with it. I can't remember it all right now… Just go to your voicemail."

Damn! Double damn! If she called her voicemail from this phone, anyone tracking her could trace her to this new number now. "Do you remember the name?"

"Hmmm, let me see…. *Ya!* Carrasco. The Carrasco Group. Antonio Carrasco. I don't have the address…. Hmmm."

"Yes," he continued. "I *think* I've seen the place, in fact, just in the last few days. There's a tremendous mansion close to the Espolon River. It wasn't there before. It must have been built in the last year or so. It looks like a hotel. The top floor appears to be encased in glass. I thought about you when I passed it the other day. It's close to the mine. I think that's it. I left the address on your voicemail. You need to check your voicemails, young lady."

"The gold mine is close to the Espolon River?"

"Yes."

"Isn't that a popular site for whitewater rafters?"

"Yes, it is."

"And you can whitewater raft in water processed for gold cyanidation?"

"Good question. I don't think they would …" He hummed again. "I don't know … Maybe they haven't started processing yet, or … *osea*, whatever it is they do. The property is all fenced up. It's toxic I guess, no? There should be warnings, *ya*?"

"I don't know. You tell me. You're the Chilean lawyer. What does the law say?"

"I never thought about that, Señorita Solis."

Yes, you and most people.

"So, when can I see you?"

"Uhh… I am leaving Chile… tomorrow." Lying was becoming second nature now. "I plan to be back in a few months. I'll call you." She hung up and glanced back at the door again, her pulse pounding furiously. She had one more call to make. She needed to get the address. She flipped hastily through pages of her address book. She dialed the number. He answered on the second ring. *Thank God!*

"Nahuel, this is Emmanuelle Solis." Her voice was a whisper.

"*Ah, si. ¿Como estas*, Señorita?"

"*Más o menos*, Nahuel."

"*Yo también, más o menos.* Carabineros suspect Mapuche involvement in the murder of Padre Rodrigo. They have made some arrests. I will probably be next."

"Wait. I am close to resolving this. I am sure the cases are linked. I need your help. I'm close to Villa Santa Lucia and I need to get to an address in the Futaleufú area urgently. Close to the Espolon River. It might not be easy to find. I need someone who knows the area. Could you possibly pick me up if I can't get there any other way?"

"You are at Villa Santa Lucia? Hmmm …you are *quizas* … maybe an hour and a half away from me. I am sorry, Señorita. Padre Dionisio, he is not well. He might fail. I am at the Don Bosco Mission in the Futaleufú. I don't want to leave him. If I am arrested, I might never see him again. *Lo siento.*" His voice faltered. "I owe him my life ... He's been like a father to me. We think it's his heart. He is refusing to go to the hospital. He's asked for Padre Felipe to say his last rites. He's on his way."

"Dear God. That's terrible. I am so sorry." She felt like a malediction was swirling in the air. Maybe even a curse she brought with her. Didn't her landing in Chile precede all of the horrible events of the last few weeks? She rubbed her temples. Sebastián would be wondering what was taking her so long.

"I am sorry too," he said somberly.

"Nahuel, listen to me. I know the cases are linked. But I need to prove it. I'll help you."

"*Mira*, I'll talk to my brother. Tell me where you are exactly."

"I will call you back in a few hours and tell you."

"*Ya listo*, I'll ask my brother to pick you up and bring you here. I am close to the Espolon River. I will have him head down there soon. *No se preocupa, Señorita.* We will get you where you need to go. *Que dios te bendiga.*"

She hung up and turned around.

Sebastián was at the door, staring at her.

How much had he heard?

"Are you finished?" he asked. He was holding her laptop and backpack. He handed them back to her roughly as she stepped out of the restroom. He was different now. She felt it. He was rabid with distrust.

"Have you paid?" she asked.

"Move. Let's go. To the car."

The cop in him was back.

Chapter 78

"GIVE ME YOUR phone," he said, staring at the windshield.

"Just ask me Sebastián. All you have to do is ask me. I was talking to Bernardo Jara Carcura. The notary public."

"Give me your phone!" His teeth were clenched.

"Fine." She yanked it out of her purse and dropped it on his lap.

He glared at her.

He dialed the first number she had called from his cell phone.

"This is Prefecto Cienfuegos of Puerto Montt. Who is speaking?"

"Bernardo Jara Carcura, Prefecto. *¿Que tal?* What can I help you with?"

"I'll call you back in a little while."

"Certainly Señor Prefecto."

He hung up and scrolled through the dialed list. "Who was the other call to?"

She wasn't going to offer the name. She said nothing.

He dialed it, shooting her a cold look.

Oh, please don't pick up Nahuel. Oh Christ. She was implicating the usual suspect in something he knew nothing about. She felt swept by a wave of guilt.

Sebastián dialed the number. It rang and rang and then rolled over to voicemail.

Thank God. She thought, relieved. *He probably recognized the number and chose not to pick up.* Or maybe Padre Dionisio was continuing to decline. She closed her eyes and prayed he wasn't.

A young man dressed like a *huaso* was leaving the restaurant, an elegant woman dressed in the traditional folkloric *duena del campo* outfit beside him. Sebastián and Emmanuelle watched in silence as the man gallantly opened the passenger door and helped the woman into his truck. They were smiling, laughing like they had just spent the best night of their life. The man slid into the driver's seat and they drove away, taillights melting out of sight in the fog.

"Who else did you call?" His voice was low, husky with anger. Maybe even revulsion.

Her mind raced. "I dialed a wrong number." The rain started up again. It sounded like thousands of tiny pellets were falling on the car.

He was staring at the phone. "You were on the call for three minutes. Who did you call?"

"I *said* I don't know. It was the wrong number. I was trying to dial Don Bernardo. Someone picked up. There was a lot of noise. He told me to wait. He couldn't hear. When he finally got to a place with less noise, we both realized it was the wrong number. We hung up." Lying had become easy enough to swear by.

He put the key in the ignition. "You called him *after* you spoke to Don Bernardo."

"Where are we going?" she asked.

He turned on the engine, then the lights. No answer.

"I called Don Bernardo because I wanted the address of the attorney who handled the legal work for the mines. Don Bernardo had the number. His office in Futaleufú notarized all the documents pertaining to the mine. When I went to see him last week, he said he would try to find the information for the

Chilean attorney who handled it. He just told me the man's name is Antonio Carrasco."

"Antonio Carrasco?"

"Yes. Do you know who he is?"

Silence. The look on his face said he knew exactly who he was.

"Where are we going?" she asked again, as they pulled out of the parking lot.

"Somewhere where we can read the files on the USB drive."

They drove for about thirty minutes in silence. The rain had stopped, but the air in the car was thick and moist.

"Bernardo said he'd called me several times," she finally spoke. "But my phone was turned off. He said he left messages on my voicemail with information about the stock certificates. He also said he left the attorney's address on my voicemail. It's somewhere on the Espolon River in Futaleufú. He didn't have the information with him when I called just now. But he thought it was a house he'd seen somewhere while he was out rafting. A mansion in the middle of nowhere. The top floor is encased in glass. You took my phone from me. You can have your people check my voicemail. My password is 2229."

Fifteen minutes up the road, he pulled over to a gas station. She asked if she could get coffee. Reluctantly he agreed. He asked the gas station attendant to fill the tank and they went inside. Sebastián ordered two large cortados and took them to go.

They came to a sign that said *"Cabañas a Arrendar"* and turned onto a dirt road leading up to a site with cabin rentals.

"We need the Internet."

"They *have* Internet service."

Chapter 79

THE CABIN HAD one room with a single set of bunk beds, a kitchen and living room. Emmanuelle set her computer on the table as Sebastián lit a fire in the woodstove.

She took a seat, opened her laptop and plugged in the USB memory stick. The first thing she needed to do was drag all the files from the USB into her Dropbox folder so they would sync online. If anything happened to her or the USB stick, the evidence would still be intact there. For the next few hours, she sifted through the files. There were hundreds of letters in English, Spanish and Portuguese between a broker and stockholders. She opened window after window. There was an equal number of emails between geologists with scientific jargon she couldn't understand, although most were in English.

She felt Sebastián's gaze and looked up. It was an expression she never could place. She searched his eyes for familiarity, but it wasn't there now. He was just waiting for her to conclude something. And her freedom depended on it. She shifted in her seat "I think maybe this document brings it all together." She scanned it again. "The findings of the geologists were subject to a confidentiality agreement." She skipped to another document. "Wait a minute … this is a sales agreement." She rubbed her eyes and leaned closer to the screen. "Did they sell the mine for three hundred million dollars?"

No answer. Sebastián's eyes were fixed on the screen. She

wished they would look at hers. She needed to feel connected to him. She needed to feel safe with him again. Where had that moment gone? She scrolled down the document to find the date. "What day was the *Antarctic Mist* sabotaged?" She leafed through pages of her notepad. "The sale was supposed to take place on July first. Two days ago. That was just a week after the ship was sabotaged. They were closing the sale of the mine at the same time the *Antarctic Mist* was sabotaged. The sale was to be completed a week later."

Still quiet.

She logged into the Internet again. Had the deal closed? "Ameriminco staked several mineral claims in the Palena province that were supposedly prospective for gold. Then they sold the land and the mine. Why would they do that?" She checked the New York Stock Exchange. *The price of stocks had gone from one dollar eight cents to thirty-eight dollars a share in the weeks before the sale.* "Why would they sell when stocks were soaring? Did they think the value would come down?" She went back to the page with the geologists' reports. The scientific jargon jarred her brain.

Then a thought occurred to her. She opened the page of her notepad with the list Juan Carlos and Karl Gustav had given her of the scientists on the expedition team. Indeed, four of the names were on the list. Four other geologists who had been involved in the sampling and analysis of the stream sediment were on the list. They had all been killed. "Karl didn't know that his own team of geologists had been the ones who were involved in the mineralization assessment for the mine."

"What are you talking about?"

"Oh my God! They were all killed!"

He stared blankly at her. His cell phone buzzed. He picked up. It was a woman. Emmanuelle could hear everything she was saying.

"Where are you, Seba?"

"What do you want, Pilar?" He sounded irritated.

"It's her, Sebastián?"

"What do you mean?"

Emmanuelle sensed turmoil in his pause.

"Solis," Pilar said loudly.

"What about her?"

"Don Martin from Santiago headquarters called back. They traced the bank transfers back to her computer."

"What bank transfers?" His eyes shifted to Emmanuelle.

Emmanuelle heard it all. Her heart began to jackhammer. This couldn't be happening. She tried to get her breathing under control.

"A painting was illegally purchased with a wire transfer made from an offshore account. It was one of the accounts being used to deposit earnings from the gigantic stock fraud operation they ran. She was working with them. They confirmed it. The wire transfer was made from her computer. You need to bring her in. We have orders to bring her in."

My computer? She felt her stomach fall to the floor. *The only people who had access to my computer ever were Stephan and maybe Maríana.* Her thoughts raced to Maríana. Emmanuelle had found Maríana in her office several times when she had come back from a meeting or stepped out for something. She tried to remember whether her laptop was on her desk, open and running. Several times after Stephan disappeared, she'd gotten back to her office and discovered Maríana in her office. Waiting for her, she would say, so they could go out to lunch. *But if authorities had traced any transaction made from the office, it wouldn't have identified her computer. It would have identified the office Internet address.* Her mind shuffled information around. It had to be someone who had used her computer from her apartment, if they were linking a transaction to her IP address. Friends from

411

the office had only been to her apartment a handful of times. "Oh, dear God." Maríana had been among them.

Now they would link everything to Emmanuelle. Every trace of evidence now pointed to her. She was doomed.

Sebastián was still on the phone. He glanced back at her. His eyes said everything. He was convinced she was the enemy.

Her heart thudded. No, this couldn't be happening. He wouldn't believe her now. He wouldn't trust her. They were so close. He turned his back to her again listening to Pilar.

Emmanuelle slipped the phone in her pocket and headed to the bathroom. She locked the door and ran the sink water, flushed the toilet and dialed. *Dear God, help me! Pick up! Please pick up!* Nahuel picked up on the first ring. '*Cabanas del Rio Santo. Numero 10*,' she whispered, giving him the address of one of the cabins up the road.

"My brother will be there in a few minutes," Nahuel said.

Sebastián banged on the door. She hung up and slipped the phone in her back pocket.

"I'm bringing you in. Let's go." His eyes expressed the kind of betrayal she was feeling right now. Like someone had just dropped a bomb on your life, blasted it into smoking shreds, and left you heaving in the dust.

Chapter 80

"Please listen to me. All of the geologists who conducted the stream sediment sampling and analysis for the mine were killed. They were on the ship. That's why the ship was sabotaged. They knew something that someone didn't want exposed before the mine was sold. Stock prices were soaring. The information on that USB memory stick is the key to the entire conspiracy. I can explain how the stock fraud was related to the assassination of the geologists, the blackmail and the sabotage of the ship. It's—" Emmanuelle tried to go on.

She would say anything now to convince me, Sebastián thought.

"Get your things. I am taking you in. You can explain it to Santiago PDI."

She looked dumbfounded. "No, please. You *have* to listen to me." She said it as though she couldn't understand why he would have to bring her in. She was a beautiful, calculating, lying monster. A rogue. A demon. Was she Sisyphus? What was she going to fabricate next? He didn't want to hear it. "Let's go." He was going to take her in. That would be the end of this nightmare.

He turned away from her.

"Sebastián, please don't do this to me. Don't you see? We are closing in on them. I'm a threat to them because I have information about their clandestine operations. I have it all now. This substantiates everything I've been saying. I…." She walked up to him and leaned her head again his shoulder. "Please. We're almost there."

He shrugged her away. "Who did you just call?"

Silence. She would stonewall him.

"Who did you call when you were in the bathroom?"

Her eyes pleaded for mercy.

"Give me your phone."

She just stood there, looking pathetically helpless. Like a teenager, frail and ailing. He looked past Emmanuelle at her rain-bleared reflection in the window. It was just a pale silhouette.

"Give me the phone now."

She looked more pale and sick by the second. If ever she'd looked like Cristina, she looked *exactly* like her now. Like Cristina in her last days now. He looked away to hide his glistening eyes. "Give me the phone!"

She pulled the phone out of her pocket and stretched it out to him, then ran to the bathroom. He followed her. She leaned over the toilet and vomited.

He watched her for a few seconds and then looked away, slamming his hand against the doorframe. Was this really happening? He passed a hand over his face, sighing loudly, wishing with all his might he'd never met her.

She was leaning over the sink gasping for air, sobbing. Just like Cristina on her very last night.

"Okay, I'll go," she said, her voice broken. She glanced up at him. She'd soiled the front of her sweater. "I'll turn myself in."

He looked away and shook his head. "*Santo Jesus,*" he said under his breath. He rarely called on Him. But now seemed like a good time.

"Can I clean up first?" Her voice was meek. The submissive voice of a child who'd been defeated.

He rolled away from the door, his back against the wall. "Go ahead."

She walked into the room and picked through her backpack and carried a few things to the bathroom. "Can I shower?"

He shrugged.

The door shut and he heard the squeaking of rusted iron, the shower faucet, then water running.

He sat down on the bed and hung his head in his hands. How many days had it been? He counted. Four days of practically no sleep at all. He stretched out on the bed and closed his eyes.

Chapter 81

He stared out the window. It was raining again. Torrentially. It had rained every day for more than a month. He prayed for sunshine every night when he said his prayers. She needed the sun. It would make her smile again. It would make her well again. He was certain. If only the sun would shine. He picked up his book Papelucho. *He would bring it to her. She always laughed when she read it to him. He would take it up to her and bring her some tea and crackers. It was all she could eat anymore. The medicine was making her sick.* Kimo Terapia *the doctor called it. What a weird name. It was witchcraft.* Brujería. *He was certain the evil doctor killed more people than he cured. He hated her doctor. He smelled like medicine and death. She just needed sunshine. Sunshine and laughter. He opened the door to her room, clutching his book under his arm and balancing a tray of tea and crackers. She looked pale. Frail and ailing. She reached her hand out to him. Cristina was dying! He backed out of the room slowly. The tray with the crackers and tea fell crashing to the ground. Cristina was dying!*

SEBASTIÁN'S PHONE BUZZED and he bolted upright, hitting his head on the frame of the upper bunk bed. "*¡Hijo de puta! ¿Que mierda?*" He'd dosed off. He looked at the screen of his phone. It was Pilar calling again. He pressed the ignore button. He glanced around the room disoriented. He could hear the water still running in the bathroom. What time was it? He looked at the screen of his phone again. Something felt weird. Something was wrong. His heart accelerated. Her computer was still on the table, her things still in the room. He got up and walked to the bathroom.

"Emmanuelle!" he called out, knocking loudly on the door.

Nothing.

He banged louder.

Only the sound of running water.

He looked around. All her things were still in the room. His heart raced. Had she hurt herself? Escaped? Where could she have gone? Thoughts hammered his brain.

He thrust his weight against the door again and again until it shattered. A cloud of steam from the running shower rolled past him.

The window was open. She was gone.

The phone buzzed again. He picked up. "*¿Que mierda quieres, Pilar?* What the hell do you want?"

"Bring her in Sebastián. Santiago sent in the order. It's on your desk."

"*¡Conio* Pilar! I can't bring her in, if I don't know where the hell she is!" His voice rumbled through the cabin.

"You don't know where she is?"

"No. She isn't with me and I don't know where she is. Got it?" He thought for a minute. "Pilar, I need you to listen to me." He forced calm into his voice. "I need you to do something immediately. It's urgent. Her phone, we sent it to Santiago, remember? The notary public left her voicemail messages on it. Her password is 2229. Listen to the messages. Don Bernardo left an address, a place on the Futaleufú River. Have someone listen to the messages. I think it's Antonio Carrasco's address. She might be headed to there. If she is, we'll need to send backup. Get the address and call me back."

"*Artiro,*" she agreed.

"Wait. Did you get Martín's documents from Isabella's house?"

"Yes, I have them all. We are going through them now. The only thing he had was a stack of reports by geologists. Nothing about climate change. Something about, *que se yo*, sampling of sediment taken from the river. Gold sampling. Oh, and the address associated with the bank account that Martín was paid from is also from somewhere in the Palena region. I wonder if it's near the Futaleufú River. If it's the same address."

"Get on it, Pilar. Call me back and work on backup. I am sure she is headed there now."

"I'll do it right now." She hung up.

Where is she? He would trace Emmanuelle on his iPad, he thought. *No.* The cell phone he'd given her was on the bed. She left without it to God only knows where. There was no way of tracing her now. A dark feeling overwhelmed him. He looked at the screen of her phone. She'd dialed the same number again.

He dialed the number. It rang and rang. No one picked up. He dialed several more times before sinking back down on the bed. He put his head in his hands. "Dios Santo," he murmured. *Where could she have gone?*

He dialed again. Someone picked up. "*Alo, sí.*"

He recognized the voice. "Padre Felipe?" He was dumbfounded. He couldn't think of what to say. He shut his eyes tight. *Breath.*

"*¿Sí, quien es?* Yes, who is this?"

"*Soy yo*, Sebastián Cienfuegos. Padre, is this ... *your* cell phone number?" he finally said, after he had collected his thoughts.

"*Osea, no.* I don't know whose phone this is. It was ringing incessantly so I picked it up assuming it was something urgent. I'm at the Misión Don Bosco in Futaleufú." His voice was mournful. "Padre Dionisio, he's not well. I just read him his last rites. He seems to be ... passing." His voice was broken. "Who are you trying to reach?"

"I ... may have dialed by accident." *Could she be headed there?*

Sebastián wondered. It was close to the Espolon River.

"Are you alright, *hijito*? You don't sound well."

Sebastián felt like he had a tennis ball lodged in his throat. He struggled to swallow.

"No, Padre, I'm not well." An avalanche was breaking inside of him.

"*Dime, hijito*. Talk to me. It's been many years since we really talked."

Chapter 82

SEBASTIÁN WAS IN the SUV on his way to the Misión Don Bosco, his foot pressing the accelerator to the floor, when his cell phone buzzed. Maybe it was Emmanuelle. He reached into his pocket, decelerating a bit. It was Pilar again. "*¿Qué?*" he growled into the phone.

"Sebastián. The address for the lawyer representing Ameriminco *is* the same as the company address listed on the bank account that Martín was paid from."

"It is?" Sebastián slapped his hand on the steering wheel. "What is it?"

"It's Camino San Francisco 598."

"Call for backup at that address."

"Shall I call Santiago…."

"*Conio*, Pilar. I need it now." He accelerated. "Just forget it."

"No, Sebastián. Wait…."

He hung up and pulled to the side of the road.

He had a friend in the Comisaría de Futaleufú. Crístian Figuerero Sanchez. He dialed him.

"Yes, I know the place," Crístian confirmed, when Sebastián gave him the address. "There's been a lot of activity over there in the last few days. It's been all lit up. They had a truck with Argentine plates in front of the house yesterday moving out boxes. I've been keeping my eye on it for the past few weeks because we've had a report from some *arrieros* that there were heavily-armed men going in and out of the house. It's totally isolated. You know people pretty much come and go easily across the Paso Futaleufú and over the border. I was wondering if there is some drug-trafficking going on."

"We have come across information linking that address to murders in Puerto Montt. I'm not out on official business, but since I was in the area I wanted to check it out. It might be wrong, but I am heading there now. I'm about two hours away. I may need backup, if anything comes of this."

"*Por supuesto.* Let me know. I'll position some men close by just in case."

Sebastián hung up and pulled out onto the highway again. Pilar was calling back. He pressed the ignore button. Where had Emmanuelle disappeared to? Why hadn't he just heard her out? In minutes, he had discovered all she had told him was the truth. Had she gone to the Misión? Or straight to the house on the Futaleufú?

He would go straight to the house.

Chapter 83

EMMANUELLE FELT LIKE a wire had cut loose in her chest and she would go into cardiac arrest, if her heart rate didn't slow down soon. *Think!* Once she'd gotten out the window, she wasn't sure how to get to the address she had just given Nahuel. Her perspective on the ground in the foggy, dark wooded lot was very different from the one she had as they drove in and around a winding path with blaring headlights. Leaves and twigs crunched under her feet. Headlights snapped on and off in the fog a short distance up the road and her instinct said to get there fast. She kept low, brushing against a tangle of wiry shrubs. She made her way to the headlights and got into the car.

"Cautaro?" she asked, raking out bits of broken twigs tangled in her hair.

"*Si, señorita,*" he said with no more than a glance. "I've been waiting a long time." He sighed with an air of impatience. "I was getting ready to leave."

"*Vamos.*"

Cautaro Carillanca was a younger and lighter-skinned version of his brother. He pulled the truck out onto the main road. On another occasion, she might have complained when he drove his pick-up on both sides of the winding road, accelerating faster around the curves, but all she cared about now was getting the hell out of there. She squeezed her eyes tight and prayed she wouldn't retch in his car.

Thoughts shifted in her head like tiny crystals in a kaleidoscope. One thought was that if Interpol had her IP address as the address from which the wire transfer had been made for the sale of the painting, someone had to have been planning to frame her even before Stephan disappeared. The painting had been purchased before his disappearance. She brushed dead leaves off her sweater and wondered whether Sebastián had already discovered she was gone.

And there was something else. Of the hundreds of transactions that appeared to have been moving in and out of bank accounts in Saint Lucia, for the police to be have been appraised of the *one transfer* that supposedly was made from a computer in her home, the FBI had to have been tipped off by someone. Her mind shifted once again to Maríana. She had been in her apartment a handful of times.

"You're going to the Misión, *cierto*?" Cautaro's words broke into her thoughts.

"Yes, I am, but I need to make a phone call. Is there a phone center on the way?"

He handed her his cell phone.

"No, I want to make an international call. I need to find an International Phone Center."

"Aaah…" He looked thoughtful for a moment. "The closest *Centro de Llamadas* is about five kilometers south of here. They have Internet service there, too."

"Could you take me there? I will only be a few minutes. Look, I want to pay you for driving me around. I know you were waiting a long time." She took cash out of her pocket. "Please take this."

He dismissed the money with a wave of his hand. "I can't take money from you. You're a friend of my brother."

"Look, I insist." She put the money in the glove compartment.

She was going to call Camilo. She would give him her account information for her Dropbox so he could access the information from the USB memory stick. She would finally tell him everything. He would turn the files over to the FBI and Interpol. Copies of the Patagonia Files were also in her Dropbox.

After fifteen minutes, they pulled up to the phone service center. The computer cubicles were all occupied, and a handful of people appeared to be waiting, but no one was in line for the phones. She told the receptionist she needed to make a call. In seconds, she was dialing. She took a deep breath and waited. The call rolled immediately over to a voicemail message.

The message sent her pulse racing. Camilo never turned his phone off.

She dialed again. Maybe he had been dialing exactly while she was calling.

Voicemail again. This was impossible. Why would his phone be turned off? He had to know what was happening to her. He must have been trying to reach her. She felt a rush of guilt and panic at the same time. Had something happened to him? She felt a crushing weight falling on her. She felt broken and utterly exhausted. One last time... *Dear God, please, please, let him answer.* Voicemail. She looked out through the window of the phone booth. Cautaro was smoking a cigarette beside his pickup truck.

She was running out of time and her mind was drawing blanks from the lack of sleep. Her brain was her only defense at this point. She couldn't succumb to the exhaustion. She had to call someone who could turn the files over to the FBI. *Oh God, think.* It had to be someone honest. She took her address book from her pocket and flipped through the numbers. *Lynn.* She dialed the office secretary.

"Hello."

"Lynn?"

"Who's calling, please?"

"This is Emmanuelle Solis."

"Yes?" Her voice was hesitant, dry. Of course it was. Emmanuelle had been on the front page of the *Washington Post*. Who would want a phone call from someone making the headlines as the candidate for an extradition?

"Lynn, I know you probably heard a lot of things about me in the last few weeks … but what you read in the papers is wrong. I was set up."

"I'm sorry, Ms. Solis … maybe another time."

"Please don't hang up. I need to ask you for a favor."

The line disconnected.

She dialed Camilo again.

Voicemail.

There was only one other person who she could call and that was Leandro. She flipped through the pages again and found his cell phone number.

"*Alo.*"

"Leandro."

"*Si. ¿Quien es?*"

"Leandro, its Emmanuelle Solis."

"Yeah. What's up?" His voice said he was as suspicious of her as Lynn was.

She told him as much as she could in a few minutes.

There was silence for a few seconds. "You're saying someone in the firm set you up?

"Yes, that's exactly what I am saying."

"Frankly, I don't know who to trust anymore. You know that I am also under investigation. My line is probably being intercepted."

"What?"

"After you disappeared, the FBI showed up at my place and

questioned me about Stephan's abduction and murder. A few days later, they show up again and I was arrested and questioned. Then, they let me go and nothing. No further questions. Silence. Just a judicial order prohibiting me from leaving the state. And they kept my passport."

"But did they say why they were questioning *you*?"

"You know Stephan asked me to arrange the flight from Buenos Aires to San Miguel?"

"Yes. Maríana told me."

"Maríana told you? She's a snake. I swear she tipped off the FBI with some twisted story about my family."

"I'm sure she gave them false information about me, too. I think she played a big role in setting me up. Go on, please. Tell me."

Leandro was silent for a minute. "You know my family runs a company that charters small private planes for flights within South America. La Luciernaga."

"Yes."

"So, Stephan asked me to arrange his flight to and from San Miguel, which I did. It was all taken care of. So I thought nothing about it. My brother runs the company. We got him there, but on the day he went missing, the pilot radioed in that Stephan had refused to take the flight back. He was there with, according to our pilot, a couple of musclemen dressed in black and he refused to get on the plane. Of course, my pilot is thinking that he chartered a separate flight and now we won't get paid for our flight. So, my brother called me and I told him not to worry. I know Stephan. I'll work it out with Stephan when he gets back. I hear nothing more. Hours later, the plane crashed. The pilot died. FBI showed up at my place questioning me about the men who supposedly met Stephan inside the municipal building in San Miguel and took him away. The same men the pilot told us about. FBI claimed that the men were affiliated with my family's company and that they abducted Stephan. So I told them what happened and how our plane crashed that same day. They said they are trying to get my brother extradited, but the government of Venezuela refused. They've tried to paint us as low-life criminals involved in some leftist conspiracy plot against US companies. It's bogus. Like we were involved in his kidnapping for money. It's absurd."

"Leandro, we can help each other." She told him about the Dropbox files and how to access them. He agreed to turn them over to the FBI.

"Were you able to make sense of the information?"

"I'm sure Stephan was killed, because he knew too much. Thorman was heavily invested in the gold mine here. He was probably a major shareholder. He sold the stock—millions of dollars' worth of stock—to partners. Five of the geologists who were involved in the array sampling were murdered. The first was gunned down in São Paulo maybe two weeks ago. Before he was murdered, the geologist was trying to blackmail someone whose alias is Sisyphus. Albert has a painting of Sisyphus in his office. In some of the emails, the geologist was threatening to disclose a sham of some sort. The emails were sent to someone with a Gmail address c.sisyphus. The emails are all in the files in Dropbox. The other geologists died when the *Antarctic Mist* was sabotaged. I believe it was sabotaged because they were on board. The value of Ameriminco mineral stocks has soared in the past months. I couldn't understand all of the reports from the geologists, but I am certain there's some fraud related to the mine. I never found out what the satellite images prove. But we know it's related to gold. Maybe it suggests the quantity that's under the ground. I don't know. The rest ... there was no time. I just didn't have the time to go through it all. If I did, I could figure it all out."

"I'll turn the files over to the FBI."

"Oh, and another matter that was evolving when I left, Stephan was supposed to be a witness in a FINRA hearing."

"I think you mean he was to defend in a FINRA matter."

"No, he was supposed to be a witness in some matter under investigation,"

"You might be talking about something else. But what I do know is that he was being investigated for conflicts of interest in the Metalico Case," Leandro insisted. His voice was firm.

"The Metalico case? Why?" Her pulse raced. She had drafted the memo he used in the three-arbitrator panel for the decision in favor of Metalico.

"He never disclosed that he represented the CEO of Metalico in other matters."

"Do you know the name of the CEO?"

"I can find it." She heard him typing on the keyboard. "Sean Michael Epstein."

"His stepbrother." She felt the wind sucked out of her lungs.

"That's his stepbrother? Wow. This is obviously worse than I thought."

"Oh Christ … I think so." She squeezed the words out. "Can you check to see if Sean is involved in the management of Ameriminco?"

"Hold on." She heard more typing on the keyboard.

"He is. He's CEO. The companies are both owned by Barretta."

"Oh my God."

"Emmanuelle, you don't think …"

"I don't know. I just don't know. Look, I have to get out of here. But please, please get the files to the FBI and tell them everything. Tell them we suspect Sean is Stephan's stepbrother."

"Where are you going to go? You could get killed. Just turn

yourself in. Tell Carabineros what you know. Those thugs will kill you if they find you."

"I think I can find the place they are operating from. I just heard that there have been people there for the last few days. I don't have an address, but I know someone who knows the area pretty well and he is going to take me there."

"I don't think you should go. I think you should turn yourself in. The evidence will eventually clear you. You don't want to lose your life, Emmanuelle."

"Look, can you call my brother for me? Tell him everything I just told you. I've been trying to call him and I can't get through. Can you tell him … can you tell him I love him and I'm sorry I never called him back?"

"Of course. I will call him immediately."

She gave him the number. "Look, I have to go."

"How can I reach you?"

"I'll get back in touch with you soon."

"Take care of yourself. Be careful. People kill for a lot less."

She hung up and headed to the truck.

Chapter 84

STEPHAN HENRI BRENT stood pensively gazing out at the river, puffing on a cigar. The moonlight outlined the trees on the banks of the river and glistened through the mist rising over the water.

His hair was black now. A skillful surgeon in Buenos Aires had altered his appearance. He had a new passport and would be headed for a new life in a matter of hours. As usual, he wore a suit tailored impeccably with luxurious fabrics.

"What time will the chopper be here?" he asked Sean Michael Epstein, shaking his head at the sight of him. All the money in the world had done nothing to improve his stepbrother's brassy appearance and garrulous manner. Antonio Carrasco stood beside him, looking thin and disheveled, his pupils dilated from cocaine. And across the room, Gilberto Pereira sat looking very uneasy, patting the breast of his jacket for cigarettes again.

"In a few hours."

The chopper would take them to the Futaleufú Airfield where a small plane would then to take them to Barriloche, Argentina. From there they would fly to Rio.

"You look so lost in thought. We'll be on the other side of the border in a few hours. What are you so worried about? A new life awaits us with more money than any attorney from Calgary could ever dream of," Sean said.

"Everything was shredded? All of the documentation?" Stephan looked at Antonio icily, puffing on his cigar.

"Yes. Every bit of evidence. Nothing can be traced to you," Antonio said, rubbing his nose with the back of his index finger. He and Sean waited, staring at Stephan in silence as though in anticipation of his next order.

"What about you?" Stephan said to Gilberto.

Gilberto nodded nervously. He shifted in his chair. For a moment, it seemed like he was going to try to bolt out the door. Everyone stared at him now. Fear was etched on his face. It took him a second to recompose his face.

"I'll deal with you later," Sean growled at Gilberto, making him flinch.

"What is it with all of you?" Sean asked. His voice was irritated and aggressive. Agitated no doubt by the cocaine as well. Then he turned to Stephan. "And what is it with you, Steph? Don't tell me you're worried about the girl?"

"Not really." Stephan stared out the window at nothing.

"The memory stick?"

"No, it's locked with encryption. Only someone with the password can get to the information. She'd have to been one brilliant girl to figure out the password."

"She'll be arrested soon," Sean said. "The press will focus on that. They'll forget about us. Trust me."

"Have all of the hard-drives been cleaned?"

"All except for the Brazilian Space Institute's external hard-drive." Sean said. "But so what? Even if that surfaces, it will be irrelevant. Scientifically, speaking. It will be years before they find out about the array sampling. *If* they find out. Someone would have to put up the money for remote sensing, mapping, and exploration all over again. They won't be in a position to do that for years with stocks crashing."

"When will the story be published?"

"Tomorrow morning. Front page of *New York Times*. It will say, *Government of Chile reconsiders the mining permit for the Ameriminco mine*. Stock values will plunge. The company will go haywire. You think anyone will be thinking of putting up money for exploration after that?" He waved a dismissive hand. "They'll never know. If the government is reneging on the permit, who cares if there is or isn't gold in the river, right? They'll never prove the ship was sabotaged. Impossible."

Antonio said, "Thorman can answer for the mining permits. He sits on the board. He knew the permit wasn't finalized before the company got listed on the New York Stock Exchange. But he sold all his shares to the partners anyway."

"Exactly," Sean agreed. "So what have you got to worry about? You're dead anyway, right?"

"Yeah, right." Stephan curled his lips into a bitter smile. "Me, forty-five scientists, a dozen volunteers, a slum dog and a priest," Stephan said under his breath. "You're a real savage."

Antonio and Gilberto exchanged a look. Neither said a word, but Stephan caught the expression in Gilberto's eyes.

Sean moved closer to him. "I had no choice. No way anyone is going to the bottom of sea to look for evidence. I think it was brilliant. Timed perfectly."

"You're a psychopath. I'm glad we're not related. Genetically speaking. Now we are all accomplices to—what fifty or sixty murders? Thanks to you. I've lost count. Tell me how many bloody murders have you ordered in the past weeks?"

Gilberto was looking very frightened now, chain smoking. His foot tapped the floor.

"What's the problem, Gilberto? You want out?" Sean asked. "I forgot you're just a simple criminal. A common thief? Not an accomplice to murder? Is that what makes you so uncomfortable? The whole thing could have imploded before we had the money in our hands. Everything we'd worked for. We now have over 950 million dollars to show for it." Sean threw a stack of papers into the chimney and watched them burn. "They'll never trace the money now." Sean laughed dryly. "It went through a maze of accounts. It'll take years to track it down. By then, we'll be so far out of reach. They can't prove anything."

"Oh right. I'm supposed to thank you?" Stephan said, without glancing back.

"You're an ungrateful little bastard," Sean said bitterly.

"You need to lay off the cocaine. It makes you talk too much. You've become a paranoid, neurotic psychopath."

"Your luxurious pockets are lined with millions of dollars of my hard-earned money."

The screen of Stephan's satellite phone lit up. No caller registered.

He picked it up. "Yes."

"Boss, she made the call. I have her coordinates." It was his FBI contact.

"She called her brother?" He'd been waiting for that to happen to know where she was. They had lost track of her.

"No. She called Piñeres."

"Leandro Piñeres? Shit." He was afraid of that. "Was the call recorded?"

"Yeah, probably. You set that up yourself."

"Can you destroy the record?"

"No sir. That's not my department. I don't mess with information from other departments. That could put me away for a very long time."

"You useless piece of shit. What are we paying you for?"

"Well, let's see here… How about for letting you know every move this office is making in the matter involving your disappearance? Oh, excuse me, your abduction and assassination.

Oh, and on that point, other bad news. The DNA report is back. It'll be in the papers tomorrow. They aren't so sure you're dead. You thought the feds would rely on an Argentine forensic report? *Tsk. Tsk.* Any chance you can get your bribe money back from the Argentine forensic team?" He laughed cynically. "But here's some good news. I got a description of the car she's in and the license plate number. I was able to call the place she called from while she was still talking to him. She used the public phone system."

"The *Centro de Llamadas*? Which one? Where is she? Give me her coordinates."

"Uh-uh. Not so fast. That'll be 200K. Same account. Call me when you transfer it. I get the cash, you get the info."

"You upped your price, eh? You little shit. Hold on. Don't hang up." He looked over to Sean. "You need to make another transfer to Vinnie. 200K."

"200K? What the fuck?"

"Do it! Now!"

Sean booted his laptop and brought up the page.

Gilberto looked at the door as though he considered running out.

"He's making the transfer. Where is she?"

Silence.

"Done." Sean said. "It's in his account." He scratched his armpit under his jacket.

"Where is she?" Stephan shouted into the phone.

"She called from Villa Santa Lucía."

"Villa Santa Lucia?" The news brought Stephan to sit. That was the crossroad from the Carretera Austral—the main highway—to where they were. She was *close*.

Nico gave him the description of the pickup and the plate number.

Gilberto's elbows were on his knees, his face hidden in his hands.

"She's figured it all out." Stephan said. The air suddenly seemed thick. Difficult to breathe.

"Now who's paranoid and neurotic? I can have Kiko and Lalo find her in no time." He picked up his cell phone.

"Have them bring her here. Alive. They can't hurt her."

Chapter 85

EMMANUELLE JUMPED INTO the pickup truck and they were back on the main highway in moments. She buckled her seat belt and squinted to fight the vertigo caused by the flashing reflections of the headlights on the landscape around them as Cautaro sped across the wet streets.

"We're still going to the Misión?" Cautaro asked.

"Yes, to the Misión. By any chance, have you heard of a mansion that was recently built in the Futaleufú?" She struggled to open her eyes. She felt like her stomach had risen to her neck. "A mansion beside the Espolon River?"

"*Bueno, sí.* You're talking about a big, white building, right? Built maybe a year or so ago. Looks like a hotel or something, right?"

"Yes. The top floor is encased in glass."

"I have been hearing about it for months now. I saw it the other day. There is hardly anything else out there. I was on the other side of the river. I never noticed it before, but it was dark and the place was all lit up. I saw it through the trees. Usually the lights aren't on like that. I guess people are there now. From a distance it looked like a disc lit up in the sky, floating over the river."

"So you think people are there now?"

"I don't know. There were definitely people there the other night."

"When was that?"

"Let me think … the night before last. No, it was last night. You lose track of time out here in the country sometimes."

"Is it far from the Misión?"

"No. Maybe twenty minutes … if you drive like I do." He flashed a smile.

"Do you think you could take me there? I mean, later tonight, after you see Padre Cristóbal."

"I don't know." He shrugged. "I can ask someone else if I can't take you there."

"I'll pay you." She knew it was now or never.

He was looking in the rearview mirror a lot. She glanced behind. A large SUV with blinding headlights was coming up behind them. For a second, she wondered whether it was Sebastián.

"It's not the money, Señorita. I don't know that side of the river. The road isn't paved out that way. It's a dirt road. It's been raining a lot. It's nighttime, you know, dangerous to get there. Let's see what Nahuel says. Maybe he'll take you. He knows that area better than I do."

She glanced behind again. The SUV was blaring its horn, swerving from one side of the road to the other as though the driver wanted to pass.

"*¿Qué onda, loco?*" Cautauro said, looking at the driver in his mirror again. "These guys are crazy."

"Let them pass," Emmanuelle said. A feeling of dread crawled up her spine.

Seconds later, the SUV slammed into the side of Cautaro's pickup, forcing it to lunge forward and spin out of control. It plunged into a drainage ditch. The terrifying sound of crushing metal and exploding glass echoed in Emmanuelle's mind for seconds after the truck had settled. Her mind scrambled to process what had just happened. She was stunned and out of breath but still alive. She tasted blood on her lips and realized it was her own. She felt warmth trickling down from her forehead. Blinking against the darkness, she felt shards of glass on her face and in her hair. She reached for Cautaro, feeling a stabbing pain in her left side as she shook his arm. No response.

He was slumped over the steering wheel. *Christ.* She could see two shadowy figures up on the road making their way to the pickup. She heard their boots crunching against the gravel. Her heart raced out of control. Did Cautaro have a weapon in the car? She blinked, but it was too dark to see. Her hands groped about the car. *His phone,* she remembered. She reached for Cautaro again, her hand searching his coat pocket. She found it. She heard voices. She dialed Sebastián, cutting off his wary answer of an unknown number.

"Sebastián, it's *Stephan.* I'm sure. Stephan is in the mansion on the Futaleufú. The men … they drove us off the road. They are coming to the car. I'm scared," she whispered into the phone.

"Emmanuelle," Sebastián said. "Where are you?"

She heard voices.

The two men were closer.

"Emmanuelle, where are you?" She heard the despair in Sebastián's voice, but she was frozen.

"Emmanuelle, where *are* you?"

"Get her out of the car!" one of the men shouted.

She heard Sebastián's desperate plea, "Who's there? Where are you? *Answer.*"

The men were approaching quickly. She held her breath and prayed as a terror she had never before experienced surged through her. The car door swung open and someone pulled her out of the truck, blindfolded and gagged her. One of the men twisted her arms behind her back and tied her hands. Her knees were trembling. She wanted to scream, but the gag prevented it. One of the men pulled her up onto the road and shoved her into the back of the SUV.

She fought for her breath, hearing a voice say, "We got her and we're on our way." Who was he talking to?

She blinked under her blindfolding and saw herself through death's eyes. Was she in the trunk? It felt like a grave. She needed air. She would die. Her heart felt like it would explode. She struggled to break her hands free, but it was futile. Powerless, she listened to the sound of the engine, the screeching wheels, the muffled voices of her captors, and her pounding heartbeat. She would soon face Stephan.

Would he kill her?

Chapter 86

SEBASTIÁN VEERED ONTO Route 231. The rain had stopped, but the air was dense. A feeling of dread seized him. Would he get there in time? He called the Comisario of Futaleufú on the police radio system and filled him in. "Crístian, men abducted her while I was on the phone with her. They're taking her to the mansion now. I'm on my way there. Call for more backup. We know they're heavily-armed."

"I'm close by. We have a few men on watch. The only way I can get more men in fast is by helicopter. I'll see what I can do. I'll call you back." Crístian hung up.

Another call buzzed his phone.

"Sebastián, this is Padre Felipe. Solis is on her way to the Misión. She called Nahuel earlier. His brother picked her up and he's bringing her here."

Sebastián's attention was drawn to a scene on the road up ahead of him. A Carabinero vehicle was pulled over, its lights flashing. A pickup truck had fallen in the ditch.

Sebastián slowed down. "What kind of car does he have?"

"A red pickup truck."

"They were just driven off the road by the same assassins who killed Rodrigo. They abducted Solis. I think they're taking her to the mansion on the Futaleufú.'

"Dios Santo," he murmured.

Sebastián pulled up beside the police car. Two Carabineros

were pulling someone out of the car. It had to be Nahuel's brother.

"¿*Esta vivo*?" Sebastián called out to the Carabineros.

"*Sí. Lesionado, pero vivo.*"

"He's hurt, but he's alive." Sebastián repeated into the phone. "I'm headed to the mansion."

Sebastián hung up and drove on. She had called less than twenty minutes ago. He could save her.

He saw with perfect clarity what Emmanuelle had been trying to tell him. How had he not seen it before? Everything she said to him after the call from Pilar. It was suddenly making sense. How had he not trusted her? He turned onto the gravel road that ran alongside the Futaleufú River. He was going to do everything humanly possible, everything in his power to save her. *Let her be alive. Let her be alive.*

Chapter 87

THE SUV SKIDDED to a halt, and Emmanuelle rolled forward and slammed against the wall of the back of the trunk. She winced in pain, struggling to hear what the men were saying. Doors opened and closed. She heard the crunching of boots on gravel again. They were walking to the trunk. Her heart pounded in her ears. She was thirsty. Her mouth was dry and the gag around it felt like a blade cutting into her face.

The door swung open and cool air gushed in. One of the men reached in and yanked her up by her arm. She tumbled from the trunk to the ground. The other caught her arm. He took off her blindfold and gag.

The lights from the mansion were blinding, but she could see the outline of the two men who had abducted her with AK-47s slung over their shoulders. The mansion was just as Cautaro had described, appearing like a disk floating over the river. She saw the silhouette of a man on the top floor. He was looking down at them. She knew it was Stephan. She recognized his build and the cut of his clothes. He was watching them bring her in. Her vision spun. She heard the hum of an engine. A generator probably.

The forest lining the landscape seemed like a wild, shadow-filled and haunted place. Blinking against the bright light, she looked at one of the two men. He was the man Sebastián had identified. Beside him, Stephan's driver from Brazil. His cold dark eyes pierced her as he removed a knife from a sheath. The blade glinted as he raised it and turned her around brusquely. She held her breath and squeezed her eyes shut. He cut her hands free. She breathed.

They walked her to the entrance of the house where two other men were waiting. One jerked the door open and pushed her inside, forcing her up the stairs, his gun pointed to her back.

Chapter 88

THEY BROUGHT HER up to the glass room overlooking the river where Stephan, Sean, Gilberto, and another man whom she guessed was Antonio Carrasco were gathered.

Stephan was waiting for them at the top of the stairs. His hair was dark. He had undergone some sort of cosmetic change—his cheeks were more prominent now, his nose straighter and thicker, but she recognized his eyes. There were other characteristics—lines around the eyes, his cleft chin, furrows around the mouth—that she knew so well.

Emmanuelle couldn't talk. Her heart slowed, perhaps from sheer exhaustion, or the feeling of impending death. Her legs were limp. She backed away from Stephan slowly, staggering step by staggering step, until she felt the cold wall pressed against her back. Entirely depleted, she slid to the floor staring at him. There were some situations in which instinct just didn't offer enough guidance. This was one of them.

Stephan approached her. "Come now. Don't sit on the floor." He held a hand out to her.

She didn't move a muscle. He reached down, pulled her up and walked her to the sofa.

"So, you finally made it." He sat next to her, peering at her through black-framed spectacles. "I hope you brought me my USB memory stick like a good girl."

She watched him, wondering if she were hallucinating. Was

this some kind of dream? Had she died in the car crash and gone to hell? Or was she in a coma and this, a freakish nightmare? She blinked hard.

She recognized his cologne. She closed her eyes and her mind returned to the InterContinental Hotel in Paris, when she first fell in love with him. The memory brought a wave of nausea. Her mouth was dry from fear, sealed shut maybe. She felt like her teeth were glued together. What did he want to do with her? Her heart took off again, but her brain was failing. It was drawing blanks. For a second, she wished she were dead. It might be better than many of the alternatives that seemed plausible right now.

She opened her eyes and saw Gilberto's pale, nervous expression. He was staring at her. She sensed something, perhaps objection to what was happening.

"I say we kill her," Sean said, opening the drawer of the desk and removing a pistol.

Gilberto stood up. "No!"

Stephan turned around and faced him.

Gilberto raised his hands in the air as though it was Stephan brandishing a gun. "*Isso é o suficiente. Ele é insano.* Your brother, he's crazy. He killed enough people. *Basta,*" he pleaded.

Stephan held his stare for a long moment. In three split seconds, the divisions in the room were clear to Emmanuelle.

"She's my woman. And I call the shots. Got it, slum boy?" Stephan said, glaringly to Gilberto. "Let me remind you where you come from, *favela* boy? You are a worm from the shantytowns. No pretending in this room." Stephan took the pistol from Sean's hand and placed it back in the drawer.

"We're taking her with us," he said to Sean. "She would follow me to the end of the world. She'll be loyal to me to the end of time. She has such qualities, this woman."

No. Emmanuelle's heart thudded. Emmanuelle realized that

the only reason he'd been attracted to her was because she had admired him so much. She was a reinforcement of his egotistical desire to be admired.

Tears streamed down her face. She prayed Sebastián would find her. Rescue her from this monster. How she wished she'd stayed with him. He would have fought for her. She was certain of that. All this would have become known.

Stephan caressed her hair. "She's worth more to us alive than dead." He picked up his satellite phone and dialed. "Where the bloody devil is my chopper?"

Emmanuelle had to remind herself to breath. Her brain would kick in again. It just needed oxygen. *Breathe. Breathe.* It was all she had. *Think. Think.*

"You staged your own disappearance. Why did you do it, Stephan?" The words finally came out. They sounded childish, meek. "You didn't need this. You didn't need more money. Why resort to crime?"

"Crime, my dear, is relative. What constitutes a crime today might not be crime tomorrow." His sharp blue eyes shifted to Sean, "They'll be here any minute. Everything ready?"

"All set to go." Sean opened the drawer again and removed the pistol, studying it carefully.

"Laws change. People change. The world changes," Stephan said. "Nothing stays the same. Laws are irrelevant. I used to wake up amazed that governments turned over their jurisdiction to us. How many arbitral panels did I sit on, deciding the fate of how many countries?" His eyes traveled to the dark world on the other side of the window. They give us the power to make multibillion-dollar decisions. We had absolute power to rule with practically no possibility of appeal, and what *we* said became the law. The power of the word. The power of decisions. Scrutiny over the conduct of governments, over decisions made by their courts, over their laws and

446

regulations. That, my dear, is power. That power made *me* the law. You see, my love, law and criminality are all relative. And more importantly, they are bedfellows." He spoke with the magnetism that drew so many to admire him. An image came to her of attorneys applauding after one of his conference speeches. A shudder of fear and revulsion crept through her.

Gilberto crossed one arm over another and bit a fingernail, his head bowed, occasionally looking up at Emmanuelle. It was clear; he was as much a prisoner as she was.

"You think you're God." Emmanuelle's words were a whisper, but Stephan heard them.

"That's irrational. I don't think I am God. Religion is exactly what Freud said it is, collective insanity. Worse yet, it's an infectious disease. There is no God. Only laws created by men. And *I*, for a very significant period of time, was one of the few men in this world who *made* the law. I decided, and governments were bound. I ruled, and nations were bound. And people, by the way, all those little people who you protested about … the people who live by rivers that you claim die from *environmental pollution*." He paused. "Yes, all those little people that color your sad stories, they are mere brushstrokes on the landscapes *I* paint. Adding color here and there." He paced as though he believed he were in a courtroom and she, a member of his jury. "Don't you realize, my love, that because of *God*, nothing is possible? So many people just can't see that simple fact. You always had fear clinging to the wings of your mind. You'll never soar, my child, with that fear."

"It's not fear. It's a sense of right and wrong," Emmanuelle said.

"Religion and morality are the ball and chain of your servitude. Without it, we are free. We are alone. Solitary as a tomb. But we are free and we are unique."

Emmanuelle's head throbbed from the blow of the car

crash. She felt her forehead. The blood had dried and was hardened along her hairline. "You are isolated and alone, because your criminality isolates you. You hurt so many people. You staged your own death to avoid prosecution. They were catching up with you, weren't they? The FINRA hearing was about you. Not about anyone else. It was about how you hadn't disclosed that Sean Michael Epstein, the CEO of Barretta, was your stepbrother and that you had significant interests in his companies. All of those decisions you made were based on your own interests. They were catching on to you. And the ship. You had the ship sabotaged because the geologists were blackmailing you. What they threatened to tell the world would have jeopardized the sale of the mine, right? Would it have sent the price of the stocks tumbling? What did Guilherme threaten to reveal? What was it, Stephan? What do those satellite images reveal?"

"You are a smart little girl. But you're wrong. I never killed, ordered or agreed to the murder of anyone. That wasn't part of the plan. That was *never* part of the plan. You can direct those questions to Mr. Epstein," he said bitterly, turning to his stepbrother. "You're trying to distract me from my point. Which is, that we are born nothing and no one. We *make* ourselves. I made you because you never had the strength to make yourself. You were nothing when you came to me. You were no one. I made you who you are. I created you."

His words echoed in her mind.

I'm not the same person you left in Washington two weeks ago, she thought.

Emmanuelle thought she saw a light in the dark, dense woods outside the window. Something that flicked on and off not too far away in the distance. A pinprick of light. Was she seeing things? She heard a distant whirring. A helicopter on its way here. Maybe it was the helicopter Stephan was expecting.

Or maybe it was Sebastián. He would find her. She knew he was coming for her.

Another speck of light glinted through the trees on the other side of her glass prison. This time closer to the mansion. Something told her it was there to rescue her.

Sean and Antonio were lining cocaine on a table and taking turns snorting. Maybe she could distract Stephan for a few more minutes. "You said you loved me, Stephan. You called me to lure me here and frame me for crimes I couldn't have even imagined. You said you loved me…"

He was angry and provoked. "My dear, what is love? It is an exchange of promissory notes with "Happiness" written on them." He winked at Sean. It was a slow nightmare. Her vision swam again. "Love is a commitment that human reality cannot fulfill," Stephan continued. "The elixir of life is not love, sweet Emmanuelle. It is power. Love is an agreement that cannot be executed. And, therefore it is null and void."

Suddenly, the lights went out, plunging them into complete darkness.

"What the fuck…" Sean cried.

She heard Stephan say, "My ride is here." His voice thickened and his breathing grew heavy. "Those idiots probably knocked out the generator. Let's go!" He was moving to the door.

She heard the door open and felt a rush of cold air. Then, it slammed shut again. Her eyes struggled to adjust. The moon cast some light in beams and shadows. She heard voices and movements. The trampling of feet on the stairs. Many people maybe. Hushed voices from below. She blinked against the darkness, asking herself if she'd just slipped into madness. She slid off the sofa, feeling her way across the room. She remembered seeing another door there. Shadows were moving. Dusky figures rushing about. The thrum and beat of a helicopter in the distance. More lights behind the trees in the deep darkness. She knew Sebastián was out there. She had faith.

She heard more shuffling sounds. More noise in the stairwell. Voices outside in the night. Then, gunfire outside. She recognized a figure at the opposite end of the room coming toward her. It was one of the men who brought her here. The AK-47 in his hand was glinting in the moonlight.

Suddenly, the door swung open again. "*¡Alto Policía!*" It was *his* voice. He was here. Sebastián had arrived.

An explosion of automatic gunfire came from the opposite end of the room. She felt an excruciating pain swallowing her, sinking her.

Chapter 89

THE LIGHTS CAME on again, white and blazing. They burned her eyes. Even with her eyes shut they were blinding. Was she asleep or awake? She felt a flutter in her stomach, warmth spreading in her body. She heard something that sounded like the flurry of wings, perhaps birds. Some large, winged creatures nearby. Everything was fading away.

Then she heard his voice. He was calling her. Camilo was calling her, but she was hiding. She suppressed a giggle. She smelled the perfume of irises. She wore a crown of cherry blossoms in her hair. She was peering at her brother from behind the massive trunk of the tree in the simple garden of their house in Switzerland. The simple but exquisite garden of her childhood. With the trees that had cradled all of her dreams. A lush carpet of thick grass tickled her toes. Their parents were inside. Her mother waved from the window. Emmy! Camilo cried. He was growing desperate. He was worried now. Emmy! he cried. She heard the beating of wings. They were beating more forcefully. He wasn't playing anymore. He was worried. The winged creature was there to take her away. She heard his cry, Emmy!

She forced her eyes open, waking from a free-falling dream. It wasn't Camilo. It was Sebastián. She'd been shot. The pain was excruciating. She was floating. Conscious, but floating. Sebastián was cradling her in his arms. Carrying her. Running. She heard the thrumming. The rhythmic beating. Was it the large, winged creature or had the helicopter arrived? A blasting cold wind, swirling and sweeping. Her guardian angel had arrived. They were transferring her to the helicopter. She was floating. In her last seconds of consciousness, she saw Carabineros, PDI and *arrieros* had surrounded the mansion on the Futaleufú below her. Inside the mansion, Padre Felipe was kneeling beside Gilberto. Was Gilberto dead? Struck by the gunfire as well? She felt Sebastián's warmth. His face was close to hers. He was talking to her. Her vision swam. She closed her eyes again. The noise of the helicopter faded into a whirring sound, a faint melodic wind concerto dissipating in the misty air. He was holding her hand.

He was her guardian angel.

Chapter 90

BRIGHT LIGHT FILTERED through Emmanuelle's eyes bringing her to her senses. She felt a whirl of disorientation. She was in a hospital. The trees outside her window were brushed by dappling sunlight. She heard men talking in hushed voices. She lifted her head. Pain in her shoulder lanced through her body. Sebastián and Camilo were beside her bed.

"Hey you," she said weakly. "I tried to call you so many times…."

Camilo rushed to her bedside. He kissed her on the forehead and stroked her hair. "I know. I was on the plane on my way here. That's why my phone was turned off. You can't imagine how worried I've been." His eyes welled with tears.

Sebastián moved to the other side of the bed. She reached for his hand. He took hers and kissed it. "How does your shoulder feel?" He had several days of stubble on his face, and he was wearing the same clothes. Had he been at her bedside all the time?

"It hurts."

"The surgery was successful. The doctors believe they removed all of the bullet fragments … but it will take months to heal."

She looked out the window. "Cloudless days are a luxury in these parts."

Her brother smiled.

"Are Stephan and Sean in custody?" she asked.

"Stephan was shot. He died last night. Sean Michael Epstein and Antonio Carrasco are in custody along with their assassins. Brazilian authorities have a warrant out for Lucas Braga's arrest along with a few others from GM."

"Gilberto?"

"He's here in another wing of this hospital. He was shot, but he's recovering. Carabineros are waiting to take him into custody as soon as he's well enough. He's cooperating with us. He's given us an incredible amount of information about the investment fraud. If he continues to cooperate, it's likely his sentence will be considerably shorter."

"He tried to defend me. Sean wanted to shoot me." She closed her eyes. "What day is it?"

"It's Wednesday. Your extradition hearing has been indefinitely postponed. Santiago is working with the US Federal Prosecutors Office. I'm confident it will be withdrawn soon. They have already moved to extradite Sean to Canada, although Chile will not likely allow it. He will be tried here for the crimes he committed."

"And Padre Cristóbal?"

"He passed away yesterday. Funeral services will be held tomorrow."

She closed her eyes. "I want to go."

"I don't think your doctor will let you."

"What about Thorman?"

"He claims to be a victim. He has North American authorities convinced."

"That's absurd. He is as guilty as Stephan and Sean. The proof is in the Patagonia Files. He hired GM to falsify reports so that they could get a favorable environmental assessment and the dam project could be approved. It's the same organization that had falsified the stream sediment sampling for the gold mines. Martín worked for both Stephan and Thorman. Thorman had as much interest in the gold mine fraud as Stephan. He held most the shares."

"He claims Stephan fed him that information and that he was just relying on Stephan's contacts. That Stephan insisted they were legitimate. That Stephan lured him into investing in the gold mine, along with other companies that were mere shams. He apparently advised FINRA of Stephan's failure to disclose his conflicts of interest in the Barretta case."

"It's not possible. He can't get away with this. He was on the board of Ameriminco. He got it onto the New York Stock Exchange knowing the Chilean government hadn't finally approved the mining project. He duped his partners and sold them stock knowing the price would drop when news broke that the government was reconsidering the permit. And he was going to see to it that the commission deciding on the dam project relied on a falsified report. He's a criminal. He *has* to be tried."

"Interpol and the FBI agents are here and they are combing through the evidence. Maybe they will find something that they can use against him. It will be weeks, maybe even months before it's all sorted out. But Gilberto Pereira is cooperating. We think Antonio Carrasco may cooperate as well when he realizes that he could spend the rest of his life behind bars," Sebastián said, stroking her face gently. "But you have nothing to worry about now. You have practically been cleared from all suspicions. You can relax now."

"Thorman must be put away. I know he's guilty. I won't relax until that happens."

"You need to recuperate and cooperate with your doctors so we can get you out of here."

She knew the story would be all over the papers now and in the news across the world. "You know that they sabotaged the

455

ship because the geologists who did the stream sediment sampling were on board. They didn't want them to disclose the findings to the public."

"Yes, we know. The company was distributing hundreds of bogus assay results to boost the share price of Ameriminco gold. The geologist who was gunned down in Rio was in charge of the exploration program. He also worked for GM. He wasn't supposed to be using satellite imagery from the Brazilian National Space Research Institute for private organizations, but he did. They went after Karl Gustav because they knew he had the system archives on his backup drive. Karl Gustav didn't know a member of his team was involved with Ameriminco."

"What did the satellite imagery reveal?"

"That there was no likelihood that the quantity of gold represented to the public existed in the area of the mine. That's why they were desperate to sell before that became known. That was the blackmail."

"Thorman *has* to be prosecuted. He's just as guilty as the rest of them."

"It will be difficult to make a case against him. He is lining up his political friends already."

"But in the very least he can be prosecuted for securities fraud."

"Difficult with his connections. He was a former Commissioner of the United States Securities Exchange Commission. You know that."

"I can't believe the bastard can get away with this." She knew it would be difficult to prosecute Thorman. Stock in mining companies was often traded long before minerals even got out of the ground and often even before permits were issued.

"We'll try from all angles. But promise me you will rest."

"We have to reveal the truth."

The word rang in her head. Truth was something Stephan

and Thorman had scattered to the wind for money and all of its implied delights. The inescapable contradiction was the brevity and illusion of it all. But that was someone else's problem now. Her mind was drifting. She closed her eyes. The two men she loved most in the world were beside her. And that was all that mattered.

Chapter 91

THREE MONTHS LATER, Sebastián watched as Emmanuelle made her way to the door. She'd been cleared of all the charges and prosecutors transnationally were piecing the evidence against Stephan's surviving co-conspirators in what had become one of the most publicized crimes in international investment. Emmanuelle was returning to Washington with a wounded shoulder, a healing but painful reminder of a nightmare that had spun her life into frenzy. Sebastián was under investigation by his superiors in Santiago PDI for not following orders. Demotion seemed possible.

The flight was called for boarding and passengers were lining at the gate. Neither had exchanged a word, but he sensed they both felt the same way. There were some people who came into your life and changed it forever, shrinking what used to seem important, sweeping through it like a gale force wind, violently shifting your perspective of the world, altering your mind, your emotions, reorganizing thoughts. Like a new pair of spectacles, the encounter gave you a sharply redefined vision, a new and all-embracing perspective of the world around you. As though that person had altered your blueprint or simply unfurled some yellowing paper in a well-worn, crinkly-edged folder that was archived in some seldom-opened drawer long ago. And now, seeing it anew, it is as clearly yours as a hand-drawn map tracing your journey up to the present, indicating each and every place of your childhood, the mountains, the streets, the backyard, the summers, the trees that cradled your dreams. Tracing the trail right up to this moment.

It all came to him now, falling over him in blustering, thunderous silence. A familiar emptiness swept over him. She was leaving. He was letting her go.

He didn't want that.

"Stay with me," he said.

She turned back looking stunned, stopping inches away from him. He wrapped his arms around her waist and pulled her close, careful to not put pressure on her injured shoulder.

"Don't go. Stay with me."

"What would I do here?" she asked, surrendering in his arms.

"The same as me. Look for work. You know I have no interest in remaining on the force with a demotion. I've outgrown this position anyway. I could never be happy returning to that life after all that has happened."

"You risked it all for me."

"No. I put all of my bets on you. And I would do it again. What will you do if you go back?"

"I don't know."

"Then stay with me. We can apply for jobs with Interpol. Maybe work together as a team. Maybe stalk Thorman. Finally get the monster behind bars."

"Now that's an idea."

"Please, Emmanuelle, stay here with me."

It was that easy. A few words, and the whole world fell away.

They stepped through the glass doors of the Tepual Airport and back out into the rain. Only this time they were both laughing.

About The Author

Mary Helen Mourra is an international lawyer and adjunct Professor of Law at Georgetown University Law Center in Washington, D.C. Her paternal grandparents migrated from the Middle East to Chile in the early 1900s, thereafter settling in Haiti where her father was born and raised. She grew up in Haiti and lived in Chile for several years where many of her relatives still live. Her mother is an American who lived most of her adult life in Haiti and many years in Chile. *The Patagonia Files* is her debut novel and its sequel; *Eryxile's Garden* will be released in 2017.

9 780692 789209